LIGHT MY FIRE

Since he kept his arms at his sides, she said, "Your choice. Dance or talk."

"Okay," he sighed a mock sigh. "Logic wins every time."

Ben turned from the fire and encircled her waist. Heat shot through her. Logic evaporated. Holding onto his neck, she arched backward, grabbed the CD remote and flicked it. Bass and piano melded in slow, easy jazz.

"Nice," he murmured.

"No mushy lyrics."

"Mush can be . . . nice." His breath seared her ear.

Feeling almost petite, Risa raised her arm, placed her hand lightly on his nape, and swallowed the growl deep inside her. His hiss of indrawn breath, as his arm tightened around her waist, was like a match to dyna-mite.

Holy Hedda, she'd lost the last bit of her teeny, tiny mind.

BOOK YOUR PLACE ON OUR WEBSITE AND MAKE THE READING CONNECTION!

We've created a customized website just for our very special readers, where you can get the inside scoop on everything that's going on with Zebra, Pinnacle and Kensington books.

When you come online, you'll have the exciting opportunity to:

- View covers of upcoming books
- Read sample chapters
- Learn about our future publishing schedule (listed by publication month *and author*)
- Find out when your favorite authors will be visiting a city near you
- Search for and order backlist books from our online catalog
- Check out author bios and background information
- Send e-mail to your favorite authors
- Meet the Kensington staff online
- Join us in weekly chats with authors, readers and other guests
- Get writing guidelines
- AND MUCH MORE!

Visit our website at
http://www.kensingtonbooks.com

PRINCE OF FROGS

BARBARA PLUM

ZEBRA BOOKS
KENSINGTON PUBLISHING CORP.
www.kensingtonbooks.com

CHAPTER 1

"What the hell's the holdup?" Ben Macdonald made zero effort to curb his impatience. A bad habit grown worse lately.

At 5:46 A.M. on the second of December, the line at his neighborhood Starbucks stretched out the door, onto the sidewalk, and into the parking lot. Where he stood shivering. A nippy, predawn breeze snaked down the collar of his ancient London Fog trench coat. God, why not forget coffee? Forget work? Hightail it home and send Molly off to school after a bowl of hot cinnamon oatmeal? A gust of wind stung his face and woke him up.

"Brrr. Any chance of a white Christmas?" a woman asked.

"With all the hot air in Silicon Valley?"

Laughter. Ben grit his teeth.

"Not even at Christmas."

At the second mention of Christmas, acid spewed into Ben's stomach. The sudden pain knocked the air out of him, and he staggered, bumping the woman ahead of him. Before he could apologize, she swung around.

Almost as tall as him and big, but not fat. Statuesque came to mind. So did a blur of near-naked, voluptuous women in museum paintings. Ears scalding, Ben focused on the *big* woman in front of him. Red hair pulled back from nice, regular features. Not the classic nose and high cheeks of Amy, but pleasant.

"Hey!" The laser smile Red flashed him lit up the whole parking lot and bathed him in heat. "Five, ten minutes, you'll be on your way."

"Yeah, on my way to rush hour gridlock," he snapped, not sure why he vented his frustration on this cheery, carrot-topped stranger. Deliver him from bright-eyed and bushy-tailed this early. Not to mention the inevitable Christmas cheer she'd probably start spouting any minute.

"I bet in ten years we'll have rush hour twenty-four/ seven." Her deep emerald eyes positively glowed. Obviously, she didn't have a worry in the world.

"What a cheery thought." He scrubbed his eyes. They felt like fried eggs.

"Sorry. My brain stays flat till after my first three cups of coffee."

"Uh-huh." Another arctic blast froze his ears. He scrunched his shoulders. God, he hated the cold. Amy, on the other hand, had loved it. His chest tightened.

"Don't you love this weather for a change?"

"I'm a sunshine kind of guy." Teeth gritted, Ben glared at Red. She wore a navy turtleneck with matching tailored slacks. No jacket, no coat. What was she—part polar bear?

Not with those curves.

Quickly, Ben brought his wrist up and checked his watch, sucking in his gut. Maybe he could create another inch of space between him and the woman. Even half an inch would prevent any accidental touching while she yakked about skiing and he stared.

Jesus, her breasts were magnificent. Big. Round. Soft. Just like everything else about her.

Soft like his brain—now as mushy as an overcooked pea.

Breathing hard, Ben positioned his watch closer to

his nose and bought a moment of sanity. Jesus, did testosterone spike when the temperature dropped?

It must. Probably how Mother Nature ensured preservation of the species. Widowers and bachelors had the same number of sex hormones. Hormones made guys visual animals. Men looked. He was male. Ergo . . .

Suddenly, the bones in his wrist melted. Red's left breast had grazed the cuff on his coat as she leaned into the extra space he'd so brilliantly created. The air around them hummed with high-octane pheromones.

Watching him clutch his wrist like an idiot, Red lowered the wattage on the smile-o-meter. "You drive 101?"

"Along with the rest of the herd." He jammed his hands deep into his coat pockets, shuffled his feet, and spoke fast. "Big—" He heard the word and stammered, "My—my important meeting starts at eight. On the dot. Downtown San Francisco."

"Ouch. You make that commute every day?" Her voice washed over him like the deep, rich notes of an oboe.

Against his better judgment, knowing he should ignore her attempts at casual conversation, Ben nodded. Like any other sociable being—whose wife hadn't died eleven months, twenty-nine days, and nineteen hours ago.

"Rough. 280's not an alternative?"

"No, 280's not an alternative," he snarled.

With a shrug, the redhead gave him her back. Her truly ugly gold frog earrings swung back and forth.

She was pissed. Tough. Dammit, one nod did not mean he intended to talk about the God-awful traffic or freak weather or anything else that qualified as social chitchat. Period. Red definitely wasn't his type. Too tall. Too fair. Too damn jolly. Nothing like his petite, golden, composed Amy.

'Tis the season to be jolly. Ben bit back a snort. He should apologize, but why? A year ago, he'd have debated the merits of both freeways with Red, making his point right

up until they each paid for their coffee, and then gone their separate ways.

A year ago, he didn't have Clue One how sweet his life was.

Today . . . he stared at the wiry tendrils coming loose from Red's thick braid. He'd never see her again. Never seeing her again didn't matter. Never seeing Amy again . . .

An invisible vise squeezed his heart tighter. He clamped his mouth shut. Too late—the moan in the back of his throat escaped. Red glanced at him over her shoulder, made eye contact, and slowly turned around. Patting his arm, she whispered in a loud stage voice, "How long since your last caffeine fix?"

A chuckle rippled through the line.

Her fingers burned a hole right through his coat. Only down to the top layer of skin this time. "If it's been more than twenty-four hours, maybe you can go to the head of the line."

Bathed in sweat, Ben jerked his arm behind his back. "I can wait." Sure everyone was staring at him, he whispered loudly, "At least five minutes. It's not like I'm addicted."

More laughs.

"Uh-huh." She nodded.

"I can quit any time." He held up three fingers, fascinated by a dozen freckles dusting the bridge of her nose.

"Of course." She leaned closer, her breath a silver puff.

Essence of woman and the scent of roses filled his nostrils and spread through him like a fever. Her frog earrings smirked. He ground his teeth. Thank God, he didn't have coffee yet. The state he was in, he'd probably bite right through the cup.

"I, myself," Red slapped a hand over her heart, "could quit this instant."

All at once, the urge to lay his hand on top of hers

seemed logical. Ben swallowed a groan. God, it had been so long.

Obviously unaware of his lust, she said, "This close to ordering, I'm sure I'd hurt their feelings if I left now."

"My thoughts exactly," he lied, surprised he didn't thump his chest, bellow, and jump around in a circle like an alpha ape.

Feet shuffled. They moved but got no closer to the door. Unless he was careful, he could still make an ass of himself. His stomach clenched. Dammit, he knew how to cope with his hormones. Hadn't he survived eleven months by pretending Amy was on an extended trip? Easy enough, considering business had—too often—taken him away from her and Molly.

A glimmer of reason took hold. He pulled some notes from inside his jacket pocket. Reading required more light, but he could fake it. In less than a year he'd become an expert at faking.

Too happy to bear a grudge, Risa Taylor smiled to herself. This guy reminded her of her two-year-old patients. Okay, so he was taller, darker, and downright handsomer than any of the cute two-year-olds who visited her. But like them, he wasn't quite sure if he wanted to trust her or not. No question he didn't sleep enough—which might explain the tic going at warp speed under his left eye. Or a craving for caffeine might explain it. Or it might be something entirely unrelated.

Whatever. Not her problemo. She fingered the gold frog around her neck. Her only problem was controlling the happiness bubbling inside her. Start talking babies and a hunk like Mr. Cautious would turn tail faster than a spooked cat.

In truth, these days, most of her friends ran when they saw her coming, because she exercised no judgment. She wanted them, along with everyone else—her mother, her patients, perfect strangers—to share the dream that was about to come true for her.

Spread the joy. That was her philosophy.

Risa hugged her waist. This time next month she'd happily forego coffee breaks at Starbucks. She'd be at home feeding three newborn infants. Her very own adopted sons. Triplets.

Close to dancing a jig, Risa reined in her imagination and grabbed the first thought that floated by. "Once, long, long ago, I drank only hot tea." She stopped. "Are you okay?"

He didn't look okay. He looked ready to pass out. Green around his wide, sexy mouth. Sweating—in spite of the cold. Like someone close to shock. Heart attack? The pulse in his temple pounded visibly like a jackhammer. Stress, she diagnosed. Commuting zapped everyone sooner or later.

"I'm a doctor." She laid her hand on his wrist.

He flinched. "What kind?"

"Pediatrician. Risa Taylor." She stuck her hand out.

For a second, she was sure he wasn't going to shake it. His icy fingers slowly closed around hers. "Ben Macdonald."

No wimp at handshaking, she wrung his hand, pretty sure he wasn't having a heart attack after all. Straightfaced, she said, "Almost everyone calls me La Ti Da."

He blinked, surprise reflected in the way he cocked his dark head at her. "Okay, I'll bite. Why?"

She laughed. "According to my mom, I was the most extraordinary baby ever born at St. Claire's Hospital."

"Uh-huh." He grinned, leaned in toward her, and brought with him a whiff of citrus-scented aftershave.

Uninvited, the wheels in Risa's head rolled out a technicolor video, frame by frame. The two of them. In a garden of lemons and oranges. Naked. Dancing. Drunk on each other and the perfume of citrus.

"The most extraordinary baby ever born?" he cued.

Blushing, she sucked in fresh air. Was she nuts? Let him see her naked, and he'd disappear faster than a puff of smoke. She exhaled. Caffeine vapors jump-started her brain. Somehow she picked up the threads of her birth story.

"Besides having ten perfect fingers, toes, powerful lungs, and a brilliant mind at birth, I had a headful of red curls."

No use mentioning she'd weighed in at ten pounds eleven ounces. He could see with his own big brown eyes that she wasn't in the running for Miss Petite USA.

Holy Heloise, why had she jumped in to cheer this guy up? He looked as if he expected her to start tap dancing at the very least, so she said, "The nurses went gaga. They tied a sausage curl with a huge pink bow. Very La—"

"Ti Da," he finished, snapping his fingers.

"Bingo!" Risa said, encouraged the tic under his left eye had slowed.

His small smile filled her with the same pride and joy she felt whenever she soothed an angry or scared patient. Of course, Ben Macdonald wasn't crying. Or throwing a temper tantrum. At least not on the outside. And it was none of her business if he felt sad. Give him his jolt of caffeine and he might turn into Mr. Sunshine right in front of her eyes.

The silence between them stretched out too long. A precocious talker—full sentences at birth, according to her—Risa had all at once run out of things to say. Brooding men baffled her. Ask Dr. Tim. Her ex-husband had brooded about everything—especially her weight. Yet he'd married her.

Ben Macdonald cleared his throat. "How's your ego?"

"Pardon?" Her ears and cheeks burned. How the heck had he turned the tables on her so fast?

"Suppose you weren't the most extraordinary baby ever born at St. Claire's?"

She exhaled. Whew! He'd had her going there for a minute.

Warm all over, she tapped her forehead. "Let me guess."

She stepped backward, her heel skidding on damp pavement. She grabbed at the air. In a daze she felt his arm around her waist. Hot and cold at the same time, she relaxed against him. His body—lean, but hard in all the right places—supported her with no obvious effort. She imagined him picking her up and holding her in his arms just as effortlessly. *Without getting a hernia?*

He responded to the catcalls and released her too fast. "By the way," he said quietly, "the most extraordinary baby? Not me."

His grin spread, crinkling around his eyes, loosening the tension in his jaw. He wiggled his black eyebrows. His silliness stoked her embarrassment. A tingle started in her toes, then raced up her back. A neuron fired deep in her brain. She hung on his every word with heart-fluttering anticipation.

"Check with the nurses. They'll tell you," he said.

"Tell me *what?*"

He shook his head. "Not what. *Who.* My daughter."

Though it nearly choked her, Risa swallowed her yelp. *Daughter?* Why in the world had she assumed he was single? So he didn't wear a wedding band? Tim wore the ring she'd given him from Day One. By Day Two he'd started his first affair, with a student nurse weighing about ninety pounds.

"She'll be five in April."

The picture in Ben Macdonald's open wallet was in a plastic protector. A glossy, studio photo of mother and daughter smiled at the world. The camera had captured his wife's serene beauty. Somewhere between Grace Kelly and Audrey Hepburn.

After a quick swallow, Risa said, truthfully, "She's drop-dead gorgeous." Another swallow. "So's your wife."

Her beeper saved her from saying more. While she fumbled it free from her waist, he snatched the wallet away. From his frown she guessed she'd offended him. Again. Too bad. There was a real child—not a bratty adult—who needed her.

"The deliveryman said it's a good thing it's not a Venus flytrap."

Neck craned, Emily Brown, Risa's motherly front desk nurse, stood in the middle of the empty waiting room, gaping at the ceiling-high poinsettia. Risa stood on tiptoe, stretching her five-foot ten-inch frame, and still couldn't see over the sucker.

"Who's Ben Macdonald?"

Risa ripped the small white card from a startled Emily's fingers. "Sorry I was such a grinch. Happy Holidays, Ben Mac . . ." Her voice trailed off.

"Is he cute?" Emily demanded.

"No." He was, in fact, handsome. Rhett Butler—as played by Clark Gable—without a mustache.

"So what's wrong with him?" Emily started around the poinsettia. "Is he crazy? Dangerous?"

"He's married."

Recalling her fantasies starring the handsome, crazy, dangerous, *and* married Ben Macdonald, Risa spoke in her noncommittal, medical–science tone. Aware that her blazing face contradicted her ho-hum inflection, she bent over and examined a leaf. Her braid swung over her shoulder but gave no cover whatsoever for the heat scalding her cheeks.

Em's trip around the poinsettia seemed to take longer than an expedition around the world. Time enough for Risa to gird herself for what she knew was coming next.

"How'd you meet him?"

"Jogging buck naked in the park." Risa sniffed a leaf.

Em arched a brow. "Maybe I'll stop by Starbucks to-morrow."

Risa clamped her mouth shut. No way she'd say another word about the fiasco with Ben Macdonald. In some ways Em was like family. Full of questions. Full of advice. Fiercely loyal.

How many times had she said, "Go ahead. Starve yourself. And forget ever getting married again. Men want to make love to a woman—not to a toothpick."

Maybe. But Tim had preferred the toothpick type. Em backed her divorcing Tim once Risa admitted her fears that he'd never be faithful. Em supported adopting triplets a thousand percent—as long as Risa found a daddy for them.

At the very least, Em would figure out a way to learn if Ben Macdonald had a single brother.

"I'm not sleepy, Daddy. I want to stay up and talk to you." Molly kicked the pink coverlet away and tried to push up to a sitting position. Dozens of stuffed bears made that a challenge.

With a little groan, Ben pulled his daughter onto his lap. He hooked a black curl behind her ear and tried to ignore the fire in his stomach. It had started smoldering the instant Molly's nanny interrupted him in a meeting earlier that afternoon. Molly had another stomachache.

"She won't go to the doctor," Maryann had sighed. "She hates Dr. Judy's sub. Says she'll feel better once you're home."

A stake through the heart couldn't have hurt Ben more. He tore out of the meeting, talking to Molly on the cell phone as he raced down eight flights of stairs. Stalled in city traffic, he'd tried cajoling her into meeting him at the doctor's office.

"No, Daddy. Talking to you makes me feel lots better."

Her declaration had made him feel like a dog. Dammit, he should be there for her. Problem was, how could he be in two places at once? Maryann sure as heck wasn't the answer. No nanny could ever take Amy's place. He didn't expect that. So what did he expect after almost a year?

Stomachaches, more and more frequent. Instantly eased by his presence. Dr. Judy had gently suggested counseling, but there Ben balked. Spill his guts to a stranger? No way. Besides, what would counseling accomplish? The hard, cold truth was that Amy was dead. She wasn't coming back. Wishing wouldn't bring her back. Molly would be fine. He'd take care of Molly.

Except gridlock on Highway 101 had stranded him. For over two hours he'd repeated every fifteen minutes, "I'll be there for a bedtime story for sure, sweetheart."

He took no comfort in this promise. He'd believe she was okay when he saw her, held her, kissed her. He replayed the doctor's assurances every mile of the way home. No physical reason for the stomachaches. Losing a wife was hard. How hard was losing a mother for a four-year-old girl?

A four-year-old girl whose daddy needed to work less and pay more attention to his daughter.

The unspoken rebuke ate away at Ben's stomach morning, noon, and night. Something had to give. He knew that. He just didn't know *how* to change his life. Amy had anchored him. Shown him how to balance work and time for his family. After the accident, work offered a refuge. Work became the one place where he forgot for awhile the night that had ripped his life apart.

Molly squirmed in his lap, and his mind returned to his body. Shaken by a rush of love, he nuzzled her left ear.

A giggle. "Another story, please, Daddy?"

He snuggled her close to his heart. "Okay, but tomorrow we go to the doctor."

"Nooo, Daddy." Tears welled in her dark eyes.

"I'll go with you, sweetheart." His mind scrambled, trying to recall his schedule for the next day.

"No, Daddy! Tomorrow's my holiday pageant." She shook her head back and forth. "Did you forget? Aren't you coming?" Her voice rose, and tears spilled down her pink cheeks.

His chest tightened. God, he had forgotten. Completely. Weren't holiday pageants unconstitutional? They should be. How did other working parents manage?

"Of course I'm coming, sweetheart. He kissed her tears away, tasting salt. Still edgy from the commute, he all at once felt like a train had run over him.

Somehow he wove working at home into a story so silly he couldn't follow half of it. Molly, on the other hand, ate it up. Snuggled against him, she giggled till she ended up with the hiccups—a legacy from Amy's bedtime stories.

The fire in his stomach cooled to ashes. Molly's head nodded. He held her till his arm went numb, then tucked the pink coverlet around her chin and laid her favorite bear next to her.

Ten minutes later he sent e-mail to his managers. What a mess to dump on them. He took a slug of coffee. The bitter taste triggered memories of his encounter with Dr. Risa Taylor fourteen hours ago in a parallel universe. God, she was so . . .

Statuesque? Unwanted, the memory of her came to him. Wild red hair. All that damn cheer. Nothing, nothing like his lovely, serious Amy.

The ache in the back of his throat spread. Impossible to swallow the coffee. He dumped the remains in the sink, watched the brown liquid slide down the drain, then rinsed his cup. Dr. La Ti Da had turned silent as the sphinx after he bit her head off. He stuck his cup in the full dishwasher and started the wash cycle. Why the hell had he shown the doctor—a total stranger—a picture of Amy and Molly?

'Tis the season to be jolly.

There was that. He felt the familiar tightness in his

chest, but repressed memories from Christmases past. Had the doctor received the plant? How big was the biggest poinsettia in the florist's shop? He grinned. What a Kodak moment—her face when she read his card. He'd bet she hit the moon laughing.

His stomach growled. Damn, he'd forgotten to eat. He zapped leftovers. God, he missed Amy's gourmet meals at a candlelit table. Molly asleep in her bed. Breakfast together the next day. Blueberry pancakes, Molly's favorite.

Scraping his plate, he surveyed his backyard. When was the last time he'd played outside with Molly? Gone to the park?

"Molly, Molly, we will get through this," he muttered.

First, make sure she didn't have an ulcer. *Or worse.* He gripped the edge of the sink. He had to find another doctor till Dr. Judy returned from maternity leave. He scrubbed his face. His secretary had checked the yellow pages for Dr. Risa Taylor's office address. Why not let *his* fingers do the walking?

Several pages of the phone book stuck together, but he found the number, dialed, and spoke clearly into the answering machine. "This is Grinch. Do you make house calls?"

CHAPTER 2

Molly Macdonald.

The name jumped off the holiday pageant program and hit Risa between the eyes like a two-by-four. Praise Jupiter, with all the noise of parents arriving and getting seated, Kelsy didn't hear her squeak. Kelsy, mother of Risa's godson, Jason, was too busy reading the program.

Heart fluttering, Risa scanned the seats in front of her. Poinsettias, tinsel, and bee lights faded in a blur. The world couldn't be so small, could it? What were the chances this Molly Macdonald was *that* Ben Macdonald's four-year-old daughter?

Risa checked the first row. The knot in her neck hardened. Holding her breath, she stared at the back of a man's dark head.

Turn around. She leaned forward on her chair. A chair obviously made for children and women no bigger than dwarfs. A chair that made her feel like an amazon.

"Aren't these seats awful?" Kelsy murmured.

"Awful."

"Is that why you're all flushed?"

"I'm not flushed." Sweat beaded Risa's hairline.

"I forget." Kelsy laid down her program. "As a doctor, you can see yourself, right? Whether you're flushed or not."

"Now I'm flushed," Risa hissed. "Funny how sarcasm has that effect on me."

"Did you know your eyes squint when you lie?" Apparently worn out from their scintillating exchange, Kelsy returned to reading the program.

Careful not to look at the front row, Risa waited a couple of breaths, feigning fascination with the menorah on the nearest wall. Kelsy had the intuition of a TV talk-show host. The instant she picked up on Risa's interest in the man who might be Ben Macdonald, she'd drive Risa crazy digging for details.

On stage, tiny feet scurried back and forth under the maroon curtain. The audience buzz grew. *Turn around.* Unmoving, Ben Macdonald's clone stared straight ahead at the stage. Why didn't he turn around?

The shuffle of feet behind the curtain probably put his radar on the fritz, Risa decided, her own radar on high alert.

A thorough exam of his hair and ears convinced Risa this was not her Ben Macdonald. Her Ben Macdonald had longer—

Her mind screeched to a halt. *Her* Ben Macdonald?

Okay, okay. *The* Ben Macdonald who'd sent her that Leaning Tower of Poinsettia now blooming at St. Claire's. *The* Ben Macdonald, whose phone call she hadn't returned the night before. That Ben Macdonald was not the man in the front row.

More disappointed than she wanted to admit, Risa choked her frog pendant. Was she insane? Ben Macdonald was married. *Deeply married.*

Kelsy squeezed her elbow. "You are an angel for coming."

"I promised Jason weeks ago."

"Yes, but I know how busy you are. You're working too hard. No wonder you're flushed."

"Give it a rest, Kel." Pushing Ben Macdonald to the back of her mind, Risa continued, "Flushed or not, even if I had a hundred patients today, I wouldn't miss my godson's debut as a tree."

Kelsy laughed. "You know Jason only agreed to let Sam go on his business trip because you were coming."

"I'm flattered."

A warm feeling filled Risa. If only all males stayed four-and-a-half forever.

"Three boys the same age." Kelsy clucked and shook her head. "Just think what you have to look forward to." Her voice rose over the buzz of the crowd.

The man in the front row turned his head their way and looked at them. Risa felt her cheeks sting. "Shhh," she admonished Kelsy.

Holy Harriet, it was him. *That* Ben Macdonald. *Her* Ben Macdonald. *Where was his wife?*

"You aren't leaving?" Kelsy's tap on the shoulder stopped Risa halfway out of her chair. In her head she saw herself getting up and floating gracefully out of the auditorium.

"What's wrong?" Kelsy demanded.

"It's hot in here. All these people."

"I bet you're coming down with something."

Since she couldn't so much as squeak, Risa swallowed her protest. Let Kelsy keep talking. Do not let her notice Risa had lost her mind.

Smiling that slow, sexy smile at her, Ben Macdonald nodded. Her heart spiraled upward so fast she felt lightheaded. Holy Henrietta, one more smile from him and she'd leap over the chairs and rip off his shirt.

Riiight. Her heart felt like a yo-yo. Leaping did not figure into her daily treadmill routine. During her two-minute marriage to Tim, he'd nagged her to spend more time jogging and less time eating. She ground her teeth. *Don't go there.*

Inhaling deeply, she locked eyes with Ben Macdonald. Confused, bewildered, she started blinking. At warp speed. Like she was caught in a desert sandstorm. *Lame, lame, lame.*

After several more blinks, logic still didn't come to her rescue. She sank back into the chair, causing severe damage to her kidneys. Hands shaking, she fished a tissue out of her pocket. Her mind raced, piling up question after question. Why was he alone? Was his wife out of town? Was that why he'd called Risa last night? Had he picked up on her raging hormone attack and forgotten *he* was married?

Well she hadn't. Common sense had told her yesterday morning that he reeked of trouble. Hadn't his aftershave almost sent her over the edge? Imagining them naked in the Garden of Eden, she sniffed. That scenario spelled trouble with a capital *T.*

Admittedly, in the throes of a hormone attack, she'd sent him mixed messages in the parking lot, but what was his excuse for calling her at home last night?

Did she make house calls? Honest to Pete, what kind of line was that? Mercifully, late at night in her own home, reason had prevailed.

"Should be starting any minute," Kelsy boomed.

Startled out of her reverie, Risa felt her heart hit her skull. Several people clapped softly. Ben Macdonald twisted all the way around in his seat. His dark gaze zeroed in on her. The scent of lemons and limes drifted her way, shorting out the logic circuits in her brain. Like someone partially electrocuted, she suddenly tingled all over. She rubbed her sweaty palms down the sides of her slacks. His mouth curved into a wide grin, and he gave her a two-fingered salute.

Cheeks stinging, she ducked her head and struggled to corral her hormones. *Think. Think.* Okay, he exuded sex appeal. Her response was purely biological. At some deep level her mind knew that adopting three newborns would take her out of the mating game for a long, long time. To instill sympathy with the birth mother, tricky Mother Nature had tweaked Risa's hormones a little too hard. After all, men hadn't knocked each other down to get to her since divorcing Tim.

Reason kicked in. What sane man would volunteer to take her *and* three infants? Not a man married to a babe like Mrs. Ben Macdonald.

The tingle in Risa's cells stopped. The scent of lemons and limes faded. Her heart rate came back to about 200. Ben Macdonald might be on the prowl, but he'd turn tail once he heard about Charlie, Tom, and Harry.

Smiling to herself, Risa inclined her head toward El Jerko. His eyebrows shot up, and her pulse shifted directly into high. He frowned. Before she went off the deep end again, she dug her short nails into her palms. On the phone, his words had slurred. She'd thought he sounded drunk. Maybe he still was.

Why did he keep staring at her? Like no one but the two of them existed in the room.

She fought the urge to touch her hair, finger a strand brushing her cheek. She clamped her jaw shut. Holy Hermione, she'd give anything to lick her lips!

The noise in the background faded in and out. Aware that he was still looking at her, Risa felt dizzy. Too many people in the auditorium. Too much body heat. It was so hot she couldn't breathe. Couldn't think. Sweat pooled between her breasts. A mental image of Ole Ben removing her bra played out in her brain. She felt his breath in the hollow of her throat. Three rows away, he cocked an eyebrow.

Someone behind her sighed, then giggled.

All at once Risa felt like an idiot. A fool.

Please, please, let the floor open up. Let her drop down, down, down, to the lower regions of hell. The place reserved for women daydreaming about another woman's faithless frog of a husband.

Another giggle. His eyebrow arched higher. Truth came in a blinding flash. Breathing hard, Risa squeezed her frog pendant.

The man wasn't staring at her. He was trying to see around her, since her shoulders belonged on a wide-end receiver. Obviously, he was staring at his wife. She must've arrived late and now had to sit in the back.

Risa's throat filled. *Forget Ben Macdonald. Think babies.* Her pulse slowed, but she still wanted to turn around and check out his wife. Did she exude the same radiance in the flesh that she did in a studio portrait? Why not find out?

She knew why not. Ben Macdonald would see, and her pride would shrivel to the size of a pea. She'd die of humiliation.

"You skipped lunch, didn't you?" Kelsy shoved a PayDay candy bar at her. "Peanuts have lots of protein."

"I'm not hungry."

Mouth wide open, eyes round, Kelsy blocked Risa's peripheral vision. "You're not?"

Her look of astonishment grated on Risa's nerves almost as much as the crackle of the candy wrapper. Why didn't the man turn back to the stage? Was he so crazy about his wife he couldn't look at anything but her? The smell of caramel and salty peanuts made Risa's mouth water, but she kept her hands squeezed in her lap.

"You heard me." Absolutely certain that Mrs. Macdonald weighed ninety-five, ninety-six pounds soaking wet in a winter coat, Risa swallowed, tasting the bittersweet sting of envy and lust.

"I'm not hungry," she repeated edgily.

"I heard you." Kelsy bit off half the candy bar.

Swallowing, Risa could almost taste the salty–sweet morsel, and she clamped her mouth shut before she started salivating.

"Of course," Kelsy mumbled, "I wouldn't be hungry either if I weren't a happily married woman."

"Pardon?" Risa watched Kelsy out of the corner of her eye.

Mouth full, her best friend nodded toward Ben Macdonald, chewed, then swallowed. "He'd take my appetite away for sure," she said, "if I weren't a happily married woman."

Luckily, Risa saw the trap Kelsy hoped to spring. She patted her best friend's arm. "To paraphrase that old song . . ."

Her mind blanked out. Dead in front of her, Ben Macdonald mimed something. Something secret and private . . . apparently understood only by his wife.

"Yesss?" Kelsy prompted. "To paraphrase . . ."

Blushing, Risa said, "Oh. He only has eyes for his wife."

A peanut fell out of Kelsy's gaping mouth. She choked, then exclaimed softly, "For his wife?"

"Don't tell me you thought he was single?" Feeling almost sorry for her matchmaking pal, Risa patted Kelsy's wrist again.

Ben turned and faced the stage the second the curtains parted. A child dressed in green like an elf appeared. A hush fell over the audience.

Waiting for Molly's number, Ben settled into his chair, puzzled by Dr. Risa Taylor's aloofness. So much for thinking a poinsettia made up for his rudeness yesterday. He must've offended her more than he'd realized. That might explain why she didn't return his call last night and why she gave him the cold shoulder today. So much, too, for her helping Molly—those hopes floated away like a balloon let loose. Christ, would he never learn to play nice?

The white noise of the crowd soothed his brain and

gave him an opportunity to regroup. His ten years as a dot-com CEO kicked in. What if he was wrong about Dr. Taylor? He hadn't even spoken to her yet about Molly. There could be a logical reason why she didn't return his call last night.

Tired as he was, maybe he'd mumbled. Had he left a correct phone number? What if she simply didn't recognize him in this environment? Unlike her, he didn't stand out in a crowd.

With a blast of horns, Molly, dressed in her angel costume, her cheeks scarlet, ebony eyes sparkling, appeared on stage. Ben's breath caught. She looked so much like Amy. Bursting with pride, he sat up straighter. God, how he and Molly had laughed trying to get her halo on straight. And no tummyache. Not even butterflies.

"I'm too jazzed," she'd confided in such a serious tone he hadn't dared laugh.

After singing her little song, she took a slow bow, then moved out of the spotlight. She looked straight at him and said in a stage whisper, "Hi, Daddy."

The audience broke up, and Ben's heart swelled with love.

"Shhh." The woman in front of Risa and Kelsy turned around for the second time.

Oblivious to her impatience and to Risa's shock, Kelsy went right on whispering her story about Amy Macdonald in the dark auditorium. The New Year's Eve party. The drunk driver running the red light. Amy Macdonald killed instantly. Her husband walking away without a scratch.

"He was a basket case," Kelsy said. "He finally snapped out of it. He had to. For Molly."

Jason came on stage then, and Kelsy shut up. Finally, before Risa made a fool of herself by gasping. Gasping because, though she'd heard every word Kelsy said, her brain cried, *Oh, that poor family!* She also wanted to gasp, *I wish I'd known yesterday.*

What if she had? How would she have behaved differently?

The lights came up, and the children filed across the stage. *Had some patience,* she thought fleetingly, joining the audience in a standing ovation. Holy Hedda, at least she'd done one thing right yesterday. She'd said Molly was—her words came back to her: *drop-dead gorgeous.* Her face burned. Open mouth, insert foot. She stared miserably at Molly.

The little girl's beauty took your breath away. What must that be like, every day kissing your child and seeing your dead wife's image?

Risa spoke in Kelsy's ear. "I need to leave. I can't face the man."

"You'll break Jason's heart," Kelsy protested. "I promised him we'd go for ice cream afterwards."

"Stop that," Risa ordered, clapping harder. Kelsy wasn't playing fair. "I don't need any more guilt today."

"You think Ben Macdonald expects everyone in town to know about the accident?" Kelsy asked. She rushed on, not waiting for Risa's answer. "I remember because Jason and Molly're in the same class."

"Yes, well, I must've known. I read the paper."

"You gotta read it every day, Toots. And you can't just read the comics."

"You think it's any comfort to him, knowing I read about it, then forgot?" Risa's hands stung from clapping. Molly Macdonald took a second bow.

"Why should the subject of his wife's death even come up?" Kelsy whooped Jason's name as he took another bow.

Put that way, the question mocked Risa. If she admitted her parking lot fantasy about Ben Macdonald, she came off sounding like a nutcase—even to herself. Ad-

mitting she still tingled from their stare-off before the
play, she sounded certifiable. For crying out loud, the
man was a widower. A recent widower. And having been
friends with her since kindergarten, Risa knew in
Kelsy's mind widower translated as *eligible*.

Loyal, competent, a wonderful mother, Kelsy whole-
heartedly supported Risa's decision to adopt. At the
same time, she believed a woman needed a man to help
raise kids. It went without saying a man needed a mother
for his children. Nothing complicated. The world according to Kelsy, who also believed everything happened for
a reason.

Voilà! A dim bulb flickered in Risa's head. Enter Ben
Macdonald and Risa Taylor. Brought together by fate.
Kismet. Karma. Whatever. Kelsy would take on getting
them married as a personal challenge. She would race
down the track like a freight train. Risa'd never know
what hit her.

A poke in the ribs brought her mind back to earth.
Kelsy all but knocked her down trying to get into the
aisle. Waving over the sea of heads, she called, "Here we
are, Jason. Hi, Molly. Hi, Ben."

Risa grabbed Kelsy's elbow and hissed, "For two
cents, I'd wring your neck."

Ben wasn't blind, and he saw from the get-go that Dr.
Risa Taylor would rather kiss a snake than spend a nano-
second chatting with him. Maybe she hated poinsettias.
Maybe he'd figured her all wrong. Why should she help
Molly?

She didn't even know Molly. She didn't know him either. He offered his hand. After one meeting, during
which he had acted like a jerk, she'd decided he was a
jerk. The wisp of optimism he'd nurtured throughout
the pageant evaporated when she avoided his gaze and
dropped his hand like it was slimy.

His stomach clenched. In business, he never gave an inch. When it came to Molly, he never gave even a fraction of an inch. He'd find a doctor. Dr. La Ti Da Taylor sure wasn't the only pediatrician around. He'd find someone. Someone genuinely cheery. Someone who returned his phone calls. Someone who didn't scramble his brains just by looking at her.

For the hell of it, he drawled, "Why doctor, we have to stop meeting like this."

Her wide mouth thinned out to a flat line. Her ears and face flushed bright pink, but she didn't take the bait. Before he could figure out if he was disappointed, Kelsy Chandler jumped in with her two cents. "The world's the size of a pinhead, isn't it?"

"La Ti Da!" Jason Chandler tugged on Risa's hand. "Molly'n me were great, weren't we?"

Smiling from ear to ear, Risa gave both kids high fives, then hunkered down to their eye level. "You were awesome. I've never seen a better tree, and, Molly, you sing like an angel."

"My mommy's an angel, you know." Molly hugged her waist.

The noise of the milling parents ebbed, and Ben heard a roar in his ears. *Thank you, Dr. La Ti Da.* He didn't trust himself to bend down and swing Molly up into his arms. Still down next to her, Doc said, "I know your mommy's an angel. Do you think that's why you sing like one?"

"Uh-uh." Molly shook her head. Her eyes rounded and her childish vibrato sank, squeezing Ben's heart. "Mommy said I always singed like an angel."

Fragments and remnants of Molly and Amy singing together fell over each other in Ben's head. His chest tightened. Amy should be here now. Celebrating. Would be here, if he'd seen the other car coming. . . .

"Did you and Mommy sing together?" Doc asked.

"Uh-huh. And I writed lots of our songs." Molly tapped

a finger on her chest. "Daddy sings like a rusty pipe," she whispered behind her hand.

Doc kept an arm around Molly's waist, but shot Ben a laser smile over her shoulder. His lovely daughter was only repeating what Amy had said teasingly a hundred times. He shrugged, palms up, heart beating fast. "What can I say?"

Arching a brow, the doctor snickered. "Silence is gold—"

"I write lots of songs, don't I, La Ti Da?" Jason crowded closer to the doctor.

Too close. In his exuberance, he leaned on her shoulder. Knocked off balance, Doc squealed, threw her hands out and swayed to one side. Molly screamed, then grabbed one of Doc's hands. Jason grabbed the other. Too late, Kelsy Chandler whooped, "Watch out!" Mr. Rusty Pipe's feet stuck to the carpet.

Pulled from two sides, the doctor didn't have a chance. She fell backward. Flat on her back, she looked up at them with a dazed expression in her wide green eyes. She managed a weak smile at the ceiling. "Invisible banana peels get me every time."

"*What* invisible banana peels?" Jason screeched.

"You can't see them, Jason. They're invisible." Molly flung herself on the floor next to Doc.

Jason immediately sprawled on the floor, too. The doctor laughed, setting the kids off into gales of giggles. Half a dozen parents and teachers materialized from out of thin air. Tempted to haul the good doc to her feet and shake her, Ben muttered to Kelsy, "Time the adults took charge."

"Okay, I'll corral the kids, you help Risa."

"I don't think so." Ben waded into the fray. "C'mon, Molly."

Like linebackers, the looky-looks blocked his path to the trio on the floor. A white-haired grandfather type tapped Ben on the shoulder. "Should I find a doctor?"

"Get up, Jason." Kelsy waved over the small crowd.

"No doctor necessary," Doc called. "Thanks, anyway."

"Thanks, anyway," Molly and Jason echoed.

"Excuse me." Ben broke through the circle of on-lookers.

Once inside the circle, everything sped up. Kelsy wiggled between two curious bystanders, dropped to one knee, and threw Ben a look that said, "You're the man, take charge." Giggling, the kids came up to hands and knees on either side of Doc, chattering at her like little monkeys. Ben's mind hiccuped.

What'd Kelsy expect him to do? Unlike Amy, who he could pick up almost as easily as picking up Molly, Dr. Risa Taylor was definitely an armful. *A curvaceous armful.* Those curves made taking charge that much harder.

A loud whistle pierced the logjam in his brain. On the floor, Doc shook her head when Jason demanded she show him how to whistle through his teeth. "Later, honey."

Somehow—how eluded Ben—she managed to look dignified flat on her back. She waved to the crowd. "Nothing broke but my ego, folks."

"Where's your ego?" Molly demanded.

Someone chuckled. The doctor rolled her head to one side and mumbled something Ben didn't catch. Kelsy snickered.

"Yeah, where's your ego?" Jason parroted.

"Let me get back to you on that one, honey." Doc's shoulders heaved.

Titters from the onlookers. Ben even felt his lips twitch. *The lady has spunk.* Giggling, she turned on her right side. Her long jacket inched up. White wool slacks accentuated the full roundness of her hips.

Unable to tear his eyes away from her frog ankle bracelet, Ben slipped one arm out of his jacket. Her jacket rode higher, and a sudden fire ignited in Ben's groin. He stopped just in time. Any attempt at chivalry, he realized regretfully, would only draw attention to the erection betraying him. *Christ! What was wrong with him?* He jerked his jacket back on in disbelief. Dr. La Ti Da propped herself up on one wobbly elbow. Wobbly because she couldn't stop laughing.

Her laughter was contagious. Like bugs on their backs, Molly and Jason kicked their feet in the air and giggled. Convulsed by cackles, Kelsy offered no help to her friend. The onlookers howled, but the circus atmosphere turned Ben off. His testosterone rush ebbed. Sane again, Man-of-Action Macdonald broke through the bystanders. Jason jumped to his feet and ducked under Ben's outstretched hand. "Why're you laughing, La Ti Da?"

"She's having fun!" Molly followed right behind Jason, clipping Ben's right knee. The next thing he knew, he bounced off Doc, who was midway to standing. Their heads cracked. As his ass hit the floor, Ben saw stars.

"Ouch." Knocked flat again, Doc rubbed her forehead.

Teeth gritted, Ben said, "What's life without a concussion?"

"Daddy! Daddy!" Molly tumbled on top of him, patted his head wound, asked, "Where does it hurt, Daddy?"

Jason piped up, "Did you hurt your ego, Mr. Macdonald?"

CHAPTER 3

Twenty minutes later, the sun-splashed school corridor was empty except for Risa and company. She and Kelsy dawdled, admiring the artistic endeavors of budding Picassos. Mother and godmother oohed and aahed each time they found a masterpiece by Jason or Molly. Not one to linger, Jason raced for the exit sign, urging Molly to hurry. She, in turn, dragged her father down the hallway. He called a halt a few feet from the front door.

Despite the distance, Kelsy cupped her mouth next to Risa's ear. "Did you ever, in your wildest, kinkiest fantasy imagine tying a child's shoe could be so sexy?"

"Have you lost your mind?" Risa jerked her head away and planted both feet on the carpet. No way she'd risk getting close enough for Ben Macdonald to overhear this conversation.

Distance, though, didn't keep a vague panic from uncurling in the pit of her stomach. She had to derail Kelsy. Now. Before it was too late. Otherwise, Kelsy would have Risa and Ben Macdonald engaged by the time they reached the parking lot.

"Isn't Jason darling?" Risa heard the desperate note in her sissy attempt at derailment.

"Darling." Jason supported Molly by the elbow while Ben Macdonald held his daughter's left tennie on his thigh and looped the long strings together with exquisite precision.

"Think he has a foot fetish?" Kelsy asked. "And please don't ask me if I mean Jay."

"I know who you mean, and I think you have a screw loose."

"What's wrong with a foot fetish?" As if in the Louvre, Kelsy examined a drawing of purple and orange scribbles.

"One more word, and I wring your neck." Risa charged, but Kelsy stuck her tongue out and danced away.

"You think he's got super hearing in addition to a super—"

"I will kill you." Despite her soaring pulse, Risa lunged.

Kelsy ducked out of reach. "Who invited him for ice cream?"

"*Them.* I invited *them* simply as a courtesy gesture after—"

"After falling on top of him in front of thousands of people?" Canary feathers floated out of Kelsy's mouth.

"Stop exaggerating." An instant replay of the fall-down scenario unwound in Risa's head. Hot blood rushed to her face. "It wasn't thousands, and I did *not* fall on top of him."

"Right." Kelsy snapped her fingers. "You skidded on an invisible banana peel, lost your balance and—"

"And crashed down like an elephant nosediving off a high wire skinnier than dental floss." Risa crossed her fingers and hoped Kelsy didn't hear the bitter edge to the elephant comment.

"You didn't crash down like an elephant."

"Okay. Like a rhino, then." *Whine, whine.*

"No." Kelsy shook her head. "Like **a big** kid having fun."

"Emphasis on *big.* "

Kelsy made a noise in the back of her throat.

"Hey." Risa laced their fingers. "Big isn't a four-letter word. You can say *big* without me going into shock, okay?"

"Okay, but I'm sorry. Sometimes my mouth doesn't consult my brain. Asking Ben Macdonald and Molly for ice cream was a nice gesture. I respect you for it."

"Uh-huh." Wary, Risa eyed the other end of the corridor. Kelsy never gave up without the last word.

"Just like I'm sure Ben Macdonald will respect you in the morning," Kelsy added. "But wouldn't you trade his respect for a night of mad, passionate lovemaking?"

Risa took off at a gallop. Praise Jupiter Ben hadn't moved. He was too busy working on Molly's other shoestring.

"Admit it." Huffing, Kelsy fell in step. "He looks like the prototype for Prince Charming, down on one knee like that."

A scream threatened. Risa swallowed, then spoke through gritted teeth. "I admit you are hallucinating. Plus, you're out of your mind if you think he and I are soul mates."

"Did I say anything about soul mates?" Kelsy arched a brow.

"No, but I can read your itsy bitsy mind."

"You'd do better to read your horoscope. All this week—"

Risa stopped and clapped her hands over her ears. "Don't give me that planets-in-perfect-alignment mumbo jumbo."

"Didn't the stars foretell that marrying Tim—"

"The stars and everyone in the universe but me knew marrying Tim was stupid." Pride alone helped Risa sound so casual when she could barely breathe.

She checked behind her. No one in the sun-filled

corridor but her, Kelsy, and the ghosts of bad memories. On a distant planet, Ben Macdonald didn't even glance their way.

"We should charge your jerky ex for oxygen." Kelsy narrowed her eyes.

"No argument from me." Tim's jokes about liposuction and breast reduction still hurt. Risa sucked in air and vowed silently to raise sons indifferent to a woman's breasts and weight.

"Here's a better idea." Kelsy tapped the side of her head. "I bet I could find someone, somewhere, who'd offer to reduce the size of Tim's balls as a favor to women everywhere."

Temptation won. Risa laughed, then said, "Remind me never to get on your wrong side."

"Remember that when when I find Mr. Right for you."

Risa rolled her eyes. "I didn't even see that one coming."

Hand over her heart, the drama queen pointed at Ben Macdonald. "See the way he's holding Molly's shoe?" she whispered.

"Uh-huh." The little hairs at the nape of Risa's neck prickled. The look of love on his face took her breath away.

"Wouldn't you give anything to change places with her?"

"No." Shaken, Risa shook her head for emphasis, then added, "They don't make glass slippers in size eleven triple As."

"By the way," Kelsy whispered, "I think he reads lips."

"Whaaat?" Blood drained out of Risa's limbs.

"Easy." Kelsy clamped down on her arm with the ferocity of a Gila monster and hummed the first notes of "Embraceable You."

Down the hall, the kids broke away, racing toward Kelsy and Risa. Their high-pitched excitement boomeranged off the walls. The noise jangled Risa's nerves. Leisurely, like a movie in slow mo, Ben Macdonald rose. Desire, uninvited, slammed Risa behind her knees.

"You're drooling," Kelsy whispered.

Mouth dry, Risa swallowed. "Doctors don't drool."

Proud she'd come back at Kelsy, Risa wished her doctor's brain didn't feel like cottage cheese. The slow, sexy way Ben Macdonald loped toward them triggered images of cavemen dragging women through the underbrush. A tiny smile played around his mouth. Nerves tight, Risa moistened the corners of her mouth. Feeling like a fool, she tried to recover by coughing.

Too late.

More canary feathers floated around Kelsy as she elbowed Risa in the ribs. Since the man was now less than an arm's length away, Risa chose not to retaliate. For the moment. In truth, she couldn't lift a finger against Kelsy because the scent of lemons and musk Ben Macdonald emitted had leaped the distance between them like a forest fire jumping a river.

He fell into step next to Risa, putting her in the middle between him and Kelsy, who spit out canary feathers the way Risa imagined shovelers in hell spit out jalapeño peppers. Legs trembling, she listened with half an ear as Kelsy agreed Jason was, like Molly, jazzed.

"Jason loves an audience," Kelsy bragged. "He definitely got his daddy's genes in that department."

The almost inaudible crack of Ben Macdonald's jaw stopped Risa's smart-ass comeback. Tiny, invisible antennae silently rose like periscopes behind her ears. They slithered up through her hair, snapped into place above the top of her head, and took a quick reading.

Back rigid, eyes straight ahead, Ben Macdonald gave no visible sign of the struggle Risa's antennae intercepted. Since his silence made the Great Sphinx appear chatty, Risa made social noises that kept Kelsy talking. A nod from time to time, accompanied by a mumble now and then, bought him time to regroup. All the while, through her lashes, Risa watched him like a hawk.

The man was wound tighter than new wire.

Yes, he smelled good.

Looked good, too.

His knuckles didn't drag the ground.

All qualities, in Kelsy's warped mind, for Risa's ideal husband.

Except even a child could see Ben Macdonald had miles to go before he accepted his wife's death.

The kids careened back into the adults' orbit, and Ben came out of his funk, grateful Dr. La Ti Da hadn't chewed his ear off. Molly, her eyes shiny, tugged his hand.

Could she, *pu-leeze, Daddy, pu-leeze,* ride with Jason in La Ti Da's car?

A sharp pain punched Ben in the gut, but his computer mind whirred. Three miles to Main Street. Perfect weather. Five stop signs. No lights. *If* the good doc avoided El Camino. This time of day meant fewer drunk drivers. . . .

His hesitation sucked the radiance out of Molly's upturned face. Out of the corner of his eye, he watched Dr. La Ti Da go very still. Their eyes locked. Expecting curiosity, Ben bristled, pissed at the winter sun jitterbugging on the tiles and Jason's unleashed excitement boomeranging down the lemon-yellow hall.

"You're welcome to ride shotgun," the good doc said so softly Ben almost missed it.

The fact she didn't push bought him another second. Doctors—especially pediatricians—got called out at all hours. In all weather. It stood to reason. They had to be good drivers. Deep in his brain, the flashing red light faded. Slowly, he said, "Okay, Molly, we'll ride with Dr. Taylor."

Jason barely waited for the words to fall out of Ben's mouth before the kid screeched loud enough to peel the enamel off Ben's front teeth and loud enough to infect Molly with a case of ear-splitting giggles. Sweet Jesus, how could anyone drive with so much chaos in the backseat?

Ben knew how. No way. He opened his mouth to say forget it, but Dr. La Ti Da suggested, "How about fifteen minutes of tag before we hit Baskin-Robbins?"

Kelsy clasped her hands under her chin. "Thank you, O Wise One."

With Molly snugly on his hip, Ben said to the good doc, "I bet you're first in line at the roller coaster, aren't you?"

Sunshine drenched the parking lot, so they ended up walking to Barron Park. At least Ben and Kelsy walked; Doc chased the kids through piles of dead leaves the entire four blocks. Once in the park, Molly went ballistic. She couldn't get enough running and jumping. Ben joined the game of tag but lasted about ten minutes before stumbling across the field to catch his breath next to Kelsy.

"Amazing, huh?" Kelsy jerked her thumb at the good doc.

"Amazing." Ben watched a couple of people on Rollerblades in the distance. Christ, from washboard abs to Mr. Flab in eleven months. His mind veered away. "She always been nimble as a racehorse?"

"Always. Comes from having great legs," Kelsy said.

That seemed a little personal, so Ben just nodded.

"You should see her ankles."

Feeling like he'd crossed a line, Ben feigned intense interest in a woodpecker on a nearby pole. Why admit he'd seen her ankles? Not as great as Amy's, but surprisingly trim.

"Jason gave her the ankle bracelet," Kelsy volunteered.

"Nice." If you liked frogs.

"I keep telling her she should give up wearing pants. Wear only skirts. Micros. They're in fashion, you know."

Inwardly, Ben snorted. "I'm not exactly a fashion maven."

Kelsy waved a limp wrist. "Most men don't have a clue about buying women's clothes. Personally, I blame Adam."

"Yeah, fig leaves are pretty drab." Ben grinned to show he was kidding.

He'd loved Amy's soft, feminine blouses and skirts. But he never shopped for them. Whenever he took time off from work, Amy had insisted they spend the time playing with Molly. Or making love. He closed his eyes against the rush of pain.

On the slide, Molly shrieked, "Daddy!" His heart lifted, and his eyes flew open. Lord, hearing her laugh, who'd ever think she might have an ulcer?

Sliding down after Molly, Dr. La Ti Da taunted, "Wimps!"

Kelsy sighed. "Makes me tired just watching them."

"She's barely sweating," Ben observed.

"She's one of those women who glow."

Ben clamped his mouth shut. He'd almost said she glowed. The roses in her cheeks and the flash of her green eyes made the observation true. Intent on watching Dr. La Ti Da's sweater ride up, revealing a patch of ivory skin above her belly button, Ben almost missed Kelsy's next question.

"She'll make a great mother, don't you think?"

Once the question registered, Ben felt something snap inside his head. Something basic. Every muscle stiffened. A red mist blurred Kelsy's features. He wanted to grab her. Shake her.

Goddamn matchmakers. Ghouls. He heard his jaw crack.

"Daddy! Daddy!" Suddenly, arms around his knees slowed his racing pulse. Like a sleepwalker, he blinked away the red haze.

"Did you see me, Daddy? Did you?"

Doc saved him.

"What'd you think of that landing off the slide, Dad?" She twirled Molly around. "Molly's a regular Miss Twinkletoes."

"She's awesome," Jason chimed in.

The fog in Ben's brain lifted. He threw the good doc a goofy smile that drew a confused look from her. He scooped Molly up into a bear hug and nuzzled her neck. "Is that you, Molly? Miss Twinkletoes?"

"Uh-huuuh." She stuck her little chin out.

"I want ice cream," Jason demanded loudly.

"Me, too." Doc grabbed Jason's hand. "Race you!"

"Me, too!" Molly slid out of Ben's arms like quicksilver and roared after Jason and La Ti Da, who hung back till Molly caught up.

"Too bad I don't have a video camera." Kelsy stretched.

"Why's that?" Ben grunted, not giving a damn.

With an imaginary camera to her right eye, Kelsy took a couple of steps toward the jogging trio, then stopped. "To show La Ti Da in about a month."

Still smarting from Kelsy's stupidity, Ben shrugged.

"You know. When she's so worn out she can barely stumble—let alone frolic," Kelsy finished.

For half a nanosecond anxiety took root in Ben. Had worry over Molly, coupled with insomnia for the past year, finally caught up with him? Unwilling to let on that he didn't have a clue what Kelsy was yammering about, he mumbled something.

She went on as if he'd said something brilliant. "No one's greater with kids than La Ti Da. I believe with all my heart she'll be a wonderful mother."

"Wonderful mother?"

His chest tightened. Didn't this woman ever give up? Here he was, convinced he had an inoperable brain tumor—provided they could find his brain when they opened his skull during exploratory surgery—and Miz Matchmaker brings them back full circle.

"Wonderful mother?" Brain tumor or not, he couldn't kill her.

Kelsy flung her hands toward the blue sky. "Are we in a loop?" In a rush, Kelsy said, "*We* know that being a doctor is not the same as being a parent, right?"

Head swimming, Ben nodded. Not because he agreed, but because he now knew with one-hundred-percent certainty that he'd fried his brain. Rage did that to you—fried your brain.

"Having one baby," Kelsy continued, unaware she walked next to a mental midget, "is about the hardest thing in the world. Having triplets has to be three quantum leaps harder."

"Triplets?" he croaked.

What the hell was the matter with him? Dr. Risa Taylor was pregnant with triplets? Sweet Jesus, he'd been fantasizing about a pregnant woman.

"When?" His throat closed on the single word.

"Due the week after Christmas, can you believe it?"

He could not. Okay, so Doc's lush body reminded him of a ripe pear. But if she was pregnant with triplets, then he, Ben Macdonald, needed immediate eye surgery. Right after his brain transplant.

Cautiously, he said, "I didn't think she was married."

Not that a woman needed a husband to get pregnant.

"All the more reason I predict she'll be so worn out she won't be able to see after the first week."

Ben couldn't figure out why he was surprised—no, shocked. After all, he was living in the twenty-first century.

"Starbucks can't make enough coffee to jump-start your brain after being up every night with three babies," Kelsy opined.

"What about her practice?" he gargled.

A sniff. "She's using her brain there. There's no way she can take care of triplets with her practice. So she's taking a leave of absence. It only makes sense."

"Yeah," Ben said. "It only makes sense."

Despite the heat wafting off the freshly baked waffle cones, Ben Macdonald's icy stare froze everyone within a mile of the pink-topped counter. Risa fumbled a twenty out of her billfold with numb fingers. "Exactly what the doctor ordered." She smacked her lips.

His grunt reminded her so much of Tim's disapproval that she said, "Once upon a time, I knew how many calories I saved eating single dips of fat-free, frozen yogurt like Kelsy."

"I understand you're eating for four." He snatched his own double-dip vanilla cone from the tonsured, teenage clerk.

A mega-jolt of joy zapped Risa. Her brain hummed. She couldn't help herself. Expecting congratulations, she ignored his grinch scowl and blasted Ben Macdonald with her biggest smile. "Kelsy told you."

By way of an answer, his tongue flicked over his small mountain of ice cream, and—Holy Hedda—her breasts swelled as she imagined him licking them. Blinded by lust, she tottered to the pink plastic booth. Molly and Jason, busy devouring their sundaes, sat wedged between the wall and Kelsy.

Surprise, surprise. First a hormonal attack, then a Kelsy assault. "Where should I sit?" Risa asked her sneaky, matchmaking, former best friend, who smiled as beatifically as a contemplative Belgian nun.

"Right there, La Ti Da," Jason bellowed.

"Next to Daddy," Molly brayed.

Daddy flinched, but slid in next to Risa. Between the scent of him and the heat arcing off her, she gave up

trying to get the cone to her mouth. No matter. Kelsy
started the conversational ball rolling.

"They say our choice of ice cream says a lot about our
personality."

"Sounds like a theory I'd take to the bank." Daddy
rolled his eyes.

His rudeness went right over Kelsy's head. Risa kicked
her under the table to shut her up, but it was Jason who
came to his mother's rescue. Whoever *they* were didn't
grab his attention either. He pushed his empty cup toward Kelsy. "More please."

"Try a little of my yo—"

"Yuck!" Jason wrinkled his nose.

Silently, Risa gave thanks for little boys. Please let her
raise three sons who appreciated women in their fullness, yet still knew their own minds. Before she could
offer to share with Jason, Molly handed him her cup.

Tension—the kind Risa picked up from parents of ill
children—instantly vibrated from Ben Macdonald's
every cell. He swallowed twice before speaking. "Does
your tummy hurt, Molly?"

Up periscope. The invisible antennae rose out of Risa's
head. She swallowed a lump of ice cream. With black
eyes bright as polished buttons, Molly sure didn't look
like a kid with a stomachache. The four-year-old shook
her head, then pointed at Risa's cone. "I like chocolate
better'n strawberry."

"I like both," Jason announced.

With a laugh, Risa held her cone in the middle of the
table and watched Ben Macdonald through her lashes.
What was his problem? Molly scooped out a heaping
spoonful of Rocky Road.

The lines faded in her dad's forehead and his bleak
eyes danced. Risa's heart clutched. Poor man. Someone
should tell him that the role of the Pied Piper belonged
to parents—not to the child. Their eyes locked. He narrowed his to slits, silently telegraphing, *No mind peepers.*

"La Ti Da?"

"Yes, Jason?" Risa gave herself a mental shake. The last thing Mr. Uptight Macdonald wanted was advice on raising Molly.

"Will you have supper with us tonight?"

"I'm working tonight, Sweetie." Risa squeezed his fingers.

"Tomorrow?"

"Tomorrow I—" Risa took her cue from his squinched-up face. "Why don't you come help me with the nursery tomorrow?"

"Daddy, did you know La Ti Da's going to 'dopt triplets?"

Confusion, doubt, and what finally looked like relief slam-danced across Ben Macdonald's face. Open-mouthed, he stared at Risa, who glanced at Kelsy, who rolled her eyes, then made half a dozen little circles near her right temple with her forefinger.

Molly asked Risa, "Can I come see the nursery sometime?"

"Tomorrow, tomorrow, tomorrow," Jason chanted.

"Can I?" Molly inched forward on the pink plastic bench.

Risa *knew* she wasn't strong enough to flat-out say no, so she waffled. "We'll have to work."

Next to her, Ben Macdonald shifted his weight, and Risa groaned silently. Holy Hannah. She'd just invited Molly to her house without checking with him first. Biiig mistake.

"I'm a good worker," Molly insisted. "Right, Daddy?"

"The best worker ever, sweetheart." He kissed her nose.

Stomach clenched, Risa saw a way out. "If you're busy—"

He shook his head. "I'd be glad to help, too. I'm pretty good with my hands."

For the second time in her life—both times in the presence of Ben Macdonald—Risa was struck mute.

CHAPTER 4

"Daddy, who do you think La Ti Da likes better: me or Jason?"

The question came two seconds after Ben punched the good doc's frog-shaped doorbell on a foggy morning way too early for such questions. Also way too early for "Oh, What a Beautiful Morning" blaring at him from the doorbell.

Under his breath, he moaned. Aloud, he said, "Don't you want to know the latest theories of quantum physics?"

"Oh, Daddy." Mercifully, Molly giggled.

On a roll, Ben pointed to the Santa Claus wreath. "Tell me, do those elves look like frogs?"

"They do, Daddy."

"See how brilliant your old man is?" So brilliant he knew the first words out of his mouth to La Ti Da had to be an apology for that stupid, adolescent crack yesterday. *I'm pretty good with my hands?* God, what had been in that ice cream?

"I think La Ti Da likes Jason better," Molly said solemnly.

The doorbell music didn't even strike Ben as ironic. He dropped to one knee, wrapped his arm around Molly's waist, rejoicing in her sturdy little body, and cursed his brain.

"You know," he began, "she's known Jason a lot longer."

"Uh-huh."

Uh-huh, yes? Or, uh-huh, what? Ben didn't have a clue.

"You don't have to know someone forever to like them a lot, do you?" Worry clouded Molly's eyes.

"No, sweetheart." God, he was already in over his head.

Maybe, since the good doc didn't know him, she didn't take offense at his dumb double entendre yesterday. Maybe there was no reason to open a can of worms by apologizing.

"You like La Ti Da a lot, don't you?" Molly patted his hand, stopping his mind's free fall.

"Welll, sweetheart . . ." Sweet Jesus. Had Molly picked up on his testosterone attack yesterday?

Smart as she was, she'd sensed something. Maybe not the gist of his dumb-ass wordplay, but *something*. A sudden crick in his knee demanded he shift his weight. He stretched for the doorbell and took a deep breath. Where the hell was Doc?

"Do you like La Ti Da or Jason better, Daddy?"

"Sweetheart, I don't really know either one."

"Could we invite La Ti Da for pancakes some day so you could know her better?" Molly dazzled Ben with the kind of smile he'd almost forgotten.

Sweat dripped off his brows. He swiped it away. Careful. He was teetering on the edge of quicksand here. "You know, she's pretty busy, sweetheart."

"I know, Daddy. She's a doctor."

"Doctors are pretty busy." Especially doctors about to adopt triplets. Salt stung his eyes. He blinked, repeatedly.

"Could you like La Ti Da the way you liked Mommy—if you knew her better?"

His heart dropped.

Coffee. Preferably by mouth, but he'd take it through a vein if necessary. "You know, sweetheart—"

His mind stumbled. It had been one of those mornings. Molly up at the crack of a sunless dawn, urging him to hurry up so they could go to La Ti Da's house. Not even blueberry pancakes slowed her incessant comments about the woman, who—Ben wasn't sure, but he intended to check—apparently walked on water.

"Daddy, she can talk without moving her mouth." Blueberry syrup had dribbled down Molly's chin during this announcement. "She only does it for special people. Jason said she's teaching him. Do you think she'd teach me, Daddy?"

In the same breath, his child then launched into a barrage of deep questions that continued nonstop right up through the doorbell blaring.

Where the hell was Doc? Surely, with all her other magical powers, she wasn't deaf. Why didn't she answer the damned doorbell and save him?

"Maybe she's still asleep, Daddy." Molly reached for the doorbell again.

With flashing thoughts of Doc asleep in the nude, Ben caught Molly's hand. "Maybe she's getting dressed."

Molly sighed. "I hope she didn't forget."

"Maybe she did forget." *I'm pretty good with my hands.*

"No." Molly shook her head. "She didn't forget, Daddy."

Her certainty shook Ben, and he decided that one more verse of "Oh, What a Beautiful Yada, Yada, Yada" wouldn't send him 'round the bend after all. He suggested ringing the bell again, but Molly cried, "She's coming! I hear her, Daddy!"

Then, there she was. Exuding the scent of roses. Damp, red ringlets framed her face. Huge green eyes. Lavender shirt buttoned all wrong. A hint of lightly freckled skin under the open collar. Jeans, tattooed to her lush female hips, tapered down those long, long legs. Stopping at the ankle. Accenting elegant, bare feet. With fire-engine red nails.

His breath rumbled in his throat. He couldn't take his eyes off her silver frog toe ring. What the hell was wrong with him?

Scrunching her toes under, Doc threw Ben a look. "The intercom doesn't work, and I was in the shower."

Uh-huh. An image flashed. Water cascading off her curves.

"We rang the bell," Molly said.

"I—I didn't hear the bell till I was drying off."

Without warning, a flash fire engulfed Ben. He imagined her ritual of drying off. Bending over. Water droplets sliding down her throat, pooling in the hollow, glistening between her breasts.

Molly saved him from working himself into a lather by saying, "I don't like showers. I like baths."

"Me, too." Risa nodded. "Come on in, and I'll show you the rubber frog Jason gave me for my birthday."

"You kiss him every night before bed?" The words popped out of Ben's mouth, bypassing his brain altogether. Then, God help him, he grinned.

Thankfully, Molly laughed and began retelling *The Frog Prince*. Doc nodded at Molly but threw Ben a look that told him he should pay for his daily intake of oxygen. And damn if her contempt didn't excite him, make him want to thump his chest.

Over her shoulder, Doc said, "Fresh coffee's in the kitchen. To your right. Help yourself—since you're so good with your hands."

"Thanks." Red-faced, he waited till he heard her footsteps on the stairs before mumbling, "I'd rather meet the frog."

* * *

"Daddy's funny, isn't he, La Ti Da?" Molly held Risa's hand in a tiny vise.

"Uh-huh." So funny his frog crack made getting up the stairs a minor marathon for Risa. Her pulse rose with every step.

"I like it when he's funny, don't you?"

Lying stuck in Risa's throat, but she nodded, averting Molly's face so she wouldn't speak the truth. Molly didn't know the difference between nervy and funny. Where did her father get his nerve? Arriving before eight on a Saturday morning and giving Risa grief before her second cup of coffee?

"He always made Mommy laugh a lot."

Heart racing, Risa didn't see what choice she had except to keep climbing. Even if she had a coronary. "What about you? Did Daddy make you laugh a lot, too?"

Her heart missed a beat. A coronary wasn't that farfetched.

"Uh-uh. I giggled." Sure-footed as a mountain goat, Molly dragged Risa up the stairs and confessed, "I hiccuped, too. Sometimes Mommy gave me a paper bag, and I blowed in it."

And what was Daddy doing? Risa bit her bottom lip. Who cared? He reminded her a little too much of Tim, who had spent ninety seconds of their two-minute marriage *teasing*. When Risa complained, he'd said, "What's the matter, Big? Can't take a little teasing?"

Forget Tim. He's out of your life.

Generally, forgetting Tim was not a problem. Especially with a cute kid like Molly jabbering at her a mile a minute. But this morning, past and present came together in Ben Macdonald's question. *You kiss him every night before bed?*

Had he meant she didn't have anyone but a frog to kiss?

Had he meant a kiss from her didn't turn frogs into princes?

At the top of the stairs, Molly surveyed the hall, gloomy despite the recently installed skylight. Risa believed kids thrived in sunlight. In moderation, of course. Moderation was the key in all things. Too bad her raging hormones didn't agree.

"Which door, La Ti Da?"

"That one—through my bedroom . . ." A mess because they'd come so darned early.

"Daddy has a big bed like yours." Molly pointed to the king-size bed with its twisted sheets. "I help him make it."

Risa dropped Molly's hand and quickly pulled the comforter up over the tangled bed linens. Holy Hannah, what a miserable night—thanks to X-rated dreams starring Ben Macdonald.

"Are you going to read bedtime stories to the babies?" Molly handed Risa a stack of medical journals, which she shoved under the bed, saying, "Sure am. Want me to read you and Jason a couple of my favorites?"

"After we see your frog?"

"After we see my frog." Risa stuffed her raggedy UC Davis nightshirt between the pillows, then opened the bathroom door.

Molly wiggled her nose. "Ummm. Roses."

Risa inhaled and felt her nerve endings lengthen, relax. She handed Molly a bar of soap. "It's made of rose petals."

Sniffing it, Molly said, "My soap makes lots of bubbles."

"Bubbles are good." Risa kicked aside the towels she'd left on the floor in her desperation to jerk jeans up over her damp legs and butt. "I like lots of bubbles in my bath."

"Me, too. I looove lots of bubbles in my bath."

This revelation—and the little girl intensity with which Molly revealed it to Risa—fast-forwarded images of the future knockout teenager and young woman Molly would become. Awed, Risa bent down. "Bubbles are what baths are all about."

Without warning Molly threw her arms around Risa's neck and whispered, "My mommy said bubble baths are a girl thing."

"Absolutely." Risa swallowed hard.

The sweet, clean smell of Molly was enough to reduce Risa to putty. It took all her willpower to let go when Molly moved out of her arms. For a couple of heartbeats the room swayed after she stood. *Easy.* She flipped on a soft spotlight over the Jacuzzi. Careful of her spinning head, she reached across the unlit candles and lifted a big green rubber frog out of his corner on top of the tub.

"Ohhh, La Ti Da, he's soooo cute."

"His name's Fergus. Fergie, for short."

"He's so biiig." Molly's eyes looked like dinner plates.

"Indeed, I am." Risa moved Fergie's head from side to side and adopted his froggy voice. "Want to hug me now, do ye?"

Molly clapped a hand over her mouth, then threw open her arms. Risa fought back a smile, handed Fergie over, then said, naturally, "He's almost bigger than you."

Rocking back on her heels, Molly nodded. "I love his little sunglasses."

"Fergie's a cool dude. But he's ferocious." Risa patted the frogs's blubber belly. "That means he scares away all the spiders in my house."

"My teddy bears are frocious. They scare away all the monsters in my room."

A tiny quaver, almost inaudible, squeezed Risa's maternal heart and set alarms clanging in her physician's head. Daddies, not teddy bears, should keep monsters away.

Carefully, she knelt next to Molly, who, with total concentration, smoothed the fake beads on the collar of Fergie's dark green morning coat. Teeth clenched, Risa asked quietly, "Where are the monsters your bears scare away?"

Molly examined the gold rings on Fergie's long, spindly digits. "In the closet."

Making no sound, Risa waited.

"Under my bed." Molly cuddled Fergie's gangly body.

After two full heartbeats, Risa repeated, "In the closet. Under your bed." She stopped. Waited.

"In the bathroom, too." Molly met Risa's gaze.

Breathing normally, Risa gave away nothing as Molly continued. "In the hall. Everywhere."

Red spots danced behind Risa's eyelids. "Even with a light on in your room?"

"Uh-huh." Molly caught her bottom lip between her teeth, patted Fergie's cheek, then said, "The monsters don't come every night. Only the nights when Daddy works late."

A surge of anger erupted inside Risa. What was the matter with the man? After mentally counting to two, she swept aside her normal caution. "So Daddy doesn't work late every night?"

She kept her voice neutral on *every*.

"Uh-uh. I 'member, before Mommy . . . before—you know—when she lived with us, Daddy comed home early 'most every night." Molly blew her bangs out of her eyes, then kissed Fergie. "Can I show him to Daddy?"

Right at that moment, Risa wanted to show Daddy the door. No way she'd allow a jerk who neglected his only child to invade her private, rose-scented sanctuary. On the other hand, no way could she categorically say no to such a simple request. Not when Molly looked at her with the soft, trusting eyes of a cocker spaniel and simply waited.

Risa swallowed. She'd met her match. She said brightly, "Okay, but let's take Fergie downstairs and wait for Jason."

* * *

Smoke streamed out of Doc's ears. Not to mention there was blood in her eye.

Two cups of coffee curdled in Ben's stomach. He set his mug—frog-shaped, naturally—next to the coffee pot and watched his grinning daughter race toward him.

"Look, Daddy, look."

"See Molly run. See Molly run." Hard to miss the big, ugly rubber frog she clutched. Not to mention the death glare the good doc trained on Ben's balls.

"Isn't he cute, Daddy?" Molly cooed.

Wisely, Ben agreed. But he drew the line at cooing. On occasion, after getting home too late for a bedtime story, he would kiss Molly good night and coo at the menagerie of teddy bears on her bed. In Doc's kitchen, with her coming at him like a stealth bomber, cooing put him at a big disadvantage.

"Do you know any frog jokes, Daddy?"

"No, I don't, sweetheart." Ben avoided looking at Doc by pretending to pay attention to Molly.

"Did you *ever* know any frog jokes?" Doc arched a brow.

"I suppose that's debatable."

"I bet it would be a very short debate."

"Hey, I'm not afraid to admit my frog joke hit a little close to home—given your thing about frogs."

Doc stared at him, then snorted. Just in case he missed her message, she tossed her head and rolled her eyes. *So much for apologies.*

"Do you have a thing about frogs, La Ti Da?" Molly squealed.

"I sure do. Toads, on the other hand . . ."

Ben's survival instincts kicked in at that point. Pulling Molly against his knees, he raised his empty mug toward the good doc. "Great java."

"Too bad I forgot the arsenic."

"Never use it or cream. Take mine black every time."

"Nothing *soft* about you, is there?"

Before he could ask her what that meant, Molly tugged his hand, chattering faster than a baby monkey, going on and on about Fergie and La Ti Da's bathroom, conjuring up the previous mental snapshots of her up there naked.

Whether it was the almost inaudible groan that escaped his throat or his heavy breathing that betrayed him, Doc must've read his mind. Her eyes flashed fire.

Thank God, Molly stood between him and her.

Ben Macdonald, Best Daddy in the World. Red-faced, filled with disgust, he forced himself to take Doc's withering gaze like a man. After a decade, he said, "I owe you an—"

"Oh, what a beautiful—" The brassy notes of the doorbell mocked Ben. "Yeah." He rolled his eyes. "I've definitely got the feeling everything's goin' *my* way."

Mouth primped, the good doc sailed past him. The sexy sway of her luscious backside sent his pulse skyrocketing. Her hips narrowly missed a corner on the kitchen island. "Excuse me," she said in a tone frigid enough to frost the little hairs in his ears, "that must be Kelsy and Jason."

Molly let go of Ben's hand and adjusted the damn frog under one arm. "Can I open the door?"

"Ever think about a different tune on your doorbell?" Ben raised his voice above the violins and trumpets and drums swelling in another chorus. "How about something upbeat—like 'Froggy Went a Courtin'?"

For a second, he'd have sworn he saw Doc's mouth twitch. Then she gave him her back and spoke to Molly in a deep, froggish tone. "On a beautiful day like today, of course ye can open the door."

"Yay, yay."

Molly slipped her hand into the good doc's and skipped toward the hall without a backward glance at

Ben, who decided he should use the time alone to rehearse his apology.

Apologize first, then ask Doc to take Molly as a patient. He sloshed coffee into his mug, looking for holes in his logic.

God, if this was a beautiful morning, show him a bad one.

The morning after Amy died.

The memory slithered out of the darkest corner of his mind, caught him by surprise, filled him with the urge to run—the way he'd always wanted to do when he'd startled rattlers as a kid. Without warning, his chest tightened, until he could scarcely catch his breath.

Goddammit. What the hell was he doing, playing at being whole again? Making sexual banter? Running toward fire? Grief tightened the wire across his chest. There would never be another woman for him—whether Dr. Risa Taylor accepted Molly as a patient or not.

A screech in the hall jerked Ben to attention. Jason screamed, "You give me that, Molly. Now!"

"Molly?" Ben bolted across the kitchen, rounded the corner, and raced across miles of marble tiles.

"It's okay, Jay." Hunkered down at kid level, Doc had one arm around Jason and the other around Molly, which should've reassured Ben, but didn't. He knew he was overreacting, but he picked up speed, calling, "I'm right here, sweetheart."

"Honey." In the open door, Kelsy peered over an armful of grocery bags like one of the ugly stepsisters waiting for Prince Charming. Ben passed by her without a twinge of guilt.

"She can't hold Fergie," Jason insisted, glaring at Molly.

"Can too," Molly said.

"Can not."

Ben ground his teeth. Why didn't the good doc work her magic on that kid? He was out of control.

"You're not the boss of me."

"You go, girl," Ben mouthed under his breath, awed by the way Molly jutted her chin at Jason, who was red-faced with rigid shoulders and fisted hands.

"Hey, guys," Kelsy called.

Wiggling her nose, Doc gently uncurled Jason's fingers one by one. "Let's talk this over," she whispered.

Without warning, Jason dodged around her and jerked Fergie out of Molly's hands. "This is La Ti Da's."

"Now just a damn minute." Ben's hand shot out. His fingers hooked around a skinny frog leg.

The good doc glared and hissed, "Are you insane?"

"Hey!" Jason dug his heels in and hung on for all he was worth.

"Here, Molly." Motioning his open-mouthed daughter toward him, Ben gave a good yank on the frog. Jesus, he was insane.

"La Ti Daaa!" Jason held onto the frog but came about an inch off the floor, kicking like a demon before he dropped onto terra firma and immediately smacked into his mother.

She yelped. *WHAAP.* The grocery bag she carried hit the floor. Dozens of green grapes rolled across the tile like marbles. Ben froze as Molly, a dead weight, gloamed onto his free arm.

"Oh, for cryin' out loud." Doc lunged for Jason, who grabbed another frog leg, hollered, *"Yahoooo,"* and took a running slide across the grape-splattered tiles.

"All yours, kid." Feeling caught in a bad dream, Ben let go of the frog and prayed Molly didn't knock him off balance.

"It's okay, Daddy." Molly sighed and released her vise grip on Ben's arm. "Jason can have Fergie."

"Yahooooo!" Jason spun around on a couple of grape skins.

"Cool it, Jason." Doc held up her hands like a traffic cop, and damned if the kid didn't stop and go to her like a hungry calf to its mother. He even let her work his fingers off the damn frog and lay the stupid thing in the middle of the hall.

Down on her hands and knees, Kelsy said, "Any time now, I could use a little help here."

"I'll help," Molly volunteered.

"Not me." Jason bussed Doc on the cheek.

Me either, Ben decided and tapdanced out of Molly's path. Where was the payoff in helping clean up? Doc sure as hell wasn't cutting him any slack. The look she shot him could fell an elephant.

Hell, she probably hoped he'd fall on his ass.

Snug in her embrace, Jason stuck his tongue out. Ben heard something snap in his head. Furious, he reached down, scooped up the frog and tossed it to Molly. "Here you go, sweetheart."

Instantly, she fell on top of the green plastic body. With a shriek, Jason dog-piled on top of her. Instead of protesting, Molly giggled. A beat later, so did Jason.

"Score one for the kids." Doc licked her finger, then dragged it through the air.

Her comment sent the kids to the moon. Sidestepping the melee at his feet, Ben imagined her fingertip—poker hot—in his mouth. Spontaneous combustion ignited the back of his throat. He mewed. She stared at him. The next thing he knew his feet started going round and round like a hamster in a cage. His body, in the meantime, forgot to follow.

Oh, shiiit. Not again.

CHAPTER 5

"Some days it just don't pay to get out of bed." At the kitchen island, Kelsy unpacked two unbroken grocery bags and tried not to grin.

"Don't start with me." Risa slammed a picnic basket down on the counter.

"Oops. Did I touch a nerve?" Kelsy backed up.

"Don't be ridiculous." Risa opened the basket.

"Ridiculous, huh?" Kelsy tiptoed to the door and peered at Ben, Molly, and Jason scrubbing grape juice off the hall floor. "The sparks zinging between you two sure weren't ridicu—"

"You're hallucinating." Risa rattled knives and forks.

"Okay." Kelsy shrugged. "I just think—"

"You should check on Jason instead of matchmaking."

"He's cooperating beautifully. He knows Ben has his number." Kelsy leaned a hip against the island.

"I thought you'd take the guy apart for jerking—and I do mean jerking—Jay around like a kite on a string."

The tone, more than the words, spoke volumes. Kelsy felt a little flush of doubtful curiosity. "Is that what this is all about? You think Ben was too rough with Jay?"

"Don't you?" Risa crossed her arms over her chest.

"Nope. I think Jay needs a little roughhousing from time to time."

"What?" Risa scowled.

"I don't mean spanking." Kelsy felt her heart miss a beat. "But Sam travels too much, and boys need men in their lives if they're going to grow up to be men and not pseudowomen."

"Pseudowomen?" For a second, Risa bristled, then met and held Kelsy's gaze. "I'll say this, then, we can agree to disagree. If any man ever *roughhouses* my sons the way that—that *jerk* jerked Jay around . . ."

Her voice trailed off, and Kelsy tensed, trying not to let her imagination get away from her and tempt her to interpret the unfinished sentence as a slam against her mothering. After all, she'd pretty much just said Charlie, Tom, and Harry wouldn't grow up to be *real* men if Risa never married. Taking a deep breath, Kelsy said, "Is this the worst argument we've ever had in thirty years?"

"Hardly." Risa shook her head. "The worst was seventh grade when you stood me up to go to the movies with Scott Douglas."

"What can I say?" For at least the millionth time in thirty years, Kelsy coveted Risa's mop of copper curls and her best friend's boobs. "It was two days before my first period."

Risa made a rude noise. "The old hijacked-by-hormones argument, right? No wonder men think a woman can't be commander in chief. Next mood swing: six minutes."

Kelsy chuckled, glad Risa hadn't lost her sense of humor. She drawled, "Uh-huh. And who taught *you* how to figure out where to put your nose when you kiss a boy?"

"Go ahead, brag. I bet if Tim knew I'd practiced kissing with you, he and I'd never've walked down the aisle."

"C'mon," Kelsy protested. "Admit it. You learned a lot from those lessons."

"It's a wonder people didn't think we were lesbians." Risa shook the empty picnic basket over the sink.

"Guess what, Toots? Merilee Simpson and Alana Michaels told everyone we were."

"What?" The picnic basket slipped out of Risa's hands, but she caught it before it hit the floor. "Why didn't you ever tell me? Best friends tell each other every—"

"Like you're telling me how you really feel about Ben?" Kelsy arched a brow and savored the tingle of victory, but the urge to gloat died quickly.

Whatever her reason for holding back, Risa would open up when she was ready. Kelsy took a step back from an invisible line. "You know I love you, right? You're my best friend."

"I know." Risa opened her arms. Filled with relief, Kelsy stepped into the hug. Sniffling, they held each other tight. They'd been here before, and they'd be here again. Of this, Kelsy was absolutely certain. After they patted each other between the shoulder blades a few more times, Risa whispered, "It's awfully quiet out in the hall. Should we check?"

"Can't keep your eyes off the hunk, can you?"

Risa straightened with a jerk. "Earth to Kelsy. Ben Macdonald and I will *never* get together—even if it means saving the human race. Believe me, the man's trouble."

"Trouble can be fun." Kelsy wiggled her eyebrows, confident Risa would take the bait.

"Don't be dumb. I'm clueless about having fun with a wolf in sheep's clothing."

"What better time than the present to learn? You could use some fun in your life. Maybe even an orgasm."

Risa rolled her eyes. "If I wanted that kind of fun, would I adopt triplets? I'm ready to settle down, Kel, have a family, forget sex."

"How can a smart, sexy, thirty-six-year-old female say 'forget sex'?" Kelsy folded one of the brown bags.

"I can say it because I married Tim. Trust me. Sex is overrated."

Kelsy threw her hands up in the air. "Your ex is not Ben."

"No, Ben is . . ." Risa threw her hands up, too.

"T-R-O-U-B-L-E?" Kelsy smoothed the label on the thermos, set it aside, and tucked three Tupperware containers under her chin. She mamboed toward the fridge. "See this?"

"Your point being?" Risa glanced at the plasticware tower.

"My point being, it's like your life—trying to raise three kids without a father."

Risa rolled her eyes. "Shaky," Kelsy clarified, returning to the real subject. "Now you tell me why Ben's trouble." Afraid the tower would topple, she spoke carefully. "He's too good-looking? Too smart? Too hot?"

Throwing her arms out wide, Risa got right in Kelsy's face. "Do you have ADD? Didn't I just tell you why I have as much interest in that jerk as . . . as . . ." She wagged a finger. "Forget matchmaking, Kel."

"You're just cranky 'cuz you haven't had sex for so long—"

"Shut up." Risa clapped her hand over Kelsy's mouth. She checked over her shoulder, her eyes rolled so far back in her head that Kelsy instantly thought about the old *Exorcist* movie.

The middle container teetered but miraculously didn't fall. Risa's hand tightened. Kelsy crossed her eyes. For once, the ploy didn't work. Risa held on tighter, speaking through gritted teeth. "What you know about my sex life is privileged. Nod if you understand."

Kelsy nodded and Risa took her hand away. "Whoa." Kelsy sucked in a deep breath. "You've got it bad, Toots."

Naked misery stared her in the eye. Heart thumping, Kelsy swallowed the banter. "Sorry," she mumbled. "Truly."

Risa jerked the fridge door open so hard a couple of ice cubes fell through the ice maker. "Are you sure you can't go on this picnic with us?" she demanded.

"When was the last time you cooked?" asked Kelsy, sliding the Tupperware onto the top shelf, which was empty like the other three except for six little white packets of hot mustard and a bottle of Dom Perignon. Without guilt, Kelsy read the attached card, made a noise, and said, "You're eating junk food again, aren't you?"

"Do I look as if I'm starving? Are you coming or not?"

"I trust the freezer's brimming with goodies." Kelsy opened the freezer door, sighed, and sniffed the lidless, half can of orange juice concentrate.

"Oh goody. Nutritious ice crystals." Her heart ached. She returned the can to the top shelf and shut the door. "I made other plans. Besides, five's a crowd."

Risa snapped her fingers. "I'm glad you can't come. At least I'll get a break from your darned matchmaking—"

"Tell me again why that'd be so bad?" Kelsy opened her hands wide. "Your sons need a daddy. Molly—"

Risa shook her head so hard it made Kelsy dizzy. "Whatever Molly needs, I'm not the one to give it to her, Kel. And Ben Macdonald sure can't take on three more kids."

"Who says?" Kelsy felt like shaking her best bud. Risa would find fault with a saint.

"I say." Risa lifted her chin. "You think he's hot? I think he's probably the coldest man I've ever met. He is not daddy material, so once and for all, will you give it up?"

For now. Afraid Risa would read her mind, Kelsy ducked her head before saying, "Will you remember men are not like copiers? We do need them for more than reproduction."

"I'll remember." Risa tossed her head. "I'll remember men are like mascara—they run at the first sign of emotion."

At 9:11 A.M., Ben waited a couple of decades in the hall while the kids and Doc said their good-byes to Kelsy at the front door. In no hurry, she checked out the floor, then asked, "Do you do windows, Ben?"

For some reason, Molly thought this was hysterical, which, of course, set Jason off too. Doc looked ready to strangle Funny Girl. Which could've been fun, except Ben didn't want her to go to prison till he'd asked her about Molly.

Feeling murderous himself, he said, "Windows fall outside my expertise. I'm a man of limited skills."

"Modesty becomes a man, don't you think, Risa?"

Doc shrugged, but pushed Jason toward his mother. After a quick hug, she spoke over his head to Ben, "Have fun."

A camera in his head clicked a snapshot of him and Doc climbing the stairs, hugging the frog, then falling on each other like rabbits. When the front door closed, Ben went cold, then hot all over. What the hell was wrong with him? Had that cleaning crap zapped a bunch of his brain cells?

The second Doc shut the door Jason screeched, "Me 'n Molly are bored, La Ti Da."

Ben jumped. Doc's eyes widened. Then, her mouth twitched. *You better not laugh,* he thought. What was laughable about reacting normally to a four-year-old banshee? He drawled, "We're all bored."

In case she missed his point, he yawned. Ignoring his bad manners, she went down to Jason's and Molly's eye level. "Are you too bored to help me with the nursery?"

"Do we hafta?" Jason whined, grating on Ben's nerves. Thank God Molly never whined. Not even when her stomach hurt. "Can't we play?" Jason looked ready to bawl.

"Of course," Doc said in the gentlest tone Ben had ever heard. His nerve endings stopped twanging. "You worked real hard cleaning the floor."

"I worked hard, too," Molly said shyly.

"I know you did." Doc touched Molly's cheek. A sudden stab of jealousy caught Ben by surprise. He took a step toward Molly, but she snuggled closer to Doc, who whispered, "Thank you."

Molly's face lit up. "You're welcome."

The woman can charm the birds out of the trees. Ben bit his tongue. Well, he wasn't a bird. Just the dummy who'd ended up scrubbing tile with two four-year-olds while the women conveniently disappeared.

"Let's play," Jason demanded.

"You really are bored." Doc hugged her godson.

Not half as bored as Ben, whose left eye started ticking as the good doc included his kid in a group hug.

"I'm not bored." Molly looked up through her lashes at Doc, then smiled at Ben, twisting his heart in knots and giving him some comfort that she didn't have a stomachache.

"I'm ready to work. Are you ready, Daddy?"

"I can hardly wait, sweetheart." The smirk on Doc's mouth stopped him from embroidering his lie.

"What should we do, La Ti Da?" Molly bumped up against Doc like a kitten.

Remembering he'd catch more flies with honey than with vinegar, Ben said, "Leave the heavy lifting to the men."

His smart-aleck attempt at humor fell on deaf ears.

In whispers too low for him to overhear, Doc drew both kids into a tight circle that shut him out. Their giggles taunted him, but he didn't care. So what if she was throwing her voice? Such theatrics didn't intrigue him. On the other hand, he felt royally pissed when, like the Pied Piper, she led the kids up the stairs and left him staring at her sexy behind.

For half a nanosecond, Ben toyed with the idea of stalking out with Molly, but common sense kicked in before he took a step. Molly might not be a whiner, but she'd pitch a fit if they left now. And once they left, when could he convince Doc she should take Molly as a new patient?

Shoulders back, he marched up the stairs. Crossing

the threshold into the nursery, he broke up a gigglefest. Doc looked through him like he was invisible. He snapped his heels together and threw her a salute. "Private Macdonald reporting for duty, *ma'am.*"

Her eyes narrowed, and it was obvious he'd punctured her famous sense of humor. Which, frankly, gave him a small sense of power. Self-discipline took a backseat to gloating. He grinned at her. Mouth tight, she pulled Jason closer. Her body language said to Ben, *You fool, you're not even in this room.*

Patient as a saint, Ben waited while she showed the kids three shelves and a trunk filled with toys. While they sorted books and blocks, Doc spit out instructions to Ben faster than bullets. Burro work, but he didn't complain—not even when the kids got underfoot every time he turned around. He just traipsed up the stairs, down the stairs, up the stairs, down again. Like a robot, he carted, hauled, and lugged enough furniture, toys, and baby stuff to qualify for a union card.

After Ben's eleven millionth trip, Jason announced, "No more toys. Now can we play?"

Without so much as a by-your-leave, Doc sashayed out of the nursery, taking the kids into another room. Ben took a break without asking. When Doc returned, she didn't bother explaining a thing. Pulse thudding in his ears, Ben held his temper in check. She'd never take Molly as a patient if he went off like a stick of dynamite. Inhaling through his teeth, he kept on truckin'.

"Tote that barge, lift that bale," he chanted.

Doc rolled her eyes, but in a demonstration of grace under fire, Ben lined up the bassinets under the window for the fourth time without making a single smart-aleck crack.

Sun danced on the ugly frog wallpaper. If her kids never slept, he could tell her why. The morning sun would blind the poor little guys. Of course, the sun would rise in the north before she listened to his logic.

He wailed, "Here we go 'round the mulberry bush, the . . ."

Not even a flicker of an eyelash this time.

"Any song requests?" he asked, his pulse kicking up a notch.

It didn't seem unreasonable to expect that a woman who probably yakked in her sleep might ask what Molly's nursery had been like.

Smarting from Doc's indifference, Ben felt his cool slip away. Determined not to lose this battle, he sidled closer to Doc, making his tone friendly. "We painted Molly's nursery some kind of pink—apricot I think they call it."

"Really." Doc shied away from him.

"*Really.*" Her icy tone fried him. Past the point of no return, he demanded, "What the hell's the matter with you? You act like I'm a serial ax killer."

As if he could wield an ax, after falling down every time he turned around.

"Don't flatter yourself." The sun bathed her in a pool of golden, righteous wrath.

Christ, she looked like a red-haired Norse goddess. Involuntarily, he took a step toward her. "What does that mean?"

Her hair, a mass of wild curls, fanned out behind her as she jumped back. Her hand grazed his wrist. "It means I'm not interested."

Of its own volition, his libido wove a fantasy of her hair spread out on a pillow after making love. "I must've missed that." He raked her from head to toe.

"There's a lot you miss."

She'd buttoned her shirt up to her chin, but the jeans still hugged her hips like cellophane on ripe fruit. Black and white high-tops, ugly as a schoolmarm's orthopedic shoes, encased her elegant feet, hiding her crimson-painted toenails. She gazed down her nose at him, and he felt his heart shrink. Mentally, he smacked his forehead. God, rabbits had longer attention spans.

Guilt hit him between the eyes. She was all business. Exactly the way he wanted her, right?

"I think this arrangement works." Her tone froze the short hairs on the nape of his scalding neck.

"Hallelujah!" Sanity returned, and he didn't point out he'd used the same config the first three arrangements.

"If you'd like to leave now, catch up on some of your own work, I'm sure—"

Sniffing trouble, his reptile brain twitched. "I don't leave jobs half finished, Doctor."

"Really?"

"Anyone ever tell you you really use *really* a lot?"

"No one's ever pointed that out." She jutted her chin at him. "But few people I know have minds smaller than postage stamps."

"Really? With your huge mind, how come you implied I work weekends? Weekends are my time with Molly."

"You think weekends make up for the time you're gone during the week?" She slammed a dresser drawer shut with her hip.

Tempted to slam something himself, Ben held up both palms. "Where the hell does that question come from?"

"From a concern for your daughter."

Mind your own damn business. Dry-mouthed, he realized her concern was precisely why he wanted her for Molly's doctor. Back rigid, she held up a tiny white shirt, then folded the sleeves under without taking her eyes off him. "You are aware she has frequent nightmares?"

What had Molly told her? His heart slammed into the top of his head.

"Not to mention," Doc added softly, "those stomachaches you're worried about."

"Wait till you have kids," he said through gritted teeth. She gasped. He exhaled loudly. Ahhh shit. Her face flamed. *Go for the jugular, you sweet-talker.* "I am *aware* she has nightmares," he said hoarsely. "I am her father, dammit."

"And I'm nothing." Her harsh tone stung like a bull-whip. "But if I were . . ."

Unnerved by the familiar feeling of panic squeezing his guts, Ben straightened, stuck his hands in his pockets and rocked back on his heels, morphing into his "Don't mess with me, I'm a CEO" persona. "Want to cut to the bottom line, Doc?"

She blinked but didn't back down. "If there's a problem with a child—any kind of problem—I *always* hold the parents responsible."

Enlightenment flashed, and he connected the dots, figuring out her unspoken accusations. No wonder she treated him like he didn't deserve food and water.

"Molly said something, didn't she?" His gut burned. Two red spots stained Doc's cheeks, confirming his suspicions. "What'd she say?"

"You're gone too much."

"Anyone ever complimented you on your bedside manner?"

"You asked," she said, in a tone that, by law, should be used only when dealing with registered sex offenders.

Panic made his throat tight. He swallowed. "She said that?"

"No, but that's the bottom line."

"The bottom line is I—I've got a company to run. Molly understands. . . ." He heard his defensiveness and felt his heart dip.

Christ, Amy could handle this. Amy could soothe Molly's fears, assure him he was a good father and understand he didn't neglect his kid, for God's sake. Obviously, Doc didn't get it.

She touched the frog pendant, opened her mouth, then shut it again. "Don't hold back," Ben barked, then added, "I can take it."

He'd swear he saw a flash in her eyes. Pity, or the sun? Whichever, she took him at his word and didn't hold back. "Molly understands a lot. She understands she's lost her mommy *and* her daddy. She understands if she has tummyaches, he'll come back."

Ben pinched the bridge of his nose and tried to straighten his back while searching for an explanation that didn't sound like whining. Or worse, like blaming Molly. Discounting whatever Molly had said.

"Believe it or not, she does come first." Ask his staff. But *don't* ask his board of directors. They wanted all of him.

A shrug and pursed lips told him what Doc thought. Certain she'd never take Molly as a patient now, he grabbed her shoulders and pulled her so close he could taste her breath, warm and sweet. Her eyes widened, but she didn't jerk away. Her scent of roses brought back memories of Amy sniffing bouquets of violets. His pulse dropped to racing instead of galloping.

Holding on to both of Doc's strong shoulders, Ben didn't back down. He could do this. He could ask for what he wanted. "I—I want you . . ."

"What?" She reared back. Ben's stomach lurched. "I don't mean I want *you*—" She held her hands up, warding him off like he was Dracula. "Hell, that's not what I mean. . . ." With both feet in his mouth, his intention came out as gibberish.

The floor shook under their feet. "La Ti Daaa, we're bored," Jason screamed. "Can we go outside?"

"Can we play in the park?" Molly careened into the nursery a second before Ben dropped his hands to his sides.

Heat arced off Dr. Risa Taylor like lightning, and Ben stood absolutely still, sure a single spark would sear him like fresh tuna.

CHAPTER 6

Getting ready for the picnic, Risa made sure Molly or Jason stayed at her side every heartbeat. Being in the same galaxy with Ben Macdonald was impossible now. Risa jumped every time the man breathed. Assigning him to carry the picnic basket gave her more sophomoric satisfaction than she wanted to admit. Packed with gourmet booty from Kelsy, the basket weighed a ton. Unless he wanted a hernia, he couldn't possibly keep up with her and the kids charging through piles of crunchy leaves.

Frolicking and cavorting helped short-circuit the video endlessly looping in Risa's brain. Holy Hannah, she'd come so close in the nursery to putting her arms around a man she didn't even like, cradling him close like a hurt child, promising she'd take his pain away. Did he suspect she'd been a heartbeat away from kissing him? Heat scalded her face.

Had she lost her mind?

The man neglected his only child. He was a world-class workaholic. And big reminder: he still loved his dead wife.

Praise Jupiter, Jason had been bored. Otherwise . . .

Despite a nippy breeze, Risa went hot all over. Hot for a man who couldn't tell you the color of her eyes if he stared her in the face. Jason zoomed by tagging her, and she clamped down on her thoughts.

Sunshine, a smog-free sky, and tag helped clear both her sinuses and her brain. Her stomach, on the other hand, fluttered whenever she turned around to check how far Ben Macdonald trailed behind. The picnic basket had to be testing his shoulder joints to the max. *Poor baby.*

"Hey," he called for the third time. "Wait up."

Temptation ignited a bonfire in the pit of Risa's stomach and stopped her in her tracks. One thing in his favor, he didn't whine. Had she judged him too harshly? Shouldn't she at least attempt to be fair and give him a chance to respond to Molly's account of monsters?

"Shouldn't you get a life?" she mumbled, then whirled around in hot pursuit of Molly, who taunted, "You're it, La Ti Da."

Risa chased the kids till her pounding heart overrode any sympathy for Mr. Macdonald. The delight of two four-year-olds drove her onward. Hell-bent for the swings, she pumped her arms, gaining on Molly. They barreled across a grassy field, shouting and whooping.

On the perimeter of the park, a puppy that looked like a cross between a small pony and a big raccoon caught their fever, and he barked and strained at his leash. The puppy's exuberance didn't slow Jason, but Molly stopped too close to the yipping, jumping ball of golden fur and spindly legs for Risa's comfort. She stopped, too, a little in front of Molly. A second later, Jason roared back and demanded to know what was going on. The puppy lunged. Jason danced away.

"Sit." A well-dressed, blond, twenty-something guy yanked on the leash, and the puppy fell forward in the grass.

"Doesn't that hurt?" Jason ran toward the puppy and stuck his hand out to pat its head.

"Stay back, Jason." Risa grabbed his elbow, but he

twisted toward the dog. It slobbered and whined, struggling to lick a hand so close to its mouth.

"I said, *sit.*" The blond guy smacked the puppy on the nose. The animal whined louder, but sat back on its haunches, its massive head down, its eyes on Jason.

"Oooh." Molly hid her face in Risa's waist.

Nerves in her neck twanged. She stroked Molly's hair and met the guy's eyes. "Is he yours?"

"Not for long." The guy fumbled a package of Camels out of his shirt pocket and popped a cigarette between toothpaste ad teeth. "Landlord says he makes too much noise."

"Puppies tend to do that." Smoke rings drifted between Risa and the guy, then into the sapphire sky. Her throat tickled.

"What're you gonna do with him?" Jason asked.

With a shrug, he answered. "Sell him. Take him to the pound. Whatever."

"What's the pound?" Molly asked.

Hell, Risa almost said, then explained, "A place where people take animals they can't take care of anymore."

Rolling his eyes, Joe Cool sucked more smoke into his lungs.

"How much do you want for him?" Jason asked.

"A hundred." Joe Cool squinted at the sun.

"A hundred what?" Molly asked.

"Barbie dolls." The guy rolled his eyes. "Bucks," he said.

"That's a lot." Jason eyed the puppy, then looked up at Risa, who felt what was coming in the pit of her stomach but said, "It is a lot."

"He's worth a lot. He's got papers."

Riiight. Risa stared the jerk down.

"I don't have any money," Jason said.

"Me neither," Molly said, "but I bet Daddy does." She waved at her father, still half a block away.

And he'll fork over a hundred bucks for this mutt when pigs fly. Convinced she'd lost her mind, Risa went down on one knee. She ripped back the Velcro strip on her right shoe and removed a miniature coin purse stuck to the laces. She fished a bill out, unfolded it, and flashed it at Joe. "I'll give you twenty."

"Deal." He dropped the leash, grabbed the twenty, tucked it in the pocket with his smokes, then sprinted away. "Lotsa luck."

"Is that his name?" Jason screamed.

"Is he a boy or a girl?" Molly yelled.

"We'll figure it out," Risa said, glad Joe kept going, afraid she'd return the puppy if he turned around.

About to bend down and examine her new purchase more closely, she inhaled a whiff of lemon-scented smoke. Molly and Jason pushed past her. *Get a grip.* Her head swam. *Don't turn around yet.* What could she say—that would make sense—to Ben Macdonald? The man probably can't even spell spontaneous.

Catching up to them at last, frowning, he set the picnic basket next to Risa's feet.

"Daddy, La Ti Da bought a puppy. Isn't he cute?"

"He sure is, sweetheart." In an aside, he said, "A pup *and* triplets? I'm surprised we don't call you Wonder Woman."

"No more surprising that we don't call you Motor Mouth."

"Can I pick him up, La Ti Da?" Amazingly, Jason waited for permission. Risa said, "If you and Molly sit side by side, you can hold him on your lap. That way you won't squeeze his tummy."

The kids squished their legs and hips together and pulled the wriggling puppy toward them, warning each other against squeezing his tummy. Risa raised her chin. "He is cute."

"If you're fond of raccoons." Ben added with a sigh. "Didn't your mother ever warn you about guys in the park with cute, furry puppies?"

"No." Risa edged away from the heat he threw off. "She did warn me about guys with big teeth—on the way to Grandmother's or wherever I met them."

"Sound advice." Grateful she couldn't see the sweat sliding down his spine, Ben couldn't stop yapping. He grinned. "Ever see such small teeth in any adult male's mouth?"

When she didn't move toward him, he raised his top and bottom lips like a jackass about to bray, mumbling, "See for yourself."

"I see." Mouth twitching, she kept her distance. Before she laughed in his face, he said as fast as he could, "You probably think I'm lying through my teeth, but I'm harmless."

She stared at him—as if she didn't realize he hadn't pressed his advantage in the nursery. "It's the truth," he lied, straight-faced.

"Uh-huh." She slipped the frog pendant out from under her T-shirt and fingered its gold legs.

The gesture drove him nuts. His nerves hummed from remembering how dumb he'd sounded in the nursery. More like a pervert than a worried father. "I swear." He held his hand up.

"Okay." She looked like she'd decided the distance between them wasn't enough.

"Really." He winked, hoping she realized he was teasing her.

"If you say so." She looked a little bewildered. Natural, since he was staring at the steady, even pulse in her throat. Less than an hour ago in the nursery, he'd declared he wanted her. The wild rhythm of her heartbeat mesmerized him, drove him toward decisive, logical action. Kissing her still made sense.

Flushed, she fanned her face. As if reading his mind, she said, "This isn't the time or the place."

"For what?" He started to smile, then thought better of it.

Slipping the frog back under her T-shirt, she glanced at the kids and the puppy. "For finishing our earlier conversation."

"Since I'm harmless?" Since she didn't have a clue he'd proven what a lousy dad he was. In the nursery, he'd fantasized about kissing the hollow of her throat and completely forgot Molly.

"Right." Doc pushed a strand of hair out of her eyes, and the sun danced on her elbow. It made him so hot, he took a step backward. "Since you're harmless."

God, she had sexy elbows. Christ, he had a disgusting lack of scruples. Sweat sluiced down his sides. Her look of confusion warned him he'd hit the wall. Again. How else did he rationalize daydreaming about dragging his mouth along her elbow? Down her arm . . . to the inside of her wrist.

Dry-mouthed, he swallowed, then said, "Look at the kids."

Oblivious to his teeth—now a foot long and growing—Doc looked at Molly and Jason, who were in ecstasy with the weird-looking pup between them, on its back, feet in the air.

Doc chuckled. "Ever feel like chopped liver?"

"Yep. Ever since Molly met you." He pitched his voice light, but she took a step toward the kids anyway.

He touched her elbow, shocked by the jolt that ran up his arm. She slipped away like quicksilver. He looked at her retreating back and felt dumb. "You're avoiding that conversation we need to finish."

"Life is a timing problem." She stopped and faced him, her eyes hard. "Your timing sucks."

"Thanks for sparing my feelings." He gave her a bigger smile than he felt, pretty sure she'd bolt if he morphed into one of those sensitive male types and started blubbering.

Her mouth worked. Expecting a tongue-lashing about his ego, Ben braced himself. She said, quietly, "We brought the kids to play."

"Got it." Buoyed by her restraint, he held out his hand. "In the meantime—for the kids' sake—how about a truce?"

Sweating like a pig, he didn't blame her for hesitating. Since he didn't want to spook her, he didn't start peeling off clothes. He held her gaze. A twitch of her fingers eased the tension in his back and neck. She put her hand in his, and Ben relaxed a little. He pushed his luck.

"Since we're here to play with the kids, how about a game of Frisbee before lunch?" Self-conscious, he started pulling his sweater over his head.

Doc didn't blanch till he unbuckled his belt. Amused, he said, "Haven't exercised for a while." Eleven months of eating, working, reading Molly a bedtime story, then falling into bed had taken a toll on his gut.

Already jogging away from him, Doc called, "I'll check with the kids."

Glad she couldn't see how many notches he had to expand the belt, he said, "Give me a minute."

Screams and yips boomeranged over Ben's head. He felt a twinge of alarm. Lord, Jason and Molly were wired. The pup, too. Tongue flapping, he tore around the field, his excitement spilling over to the kids.

For a second, Ben felt trapped. Did he remember how to play with little kids?

"Here I come! Ready or not," he shouted with male bravado.

Eyes wide, Doc raised her head like a deer scenting danger. Good, he'd unnerved her. Waving at her, he grinned. She raised her arm. The folds of her bulky T-shirt doubled in, delineating the contours of her breasts, clinging to their lushly feminine shape like something sheer and silky.

Lust slammed into Ben. God help him if he had to move his legs.

"Hope you're ready," Doc yelled.

Ben groaned at her word choice. She lowered her arm, leaned forward, and threw the Frisbee right at Molly, providing Ben with a flash of Doc's belly button that shifted his heart into jackhammer mode. *Let's hear it for Frisbee.*

Still stunned by his Peeping Tom luck, Ben stepped out of Molly's way. He yelled his head off when she caught the Frisbee. He held his hands out. She threw him an easy catch. A disappointment, since it nipped his chance to demonstrate his primo Frisbee skills. Ace Frisbee Player drew back his arm and then let it fly.

Faster than lightning, the mutt jumped up, snatched the purple disc in midair, then raced in circles around Ben. Molly squealed, and Jason squealed louder. At Ben's command, the puppy went down on its forepaws. He offered no resistance when Ben reclaimed the Frisbee.

With a whoop, Molly intercepted the next throw. Ben's heart filled with pride. Arm back, she lost control, and the disc bumped to the ground. Lunging for the prize, Jason barely beat out the puppy. He preened for a second, then threw Ben a wild triple loop. "Catch!"

"Don't think so!" Doc came out of nowhere and leaped over the pup, which ran toward Ben like a long-lost lover. Ben jumped out of the canine's path—a second too late.

"Auuugh!"

The musty taste of dirt filled his mouth. Blood dribbled out of one nostril. His bottom lip felt like a small filet mignon.

"Daddeee!" Molly stopped in her tracks.

"Time out," Doc called.

"No." Ben scrambled to his feet. Swallowing a groan, he stood and forced a smile at Molly. "I'm fine, sweetheart." He tasted blood. Panic soured his stomach as Molly—white-faced, eyes huge—stood absolutely still, staring at him.

Do not scare her. Praying Doc could read his mind, he pointed at her. "Am I fine or what, Doc?"

"I'll let you know in two seconds." Quicker than his eye could follow, she immediately tagged Jason. Her froggy voice came from someplace behind the kids. "You and Molly play with the puppy while La Ti Da checks out Mr. Macdonald's boo-boo, okay?"

Maybe it was her low-key approach or her nothing-to-worry-about ventriloquist's performance. Or, maybe it was because kids recovered from dozens of boo-boos every day.

Whatever. Molly and Jason roared off without a backward glance.

Ben's chest got tight, but a little piece of his heart jumped with joy. He really didn't want Molly burdened by fears for him. A deep sadness took the edge off his heart-stopping relief. She needed him, but at almost five, she possessed a wisdom that eluded him. Leap forward to the future with fervor. Leave the past behind without regret or guilt.

Doc dabbed the blob of blood on his lip. Despite her spellbinding rose scent, Ben grimaced. "Boo-boo?"

"Boo-boo." Her emerald eyes glinted with laughter.

The glint teased and provoked, intimating they shared a secret. Unspoken. Delicious. Mutually understood. With their repetition of *boo-boo*, which by necessity forced their lips into taunting puckers, each dared the other to take the next step. Just for the hell of it, he dropped his head forward, rested his ear over her heart, and soaked up their closeness with gratitude.

"Boo-boo," he whispered. "Who am I to argue with such a sophisticated medical opinion?"

Snorting, she moved his head back up and anchored it in place with one hand. "How about helping me out here?"

Right in front of his eyes, her clothes fell off. His breath caught. The ground tilted under him. Sir Galahad, he helped her out of white slacks pooling around her ankles. Dry-mouthed, he said, "Whatever you say, Doc."

"What I say is this will only take a minute if you cooperate." Gently, she swept the hair out of his eyes.

Did she feel his heart thundering? He squirmed under her serene scrutiny. She lifted an eyelid. "Hold still."

"That's a little harsh, isn't it—since I'm wounded?" Once she'd checked both pupils, he cocked his head and tried a hurt puppy look.

Hurt puppy did not distract her. Her fingers grazed the cut on his bottom lip. A hundred prickling pins vaporized his fantasy of catching her fingers between his teeth and kissing them one by one.

"You are wounded enough to need a couple of stitches."

"No way." He pushed his bottom lip out. It felt as big as a saucer. "As I recall, the best medicine for boo-boos is a kiss."

"In your dreams." *Tsk*ing, she checked his front teeth.

"That makes me feel like a horse."

"How would you know how a horse feels?"

Because aside from Amy, his horse Lightning was the only friend he had growing up—a fact he didn't intend to share with the lusciously sensitive Dr. Risa Taylor.

"I fell off my first pony when I was three."

"Where in the world do they let a three-year-old ride a pony?" She thumped his chest.

"Montana. The nearest doctor lived two hundred miles away. I was almost seventeen before I had my first stitch."

Her left breast brushed his bicep, and a vital neuron in his brain hiccuped. Suddenly, he was on fire, and not just where she'd inadvertently touched him. But in places she'd notice any minute now, if he didn't put on the brakes.

Apparently unaware of his condition, she asked, "So why'd you need a stitch at seventeen?"

He heard the question from a long way off, like a swimmer under water. He prayed for brilliance. Brilliance—*not* runaway lust—would impress her. Brilliance would forge a connection between them. Brilliance would make the case for Molly. A dim bulb flicked on in his head.

"A hockey puck and I had a close encounter." His memory brought back the ice rink, the team doctor, and Amy's anxious face.

In real time, Doc cupped his chin and turned his head left to right, up and down. He blinked. The memory faded.

"Where and when did this close encounter take place?"

"All these questions—are they your subtle way of checking me for brain damage, Doc?"

"Are you worried about brain damage?"

Only when you get too close. "Nope. I survived hockey at Stanford twenty years ago, so I'm not concerned about a boo-boo."

"How'd you play hockey at Stanford?"

"Ahhh, still checking me out, huh?"

"Actually, I'm curious."

"Hi, Curious. I'm Ben." He held his hand out.

She tugged on his right ear and spoke directly into it. "Well, now we know you're humor impaired."

It wasn't that funny, but it felt good to have her tease him. Better to have her touch him—even on his ear. He said, "A bunch of us from places like Minnesota, Michigan, Montana—places where it snows a lot—played on the team."

"I had no idea Stanford has a hockey team."

"I'd bet eighty percent of the faculty and students don't know. Think Montana, think ice hockey. Think sunny California, don't think ice hockey."

"Stanford must've been a big change from Montana." She started in on his cut lip again.

"Took some adjusting." He sat perfectly still.

The pain receded, replaced by images of Stanford popping like flashbulbs. Palm Drive. The Main Quad. Memorial Church. Another lifetime. The beginning of his life with Amy. He moved, jiggled Doc's hand, and jumped—though he welcomed the momentary sting of pain. It short-circuited the memory of Amy floating down the aisle in Memorial Church.

"Sorry." Sympathy clouded the good doctor's emerald eyes.

Sympathy for his boo-boo, he assumed. "Not your fault, Doc." Disgusted, he sat up straighter. "Did it to myself."

Why the hell was he chasing the past? Now he'd missed his chance—again—to ask her about taking Molly as a patient.

"You satisfied I only have a boo-boo?"

In fact, he wasn't sure he hadn't cracked his head when he hit the ground. Dreaming would not bring Amy back. How long before he figured that out?

"Humor me. Tell me about Stanford." Doc laid warm fingers on his racing pulse. "How old were you? What'd you study? Et cetera, et cetera."

Luckily, she kept her distance this time. No chance of her breasts grazing any part of his anatomy. Even so, he had to think a minute before picking up the thread.

"When I hit Stanford at sixteen, I felt like I'd warped into another galaxy."

"You started Stanford at sixteen?" She arched her eyebrows.

"Sixteen-and-a-half," he clarified, memories unwinding of him and Amy at the train station in White Fish. Both baby-faced, anxious, excited.

His heart contracted. Dammit, he was looking back. He switched gears. "What about you? Where'd you attend med school?"

"Davis. Took me three years to decide if I wanted to be a vet or a pediatrician."

"What tipped the scales?"

Her whole body softened. "Getting practice with someone else's kids before I had my own made a lot of sense at the time."

"You knew in college you were going to have kids?"

"Always." Her steady, unflinching gaze convinced him. "I was an only child." Close enough to the truth.

"Me, too."

"We—Amy and I—wanted four kids." His throat filled. Why was he telling her this?

"I'm sorry." She laid her hand on his shoulder, not squeezing, saying no more, but silently filling him with a comfort he'd given up on ever feeling again.

CHAPTER 7

"Yoo-hoo!" Kelsy strolled across the field waving, smiling like Miss America, even at a distance.

Panic slithered into Risa's stomach. She jerked her hand away from Ben Macdonald's shoulder at the same time he shifted in the opposite direction.

Praise Jupiter. With any luck, eagle-eyed Kelsy had seen nothing to raise her suspicions. Of course, after her comments in the kitchen, Kelsy didn't need anything concrete to weave her matchmaking threads into a church wedding with twelve bridesmaids, Molly as flower girl, and Jason as ring bearer. Risa could only hope she and Ben Macdonald were safe—for the moment.

"What's she doing here?" He sounded more scared than safe.

"Who knows?" Risa's heart caught. Somehow she'd have to head Kelsy off and rescue the wounded Frisbee player before he lost his cool. Or his mind. Or both, since Kelsy could bring a saint to his knees.

"I could make a run for it." He glanced at a squirrel digging in the dirt.

"You could . . . but how do you feel?"

"Good enough to make a run for it."

Risa laughed. "Why don't I send Kelsy home for aspirin?" she offered. It was the best she could do on such short notice.

"Aspirin's for the swelling, right?"

"Yes, and an aspirin mission sidetracks Kelsy."

"How about iodine?" He frowned, as if arguing with himself.

"You don't want iodine that close to your mouth."

"Antiseptic?" He watched Kelsy like a trapped fox.

"Antiseptic won't close that cut." Risa felt a little flutter in her stomach. If he were under twelve, she'd hug him.

"No stitches." He grimaced and switched his gaze to Risa. "Hospitals . . . scare Molly. She thinks her mommy . . ."

Face burning, Risa interrupted. "I'll handle Kelsy."

Holy Heloise, of course hospitals scared Molly.

Hand trembling, she fished the house keys out of her pocket. "Don't sit down yet, okay? Unless Kelsy goes stubborn on me, this shouldn't take more than a minute."

"Better idea." He held his hand out. "I'll go myself."

"You mean walk? To my house?" She blinked at him, her pulse missing a beat. "What if you pass out?"

"I won't. I'll sit down. I'm not trekking to Tibet."

Heart thumping, Risa gave him the keys, exhaling softly when she avoided skin contact. Because, she knew, if she touched him, she'd have to hold him. Try to ease his pain. Pain she'd caused, since common sense would indicate where the EMTs had taken Amy.

He pocketed the keys, then glanced toward the kids being chased in circles by the puppy. "Doesn't look as if Molly would miss me, but I'll let her know anyway where I'm going."

Whether his small sigh came from the pain in his lip or from pleasure at watching Molly, Risa wondered if she shouldn't reconsider her thoughts about negligence.

"Doctor's opinion?" She went tense when he cocked a brow.

"With that lip, I suggest you let Molly do the kissing."

He mumbled something inaudible, nodded to Kelsy, then beat a hasty retreat. His long legs covered the ground in sure, smooth strides. Risa had seen him take three tumbles in two days. Hard muscles and sinewy strength dispelled any idea he was clumsy. For a minute, she took pleasure in simply watching him move.

Kelsy demanded, "What'd I miss?"

"Not a thing, except I now own a puppy."

"Oh, is that a puppy?" Kelsy waved at her son and called his name. "I thought that was a large goat."

"You did not," Risa snapped.

"Did you and Ben argue? Is that why you're so cranky?"

"Of course not. He cut his lip and—"

"You kissed it and made it alll better, right?" Kelsy lowered her voice to a sexy drawl.

"Don't be ridiculous. I barely know the man."

"What better way to get to know him?"

Sighing like a soap opera heroine, Risa threw her hands up. "I surrender. You win. You want to know what happened?"

"I'm all ears."

"In a nutshell, I gave in to this wild, uncontrollable, overpowering hormonal urge—"

"Uh-huh. Details, girl, give me details."

Risa's stomach pitched, but the Cheshire grin on Kelsy's face was like a match to dynamite. Eyes closed, Risa hugged her waist and swayed. Dreamily, she continued. "I knocked him off his feet. That scene at school yesterday? Dress rehearsal. Warm-up practice. This time"—she dropped her voice to a whisper—"our lips locked. He nibbled my ear. I took a bite out of—"

"You should see yourself." Kelsy tilted Risa's chin up half an inch. "You're glowing. Roses in your cheeks. Eyes bright as emeralds. You look like you just had sex. Great s—"

"Kelsy!" Risa grabbed her and shook her. "For cryin' out loud. Keep your voice down. The kids—"

Chortling, Kelsy shielded her eyes. "The kids are playing. They're more interested in the puppy than in us." She grabbed Risa in a headlock. "You like him, don't you?"

Risa bucked. "Dammit, Kelsy, you're choking me."

Instantly, Kelsy let go. Wagging a finger at Risa, she did a little jig. "See? See? That proves it. You never swear. *Never.* Can't corrupt little kids, you always say. Admit it, you only swear when your emotions are totally out of control."

"My emotions are not 'totally out of control.' 'Damn' is not swearing. *You* are totally . . ." Risa rubbed her neck.

"Take a lesson." Kelsy threw her blond head back and danced around Risa. "Just think! A father for—"

"No, Kel." Tears stung Risa's eyes and throat. "Please listen. I've already told you. That won't happen."

"You're sure?" The teasing went out of Kelsy.

Nodding, Risa swallowed. Hard. "It's a lovely fantasy, but trust me on this. Ben Macdonald is . . . still . . . without a doubt . . . in love . . . with his dead wife."

Damn! Kelsy still hadn't left.

Thirty minutes later, Ben lurked at the edge of the park, cell phone pressed to his ear. He gritted his teeth, and a dozen killer bees landed on Macho Man's lower lip.

Inhaling, he tried to recall Biology 101. If the brain was busy managing pain, did it cut back on testosterone production? Wouldn't such a tactic ensure only the fittest bred? Otherwise, too many unfit offspring ended up dog paddling in the shallow end of the gene pool.

God, he'd cracked his skull instead of his lip. He opened his eyes. Kelsy spotted him and waved. With any luck, she'd missed the testosterone ambush.

Whoa! Correction. He picked up his pace. Fire stung his lip and brought a flash of insight. He had to stop kidding himself. Kidding? How about lying?

First, his hormones didn't *ambush* him.

Yes, Doc's breast had accidentally brushed against him and fried his brain. But if he had an honest bone in him, he'd admit he didn't even try to put up a fight. He'd acted the fool and paid for it. He took a nosedive, got a wake-up call, and learned his lesson. Finally. He could handle Kelsy.

"Need a minute to catch your breath?" Frowning, Doc reached his side a second ahead of Kelsy.

"No." Ben shook his head and felt an exquisite sting.

"You were gone a long time." Kelsy peered over Doc's shoulder. "I didn't want to leave. In case Risa had to call the fire department."

Doc took the packet she'd requested during their first cell-phone call. "That bench looks like a good spot for you to sit."

"I'm okay standing." He'd take his medicine like a man.

"Humor me. You're just enough taller that I don't want to swab your chin instead of your lip."

"Better watch out for his nose," Kelsy said, then laughed.

Eyes narrowed, Doc said, "You better watch out . . . for the kids."

It sounded a little lame to Ben, but he kept quiet.

"They're fine. I can see them."

Doc clenched the packet with cotton swabs in it. "Then stop breathing down my neck, dang it."

Maybe it was the *dang it.* Maybe it was the blood in her eye. Whatever. Ben didn't want to know what was going on. He jogged toward the bench, glad his lip throbbed.

Quickly, with a minimum of motion, Doc stripped blue paper off a sterile swab, then removed the cap on a silver tube she'd instructed him to bring along. "Ready?" she asked quietly.

Kelsy arched a brow at Ben. Inviting a reaction to the inadvertent sexual allusion? *The woman has a dirty mind.*

He'd bet she didn't like gross, though. He sniffed his armpit like a baboon, then said, "Sock it to me, Doc."

Intent on squeezing glop out of the silver tube, Doc didn't look up. Kelsy, on the other hand, wrinkled her nose. Ben could almost hear her saying, *Gross.* Despite his lip, now the size of Tennessee, he smiled. Forget romantic illusions about guys who reveled in sweat.

Too bad, though, Doc had missed the message. The next thing Ben knew, he was falling into the deep emerald pools of her eyes. Floating down, down, he barely heard her say, "This will hurt."

"If it's any comfort to you," Kelsy moved in for a closer look, "Jason never cries when I take him to Risa. Not even when she gives him a shot."

"I'll remember that." Ben's bottom lip twitched in anticipation. God, don't let him make a peep.

"That is one ugly boo-boo," Kelsy announced.

"Thank you, Nurse Ratchett." Doc rolled her eyes, then turned her laser smile on him. "Ready?"

Head back, neck muscles stiff, Ben nodded. "Aren't you going to tell me to be brave?"

"Want to hold my hand?" Kelsy volunteered.

"Out of the way, Nurse."

Faster than a magician waving a wand over an old hat, Doc flourished the cotton swab over his head, dragged it through the air, and skimmed its tip over his bottom lip, so fast he didn't feel more than a momentary sting.

"Finito." She squeezed his shoulder, wrapped the swabs in a tissue, then looked over his right shoulder. "The doctor orders an extra dessert at lunch for your bravery."

"Bravery by four-year-olds usually merits a hug and a kiss," Kelsy said in a loud stage whisper.

Praise Jupiter, Kelsy had gone about her business.

Stomach rumbling, Risa tied the puppy to the picnic table and shooed him underneath, out of the sun. Too bad she couldn't join him, lick her bruised ego, and think kind thoughts about Ben. Steam rose off her in the golden sunshine, and Risa consoled herself with one thought. There was a possibility Ben had hit his head as well as his lip, since, from all appearances, he preferred dessert over hugs and kisses.

As efficiently as a supermarket bag boy, Ben unpacked the picnic basket. He paid no attention to her or to the puppy. Under his shelter, the pooch peered up at Risa. She scratched behind his ears and inhaled deeply. Deep breaths were the key to relaxing.

Perfectly relaxed, singing "Jingle Bells," Molly and Jason set the table. The Christmas carol blared from a house hidden by a pyracantha hedge and wild raspberry bushes.

"I like this park." Molly moved a plastic fork.

Grateful for the diversion, Risa said, "Me, too. I'll probably bring Charlie, Tom, and Harry here every day."

"Do we live a long ways from here, Daddy?"

"Not a long way," he said, "but quite a ways." Risa noticed he was sweating profusely as he unpacked her oversized wicker basket. His lip must hurt like the dickens, but she bet he'd die before admitting it hurt at all.

"Molly lives in Alta Vista," Jason said to Risa. "Lots of millionaires live there, ya know."

Risa did know, but if she hadn't, Ben Macdonald's red face would've confirmed the announcement. "Did Mommy tell you that?"

"Uh-huh, and I heard it on TV."

Hoping to distract him, Risa asked for his help filling a plastic bowl with water. He set the bowl under the table. The puppy drank like a camel home from the desert. "What'd Mommy fix us?" Risa asked.

"Lots of stuff. Spaghetti." Jason watched the puppy, then picked up his own agenda. "There's a gate all around your house, right, Mr. Macdonald?"

"Not very high, though." He stopped dishing up spaghetti and looked right at Risa, and her heart spiraled upward.

"Molly has a pool." Jason settled onto the bench.

Finished with table duty, Molly crawled up next to him. "My mommy swimmed in it 'most every day."

A lump clogged Risa's throat. She looked directly into the sun. Narrowing her eyes against the brightness, she saw, clearly, the mask come down over Ben Macdonald's features.

His mouth set, making Risa wince, as he removed foil from a plastic bowl, leaned forward, and sniffed the contents. "Now serving two first-class table setters."

Despite the sun, Risa felt a chill. She rubbed the puppy's ears. He stopped gnawing at her shoestrings and nipped her little finger with sharp baby teeth. She welcomed the sting. It helped clear her head.

Ben Macdonald's praise for the four-year-olds' table-setting skills rang with sincerity. Under other circumstances, she'd give him high marks for complimenting his daughter. Under other circumstances, she'd reconsider her concerns about his neglect.

But, dammit, hadn't she just witnessed the classic emotional withdrawal of a Silicon Valley engineer dad? A flock of crows perched on a nearby telephone line cawed loudly, like a Greek chorus, reminding her it wasn't the first time he'd changed the subject as soon as Molly mentioned her mother.

"For adults only." He passed the thermos under Risa's nose. "Want to hazard a guess?"

What she wanted was to sit on the other side of the table. Or, better, to go home. Before she lost her mind under the bright sun and forgot she didn't like him.

"No idea." She managed not to gasp at the rich, sinful aroma floating up from the thermos.

"Enough cream and butter to scare a cardiologist to death."

Nose twitching, Risa ignored her stomach's sudden

contraction. "Kelsy knows me too well. Must be something special."

"Very special."

Jason swiped at his mouth with the back of his hand, cupped his hands around Molly's ear, and rolled his eyes back at Risa. "C'mere, Molly. I'll tell you."

Uh-oh. Risa almost stepped in, but couldn't think of a good reason for censoring free speech, since Père Macdonald didn't act worried. Jason's raspy whispers came out a buzz. Molly slapped her hand over her mouth. A wild giggle got away from her anyway, and the crows joined the cackle. Risa felt a flash of envy. Kids' secrets were such fun.

"Ummmm." Oblivious, her father inhaled deeply. "Oyster stew." He poured out two steaming cups, setting one in front of Risa, and inhaled again.

Praise Jupiter, he set the mug in front of her. Because there was no way she could risk their hands brushing.

"Mommy told Daddy oyster stew is *one* sexy dish," Jason said, parroting Kelsy's intonation to perfection.

A light breeze blew through the branches, cooling Risa's cheeks, but her mind went into a tailspin. She risked a glance under her lashes at Ben Macdonald. His lip, puffy and purple, probably accounted for why his chin hadn't hit the table.

"What's *sexy*, Daddy?" Molly asked, as if on cue. Ben looked as if he'd bitten into road kill, and Risa had to look away to avoid giggling insanely.

"Sexy is—" His face went blank, his eyes glazed over.

Laying her fork on her plate, Molly asked, "What's wrong, Daddy? Does your lip hurt?"

Coward that he was, he nodded. His eyes begged Risa to throw him a lifeline. Given the choice, she'd throw him overboard. When did he plan on telling Molly the facts of life?

Probably a year or two after she graduates from college.

Poor kid. Risa smiled, smothering the temptation to

talk about the puffy clouds and instead went with the first thing that came to mind. "Sexy is how Cinderella and the Prince felt when they saw each other for the first time."

Molly chewed her spaghetti. Her father rolled his eyes, daring Risa to kill him in front of two witnesses. Molly asked, "But why are oysters sexy? They're not people."

A noise came from the coward that sounded suspiciously like laughter. Blushing, Risa stared him down with four words. "Careful you don't choke."

"Yeah, La Ti Da might hafta give you mouth-to-mouth *rustation.*" Jason slurped a spaghetti strand off his fork.

"No," Risa said sweetly. "With the size of Mr. Macdonald's lip, we'd have to call the fire department."

"Cool," Jason said.

"Shhh, Jason." Molly wagged her little finger. "I want to know why oysters are sexy."

Distraction won't work every time.

"They aren't really," Risa began.

"But Jason said his mommy said—"

"Some people, like Jason's mommy," Risa said quickly, "think oysters make a man and a woman feel like Cinderella and the Prince."

"Did Cinderella and the Prince eat oysters at the ball?"

"No. They ate ice cream." The coward father dropped a kiss on his daughter's tomato-stained mouth, and Risa's heart beat high in her chest. Suddenly dizzy, she closed her eyes, listening to him from a long way off. "This stew's too hot. I think I'll pass."

Anyone with a grain of sense would've kept her eyes shut. Taking his remark personally, Risa opened hers. Molly patted her father's hand. "If your lip hurts too much, Daddy, you don't have to kiss me till tonight."

"Sweetheart, my lip will never hurt that much." He dropped another kiss on her cheek.

"Tickles." She giggled.

Oh, yes, the man's cold as ice.

The kids fell on second helpings like starving wolves.

Ben Macdonald fanned the air over his and Risa's mugs. "Stuff's hot enough to take the skin off your tongue."

"I noticed." Her pulse skipped. She looked away, watching two ribbons of steam drift upward, intertwining, becoming one.

A whine scared her to death. Had she made it? Heart thumping, afraid to look at the man next to her, Risa jerked her gaze downward. The puppy whined, then wiggled its butt. Her face felt scalded by the steam off the oyster stew.

"Someone's in love." Ben Macdonald's mouth twitched.

"Someone's hungry," she retorted.

"I'm male. I recognize the symptoms."

"I'm a doctor. Symptoms are my speciality. It's hard to imagine . . . he's . . . not hungry."

"A lot of things are *hard* to imagine."

Suddenly mindless, Risa ducked her head, chucked the puppy under the chin, and clamped down on her loose tongue. *Helllo, Risa. Stop throwing him lines.*

"At least he's cuter than the frog," Ben offered.

"And more faithful than most princes," she snapped.

The puppy nuzzled her knee. His adoration was embarrassing, but not as embarrassing as her comeback when its fullness whacked her upside the head. Hoping distraction would defuse the moment, she patted the puppy and threw her voice. "Something around here sure smells like spaghetti."

"And here it is." Jason held up a forkful.

Risa almost kissed him.

"Do puppies like spaghetti?" Molly asked.

Her father shook his head. "That's human food."

With his mouth full, Jason expounded. "Dogs have their food. Kids have their food. Adults have their food. Why aren't you eating the 'sparagus Mommy made for you, La Ti Da?"

Before Risa could lie and say she wasn't hungry, Molly asked, "What's 'sparagus, Daddy? Is it a sexy dish?"

"It's a veggie, sweetheart. Want a piece?" Mouth twitching, he held up the biggest green phallic symbol Risa had ever seen. Then, his double entendre sank in, and she went blind from the heat rising off him.

Kelsy was a dead woman. She'd never see another birthday.

He said, "Try it, sweetheart. It's good for . . . all kinds of afflictions."

Cocky as a teenage stud, Mr. Cool glanced at Risa. She—not the puppy this time—made a mewling noise that became a phony cough. "Pine trees." She waved at the stand of redwoods.

"Yuck." Molly pushed away the Tupperware container piled high with the lewd veggie. "It's funny looking!"

"It's for you and La Ti Da," Jason said.

Mr. Cool, straight-faced, perfectly courteous, held the plate under Risa's nose, but his black eyes danced. "Doctor?"

"Not even one." Not even if he wasn't mocking her with that sly, small smile that silently told her he was enjoying the joke. "I don't have any afflictions," she stated.

Unless you counted Kelsy.

"How about a sandwich then?" He offered her a plate. The yeasty aroma of fresh bread made her mouth water. But the shape of the sandwiches made her gape. Mr. Cool said, "I can't remember the last time I ate shrimp on heart-shaped bread."

Her stomach rumbled, but her throat felt dry as an emery board. "Thanks, I've lost my appetite."

"After all the trouble Kelsy went to?" He bit into half a sandwich. To Risa's amazement—or disappointment— he didn't choke on his droll tone.

"What's for dessert?" Jason demanded.

Molly stood up and looked in the picnic basket. Her father brought out a container labeled DESSERT. He opened it and held up a glistening bunch of red grapes. "And here I figured we'd cleaned up every last grape in North America."

Without thinking, Risa mumbled, "No whipped cream?"

"Pardon?"

"Nothing." Nothing except Kelsy's imagination in overdrive, conjuring up visions of Risa feeding Ben Macdonald grapes smothered in whipped cream.

"You said, 'No whipped cream.' " Jason laid a hand on her wrist, and Risa went for sincerity.

"Thank you, Jason."

"Think he inherited his helpfulness from his mother?" Mr. Cool whispered.

"He is his mother's son," Risa said, determined to keep her tone light if it killed her.

"Do you eat whipped cream with grapes?" Molly asked Jason.

"Nope." He stuffed half a dozen in both cheeks.

"We don't either, do we, Daddy?"

Risa resisted the urge to bang her head on the table. *Next time, keep your mouth shut.*

"No, sweetheart, but I'd like to try it some day."

Jason shrugged. "I think it's a grown-up thing."

From Mr. Cool's smirk, Risa knew—without a doubt—that he knew what she'd meant by the whipped cream crack. A rush of blood scalded her face. She started gathering up plates.

"Why don't you and Molly play with Mr. Macdonald and the puppy while I clean up?"

"I'll clean, you play." In one quick movement, he removed the plates from her hand. Fiery hot icicles stung her fingertips, racing up her elbow, to her chest, to her throat, to the top of her head, then darting down both legs to her toes.

The kids, unaware she'd lost the ability to think, talk, or walk, pulled her away from his closeness. Saved, she willed her quaking legs to obey her. They responded, and she lumbered after Molly and Jason, hell-bent for safety.

*   *   *

Ben had the good sense to wait till they were out of earshot before he laughed—or more accurately, howled.

Head thrown back, he roared at the memory of Doc's face when he opened the thermos of oyster stew. Face redder than her hair. Mouth dropping open. Green eyes indecipherable behind sunglasses. Repressed laughter almost choking her. *A Kodak moment for sure.*

Ben wiped his eyes. Someone—not him, of course— should tell her never to sit down at a poker table.

To his credit, he'd pretended not to notice her struggle for control. Hell, he admired the Cinderella story. Not to mention the lesson in sex education featuring, for God's sake, oysters. Then, she saw the asparagus. Weak with laughter, he sank down on the picnic bench. How the hell could she think he neglected Molly and still be so attracted to him?

'Cuz you're such a hunk?

More likely because he had such strong maternal instincts.

Oh, yeah, that was it. Lame and totally D-U-M-B—but he'd come up with an explanation.

One more acceptable than lust.

He heard Molly's call a long way off. His father's ear registered there was no need for alarm, but his mind rejoined his body in the park. He waved. She waved back.

Doc cupped her hands around her mouth. "C'mon, Santa's here."

The sun slanted through her wild mane, so unlike Amy's smooth, black bob. A cool breeze prickled the skin on his neck. He felt the presence tangibly enough to turn.

The crows sat on the telephone wire. Silent. Watchful.

A breeze, warmed by the sun, caressed his arms. Heart aching, he stood perfectly still.

"You coming?" Risa yelled.

"In a minute," he said and checked behind him one last time.

CHAPTER 8

"Damn!" Standing next to Doc in the park, watching Molly and Jason on Santa's lap, Ben could no longer ignore the vibration on his left hip. He glanced at the message on his phone. "Dammit."

The woman in front of them turned and glared, staring at his bottom lip. "Sorry." He pointed at his cell. "Work problems."

Shoulders rigid, Doc's lips barely moved as she said, "I'll watch the kids. Make your call."

The woman's glare softened, and she patted the pager on her right hip. "No rest for the wicked, right?"

"Right." Every instinct screamed at Ben: *Mistaaake.* Make the call, fail a big test. He said to Doc, "You're sure with the pup they're not too much?"

One head shake, so brief he almost missed it, told him she was sure he was a fool. Easy call. He agreed. Did she think he wanted to make the damn call and miss Molly on Santa's lap? Of course, she didn't have a clue how important this deal was—for him and for Molly. Like half of Silicon Valley, they could go bust. . . . Then, like her, he'd take a yearlong sabbatical, too.

Fighting the urge to defend working for a living, Ben stayed put. Doc, silent, fixated on Santa, seemed oblivious to the other adults. They shushed their tired, restless kids, mostly too young to venture forth to chat with Santa. Why didn't she say something? What did she know? She didn't jeopardize a multimillion deal by spending all day in the park.

The invisible wire tightened in his chest. He took a deep breath and surrendered by speaking first. "Two, three minutes."

"We'll wait by the swings."

"I won't be that long." Already dialing the number, he stepped out of line.

"This had better be good," he snapped, the instant Jake Barnes, his CTO, picked up.

"Don't shoot the messenger, okay?"

"Just tell me what's wrong."

Jake tried.

The birds kept singing, the sun kept shining, and listening, Ben kept falling through black space. His interruptions—senseless, incoherent, disbelieving—only made grasping the problem worse. Finally, he stopped demanding answers when there were none. The details didn't matter. What mattered was that he get to the development lab ASAP.

His free fall slammed to a stop, as if he'd collided with a planet that had broken out of its orbit. "I have to bring Molly."

"Not a good scene here, Boss. The guys are pretty bummed."

"Yeah, well, they're all big kids. Molly comes first." Ben's mind raced, sorting, ordering what had to be done.

"What about your nanny?"

"She's in Tahoe."

"Tahoe?" A groan. "That's a four-hour trip. We could be toast by then."

Shock slammed through Ben. Anxiety escalated to panic. "For God's sake, don't say that where anyone can hear you."

"Give me some credit, Boss. But see why this isn't a good place for Molly?"

Ben raked a hand through his hair. "What can I do, Jake? I depend on a nanny." Several people nearby raised their heads like wild animals on the prairie suddenly scenting danger.

"I know, I know. Too bad she went skiing this weekend."

Duuuh.

Several mothers still eyed him with caution. Ben lowered his voice. "I'll get a tune-up on my crystal ball tomorrow."

"Yeah, well, personally, I'd love to be in Tahoe. Most of us came in before six this morning."

Guilt, sharp as slivers from a shattered crystal ball, sliced through Ben's nerve endings.

"Things started going south at 6:05, and there went my plans to go Christmas shopping this afternoon," Jake added.

The jab hit home, but Ben ignored it by checking his watch. "Let's not panic. Maybe Maryann's already made her last run."

Very few skiers, except novices and those nursing injuries, would make their last run at 2:30. Maryann, born and raised in Reno, fell into neither category—a fact Ben intended to keep to himself. "Till she gets here, Molly stays with me."

"Don't say I didn't warn you."

Thank you, Mister Doom and Gloom. "Give me an hour."

Jake groaned.

"Maybe an hour and a half. . . ."

Silence. Damning. Ben started to bite his lip and winced. He'd forgotten his boo-boo. Which, right at the moment, was the least of his worries. "Forty-five minutes," he said. "If Santa doesn't have traffic tied up."

The development lab was no place for Molly, but he couldn't leave her in his office alone. Forget leaving her with any of his staff. They'd all be in high geek mode. Molly would disappear off their radar screens while everyone searched for the bug that could send the company belly-up in these days when belly-up was the norm.

Barking orders, pressing the cell phone tight against his ear, Ben sprinted toward the swing sets. The sight of Doc reaching up to push Molly's swing almost undid him.

Her shirttail had come untucked and rode up, up, up, flashing a slice of pearly skin above her belly button. Stunned by the devil desire, Ben picked up speed. He couldn't tear his eyes off the good doctor. Nor could he recall what he'd told Jake two seconds earlier. Out of nowhere, a heavy cement trash container loomed up directly in his path. "Holy sh—"

Years of ice hockey acrobatics flooded his brain and woke up muscles nearly atrophied. He jumped off the ground, did a kind of double twist at the waist, and narrowly sidestepped the container. More surprisingly, he even managed to avoid stepping on his tongue. It all but dragged on the ground. A small comfort. Surely, voyeurs didn't go around with their tongues hanging out while their companies went down the drain, did they?

"You okay, Boss?"

"Long hill." The park was as flat as Kansas.

"Well, take it easy. Don't risk a heart attack."

"Nothing's wrong with my heart," he snapped. His problem was his eyes. He couldn't stop staring at Doc. And what he saw, he wanted. Which meant he was insane.

"I just mean . . . your body's pumping out gallons of testosterone to handle the stress—"

"Not importa, Jake." He punched the OFF button.

"Daddeee, Daddeee! Look at me, Daddeee!" Molly screamed.

"I'm looking, sweetheart!" he yelled. God, was he looking.

Seeing him approach, Risa crammed her shirttail into her jeans. Quick, hard tucks didn't help distract her mind. She could read him like a book. He intended to haul Molly off to work with him.

"Not our problem," she muttered to the dog, its head going back and forth in rhythm with the swings.

"I've got a problem," Père Macdonald said out of the side of his mouth.

Surprise, surprise.

"Ummm. At work?" Risa moved over to Jason's swing and gave him a good push. Her shirttail rode up, and cool air tickled her stomach. Holy Hannah, it was fun watching Ben Macdonald drool.

Did delight in his discomfort make her a tease? Unsure, she tied her shirttails in a fat knot at her waist. His instant fixation with the knot left her mindless. Talk about transparent. Why not just walk up and rub her boobs in the man's chest?

"Higher, Daddy, higher," Molly ordered while Ben pushed her.

"One more, sweetheart, then we have to go."

"Praise Jupiter," Risa mumbled. If her blood pressure went much higher, they'd have to haul her out of the park on a stretcher. She shot Ben Macdonald a sideways glance.

Giving Molly a push, he caught the look and held it. "Could I ask you a favor?"

"Why not?" Obviously, he was pretty cocky she wouldn't kill him in public. She slitted her eyes. Hadn't she expected this from the moment his pager went off?

She fumbled with the knot, but stopped as his gaze slid toward it. Heart racing, she focused on Molly and Jason, their feet pumping the swings. The puppy strained at his leash. Risa scratched his ears. How big a push did Ben Macdonald need to ask his favor?

"I know you've got a lot planned for today—"

She met and held his gaze again. "Actually, all your toting and lifting in the nursery put me ahead of schedule."

"If you say so. Under the circumstances—the picnic and the visit with Santa—you're being awfully generous."

"You don't have to flatter me. Chalk my generosity up to holiday spirit." Her tone was a little too edgy for true holiday spirit, but so what?

"Sure you wouldn't rather kiss a snake than do me a favor?"

Unsure if she grimaced or smiled, she whistled to the puppy, then said, "What's your favor?"

His lips moved, but no words came out. She was tempted to reassure him his tongue wouldn't disintegrate if he asked her for help, but Risa said nothing. Whatever battle he was fighting in his mind, he looked miserable, deep lines around his mouth and eyes, which were red rimmed and slightly bloodshot. His lip must hurt worse than he'd ever admit, even under torture. Poor guy. Her heart did its silly flip-flop.

Give him a break.

Giving him a hard time was the other option, and Risa couldn't see it. Life was too short. Hers was perfect, and his? *Not your problem.* But she could help him out.

"You want me to watch Molly while you're at work?" She shrugged but softened her tone. "I can do it. Gladly. She's a doll."

He was astounded. His mouth didn't fall open, and his eyebrows didn't lift a centimeter, but Risa could see he was surprised all the same. Maybe because she'd read his mind. Maybe because he sincerely appreciated her offer. Or, maybe he was surprised for some reason she couldn't fathom—such as being unable to ask for help, but receiving help anyway.

"Yahoooo!" He leaped about two feet into the air.

The puppy barked, almost as giddy as Père Macdonald. Dazed by his unrestrained joy, Risa shushed the dog, then smiled her best patient smile. Without warning, like a maniac, the man lunged. She squealed—the helpless, petite fairy princess whose faithful canine companion was trying to lick her face.

"You saved my life." Ben grabbed her around the waist and swung her off her feet, out of range of the moving swings, giggling four-year-olds, and a barking dog.

"More likely I gave you a hernia." The smart-aleck remark did nothing to tamp the lust blanking out her mind.

"You . . . are . . . wonderful." He kissed her on the tip of the nose—the way he probably kissed Molly every night before bed. Fondly. Like an old friend.

What'd you expect? Passion?

Passion because she volunteered to take care of his daughter for a few hours? Disgusted by her own stupidity, Risa went limp as a bag of potatoes in his arms. The puppy whined. Grinning from ear to ear, Ben set her down.

The puppy planted his forepaws in the middle of her back. She swayed. Her arms instinctively locked around Ben's neck. Perfectly attuned, they leaned into each other. Her lips parted, and she felt his breath on her face. *Careful of his boo-boo.*

"I'm jumping, La Ti Da!"

Risa's eyes flew open. The spell broke. "Wait, Jay!"

Gentleman that he was, Ben Macdonald stepped aside, giving her plenty of space to crash-land in reality.

* * *

Dark gray clouds hid the sun, and the air felt nippy. Straight from her swinging marathon, Molly graciously let Ben hug her. His heart contracted. How long before she didn't want her daily hugs? Her body hummed like a new furnace. Like Amy—*and Doc*—she was never cold. God, Molly was the same age as Amy when they first met. Hunkered down, feeling a lot like a fraud, Ben listened with one ear as she jabbered about Jason.

His other ear picked up every sound Doc made as she chatted with Jason about Santa and the pup, whose name would *not* be Rudolph. Doc had saved Ben's butt, but apparently had no idea her offer to care for Molly had restored his belief in Santa Claus.

And why would she guess? More likely, she was plain disgusted by the macho way he expressed his gratitude. No way she hadn't felt how hard he was.

Molly's arms around his neck brought his mind back to his body. She wrinkled her nose. "Santa smells funny."

"Like cigars," Jason stated knowingly.

"Cigars? Yuck." Doc handed Jason the puppy's leash. Her lush hips swayed as she led Jason and the mutt away from Ben and Molly. "What makes you think Santa smelled like cigars?"

Sidetracking Jason was, in theory, supposed to give Ben a few minutes during which he'd explain to Molly about going to work.

"Make sure she's comfortable staying with me till Maryann gets here," Doc had said. "If she's not, expect stomachaches."

Stung by her reminder, Ben tried to rationalize his oversight, but couldn't. The constant flow of testosterone washing through his system made thinking abstract. Brought home what kind of father he was. *So, get with the program.*

He lifted Molly into his arms. Instead of daydreaming about Doc's soft curves, he needed to act like a father.

Molly pulled away from him. "I'm a big girl, Daddy."

"Yes, you are." Reluctantly, Ben let her go.

"Jason gets to do everything. Why can't I carry the picnic basket?"

Ahead of them, Jason disregarded Doc's attempts at assisting with the unwieldy basket and guiding the pup. Shoulders hunched, the kid held the basket chest high for a couple of steps before his immature muscles gave out. Carried lower, in a more natural position, the basket bumped his knees, forcing him to walk like a duck. The pooch pranced in front of him at almost every step. Overall, though, Ben figured the kid managed the basket's size and shape with heroic coordination.

"I'm sure you can carry it before we get back to Dr. La Ti Da's," Ben said. "But first, you and I need to talk."

Twenty minutes after Ben Macdonald left Risa's house, her phone rang. Jason and Molly, engrossed in playing with the puppy, barely looked up. Risa trotted across the hall to her bedroom. How could two kids and one pup make so much noise?

Not even close to the commotion triplets will make.

Grabbing the phone, Risa glanced at herself in the mirrored closet doors. Except for her cheeks being a little pink, she looked pretty much the way she always looked: hair a mess, clothes rumpled. Not the kind of sexy, feminine image that drove men wild with desire.

By men, you mean Ben Macdonald?

The question flitted through her head as she said hello, expecting a peppy telemarketing pitch.

"I'm coming back," Ben Macdonald announced.

Disgusted by her heart beating at double time, she snapped, "Why? Did you forget something?"

Like taking me to bed?

"Have you seen the weather news?"

Get a grip.

"No." Taking a deep breath, she glanced out the window. The sun had disappeared long ago, but so what?

"Tahoe's snowed in."

How convenient. "I see."

"Since yesterday afternoon."

Despite the buzz in her head, Risa managed to pull a few coherent thoughts together. "And Maryann didn't call?"

"Phone lines are down. No calls in, none out."

Risa's invisible radar couldn't pick up an emotional reading from his tone. Frustration? Resignation? Neither? Both? She pressed the receiver closer. Maybe she was projecting. Because she knew exactly how she felt.

Manipulated.

He must think she was dumb as a rock if he actually thought *she* would volunteer to care for Molly all weekend.

"Molly's not going to like leaving your place."

Flattery, flattery. Still, Risa was surprised. She'd imagined a more subtle plea for Molly to stay with her while White Knight Ben Macdonald went off and rallied the champions for a new kind of software.

"I wish I had a puppy." Molly's voice carried across the hall as if she spoke through a loudspeaker.

Head cocked, Risa stopped listening to Molly's father and listened to Molly. "A baby sister would be okay, too. Someone I could take care of."

"Babies get all the attention," Jason pointed out.

"That's because they're so little. They need someone to watch out for them."

Risa swallowed.

Apparently, Jason recognized Molly's wisdom—or maybe he'd said all he intended to say about babies—because he changed the subject to what he wanted for Christmas. Inline skates topped his list. Molly insisted she only wanted a puppy, but finally admitted she also wanted a new dress for her favorite doll. Then, they both started talking at once, interrupting each other, giggling, jabbering, shrieking at the top of their healthy lungs while the puppy yipped and barked, demanding their attention.

Four-year-olds unconsciously colluding to act silly. Risa gave up trying to understand their jabber, made more nonsensical by Ben Macdonald's droning in her ear.

"Where are you?" She hadn't heard most of what he said.

"Coming up to the Amphitheater exit. I should be at your place in fifteen, twenty minutes."

"Why don't we just follow Plan A?"

Suuucker.

Unwilling to examine this judgment, Risa spoke quickly, but firmly. "Leave Molly with me till you find your bug."

"That could be this time tomorrow."

"I can always call you if she wants to leave."

"I want to say yes, but I know it's an imposition."

"Let's call it a favor."

"A favor, huh?"

"Uh-huh. Except for Jason, I haven't had much practice with kids spending the night. In less than a month, I'll have three with me night and day. A dry run with Molly is really a big favor to me."

Silence followed, awkward because it stretched out too long for Risa, who was already regretting her offer.

"You're something else, Doc."

Uh-huh. The world's biggest fool.

Unsure if she was disgusted or irritated or something else altogether, Risa used her doctor-in-charge voice. "You should tell Molly."

"Thanks, Doc. I just hope my ego's intact afterwards."

"Why wouldn't it be?"

"Because she's going to hope I work all weekend."

Risa's heart sank. What a subtle way of informing her that he probably would work through Sunday evening.

* * *

At 5:21, tired and grumpy from waiting in line at the pet store, Kelsy dragged herself into Risa's kitchen. "I can hardly wait to see you buying doggie supplies with triplets in tow."

Risa shrugged. "Why don't you videotape our first time?"

"I'm watching grass grow that day." Kelsy felt her headache rachet up. She set a dog bed filled with canned food, bowls, and a training manual on the floor. Shrieking, Molly and Jason immediately took charge arranging the food in the pantry.

Kelsy cocked her hip against the island. "That bed's a waste of money."

"How would you know? You've never owned a dog."

"Never put my hand in fire, either, but I know it's hot."

Risa rolled her eyes. "Don't start."

Kelsy filled the tea kettle. "Was the oyster stew *good*?"

"Let's talk about the dog bed instead," Risa growled.

"Fine." Kelsy measured tea. "That puppy will never use his bed because he'll end up sleeping in yours."

"No way, Mother." Risa shook her head.

"Triplets might not scare away a good man, but a dog in the bed will scare away even the jerks."

"You promise?"

"This is me laughing." Kelsy made her face go blank. "Sleeping arrangements are no laughing matter when you're out in the meat market."

Risa threw up her hands. "First, I'm not out there. Never was, never will be. Second, don't give a second thought to my sleeping arrangements. I don't think about yours."

"Maybe you should. Believe me, alone doesn't compare to snuggling up with a hot-blooded male who adores you."

"Okay, okay." Risa held her hands up like an old

maid, and Kelsy wanted to smack her. "I get the picture. But speaking of hot-blooded males who adore you, take that damn—that *danged* mountain of asparagus home to Sam."

"What do you mean *mountain?* Do you know how much asparagus costs in December? How much did you eat?"

Like two little puppets, Molly and Jason turned around to look at Kelsy, who needed more than tea for her nerves.

"Let's feed Fido."

Apparently thinking she'd slithered off the hook, Risa used opening the dog food as an excuse for a science lesson: a hand-eye coordination exercise and ethical instruction on the humane care of all animals, rolled into an interactive lesson with Molly and Jason that wore Kelsy out simply listening.

She regrouped by filling the teapot and muttering, "For someone so smart, you do the dumbest things."

Adopting triplet boys was dumb enough, but deciding to raise them alone ranked up there as dumb beyond belief, in Kelsy's opinion. Ditto for pretending Ben lived on an ethereal plane and still carried a torch for his dead wife.

Curiosity needled Kelsy. "By the way," she asked, "where's Ben?"

Chin jutted, mouth tight, Risa said, "Handling an emergency at work. I offered to take care of Molly."

End of subject. Kelsy poured a cup of tea, debated letting the subject drop, then stated the obvious. "Risa, Risa, you've got a lot to learn about men."

CHAPTER 9

"Sam's plane lands at SFO in an hour," Kelsy said at six o'clock. "A week in Tokyo, he'll be starved . . . as you can imagine."

"Let me guess," Risa teased. "Oyster stew and asparagus?"

"If we're talking about food." Kelsy winked. As she and Jason pulled out of Risa's driveway, she was laughing.

Suddenly starved, Risa let Molly set the table while she reheated leftover spaghetti, made a salad, and mused on married life. Unless an asteroid destroyed the earth between seven and nine that night, she'd bet Sam felt like the luckiest guy in the world within an hour after getting home. Envy reduced her to a series of operatic sighs. Sam must count his blessings every night.

Dressed in one of Risa's old Kermit the Frog T-shirts, Molly took the phone when her father called after dinner. "Daddy, Daddy? Guess what? Guess who I get to sleep with?"

Molly jumped up and down, punctuating the reply to her own question. "Fergus, Fergus, Fergus. I get to sleep with Fergus. The frog. 'Member?"

Folding back the sheets, Risa eavesdropped shamelessly. Molly didn't take a breath. "We get to sleep with La Ti Da, Daddy! In her bed!"

Admittedly, the shrieks could probably drive a person stark raving, barking mad after about a day. Since bedtime for Molly was imminent, Risa thought she could get through a couple of favorite stories before reserving a padded cell.

"Her bed's huuuge, Daddy! It smells like roses. I love roses. La Ti Da washed my hair with rose shampoo, too."

The staccato delivery turned to a dramatic, whispered one. "La Ti Da let me use her rose *body* lotion. I smell so good."

Afraid Molly would never get to sleep, Risa chanted, "Fergie's almost asleeep. . . ."

While Molly made a last bathroom trip, Risa reclaimed the phone and said, "Your daughter's mad about roses."

Ben's laugh sent slow shivers down Risa's spine. "She's mad about you. If you wore eau de garlic, she'd think that was the only scent in the world."

Longing filled Risa's chest with a dull ache. *What about you?* she wanted to ask. *Do you like roses?*

Afraid she'd ask him and reveal more than she intended, she swallowed, then said brightly, "In my experience, roses don't turn stalwart males into love zombies. Big advantage in about seven, eight years when you have to start beating teenage boys away with a club."

He groaned. "Seven or eight years? That means I have to send her to the convent in Patagonia in another year."

Risa laughed. "You can probably wait two years."

"Whew." He exhaled, and the sound scalded Risa's ear.

"You may have to send Fergie with her, though."

"You mean you'd sacrifice sleeping with him?"

She put her hand over her thudding heart. "Actually, I don't sleep with him. I take a bath with him."

"Is he any good at underwater massage?"

"He'll do in a pinch." *Am I really having this conversation?* Risa fanned her face.

"Does he polish your toenails, too?"

Stunned, Risa dropped the phone, but caught it before it hit the floor. She massaged her chest. "Till my prince comes along, I do my own nails."

"Don't pedicures interfere with slaying dragons?"

"No problem for a true prince." *Amazing how the brain functions during a coronary.*

"I never realized how hard—how tough, very tough *true* princes have it."

"Why do you think there are so many frogs in the world?" she shot back, but resisted saying, *Gotcha!*

Molly's return from the bathroom gave Risa a natural excuse to hang up. The verbal sparring had taken its toll. The print in *Beauty and the Beast* jitterbugged on the page. Dizzy, Risa stopped reading. Had she imagined the game she and Ben Macdonald played? Which of them started it?

No idea.

Not Miz Innocence.

Pictures and print did a break dance. Risa took a deep breath. Surprised by Molly's patience, she waited for a complaint. Kids didn't like deviations in their bedtime stories and usually corrected every slip. Unless they were asleep, which Molly now was. *A whole day without a word about her stomach.*

Gazing at the soft curls and dewy skin, Risa felt a wave of tenderness engulf her. *Please, please, let me be a good mother.*

Carefully, she dropped a kiss on Molly's cheek, then pulled the sheet up, but stayed on the bed. *No monsters here.*

Risa leaned back on the pillows. She closed her eyes, and the sexy talk between her and Ben replayed in her head. Praise Jupiter, she'd made Kelsy take the oysters home. Something cool grazed her cheek. Heart thumping, she jerked upright.

Asleep, Molly had turned on her side, pitching Fergie forward. Holy Hannah! The frog's hand slid down her cheek—like a lover waiting for a good night kiss.

Frustrated to the point of pulling his hair out follicle by follicle, Ben took a break at ten o'clock and called Doc. In the past, when he'd reached this kind of impasse, talking to Amy always helped his mental block. He never talked to her about software bugs or technical problems. He talked, instead, about the day-to-day parts of their lives—their next vacation in Montana, Amy's volunteer work with the library's literacy program, and, of course, Molly. Always about Molly.

Often, before hanging up, he and Amy indulged in what they laughingly called *phone sex*. Especially if he'd gone back to work after dinner and didn't anticipate returning till after Amy went to bed.

Fragments and slivers of those teasing moments whirred in his head as Doc's husky-with-sleep hello scrambled memory and reality. Eyes closed, feet on his desk, he pinched the bridge of his nose. His bottom lip was on fire, and he knew he had to be careful. Go with safe topics, nothing sexy. No innuendoes. "What's Molly wearing instead of a nightgown?"

"One of my T-shirts. It barely covers my bu—it's like a tent on her. But she loves it."

"I bet I never get her to sleep in nightgowns again."

"Oh, gosh. I'm sorry. I never thought—"

"Hey, I'm not complaining. Where's it written she has to sleep in nightgowns?"

"I did till about . . . thirteen. Then I switched to T-shirts. The ones with celebrities' faces plastered on them. I slept with Mick Jagger every other night."

"Tell anybody?"

"Are you kidding? *Every*body. I was the envy of every girl I knew, because my T-shirt was autographed. Big, biiig deal."

"Is Molly sleeping in that T-shirt?"

"Nope. She picked Kermit herself. Mick didn't get a second glance."

"I think I'm relieved, but what if Molly develops a frog fetish, too?"

"As fetishes go, it's pretty harmless."

"You mean she could get hung up on whips and leather and really . . . kinky stuff?"

"My only experience with kinky is my hair."

"Don't they say our appearance reflects our inner person?"

His comeback was lame, and he imagined her rolling her eyes. Her rich, throaty laugh went straight to his head, zapping him with an adrenaline surge. He slapped his hand over the receiver. God, he'd lost all self-control. What's more, he didn't care. He loved this feeling of addicted excitement.

Surrendering to lust, he asked, "Is that what you sleep in now—a T-shirt?"

"Uh-huh. Wasn't it Chanel No. 5 Marilyn Monroe slept in? Let's just say I have to change my ways once my sons arrive."

"Understood." His brain exploded with candid shots, and not the kind he thought she'd appreciate. He said quickly, "I slept in long johns from infancy in Montana. Coming to California, I thought I'd moved to the tropics. My second day at Stanford, I threw away the boxers I'd brought and switched to briefs—learning one of life's important lessons."

Listening, he'd noticed even in the parking lot at Starbucks, was one of her strongest talents. She didn't let him down, but said, "I'll bite. What big lesson did you learn?"

"Well," he dragged it out, weaving the flimsy pieces

together in his head. With the phone cradled against his ear, he stared at his computer screen. An animated image of her—naked, in bed—crooked a finger at him.

A nanosecond before the silence turned really embarrassing, he remembered. He cleared his throat. "This was back when dinosaurs roamed the earth, remember. Before all the jocks appeared in TV commercials for designer underwear."

Despite the miles between them, he felt the heat from her long exhale in his ear. "Got it," she said.

"Okay, so here I am at Stanford. A hick kid from Montana. Long johns most of the year, white boxers a few days in the summer. Never gave a thought to underwear in my life."

"So far this sounds normal." She laughed.

"Thank you." Ben looked into space. "First night my roommate calls me a perv. God, I'll never forget it."

Remembering, he made a noise that was halfway between a groan and a laugh. "Talk about fragile male egos."

"For wearing boxer shorts?" He could tell she was trying not to laugh. "You grew up with prototypes for the Marlboro Man—"

"Damn right. And they wore long johns ninety-nine-point-nine percent of the time and boxers during the three days of spring and the two of summer."

She gurgled, then said, "So what was your roomie's problem?"

Ben turned on his CEO's baritone. "No *intelligent* Stanford guy wore boxers. Boxers, white socks? Geek-wear."

Her voice went up to a squeak. "Why is that, the D-U-M Davis coed asked?"

"Boxers and white socks—both—made you a dweeb."

"Boss?" Jake, his hair resembling Einstein's on a bad day, burst into Ben's office. "We found it!"

"You'd better go." Risa wiped her hands, slick with

sweat, down the front of her terry cloth robe. "Talk to you later."

"Can I call you in an hour? Will you be awake?"

For five minutes after assuring Ben Macdonald she'd be awake, Risa stood in her bedroom with both hands firmly on top of the telephone receiver. Heat singed her palms. The damn thing was dangerous. Sinister.

"Obviously an example of technology run amok, Watson," she pitched her thrown voice in a whisper.

"Indeed, Sherlock," she answered herself in a poorly imitated English accent.

"Wouldn't you agree, Watson, that Dr. Risa Taylor, soon-to-be mother of three, has also run amok?"

"Indeed, Sherlock."

Enough. The logicometer in Risa's head kicked on. She laughed. Whatever tiny wire or chip malfunctioned and then broke loose in the phone, it hadn't fried her entire brain. She still recognized when to stop talking to herself. More importantly, ventriloquism aside, she knew when to stop *answering* herself.

Hot all over, she gritted her teeth, but the question she was thinking came out of her mouth. "Why didn't you say something totally stupid? Like, 'I'll be waiting'?"

Saying each word in a breathy Marilyn Monroe impersonation, she twisted at the tie around her waist, bumped one hip out, and flashed an acre of thigh.

Reality sheared through her fantasy. At that moment, she'd have sworn each of her thighs outweighed the Blond Bombshell.

Her mind immediately shied away from such truth. She smacked her forehead several times. "Hellooo? Has Mr. Brain gone on vacation? How about a little relief from my hormones here? Ben Macdonald's looking for sex—not responsibility for Charlie, Tom, and Harry."

Try a cold shower.

The idea took hold. Wuss that she was, she couldn't take the icy needles for more than ten minutes. The needles stung her bare skin but didn't completely wash the memory of Ben Macdonald down the drain. Teeth clacking, teetering on the cusp of hypothermia, she toweled off.

"Blue lips—that'll make him hot."

Groaning, she slipped into the terry cloth robe and massaged her leaden feet with every ounce of concentration she could muster. Every time a thought tried to surface, she focused on several acupressure points. Calm seeped into her feet, then upward.

Convinced she'd jump-started her circulation and her brain, she tiptoed into her bedroom. Still half frozen, she rubbed her hands together, trying to think where she'd put the clothes she wanted. Had she packed them last winter? She entered the walk-in closet, shutting the door so the light wouldn't wake Molly. Four boxes later, she admitted defeat.

What if de prince don't show up?

What if Sleeping Beauty don't wake up?

What if she so scared she throw up?

The sarcasm spurred her to open another box. No way she was taking any chances in the battle with her hormones. If Ben Macdonald did show up without calling first, she'd be ready.

"Make that *prepared,*" she muttered.

Despite the heat between her legs, she had no intention of being ready. Passion wasn't on her agenda tonight. She'd be dressed to survive hours of banter, eye sex, or mouth-to-mouth resuscitation.

Two more boxes and she shouted softly, "Hal-l-lelu-jah."

Afraid the frogs on Jason's ankle bracelet might catch on the silk long johns, she dropped it in a drawer. One hard yank, and the long johns clung to her hips and legs like plastic wrap to butter. She risked a look in the floor-to-ceiling mirror. Dear God, she looked like a sausage. Felt like one, too. Turning for a side view, she imagined Amy next to her. *Don't go there.*

Pulling a thermal top over her bra and adding a thick turtleneck over both occupied her mind. She tucked the extra material into jeans. She couldn't breathe, but she'd covered every inch of skin except her hands, face, and ears. Sweat dripped off her.

In search of options, her brain hummed. Her hands cuddled, comforted, massaged, tickled, soothed, and touched kids and their parents every day in her office. Her hands had a mind of their own. She couldn't risk so much as a handshake with Ben Macdonald—unless she was willing to go to bed with him.

So wear gloves.

Great idea. Except . . . wearing gloves bordered on weird. Inexplicably weird. Okay. So, she'd keep her hands clasped in her lap. Or sit on them. *How about wringing them like a Gothic heroine?* Holy Hannah! She shoved a chunk of hair behind her ear. She'd do whatever it took to make sure her fingers didn't accidentally graze his.

Okay, okay. Any other visible sensual spots? Her brain shifted.

Feet! Ears! Hair!

Rejecting the fleeting thought that she was crazy, Risa stole back into her bedroom, found a heavy scarf, and returned to the dressing room. With shaky hands and clumsy fingers, she arranged the scarf over her ears and hair, tying it in a hard knot at her throat. She tucked the knot inside her high-necked sweater. Then, she tugged. Hard, from both sides and the top. The scarf stayed in place. She laid her palm on top of her head and tried moving it backward. Nothing. The scarf stayed in place like a cement hairnet.

Good, good. Ears and hair now untouchable.

Feet next. The crimson polish on her toenails gleamed. For half a nanosecond, her mind went blank. She palmed the scarf, hoping to stimulate her brain. "Ski socks," she whispered.

Her mind shifted into high gear. No problem. She had ski socks. Thick ones. Nothing weird about ski socks and slippers on a chilly night. What's more, they'd provide a barrier in case he tried massaging her feet. She was a sucker for a foot massage. Tim hated feet. Not just hers but everyone's, and he refused to believe how sexy they were.

Ridiculous, he'd declared, rejecting the idea for all time.

Of course, right now, her own behavior was either ridiculous or hysterical or, worse, melodramatic. Why not simply go to bed with Ben Macdonald and stop acting like a demented medieval maiden?

The sound of tires in the driveway cut short any reply. Mouth dry, legs trembling, she started down the stairs.

At the door, she fumbled the frog pendant from under her sweaters. Eyes closed, she squeezed the tiny gold body for luck.

Then, she opened her eyes and turned the doorknob.

CHAPTER 10

To hell with frog doorbells and uplifting chimes. Ben knocked on Doc's front door at 11:46 P.M., reassured by the sting of solid wood under his knuckles. Finding that damn software bug had about used up all his thinking neurons for one night. But somewhere between the office—during that chat about sleepwear?—and Doc's driveway, he'd lost his mind. If he had to tell the truth? He halfway expected, hoped, prayed, she'd open the door covered in whipped cream.

Or in plastic wrap. Or in a gauzy negligee. Bare-assed naked would work, too.

Damned close to hyperventilating, he knocked again. Calm down. He had to calm down, think of a greeting. He couldn't just step through the door, knock her down, and drag her by the hair across the floor. He'd gone almost a year without sex for God's sake. He knew how to talk.

In his fantasy on the drive over, words were superfluous, so he'd wasted zero energy rehearsing what he'd say. Which might explain why his brain took a nosedive when she cracked open the door in real time.

"You going somewhere?" he blurted. *Like to Saudi Arabia?* His image of her in plastic wrap evaporated.

A gold and black head nudged into the crack. Doc scratched the pup's nose, then patted the headscarf and rolled her eyes back as if a small animal sat on her head. "My hair's a mess. It goes crazy in weather like this."

"Too much humidity?" Did he give a damn?

"Too little."

Somehow that didn't make sense. Introduction of the weather pretty much killed his whipped cream fantasy. Though Ben wasn't sure, maybe he liked the jeans and turtleneck reality better.

"Molly asleep?" Duuuh? He turned the collar up on his windbreaker, hoping she hadn't noticed his stupidity.

"Like a baby. She played hard today."

"Yeah, she was a wild woman on those swings." He blew on his hands and stamped his feet—gentle reminders the night air was nippy though he was too wired to die of hypothermia.

"I like girls who really get into playing." Doc avoided eye contact.

Ben moved closer to the door. Warm air snaked through the crack and crept up his pantlegs. "I don't want to brag, but I think Molly's got playing nailed."

"She's a great kid all right."

Another conversational chasm yawned. The pup whined.

Take control of the situation, Ben thought, *before Doc suggests a walk for Fido.* Taking control was his strong suit, right? Hadn't he just managed a major crisis at work and lived to tell the tale?

"Did I misunderstand your invitation to drop by?" She hadn't explicitly invited him, but hey, he was taking charge.

"No. No. Come in, come in."

Mentally, he patted himself on the back. This afternoon he'd have gone for the double entendre. Did I misunderstand *your invitation?* Probably would've lowered his voice on *your invitation* so she couldn't miss his meaning. Now, tonight? God, what a relief. He'd just proven he wasn't a sex-crazed pervert. Now, he could apologize for his smart-ass remarks and ask her to take Molly's case without feeling like a hypocrite.

Tugging repeatedly at the scarf, Doc backed into the entryway like Ben was a burglar she'd surprised. But surprise didn't begin to explain his confusion. He heard the furnace click on, felt warm air but couldn't figure the extra bulk on her curves. *What is wrong with this picture?*

Okay. He took a deep breath. She was nervous. Hell, he was nervous. He said, "I should check on Molly."

"Of course. Top of the stairs, last door on your left."

Surprisingly, the relief on Doc's face didn't offend him. In fact, he appreciated that she didn't go up with him. Watching Molly sleep, he couldn't always hide his emotions.

At the top of the stairs, the scent of roses drew him to a wedge of light. He hesitated at the door Doc had left cracked. Go straight to the bed, intent only on Molly? Or slink into Doc's private space like the Wolf preparing for Red Riding Hood? His pulse went nuts. How long before Doc came looking for him? He rubbed the stubble on his chin. "Oh, Granny, what big . . ."

A little carried away by his fantasy, he grazed his ankle on the door. A radiant white light shot out of his brain. Christ, what if he woke Molly?

Eyes straight ahead, he tiptoed to the bed. He dodged the temptation to explore the bedroom by leaning down and sniffing Molly's hair. His heart caught. He couldn't get enough of her sweet scent of roses. Dammit, he should've been there, poured in the bubble bath. . . . He pinched the bridge of his nose. "Next time, baby, no matter what," he whispered.

In the meantime, how could he ever thank Doc?

You'll think of some way. Excited by the possibilities, he stood. Blood rushed to his head. He caught a corner of the sheet. Molly stirred. Standing still, he felt an ache that never left him. God, if anything ever happened to her . . .

He didn't let his mind finish the unthinkable. He whispered, "I love you, Molly."

Her even breathing calmed him. He waited five minutes. Then, sure she was fine, he tiptoed out of the bedroom.

Downstairs, Ben felt as if he'd wandered onto the runway in front of a 767. The family room was so bright that the pup lay under a table with his paws over his eyes. Doc silenced Randy Travis with the click of a remote control. After she offered, and Ben declined, coffee, juice, soda, water, or champagne, they both sat down. She sank into the big wing chair next to the fireplace. Whining, the pup got up and laid his head on her knee.

Nunlike, Doc pressed her legs together. Ben settled into the overstuffed sofa, then, like an old dog, wiggled and shifted, twisted and fidgeted, stretched and squirmed. Finally, he got up and took the chair opposite her. The pup lifted his head, looked at Ben, then returned to his original position.

"A picture of eternal fidelity," he said, going for cute. He couldn't decide if the crack he heard came from the fire or from the tension in his jaw.

Doc said in the bright voice he now knew meant she was in a state of high avoidance, "Do you think he needs to go outside?"

"Yeah. Why don't I take him, clear my head?"

To his disappointment, she went into the laundry room, returned with a collar and leash, and immediately reeled off directions so he and the pup wouldn't take a wrong turn into the hills. When she took a breath, he said, "Shouldn't you examine my lip before I go out into the cold night?"

"I don't think that's necessary." Firelight bathed her eyelids in gold.

"What if I've developed complications?" He edged his chin toward her, and Risa's heart missed a beat.

The scarf, tight, unforgiving, flattened her mop of curls into something heavy as an anvil. "What kind of complications?"

"Serious complications."

"Molly's upstairs." Her mashed-down hair scorched her scalp, boosting the temperature in her skull past boiling.

"Sleeping." He cupped his ear toward the stairs.

"We think." Risa nodded, her head heavy and wobbly, her arms and legs languid.

"So examine my lip, Doc." His fingers seared through denim, silk, and flesh, straight to her frayed nerve endings.

"Looks good. Very good." He inched closer. Her heart rate revved up to pure panic.

"You must have X-ray vision." He laid his hands on her shoulders. Colonies of goose bumps popped out on her arms. "You a hundred percent sure about your diagnosis?"

"Yes. Your lip's fine." Which was more than she could say for her heart. One more bang against her ribs and she'd probably go into full cardiac arrest.

"Does that mean I get a clean bill of health?"

"If you don't consider the doctor is stark raving, barking mad." She looked away, tempted by his slow, lazy smile. Did he want to kiss her as much as she wanted to kiss him?

He threw his head back and laughed softly. "So's the patient."

At their feet, the dog woofed, but Risa barely heard it.

"I'm not hitting on you for sex, Risa." Her name on his lips sang in her ears and fueled her hope he was lying. "I bet you've heard that line before." He turned on the smile that swelled her heart, jammed her throat.

"Not that often." *Not often enough?* She swallowed.

"The sexual banter—I don't know, I can't explain." He shrugged. "It's contagious."

But fun. Dry-mouthed, she swallowed, ready to admit her guilt, afraid she'd blurt out why she was dressed for a trip to Patagonia, but determined he'd never know she thought he found her seriously sexy.

"We've dropped so many sexual innuendoes since we met, I keep expecting a subpoena from the Morals Police."

The muscles around her mouth felt stiffly fragile. If she moved a single one, would her whole face fall off?

"I don't deny I'm flirting with you, okay? But flirting doesn't have to keep us from being . . . friends, right?"

"Friends?" Which of them was insane?

"Friends." He swiped at a strand of hair that had miraculously escaped the scarf and lay across her cheek.

"Suppose," Risa said hoarsely, "suppose Amy was still alive. Could you and I be friends?"

He looked into space. "Not likely, 'cuz I'd be a dead man. Amy would kill me for flirting with anyone but her."

"Seems enlightened to me." Risa dug her nails into her palm. "First, I'd hurt you, then I'd cut you off at the knees. Or . . . maybe a little higher. Then, I'd have to kill you."

"Ouch."

"That's one of the fine points about fidelity my ex never understood. Friends *don't* flirt."

Head cocked, black eyes serious, Ben rocked back on his heels, nodding, as if he agreed with every word she'd said. The cobwebs in Risa's head cleared. She'd started these stupid games—bursting into flame every time he so much as looked her way. She could also stop the games. Right now.

Through stiff lips, she said, "If Amy was alive, you'd notice me when St. Peter served the devil ice-cube sandwiches."

The corners of his mouth twitched. He waited a beat, then said, "Not a total exaggeration."

"But you get my point?" She bit off each word.

"Got it." He tapped the side of his head. "And you're right. I wouldn't be flirting with you—here, or anywhere else—if Amy was waiting for me at home."

After Amy, no other woman will get the chance.

Unspoken, the truth punctured Risa's heart so quickly and cleanly, she felt only a momentary spasm. Her throat tightened, but one swallow and she spoke in a reasonable, natural voice. "Thank you. For not lying to me."

"I was tempted, but I'm out of practice," he whispered.

The dog whined pitifully, reminding Ben he had an escape he'd better make. Before he spilled all his guts. Walking him to the door, Doc repeated how easy it was to get lost among the cul-de-sacs and dead-end streets.

"Excuse me, ma'am." He slipped into his jacket and took the dog's leash. "But a bred and born Montana boy never gets lost as long as the sky doesn't fall."

His tone was flip, but the words cut to the bone. How many nights had he and Amy spent memorizing constellations and dreaming of worlds beyond Montana?

"Frankly, I don't expect the sky to fall," Doc said, equally flip. "But you've got your cell phone, just in case."

Her interruption broke the connection to Amy. He almost tossed the damn phone on the hall table, but realized he wasn't mad at Doc for doubting him. He was mad because in Amy, he'd had someone in his life who knew him as well as he knew himself. What's more, she loved him anyway. Cheered, he patted the phone.

"Never fear, if the batteries die, the dog and I can always kill our own food."

"Speaking of food, I'll make some hot chocolate," Doc offered at the front door.

"Don't bother." Not unless there was a little gun in the bottom of the cup and he could shoot himself with it.

Outside, two steps away from the door, he said to the pup, "Well, I thought that went well, didn't you?"

"That was fun." Risa leaned against the front door and started laughing. Here she'd dressed like a twelfth-century contemplative Belgian nun and gotten exactly what she'd wished for. "The perfect gentleman."

Yes, he'd tried—halfheartedly—flirting. Perfect gentleman that he was, he'd backed off immediately.

Had the fact that hot chocolate was an aphrodisiac scared him off? Risa had no idea how she knew he'd been thinking of Amy when he left the house, but she'd bet on it. Her throat tightened. Whether Ben believed it or not, chocolate's magical powers could heal his hurt lip, maybe even mend his broken heart.

You'll never know. But she'd still have Charlie, Tom, and Harry.

Not entirely comforted, she went upstairs. A wedge of warm, yellow light from the bathroom cut across the bed. Risa felt her heart catch. She couldn't take her eyes off Molly—an angel in a Kermit T-shirt. An angel who lay on her right side in the middle of the bed, clutching a big green rubber frog.

Still not a monster in sight. Risa hugged her waist. Sooner rather than later, she should kickstart the monster conversation with Père Macdonald. She inhaled. What better time than a night when he felt so good about himself?

She heard the front door open. Her heart fluttered.

Showtime. She marched stiffly to the top of the stairs. Afraid her voice would crack, she whispered loudly, "Back so soon?"

Five long blocks from home, the pup sat down and refused to get up again, no matter how much Ben wheedled or cussed. Once upon a time, he'd had a knack for soothing animals. After the first minute or two, this one stopped looking at him and hung its head. Guilt tempered the impatience building inside Ben. He lowered his voice. "Don't think I'm carrying you, furball."

The insult didn't work, either. After a few seconds of no eye contact, Ben admitted they were at a standoff. A light mist gave the empty street an eeriness that evoked old horror movies. Ben snorted and felt his lip sing. Shivering, he turned his collar up and snapped his numb fingers. He'd been hotter than lava in Doc's house. On the street, he felt chilled to the bone. Would Doc take it the wrong way if he walked through her door and headed straight for a hot shower?

"You think we might get back there in my lifetime?" he asked the pup, and then felt stupid for talking so loud—hoping to stop the images of him and Doc, together, in a steamy shower.

Ben glanced at his watch. Ten minutes. Should he call her? And say what? "Your pup did his business but now won't move."

The pup looked up at him and shivered. "You are," Ben said, "a pain in the ass."

Whining, the mutt looked pathetic. Positive it wasn't cold enough for frostbite, Ben surrendered anyway. He scooped the beast up in his arms and clamped down on the pithy Anglo-Saxon words churning in his brain. He hoped that by holding the pup at arm's length he wouldn't return smelling like dog. Nothing like the scent of damp dog fur to make for a memorable occasion.

He staggered two blocks under the dog's dead weight. In need of a breather, he set the animal down and swung his arms overhead, hoping to restore blood flow to his paralyzed elbows.

The cop car that pulled up next to the curb didn't alarm him. It didn't even surprise him. What else would he expect? Victory at work no longer looked like his finest hour.

A freckled young cop with a sliver of space between his front teeth leaned out the passenger's window and gave Ben's lip the once-over. "There a problem, sir?"

"A small one." *Must be a slow night in Cielo Vista.* "The mutt's out of steam and so am I."

"Cute pup. Belong to you?"

"No. I'm walking him for Dr. Risa Taylor. She lives—"

The driver leaned across his partner. "I've escorted Dr. La Ti Da to the hospital half a dozen times. She's the best."

"So'd she get the pup for the triplets?" the young one asked. "Seems like a big responsibility—a pup *and* three babies."

"Not for La Ti Da," the older cop said. "She'll handle those boys like a champ. My son begs to go see her."

"C'mon," the first one said. "Kids hate doctors—"

"Not Dr. La Ti Da. Ever know a doctor who throws her voice? Kids love it, don't even cry when she gives 'em their shots."

Feeling left out, but also growing irked by the urban myth of Doc's legendary shot-giving prowess, Ben chimed in. "My daughter's sure nuts about her."

"See?" The older cop gave Ben two thumbs up, but spoke to his partner. "By the time you have your first, she'll be back from her leave of absence."

"She gonna be gone for twenty years?"

Might as well be a lifetime.

It wasn't that funny, but, being one of the guys, Ben joined in the hilarity anyway. Then he picked up the dog, who was snoozing through it all. "Better go, or she'll think I'm lost and call the police."

More laughs, then the driver said, "Why doncha get in? We'll drop you off."

Something about the invitation bothered Ben. He didn't know whether he should be flattered or nervous. Did they doubt he knew Doc? Maybe they thought he'd dognapped the pup. Whatever, he was pretty sure they wouldn't take no for an answer.

On the two-minute ride to the cul-de-sac, the cops casually got the basics on Ben. Name, address, business with Doc—besides walking her pooch? The pup moaned in his sleep. Ben didn't even glance at his four-footed companion. Suddenly edgy, he stared at the white Lexus next to his Chevy pickup.

"Havin' a party?" the driver asked.

"Not exactly," Ben said cautiously. "That Lexus wasn't there when I left fifteen minutes ago."

"Know who it belongs to?" the young cop asked.

Ben said mechanically, "Kelsy Chandler, I think. Her son and my daughter go to the same preschool. Jason Chandler is Dr. Taylor's godson."

"Small world, isn't it?" The young cop glanced over his shoulder at Ben. "Kelsy Chandler dated my oldest brother in high school. She's eight years older'n me and the reason I'm not married to this day." He smacked his fingertips at his partner, "I had a crush on her you wouldn't believe. She is one foxy—"

"Thank you for sharin'." The driver set the emergency brake. "We'll wait," he said easily to Ben. "Give my greetings to La Ti Da. Just say Tyler Nelson's dad. She'll know."

"Need help with your pooch?" the young cop asked.

"No, thanks." What Ben needed help with was understanding what was going on. Gone fifteen minutes on a mission of mercy, and Doc called Kelsy. Why?

"Sure you don't need a hand?"

The kid in the front seat made Ben feel old, but he

shook his head. The dog, asleep next to him on the backseat, didn't move a muscle. Not even when Ben opened his door.

"Looks like La Ti Da's got herself a killer there," Officer Nelson said.

"A killer," Ben agreed.

Teeth gritted, he swore silently as he went around to the other side of the car, opened the door, and pulled the dog toward him. How hard could this be?

The pup woke up and tried washing Ben's face. The young one stopped cackling long enough to call out, "Tell Kelsy 'hi' from Finn Bishop."

"Sure." The returning hero tottered up the front steps, too pissed to be glad the door swung open immediately. "Wave at the cops," he said under his breath.

Without missing a beat, still dressed for a ski trip, Doc took Fido, stepped outside next to Ben, and waved broadly. The cop car backed out of the driveway. The mutt tried to lick Ben's face. He grabbed the dog and set him in the hall. Surly as Attila the Hun, he snarled, "What the hell's Kelsy doing here?"

"It's a girl thing," Kelsy cooed, pleased by Ben's scowl.

Head thrown back, she moved out of the shadows, stepped over Fido, and crossed to where her best friend in the world stood next to one of the enemy. She looked down her nose at Ben, then hooked an arm around Risa's waist. It was no surprise to Kelsy that Ben started backpedaling. Typical male reaction, she thought. *Cut and run when a woman shows any gumption.*

Admittedly, she was surprised he didn't, in fact, leave. Then, she remembered Molly asleep upstairs. Watching Risa out of the corner of her eye, Kelsy raised her chin about an inch from Ben's nose. "Bet you didn't know this woman learned everything she knows about noses and kissing from yours truly."

"No, I don't believe that's come up," he said, oh so

coolly. His voice didn't go up the way hers did when she was mad or upset. *Like now.* Like all men, he had to have the last word. He said, "Doc and I don't know each other very well yet—"

"Oh, it doesn't matter how well you know somebody," Kelsy interrupted, not giving a damn that he looked a little ticked. "You can know someone for ten years—especially if it's a man—and you'll never know what's in his cheatin' heart."

"Kel."

The love in Risa's tone felt like a knife—no, make that screwdriver—turning in Kelsy's heart. Tears leaked out of her eyes and trickled down her cheeks. She accepted a tissue Risa sneaked her and scrubbed her eyes till they hurt.

"I'm okay." Kelsy honked her nose louder than she'd planned, simply because Ben looked so embarrassed. Was there a man alive who realized tears were therapeutic?

"Let's go sit down," Risa said in the voice she used in the examining room with kids seeing her for the first time who were scared to death. She squeezed Kelsy's fingers gently. "I'll fix you some hot chocolate."

"Nope." Kelsy shook her head. "Forget hot chocolate. I want some of that bubbly. I'm sure Ben won't mind sharing."

Risa slid him a look, and he shrugged, looking confused in the dumb, I'm-from-Mars way only men could look confused.

"What's the matter?" Despite his fat lip, Kelsy wanted to smack him. "What do they call champagne on Mars?"

"Kel." Risa tugged her arm, but Kelsy jerked away. "Let me get this clear, first. I mean if I can't understand this, I'll never understand the heavy stuff."

Frowning at Risa, Ben said, "Naturally, I know what bubbly is. I just didn't know we were—"

Risa explained. "I put a bottle on ice after you left."

"Dom Perignon. Good stuff," Kelsy added. "Not as good as the bottle I opened tonight to welcome my sweetie home, but okay. Just what the doctor ordered, right, Risa?"

"What the doctor orders is a hot shower, then sleep. Or you can forget the shower. There are clean sheets—"

Disappointed, Kelsy tossed her head. "Did I spout clichés at you when you found out Tim was pond scum?" Risa opened her mouth, but Kelsy waved her hand—a signal Risa interpreted right on the money and shut her mouth. "Didn't I suggest you should forget your medical training and use a scalpel on him, show him there were consequences to lying and cheating and conniving and humiliating you, embarrassing you, shattering your self-esteem, and making you feel you were the dumbest, stupidest fool in the world?" Still wound tighter than new piano wire, Kelsy paused for breath, ignoring the worry Risa projected.

Damn, if she was in her own house, she could do something physical for release. She could throw something. *Like Sam's clothes out onto the driveway.*

"I need to go." She shoved past Ben, who looked disapproving, Mr. Cool-Headed Executive, a clone of her own disapproving Mr. Cool-Headed Executive.

"I don't think so." Risa stepped in front of the door.

"You're busy. I'm just in the way."

Risa hugged her. "Now who's spouting clichés?"

Ben kept his distance. *At least he's not a total idiot.*

CHAPTER 11

Ten minutes later, Risa folded the bedspread off the guest bed, laid it on the hope chest that had belonged to Mom and turned down the sheets, removing the rose sachets she kept under the pillows. Usually, such everyday chores soothed her. But tonight, she was almost as close to shock as Kelsy.

Sam in midlife crisis?

Who, besides Sophia Loren, was sexier than Kelsy?

"Did you find your toothbrush?" Listening for water, Risa tapped on the door to the guest bath.

"I'm okay."

"Then come on out." Risa gripped the doorknob but didn't turn it. "I'm not going back downstairs till you come out."

"I'm not budging till I'm eighty or ninety."

"I'll wait." Risa raised her voice over the swoosh of water and wished she didn't have to go back downstairs at all. She didn't want to face Ben Macdonald, though the good news was, he now had the sex appeal of Fergie.

The bad news? Having to give him a few details—but not too many—about Kelsy and Sam, then trying to keep up her end of a conversation she definitely didn't want to have. Too bad if he expected an apology for Kelsy's behavior. An apology amounted to disloyalty.

The toilet flushed. Yawning, Risa glanced at the clock and groaned. 1:30 A.M. Should she tell Kelsy that daylight would be tougher than darkness?

Jason would have a million questions.

And Kelsy would have not enough answers. Those answers she had wouldn't satisfy a four-year-old who loved his daddy as much as he loved his mommy.

Risa felt her heart catch. And people asked her if raising kids without a father wasn't a little radical. At least she'd consciously made her choice. Unlike millions of women, dumped, broke, and single parents almost overnight.

The toilet flushed again, followed by more running water. "C'mon out, Kel. I know you're crying. We'll get through this . . . somehow."

The door inched open. Pale and beautiful, Kelsy stuck her head out. "Must you always be such a damned optimist?"

"I've never thought of you as a pessimist."

"I suppose you can't be thirty-six, still believe in Santa Claus, and be a pessimist." Kelsy crawled into bed. She stared at the ceiling, then said dully, "How can this happen to me three weeks before Christmas?"

Her look of misery implored an explanation that Risa didn't have. Chest tight, she sat on the edge of the bed. "Talk to me, Kel."

Tears streamed down Kelsy's face. She scrunched away from Risa, then curled into a fetal position. "Tomorrow."

She scrubbed her eyes viciously. "Right now, go downstairs and ask Ben what the hell he wants from you. Otherwise, we'll both be a mess at the same time."

Toenails clicking, the pup beat Ben to his feet and to the foot of the stairs. One look at Doc, and the dog threw his head back and howled softly. The mournful sound sent a shiver down Ben's spine. Worried Molly might wake up and feel scared, he grabbed Fido, handing him over to Doc's outstretched arms.

She crooned, "It's okay, boy. It's okay. I feel the same way." To Ben, she said almost as an aside, "Molly's asleep, by the way."

Torn between checking himself, asking about Kelsy, and pretending he didn't want to change places with the dog, Ben ignored the tightness in his chest. "Want me to leave?"

"Not unless you're too uncomfortable to stay."

Her unspoken challenge got under Ben's skin, spreading to a slow burn in his guts. "Just trying to show more empathy than a rock."

"Is that what you were doing?" She laughed.

Speaking of rocks. After he bared his feelings—the demand of women around the globe—she dared to laugh.

"What's wrong?" More accurately, she snickered.

"Nothing," he growled.

"Well, Molly's fine. No need to wake her if you want to leave." Still wasting gaga noises on Fido, Doc stroked its head, her green eyes so dark they looked black.

Silence stretched out, punctuated by noises of pleasure from the dog. Logs crackled in the fireplace. More miffed than he wanted to admit, Ben saw no easy way of bringing up the idea that Doc should become Molly's doctor. Switching the focus to his own troubles instead of Kelsy's sure wouldn't help his case.

Christ, life is just one damned thing after another.

A few more groans from the dog and several foot shuffles from Ben, and Doc met his eye. "You're not taking anything Kelsy said personally, are you?"

"You mean me—a member of the Martian species, who prefers caves to commitment—is sensitive enough to take male bashing personally?"

Her eyes widened. The pup whined. She rubbed her

face in the fur on top of his little pointed head, mumbling, "Sorry. Didn't mean to squeeze you."

"No problem," Ben said.

"Pardon?" It took Ben a nanosecond longer than it took her to realize she meant the dog and not him. Feeling stupid, he waved the question away, surprised when she set Fido down.

When she stood, cheeks flushed, she brushed her hands off. "Kelsy says you want something from me. Do you?"

Caught off guard, Ben didn't back down. Defiantly, he said, "In this instance, Kelsy's right. I suppose that makes me pond scum, too."

"I can't speak for Kelsy. But for me, it depends on *what* you want. We agree casual sex is out."

Ben choked. "We do? When? Where was I?" *Thinking about Molly by some chance?*

"Friends don't have casual sex with each other." She primped her mouth.

"What about seri—" He clamped his mouth shut before he said *serious sex* out loud. Ignoring the sting in his bottom lip, he said, "What I want from you is more serious."

The dog whined and looked up at Risa as if seeking a second opinion about Ben's sincerity. In a single, fluid movement, she picked up the mutt. Again.

"More serious than what?" She patted the dog's back leg. "For me, casual sex is so serious it's an oxymoron."

"I don't even know what that is," he said, determined not to look like pond scum.

"Oxymoron? Jumbo shrimp. Totally free—"

"I know what oxymoron means. I graduated from Stanford, remember?" So why couldn't he think or speak logically? "I meant I don't even know what causal sex is."

"*Causal* sex?" She looked at him as if he were the village idiot. The pup buried his head in the crook of her arm.

"Casual, casual." Ben whacked his forehead with the heel of his hand. "I meant casual sex."

"Okay," she said warily, waiting.

For him to make a fool of himself, he was sure, but he overrode the static in his head. "A lot's riding on this, so give me a minute, okay?"

"Okay, but since you're not facing a firing squad, do you think we could sit down?"

God! Not only was he pond scum, he was rude pond scum. Women hated rudeness above all other character flaws. According to Mrs. Ferguson, Amy's mother, there was never any cause to be rude. Heart pounding, Ben slunk after Risa into the family room.

Lights still blazed. A mixed blessing. Lights made it easier for Doc to read him. At the same time, they made hiding anything from her impossible.

Fido turned around a couple of times in her lap, then raised his head toward Ben. Without moving her lips, Doc said in a gruff, froggy voice, "Relax, man. She won't bite."

Ben winced. He didn't blame her for wanting him to get off the dime. Stalling pissed him off royally, too. So there was something he and Doc had in common. *Besides lust.* Imagining a similar comment falling out of his mouth, Ben got off the dime.

"What would it take for you to accept Molly as your patient?" he asked in a rush. "I need a second opinion on these stomachaches, and I can't wait three months till her regular pediatrician comes back. She's crazy about you, trusts—"

"Stop. Stop." Doc snapped her fingers.

Ben felt his heart drop. He already saw the answer coming in her face. "Wait. Wait." His heart picked up speed. "You want to stay home with your sons for a year.

What if I make it possible for you to stay at home till they graduate college?"

"Whaat?" Her look said he'd missed the mother ship home.

"From grad school, too," he added. "I'll set up trust—"

"Will you? Shut? Up?" Fido whined. She patted him but glared at Ben. "You sound like someone in a soap opera." In deference to the dog, he assumed, she'd dropped her outrage to a whisper.

"I don't care what I sound like as long as you listen."

"Forget that. I'm not for sale."

Stung by her hoity-toity attitude, he said, "Who sounds like a soap opera heroine now? Don't tell me you have three mil—"

"I don't confide my financial status to complete strangers."

"Complete strangers? After the foreplay right here in—"

"Foreplay? Are you nuts?"

Before Ben could shoot back that he wasn't nuts, that she was into denial, big-time, Kelsy padded into the room. Barefoot and wearing a baggy, below-the-knee Davis sweatshirt, she said, "Sorry to intrude kids, but I can't sleep. How about if we break out the champagne after all?"

Over Risa's protests that the family room was more comfortable, all of them, including the puppy, traipsed into the kitchen. Smarter than the gloomy humans, he immediately crawled under the table and covered his eyes with his paws. Risa wished she could join him. She'd attended livelier funerals. Brontë novels brimmed with fun and laughter compared to this soiree.

Stiff and visibly ill at ease, they gathered around the island, recalling for Risa the crows on the telephone line in the park. Hadn't the picnic happened a lifetime ago?

Water filled the ice bucket to its rim. Reluctant to turn her back on Kelsy and Ben Macdonald as they watched each other like feral cats, Risa rummaged for a tea towel that didn't have holes in it. *Let's not all talk at once,* she almost said, feeling anxious and nervous because all of them were acting so weird.

"Here we go." She held up a new towel.

Both guests had apparently gone deaf. Unable to stop herself, Risa said, "I've never used this towel. I can't remember where I bought it. I've kicked myself for not buying a dozen, because I've never found any others with frogs. . . ."

At least Ben Macdonald had the good manners to look at her while she yammered on. True, he looked at her as if he didn't understand a word she said, but he did watch her lips move. Kelsy had a more important agenda. She examined her nails.

Face it, Risa thought. This is one of those occasions in which—cliché or not—silence is golden. She lifted the bottle of champagne from the ice bucket and wrapped it in the towel. Still smarting from the insulting financial offer, she doubted she could drink champagne without choking.

Kelsy picked up the card next to the ice bucket, read it, then waved it at Ben. "Good ole Lance," she said. "Think he'd ever cheat on Bobbye Anne?" Before Risa could point out that Ben wouldn't know either Lance or Bobbye Anne if they bit him on the butt, Kelsy said to him, "You know Lance was in love with our Risa all through grade school."

Risa froze. "That's not true."

"So why'd he follow you around like a puppy every day for six years?" Kelsy took the bottle and worked off the wire cage and gold foil.

"We were friends." Risa glanced at Ben, blushed, and refocused on Kelsy. "After you, I've known him longer than anybody. He's going to be Tom's godfather." Another glance at Ben, whose face had gone blank as soon as Risa said *friend.*

"*Friend.*" Kelsy stopped pushing on the champagne cork and nudged Risa out of her line of vision. To Ben, she said, "That's how Sam describes his bimbette—*friend.*"

"Need help?" Risa grabbed the neck of the champagne bottle, which—pointed right at Ben—could be considered a lethal weapon if the cork exploded and hit him between the eyes, causing him to fall down, smack his head, and suffer a concussion. Not that implausible, in Risa's medical opinion, after the three falls he'd had in the last two days.

Kelsy pried Risa's fingers loose, then tossed her head. "You shake hands with a friend, maybe hug her at Christmas and weddings. You don't fuck a friend's brains out."

The cork exploded out of the bottle straight at Ben's lower lip. Paralyzed, Risa couldn't believe her eyes. His hand shot up, and he caught the missile. She exhaled. He threw her a grin, then pocketed the cork.

"Fucking good reflexes," Kelsy said.

Her tone challenged Risa, whose face felt like newly set concrete. *Now is not the time for a sermon on swearing.* The F-word buzzed over the island like a bee buzzing at a picnic. Embarrassed for Kelsy, Risa focused on the vapor spiraling up out of the bottle.

"Risa doesn't swear anymore, you know. Not even when she's upset." Kelsy leaned across the island and whispered loudly to Ben. "She gave it up after med school. Didn't want to set a bad example for little kids."

"Someone who thinks logically provides a nice contrast to the real world, don't you agree?" Ben said to Kelsy.

"That's my friend Risa, a nice contrast to the real world." Kelsy handed the bottle to him, then grabbed Risa, hugging her till Risa thought her eyes would pop out of her head. "You are," Kelsy whispered, her voice husky with tears, "a true friend."

"So are you," Risa said, meaning it, but glad when Kelsy released her stranglehold.

Not at all embarrassed by this mushy moment, Risa glanced at Ben, whose face was unreadable. What would she give to see the wheels turning inside his head? Deciding that wasn't going to happen any time soon, she lined up the glasses in front of him. He poured exactly the same amount—half full—into each glass, handing them off one by one as bubbles rose to the rims.

Glass high, Kelsy toasted Risa. "To friends you can trust."

Before Ben or Risa agreed or added their sentiments, Kelsy drained her glass. Holding it toward Ben, she said, "One more and I'm out of your hair."

"You don't have to go to bed." Risa eyed Ben, who refilled Kelsy's glass, but didn't echo the encouragement to stay.

Disappointed, Risa rationalized that Kelsy was her friend, not his.

After savoring a couple more sips, Kelsy set the glass down. "I called Sam before I came down to drown my sorrows."

Risa felt the hollow in her stomach contract. She groaned in silence. "How'd it go?"

Hard to imagine that after Sam's trip from Tokyo, a phone call with anyone at two in the morning would go well.

Another swallow of champagne, then Kelsy said, "It sucked."

Surprise, surprise. Risa nodded, hoping Kelsy took this small gesture as support. Not enough support, apparently, because Kelsy's tone hardened. "I asked him to bring Jason by here tomorrow."

Oh, goody. Risa nodded again. Poor Jason.

"Prince that he is," Kelsy threw Ben a death glare, "he said he'd come by before nine. Seems he has *business* in the city."

Disheartened, but still not surprised, Risa squeezed Kelsy's elbow. "Oh, Kel. I'm sorry." Kelsy shrugged, looked right at Ben, then demanded, "What kind of business do we think he has in the city on Sunday?"

No good business, Risa decided, but shoved the thought down past her churning stomach. "Kel, since Ben doesn't know Sam—"

"Yes, but they're both men." The reasonable tone scared Risa, who protested, "True, but no man speaks for all men. Any more than one woman speaks for all of us." *Deep, very deep.*

"News flash: I don't want him to speak for all men, I just want his effing opinion, La Ti Da."

"I can do that," Ben interjected.

"Why? So she can pick a fight?" Risa demanded. *Men didn't have a clue.*

"What if I do?" Kelsy taunted. "Can't he do anything besides pour champagne and look pretty?"

Ben grinned. "Flattery will get us nowhere."

Mouth open, Risa gaped at him. What kind of come-back was that? Apparently the kind that got Kelsy's attention. Eyes narrowed, she measured Ben, then nodded. Risa crossed her fingers. Kelsy snickered.

"I don't know," she said. "Right now my ego could use a little flattery. I believed Sam would be faithful to me throughout eternity. I believed it was our destiny to be reunited in one life after another, throughout . . . yada, yada . . ." Her statement trailed off, and she looked first at Risa, then at Ben. "I didn't believe even death could separate us."

Leave 'em stunned, then make your exit.

"She's been doing this her entire life," Risa said to Ben ten minutes later. Worried he was stunned into near cata-tonia, she said, "After thirty years, I'm used to her pushing my buttons. It's part of her—her charisma, believe it or not."

It was obvious to Risa this revelation zoomed over his head. He stared at Kelsy's empty glass as if he'd never seen such a rare and exotic object. Hoping he'd look at her, Risa moved it out of his line of vision. His gaze remained focused on the spot where the glass had stood. Risa hesitated, then touched his hand.

No bells or fireworks. No tingles or goose bumps. Praise Jupiter, the earth didn't tilt on its axis.

Mentally acknowledging the flicker of disappointment burning in her stomach, Risa touched him the way she'd touch the parent of a sick child, the way she'd touch a friend.

"For what it's worth," she said softly, "I think Kelsy was talking more to herself than to us. I don't think she was referring to you and Amy."

After another minute or two, wherever he was, deep inside himself, he came back. Not all at once, but little by little. She'd sat with parents coming back from a similar place after learning their child had an incurable disease or, worst of all, died. She never knew then, and she didn't know with Ben Macdonald, where the right words came from. But, Praise Jupiter, they came.

He looked straight into her eyes. "I don't want to shock you," he said, "but if I'm up to it, I'd like to tie up several loose ends with you before dawn."

"Sure," she said serenely, because she had under her roof two cases of people clobbered by sex, certain in her serenity that his phrase, *if I'm up to it,* was a slip of the tongue and carried no sexual suggestions.

"Great," he said. "I think I could concentrate more if I didn't smell like a dog. Can I use your shower first?"

CHAPTER 12

How long did it take a man to shower?

In some distant cavern of her mind, it occurred to Risa after a third glass of champagne that she was slightly tipsy.

Dehydrated, her medical mind corrected. Not to mention hot.

Dragging the ski sweater up over her head, she stumbled to the kitchen sink. She dragged down a large tumbler, set the glass in the sink, and turned on the water. The puppy apparently didn't mind if she was tipsy or dehydrated. He looked at her adoringly. She bent over and patted him. Proof, in her mind, she sure wasn't tipsy.

The faint scent of lemons and musk drifted into the room. Nerve endings went on alert. Her breasts ached. She turned in slow motion.

Ben pointed at the open faucet. His ultra-short hair glistened with drops of water. "There a problem?"

The dog stood, stretched, yawned. On autopilot, Risa shook her head. Her heart roared in her ears. "I can't find the cellophane wrap."

"The . . . what?"

His dazed look sent a surge of adrenaline through

her, pumping every cell with power. She'd caught him off guard.

"Cellophane wrap," she repeated.

"I thought that was what you said."

"I'd sell my soul right now for a video camera." She waltzed to where he stood in the doorway and chucked him under the chin.

He reared back. "I'm lost."

"Well, I'm here to show you the way." She focused the full blast of her trust-the-doctor smile on him. "Maybe I'm moving too fast for you."

"I doubt that." His eyes widened as she fanned her stomach with the hem of her silk turtleneck. Valiant in the face of big temptation, he stood his ground.

Risa turned the wattage up on the smile that never failed to calm screaming, terrified four-year-olds. "You're sure?"

"Yes. What's more, cellophane wrap won't make me any surer. Just for the record, I'm a whipped cream kind of guy."

The room spun. For a second, she was sure she'd faint. Or go into cardiac arrest. Or say something stupid, like *I want to have your baby.* His wink swept away everything but the feeling of excitement pounding in her chest.

"Want me to carry your water?" He turned off the faucet.

"Uh-uh. Haven't laced it with my secret potion."

"Cellophane, secret potions. You've got my attention."

"Praise Jupiter."

His fingers closed on her elbow. Bones melted. The puppy made a growling noise. "Sit." Ben pulled Risa toward him.

Amazingly, the puppy sat. Risa caught another whiff of musk, magically transporting her to a cool, dark woodland. Being against his chest brought back images of them falling down at Molly's school. Aroused, she lurched away from him.

His arm shot out, steadying her. "How about that water?"

"Why? You think I'm drunk?" She gave him her chin.

"Nope. Just a little unsteady on your feet."

"Not so unsteady I can't dance." Aware in the back of her fogged-over mind that she'd crossed an invisible boundary, Risa held her arms out to him.

A lazy smile took the sting out of his head shake. "You've heard of people with two left feet? I'm the prototype. Rhythm eludes me. Except in the saddle."

Swaying to music in her head, Risa snapped her fingers. "There you go, then. Riding and dancing aren't that different. In fact, there's no real difference."

"You ride a lot?"

"Uh-uh. Never been on a horse. But I'm a hot-damn dancer, and I promise I can teach you . . . to two-step."

Since he kept his arms at his sides, she said, "Your choice. Dance or talk."

"Okay," he sighed a mock sigh. "Logic wins every time."

He laced his fingers with hers, and the puppy went on alert. Ben backed off. Impatient, wanting his arms around her *now,* Risa said, "I'll put him in the laundry room."

With her arms full of puppy, she led the way into the family room. "Don't sit down. This'll only take a minute."

After an eternity, she returned, feeling almost no guilt. The puppy needed his sleep.

"Everything okay?" Ben turned from the fire and encircled her waist. Heat shot through her. Logic evaporated.

"Everything's perfect." Holding onto his neck, she arched backward, shutting off the image of him dropping her on her head. She grabbed the CD remote and flicked it. Bass and piano melded in slow, easy jazz.

"Nice," he murmured.

"No mushy lyrics." With any luck at all, nothing to remind him of Amy.

"Mush can be . . . nice." His breath seared her ear.

Feeling almost petite, she raised her arm, placed her hand lightly on his nape, and swallowed the growl deep inside her. His hiss of indrawn breath, as his arm tightened around her waist, was like a match to dynamite.

Holy Hedda, she'd lost the last bit of her teeny, tiny mind.

"Don't say I didn't warn you." His husky baritone soothed, then sharpened, the edges of her nerves.

"I won't have to." Eyes shut, she listened in wonder to the *BA-bum, BA-bum* of his heart.

"Anyone who played hockey in college can dance." Were his muscles—or hers—quivering?

"I thought it was anyone who can ride?"

"Hockey, horseback riding. Doesn't matter."

Did he feel her breasts, aching for release beneath her asbestos suit? What if she ripped his shirt off with her teeth?

"Makes me wonder why I never took up ballet. Think what a natural like me could've accomplished joining the Bolshoi."

"Shhhh. Just follow my lead."

"Uh-uh." He settled her left wrist on his shoulder. "Even I know the guy's supposed to lead."

"What if I don't want to follow?"

"You will." He winked.

Despite her determination not to blush, heat scalded her throat and face. He smirked. Then, quickly, but with infinitesimal gentleness, he worked the pins out of her braid before she fully recovered. A rogue pin slithered down the neck of her silk undershirt and on down her spine. She shuddered, reveling in the mini-shock of cool metal on blistering skin.

Groaning, Ben placed his mouth against her ear. His tongue, a hot poker, inched downward, blazing a trail along the tendon in her arched neck. Hot and cold at the same time, she held her breath as his hand slipped under her turtleneck. Layers of clothing didn't slow his fingers. They slipped past the barrier of her waistband and found hot, steamy flesh.

"Doesn't dancing mean moving our feet?" he asked.

"I don't think I can."

"Sure you can. A capable woman like you can probably dance and chew gum at the same time."

"Walk. That's walk, talk, and chew . . ."

His fingers ran through her hair, sparking nerves and shorting out her mind.

"Drunk . . . I feel . . . drunk . . ."

"You're not drunk." He fingered the hook on her bra.

"Yes-s-s." Not from champagne. From him. His smell. His heat. His desire.

"No-o-o." He cupped her bare breasts. Her entire body sang, so light she floated.

"You're loose as a goose, but you're not drunk."

"Next you'll tell me I'm right as rain."

"Wow. You're sharp as a tack."

His silliness gave her time to catch her breath. She giggled. "Want to hear another cliché?"

"Like, dancing's easier than falling off a log?"

"When all's said and done."

Supporting the nape of her neck, he caught a fistful of her hair, tilting her head back, letting her look into his eyes—huge, dark pools that drew her down to the basement of his soul. "Have we said enough, Doc?"

Sure her banging heart would break a rib any second, Risa squeezed her eyes shut. "Enough for what?"

"For whatever. Foreplay—"

Her eyes snapped open. "Did you say—" She stopped before she made a total fool of herself. She'd heard him. He didn't have to spell it out for her.

He tipped her chin up. "You know I still love Amy."

A statement. Not a question.

"Yes."

"I won't make any promises."

"None expected." She held his gaze, glad the silk turtleneck hid her wild pulse.

"No regrets afterwards?"

"With triplets?" She gave chuckling her best effort. "I won't have time for regrets."

Neither of them blinked.

Then, he wrapped her in his arms, laid her head against his chest, and danced her backward while her heart jammed in her throat. The backs of her legs bumped the sofa. Her pulse zoomed. Tugging her hand, he sank into the cushions, dragging her.

The room spun. In a kind of trance, she watched him from under her lashes, noting his clenched jaw, the planes and shadows of his face softened by firelight, the rise and fall of his chest intensified by his stillness.

Longing to touch him filled her, pulsed in her wrists, warmed her palms, tingled in her fingers. They trembled in anticipation of running through his hair, stroking his cheek, caressing his hands. She'd save for last grazing his wounded lip with the tip of her tongue.

"What about protection?" He nuzzled her ear.

"Protection?" she repeated like a stunned parrot.

"What do you use?"

"I—I—" Momentarily disoriented, Risa couldn't recall the last time she'd needed protection. Three years at least. *For old times' sake,* Tim had said.

Blinking away the humiliation of that experience, she whispered to Ben, "Don't you carry—"

"You're the first woman I've looked at in eleven months, and Amy was trying to get pregnant again."

"Oh," Risa said, her breath taken away by a gust of happiness. Of course, she was the first woman for him after Amy.

While her heart did somersaults, she noted with almost clinical detachment the tic under his left eye, wondering what he felt after this revelation, waiting for him

to say that even though they'd agreed on no commitment, he realized they were making a mistake since he
still loved Amy and always would.

"We made love for three years in college without using
birth control." He wound a strand of Risa's hair around
his finger. "Then, on our wedding night. Pregnant. And
it had to be that night because . . ."

Eyes closed, caught up in his story, disappointed he'd
left it unfinished, Risa listened to his heart thunder in
her ear. Was he embarrassed? Holding her in his arms,
peeling away layers of his heart, trusting her to understand making love with his wife? Her own heart galloped.
"Were you . . . both . . . glad?"

"No, we were ecstatic."

She smiled, imagining their joy, remembering her
disappointment each month Tim checked to make sure
she'd renewed her birth control script. Later, she re-
joiced in his caution.

Suddenly, Ben shifted away from her, and Risa's head
rolled away from his heart. "This is pretty embarrassing." He glanced at the mantel clock.

Oh-oh. Here it comes.

Palms sweaty, face on fire, she pushed to sit up, face
him. "It is embarrassing," she said.

Okay, she'd do the right thing. Save him from being
embarrassed. Save him from saying he'd made a big
mistake. *Let him off the hook.*

"I don't know what we were thinking of." She nearly
choked on this admission.

Admitting they'd made a mistake would be a lot easier if he'd stop caressing her shoulder.

"Was one of us supposed to be thinking?" He raised
an eyebrow.

"I guess thinking while drinking champagne is an oxymoron." Clenching her hands, she repressed the need
to touch him,

"Also stupid." His mouth twisted.

"Very. Stupid." The skin on the nape of her neck prickled as he patted a strand of hair back in place.

He glanced again at the clock. The hollow in her stomach filled with regret so bittersweet Risa felt sick.

"Risaaa!" Kelsy called from the hallway in case Risa and Ben were on the sofa in an embarrassing situation.

"Shhh, Kelsy. Molly's asleep." Face scarlet, eyes huge with undisguised desire, Risa trotted into the hall.

"I shut the door," Kelsy snapped, then demanded, "Are you drunk?"

"Of course I'm not drunk."

"Well, you couldn't prove it by me." Kelsy descended to the bottom step. "What're the chances you could give me a couple of minutes of your time? I just got off the phone with Sam."

Ben appeared at the end of the hall. He had the puppy on a leash. "I let the dog out," he said to Risa. "The commotion evidently scared him."

"He was in the laundry room," Risa explained, which for some reason irritated Kelsy like a thorn in her side.

"Why was he in the laundry room in the first place?" she shot back. Ben's attitude struck a nerve.

"He kept bothering us." Ben slid his eyes in Risa's direction, and Kelsy saw the electricity that arced between them. Momentarily blind with jealousy, she said, "Why don't you shut me in the laundry room with him? That way I won't bother—"

Tears clogged her throat, and she had to stop talking. Risa's arms wrapped around her neck. "Don't be silly," Risa murmured. "You're not a bother."

Risa threw Ben a backward look, and Kelsy stiffened. She said, "Forget it. Your heart's not in it."

"No, I won't forget it," Risa said. "You want to talk in the bedroom or down here?"

Ben just had to stick his nose in. He said, "I don't mind going into the laundry room."

Of course Risa laughed. Which should've pissed Kelsy off but didn't. She laughed, too. She'd cried too damned much for one night. Ben looked at them like they held lighted sticks of dynamite.

"Hell, let's all go into the laundry room," Kelsy said.

"Including the puppy?" Risa grinned, and Kelsy almost forgot her broken heart.

"Absolutely including the puppy." Kelsy hugged her waist.

One step into the family room, and the testosterone fumes filled her with such longing she was terrified she'd throw up. How was she going to live without Sam? Without the incredible sex? She escaped into the kitchen. Turning the empty bottle upside down, she said brightly, "No more champagne?"

"How about OJ?" Out of the corner of her eye, Kelsy caught the blistering look Risa threw Ben. Her throat jammed.

"Not thirsty." He winked at Risa.

No, but you're hungrier than the Big Bad Wolf. Kelsy blinked back tears. When had Sam stopped looking at her with such an insatiable appetite? She picked up the puppy, waiting patiently for Risa's attention.

"Kel?" Risa sounded impatient, and Kelsy felt a pang for all the times she and Sam had flirted so openly and shut Risa out. "Nothing for me," Kelsy answered.

A memory of the ice crystals on the frozen OJ can in Risa's fridge came back. *God,* Kelsy thought, *that's what I'll be like in a couple of months without sex—cold and dried out.* She didn't give a damn if she had surrendered to self-pity. She hugged the puppy.

"On second thought," Ben said, "I'll have water." He arched a brow at Risa, and the fire that leaped between them was hot enough to singe Kelsy's eyelashes.

"Anyone else?" Ben glanced at Kelsy as if she were already an icy, shriveled crone. *Never heard a word I said.*

"No, thanks," Risa said. "I'm fine."

Oh, yes. Fine and hot.

"Is there anything I can get you?" Risa asked, her eyes soft, pleading.

"You mean besides a faithful and crazy-about-me husband?"

The whoosh of water at the tap sounded like Niagara Falls to Kelsy, but unless she was mistaken, Risa welcomed the noise.

"I would if I could." She squeezed Kelsy's arm the way she did with Jason just before giving him a shot.

"I know." The frog on the tea towel sneered at Kelsy, who thought she'd scream if Ben didn't turn the water off soon. How big a glass was he filling? The puppy felt like a boulder in her arms. She set him down. Her head swam.

As she stood, Ben finally turned around. The angle at which he held his head suddenly reminded Kelsy so much of Sam, she felt the floor tilt. She threw her arms out and smacked the champagne bottle. It crashed over on its side and spun around and around. Kelsy felt like a klutz and apologized weakly. Risa waved the apology away and made no move to stop the spinning bottle. Ben, on the other hand, grabbed at the neck, missed, and let the bottle stop on its own.

The mouth pointed directly at his belt buckle.

Feeling optimistically silly and about eleven years old, Kelsy clapped her hands. "Who remembers how to play Spin the Champagne Bottle?" she asked, ignoring Risa's look of panic.

CHAPTER 13

To Ben's surprise and disappointment, Doc nixed the idea of "Spin the Champagne Bottle." "I hated that game," she said.

Kelsy stretched. "I could use some air."

"At three in the morning?" Doc countered. "What about—"

"Fresh air will help clear my head so I don't call Sam again."

At least you *can* call him, Ben thought. Embarrassed by his plunge into self-pity, he said, "I'll walk with you."

"Absolutely not necessary." She didn't so much as glance at him, but her tone sounded marginally sincere. "This neighborhood's like church during the sermon: everyone's asleep. Besides, I'm sure El Puppy here can fend off any lurkers."

"Want to borrow a pair of jeans?" Doc asked. "They'll fit you like a tent, but maybe you won't get arrested."

"I should be so lucky." Kelsy laughed.

Ben winced at her bitterness, then snapped his fingers. "I forgot to tell you 'hi' from Finn Bishop. He's a cop."

"Don't know him." Kelsy shrugged. "Risa and I went to high school with *Sean* Bishop—"

"Finn's his younger brother," Ben said. "Eight years younger. Had a major crush on you, to hear him tell it."

"How cute." Kelsy stared into space for a second, then lifted one shoulder. "Where are those jeans?"

Parked at the foot of Dr. Taylor's driveway, Finn Bishop couldn't believe his luck. Two more minutes and he'd have been long gone, home in bed dreaming hot dreams. He'd already waited over an hour after going off duty, hoping to catch a glimpse of Kelsy Chandler. Not a difficult last name, but he still thought of her as Kelsy Wright.

Ms. Wright. His heart flip-flopped.

He waited till she got to the end of the driveway before opening his car door.

"Hey, Kelsy. Long time no see."

"Let's dance." Ben opened his arms and came toward Risa.

"Out of sight is not out of mind." Heart racing, Risa moved to the opposite side of the island. "Kelsy won't be gone for more than ten, fifteen minutes max. And there's no music."

"Your point being?" Grinning, Ben leaped up on the island and slid on his butt till his legs dangled next to her hip.

Over the roar of her heart, she said, "My point being—" Her mind went blank. She couldn't think with him so close. "I don't want to sound like a junior high word problem, but—"

"I ate 'em up as a kid." He laid his hand on her shoulder, and she felt faint from the current of excitement humming through him. "I can dance and do word problems at the same time."

Risa snorted. "You're pulling my leg."

"No, but that sounds like fun."

Yes, more fun than clearing the air about Molly.

"Want to pull *my* leg?" He wiggled his eyebrows, and she laughed, shaking her head, afraid he'd move away from her if she suddenly, out of the blue, switched the focus to Molly's case.

Get on with it. "You really like word problems?"

Thumping his chest, he said, "Told you I was weird."

"Do I strike you as someone impressed by ordinary?" She raised her chin at the same time he lowered his face. Their noses bumped, and Risa giggled uncontrollably. Ben didn't giggle, but he laughed. Between hiccups, she said, "Here's the deal, Word Problem Wizard. If Kelsy walks four blocks in six minutes, how long before . . ."

"You reexamine my lip?" His hand slipped from her shoulder, grazing her breast. She jumped away from him, but not far enough. He threw off more heat than a blast furnace.

Blast furnaces cause bad burns. How fortunate she was a doctor.

While Risa fought to catch her breath, Ben said, "Need help from the Word Problem Wizard?"

"Not really." *What's the question?* "You need help. . . ."

Incredible how hot his knee burned against her hip.

In the midnight mist, Kelsy felt self-conscious for about three seconds. Finn Bishop was only twenty-eight, for heaven's sake. A little stunned he'd waited for over an hour outside Risa's, she sneaked several quick looks at him through her lashes. The gap between his front teeth fascinated her. If he caught her staring, she'd say . . . Her mind stalled.

"Think I'm worth your tax dollars?" He ran his hand over three feathery auburn spikes in his ultra-short hair.

Kelsy laughed, surprised how much better she felt. "That depends," she said, thoughts of Sam already were flooding back. She blinked repeatedly. Dammit, she wasn't going to cry again.

"Is your marriage in trouble, Kelsy?" He took the dog leash from her, then tucked her hand under his arm.

"How—?" she whispered, face hot, throat jammed with tears.

"Lots of clues." He guided her steps. "No rings. You've been crying—a lot. You're out, alone, at a time most wives—"

"I bet most wives can't sleep next to a toe-sucking, skirt-chasing, lying cheat who—" Her voice broke.

"I'd kill him for you . . ." Finn said, and Kelsy choked. "But I'm a cop."

Sighing, she said, "It's the thought that counts."

"We can't count on Kelsy being gone for more than fifteen, twenty minutes max." Risa edged away from Ben's red-hot knee.

"Plenty of time." He grinned, and her heart missed a beat.

"Not for this problem."

"Okay." He brushed back a wisp of hair from her forehead.

Fire scalded her ear, but she pretended his touch was a fly grazing her cheek and swatted at thin air, moving her head from side to side a couple of times. He dropped his hand. Sweat slithered down between her breasts, but she kept moving her head as if there was something loose inside. She didn't blame him for looking as if he'd sat down next to someone mentally challenged.

Finally, she stopped jerking her head around. He

prompted, "Hard to solve a word problem when you don't know what it is."

"My point exactly." Determined to focus, she inhaled. "The problem isn't how long Kelsy's gone or what time she gets back. The problem is, do you understand I'm not accepting any new patients—including Molly?"

Frowning, he said, "You're turning down a chance to stay home full-time?"

"Yes." Short and sweet, because her nerves couldn't take long explanations.

"Why?" he demanded.

Teeth gritted, she said, "Because I'm a damn—darned good doctor." She rubbed her jaw, felt the muscles ease, and moved her fingers to her neck. She said, "Also because I went to med school believing I could practice medicine *and* have a family."

"But"—he started to shake his head, apparently thought better of it, and stopped—"how can you manage—a career, child care, Christmas shopping, play dates—the whole enchilada?"

To her ears, he didn't sound curious. She heard doubt and bewilderment. She hugged her waist so she wouldn't hug him.

"I hope you weren't counting on Kelsy," he finished, leaving unsaid his conviction she couldn't pull off caring for three babies by herself.

She bristled, but said prettily, "I'm counting on myself this first year."

"What about your mother? A sister? Other friends?"

"Mom has her own life. I don't have siblings. My friends may help out, but essentially, it's me, Charlie, Tom, and Harry."

"When are you going to sleep? Have time for yourself?"

She reached for a canister that contained her stash

of chocolate chip cookies. *He really expects answers.* For the moment, she suppressed her need for a chocolate fix. "Women around the world have kids close enough together that they might as well be triplets."

Another frown. "I'm trying to follow your logic here."

His emphasis on *your logic* begged for the back of her tongue. Trying to shut down images of dragging her tongue down his body, she wrenched the lid off the canister. "The mother of one of my patients has four kids, ten and eleven months apart each. Now *that* is tough. Far tougher than triplets." *Tougher than going without chocolate.*

Staring at her, he said, "Yes, but they have husbands—"

"Oh, puhleez." Risa felt her patience slipping, but checked another canister without rolling her eyes. "It's a fact—more and more men, primarily in Scandinavia, Canada, England, and the U.S., are becoming more involved in raising their infants. But don't kid yourself."

Ignoring his raised eyebrows, she sniffed the empty canister. "Child rearing the world over still falls ninety-nine times out of a hundred to women."

"Yeah, well," he said, "you're looking at the exception, and I'm here to tell you, raising a child alone is harder than finding a cure for the common cold."

A wavelet of sympathy washed over Risa, surprising her. She softened her reply. "I didn't say it was easy. I am not naive about this issue."

"Issue?" He snorted. "Issue sounds as if we're studying Psych 101 or Intro to Sociology. Issue doesn't begin to cover finding a qualified nanny so you can work. Issue doesn't account for the guilt, for never having enough time, for—"

Feeling misunderstood, Risa slammed the canister back in place. "I'm not talking psychobabble. If you don't like *issue,* use another word. Split hairs."

"I'm not splitting—"

Risa kept right on talking over him. "Here's my point. I'm not adopting triplets for any other reason than I think I can give them lots of love and a good life."

"How? That's my question. How will you do that?"

"For the first year, I'll be with them full time." Unless she died from chocolate withdrawal.

"What about years two through six—before they start school full time?"

"I'll be a single, working mom. Unless triplets come with a road map, we'll have to decide which direction to take when we come to the forks in the road."

The last canister contained a few cookie crumbs but no chocolate. Despite the gnawing in her stomach, Risa gave up. "Does *my* logic hold up?"

Ben met her eyes. "Thank God, Molly's not an infant. I know you don't believe it, but she is more important to me than work."

Unable to lie, Risa let the statement stand.

His eyes flashed, but he asked, "How can I walk away from the other people who depend on me?"

"News flash." Risa felt like shaking him. "I understand about dependability." Head up, she hugged her waist. "My partner nearly had a coronary after I told her my plans, and she's only thirty-five."

Frowning, he demanded, "Because you're adopting triplets?"

"No," she put some acid in the single word, then softened the rest of her reply since he obviously didn't get it. "She's upset because I'm taking a leave of absence. Which comes back to why I won't accept your attempted bribery."

"I'm breathless."

Ignoring his sarcasm, she said, "This time next year Julie expects to be pregnant with her first child. I'll come back, and she'll take a year off."

"What about your sons then?" Ben sounded so calm and reasonable. Maybe he didn't think she was totally nuts.

"My entire life will soon become a work in progress."

"A work in progress?" He laughed. "My board of directors doesn't like works in progress—especially when it comes to a CEO working less than seventy hours a week."

"Try keeping two, three hundred parents happy—especially when it comes to their kids' health. I'll take your board any day."

"Christ, I wish you or somebody would take them." His face darkened with hopelessness. "So where does that leave us?"

There is no us. After all their sharing, she decided to keep this point to herself. She said, "I'll be glad to recommend two outstanding doctors."

"Molly won't go. She trusts you, her former doctor, and no one else," he said with conviction.

With just as much conviction, Risa said, "Let me talk to her about Leah Rankin and Nora Karr. *After* I check with them."

"When?"

"Today's Sunday. Molly hasn't had a stomachache for the past two days. I think I can wait till the sun comes up before I call Leah and Nora."

Her feeble attempt at humor went past him. He said, "Okay . . . as long as one of them sees her right away."

No wonder he's a CEO. Risa held his gaze. "I think we're talking Tuesday—unless you persuade Molly to go in tomorrow."

He flushed, and the realization hit Risa. She'd implied he didn't have much influence with his child. Being sexually frustrated was no excuse for cruelty. Quickly, she said, "I've got a couple of ideas that you could probably use."

"No." He shook his head. "When it comes to doctors, she trusts you. You'll talk to her today—no matter what?"

"No matter what." Risa admired his persistence and his refusal to let his wounded ego get in the way of doing the right thing for Molly. "I guarantee she'll love both Leah and Nora. And," she added slyly, "so will you."

Doubt clouded his eyes, and he ignored her bait, demanding, "What's your ace in the hole?"

"*Aces*. Three, not one." She smiled, wishing she dared to say, *Trust me*. Knowing such a request wasn't fair, she said, "First, Leah will be Jason's doctor while I'm on leave. Second, Leah and Norah together will treat Charlie, Tom, and Harry. In case you haven't noticed, Molly's crazy about the idea of triplet infants. Third, I'll teach her how to throw her voice."

"Oh, my God." Ben grabbed her around the waist, lifted her as if she were a feather, and whirled her around the island and into the family room. "My God, that's brilliant. Three bribes she can't resist. You're brilliant. Amazing. Awesome. How can I ever thank you?"

Fuck me. She grit her teeth, ready to bite her tongue off if her brain betrayed her. Terrified he'd stumble and they'd fall, giving her an opportunity to strip him naked, she couldn't enjoy being in his arms.

When he finally did stop waltzing them around the room, she hated the stunned happiness on his face.

CHAPTER 14

Determined to kill Kelsy on the spot, Risa threw open the front door at 8:52 A.M. Unfortunately, too many witnesses lined her porch. Front and center, Jason jumped up and down, demanding news of the pup at the top of his lungs and sending Risa's nervous system into meltdown. Officer Finn Bishop, as if at attention, stood behind Kelsy. Risa felt sure she saw his white steed nibbling grass at the curb. Jaw clenched, Sam mercifully stayed in the rear. His drawn faced blended well with the dirty-dishwater sky.

Risa took a deep breath of cold air, dropped down to eye level with Jason, and muttered to Kelsy, "What a surprise."

Her godson sniffed. "Ummm, what smells so good?"

"Blueberry pancakes. Molly's making one for you."

"Better get in there, Big Guy." Sam tousled his son's hair—a gesture Risa hated, since all kids hated it—and avoided eye contact with her.

"Save me a bite, will you?" Kelsy blew Jason a kiss, which he caught and smacked on his mouth.

"Maybe." His blue eyes danced. "Bye, Daddy, see ya."

Watching Jason charge into the house, Risa felt sick.

Say what you will about raising kids by myself, at least they won't go through divorce. She waited till she was sure Jason was out of earshot then said, "I see we're all playing 'Let's Pretend.'"

"Not me," Kelsy snapped. "I just think timing's important."

Stung, Risa opened her mouth, but Sam snarled, "I'm not getting into this right now. I'll be home tomorrow night. Can you meet with the three of us, Risa, help us explain to Jason—"

"Can you check with me," Kelsy said, her voice trembling, *"before* making appointments for me?"

Finn didn't touch her, but he mumbled something under his breath that Risa didn't hear. Apparently encouraged, Kelsy nodded, then said evenly, "Don't think I'm covering for you today, Sam, making believe we're Cleaver family clones."

"Nobody's asking you to cover for me. We could've settled this last night if you hadn't stormed out of the house like the queen of melodrama."

"You shithead." Risa winced, but understood from an instant mental replay featuring Dr. Tim how satisfying name-calling felt. *You go, Kelsy.*

As if reading her mind, Sam stared at Risa. She said quickly, "Leave Jason with me for as long as you two need—"

"Well, today, we only need about fifteen seconds," Kelsy shot back. "Lover Boy has *business in the city.*"

"Business, Wifey Dearest, that's in your best interest. Otherwise, you'll only be collecting a pound of my flesh in lieu of the big bucks."

"Call me *Wifey Dearest* one more time, and I'll be collecting your life insurance."

Finn gave Kelsy two thumbs up at the same time Risa laughed.

"On second thought," Sam said, "you won't need

spousal support. Not with all the money you'll rake in from your stand-up comedy routine."

"I'm sure you and the Bimbette will laugh your heads off when I—"

"Don't call her that." Sam barged past Risa, headed for Kelsy, who egged him on by putting her hands on either side of her mouth and widening her eyes, lampooning a terrified blonde.

Quick as lightning, Finn moved in front of Sam, who curled his lip. *Pathetic.* Risa glanced back toward the kitchen, then stepped outside, pulling the door shut behind her. *Kelsy's eating this up.*

Across the street, Bitsy Johnson, still in her robe, ambled to the end of her driveway, picked up the Sunday *Mercury,* then gaped at the scene on Risa's front step. Risa gritted her teeth, waved half-heartedly, and held her temper in check. As much as she'd like to see Finn hurt Sam for the "Wifey Dearest" crack, Risa appealed to Kelsy. "Let's think of Jason. For just a minute."

Biting her bottom lip, Kelsy nodded immediately. Sam, intent on intimidating Finn by raking him from head to foot, didn't blink. Bitsy craned her neck but moseyed back up her driveway. With the hope that Finn wasn't all brawn and no brains, Risa threw him a silent order: *Back off.*

To her amazement, he nodded, then said cheerfully to Sam, "I think the doc has a damned good idea. Since it's your son she's talking about, I'm sure listening to her is more important than throwing a punch at a police officer."

Shaking with fury, his eyes too bright, Sam said, "That a quote from 'How to Defuse a Domestic Disturbance'?"

"Knock it off, Sam," Risa said sharply.

"I'd love nothing better than knocking this kid's ass off." Sam raised his chest a couple of inches. "Cop or—"

Kelsy hooted. "You're acting like a fifteen-year-old, and you call someone else a kid?"

Icicles suddenly hung from Sam's ears. Risa shivered. *Too bad, Sam, you're on your own.*

"At least I'm not bawling like a baby," he shot back.

Low blow. Risa squeezed Kelsy's hand, but Kelsy lifted her chin. "We'll see," she said softly, "who cries last."

"Ooooh, now I'm scared."

Mentally, Risa groaned. If the man had an ounce of brains, he'd run for his life before Kelsy zapped his family jewels next.

Sam didn't run for his life, but swaggered to his car like a bullfighter, past Kelsy, who for once said zip. As furious as she was with him, Risa realized she almost felt sorry for Sam. Once in his Jag, he careened around the corner at least ten miles over the speed limit. Risa eyed Finn, half expecting him to race after Sam and give him a ticket.

Instead, Finn said to Risa, "Not the best way for me to make a good impression, was it?"

"I asked him to stay," Kelsy protested.

"I'm glad Ben and Molly made pancakes for Jason," Risa said, aware she sounded stiff—more like a lecturer than Kelsy's best friend.

When she didn't open the front door, Finn waited a beat, then said, "I'm crazy about Kelsy, but I'd rather appear buck naked on *Oprah* than hurt her."

He glanced at Kelsy, who looked as if she'd been hit by lightning. "I know that sounds weird, like I'm out of control," he said, more to Kelsy than to Risa. "But ask anyone who knows me. I'm not weird. I'm not out of control."

"How about moving too fast?" Risa hugged her waist. "Under the circumstances, aren't you moving at warp speed?"

"What's your point?" Kelsy demanded. "I am an adult."

Refusing to weigh in on that declaration, Risa spoke to Finn. "I assume you're interested in a relationship and not just a good—"

"Risa!" Kelsy shook her head, then whispered, "She sometimes forgets she's not my mother."

"No problem." Finn grinned, and Risa grinned back. He said, "Relationship and commitment don't scare me."

Beaming, Kelsy arched a brow at Risa, who drawled, "Meaning?"

Shoulders back, Finn said, "Meaning, I'm definitely not interested in a good lay or a one-night stand. Not with Kelsy."

"Honestly?" Kelsy sounded truly amazed.

"Cross my heart." Slowly, he made the sign. "On the other hand, I'm not interested in hanging around for the rest of my life either."

"Say something." Sure her heart was going to break through the top of her head, Kelsy danced around the guest room like a teenage girl. "He's been waiting for almost ten minutes."

"Ten minutes don't equate to hanging around for the rest of his life. Not since he's twenty-eight." Risa crossed her legs as if settling in on the settee at the foot of the guest bed.

"Thank you for those words of wisdom." Suddenly, Kelsy stopped dancing. "Don't spoil this for me, Risa."

"Oh, Kel." Risa got up and wrapped her arms around Kelsy's neck the way they'd done since first grade. They adjusted their foreheads against each other's till they achieved their mountain goats posture. Risa whispered, "I don't want to spoil anything for you. Truth is, I'm a little jealous."

"Why?" The tears in Kelsy's throat dried up.

"Why?" Risa looked at her nose, her eyes crossing. Kelsy laughed. Which, she suspected, was Risa's goal all along.

Focused again, Kelsy swallowed her laughter. "Why?" she repeated.

"Another time, okay? We're talking about—"

"About why you're jealous. Stop trying to weasel out of it."

"But Finn's waiting."

"Stop stalling." Kelsy grabbed Risa's shoulders and shook her. "Ben's down there too, so it's not like Finn's watching the grass grow. He'll wait."

Kelsy felt in her bones that contrary to his statement, Finn would wait for her the rest of his life. But that sounded like bragging, and she figured it gave Risa a chance to avoid answering. "Let's talk in your room." She unwrapped her arms and straightened her back. "I need to pillage your closet till I work up the courage to go get my own clothes."

"Pillage away." Risa dropped her arms too. "You know there's nothing close to a size eight."

"So? You think Finn even notices what I wear?"

The drone of male laughter floated up the stairs as they crossed the hall to Risa's room. "Hurry up," Kelsy ordered.

They went into the walk-in closet, and Risa didn't need a second prompt. "I'm jealous because I wish I took risks like you." She handed Kelsy a turquoise silk wrap-dress. Kelsy held it up against her, folded her arm across the middle, and faced the mirror. She met Risa's gaze in their reflection. "Going to bed with Ben isn't a big risk."

The blue wool sheath Risa held out to Kelsy slipped off the hanger, but neither bent to pick it up. "How in the name of Jupiter did you make that leap?" Risa demanded sharply.

"Since adopting triplets falls into the high-risk category, I deduce you're speaking in code." Kelsy tapped the side of her head and grinned. They'd played this game forever. "Adopting triplets, bringing home a stray puppy, offering me and Jay a place to stay for as long as we want—those would scare most people to death. You didn't think twice. So, I deduce—"

Sputtering a little, Risa said, "Sorry, but I deduce your deduction is off the wall."

"Right on the money, you mean." Kelsy picked up the blue sheath, held it at arm's length, then laid it aside. "Where's the risk? You don't want a man permanently in your life. Ben's still in love with his wife. Hey! I'm a poet." Feeling silly and alive and in love with the idea of being in love, Kelsy did a little jig in front of an open-mouthed Risa.

CHAPTER 15

SHAZAM! Ben loaded the last plate into the dishwasher, straightened up, and saw the freight train roaring right at him.

Kelsy waltzed into the kitchen with Doc looking edgy, and time sped up. As if in a trance, Doc mumbled something to Jason about him and her going to cut a Christmas tree while Mommy had a last-minute conference with Santa.

Kelsy smiled at Finn like a kid who'd gotten everything on her ten-page Christmas list. Ben almost howled. So now Officer Bishop was Santa?

Life, Ben was the first to admit, wasn't fair.

While he battled his darker emotions, Molly put on a pitiful face. Could they go with La Ti Da and Jason, too? It would be so much fun, Daddy. They needed a tree. Please, Daddy.

Jason chimed in at a higher pitch, and Ben surrendered, wondering what would hit the fan if he suggested Kelsy and Finn take the kids tree hunting. He and Doc would stay home . . . in front of a fire, and pick up where they'd left off the night before. The dog, he thought. Don't forget the dog. He'd go with the tree hunters. What better place for a dog than a Christmas tree farm?

Doc shifted into mother hen overdrive, short-circuiting Ben's daydreams. She sent the kids off with the pup for warm clothes, ordered Kelsy to fix hot chocolate, directed the men to check the map and the weather, then disappeared—to dress, Ben assumed.

Seventeen minutes later, Finn and Kelsy didn't even wait till the car carrying Ben, Risa, and the kids turned the corner before they raced inside.

After twenty-seven-eleven repetitions of "Rudolph the Red-Nosed Reindeer" at the glass-breaking pitch preferred by four-year-olds, Ben barely heard Doc say, "Next right."

"We're here!" Jason rolled his window down, filling the car with the smell of pine needles and damp earth.

Molly whooped; the pup howled. Grateful they'd survived the switchbacks and hairpin curves of the Santa Cruz mountains, Ben decided to forego whooping and hollering. He'd gloat after he got Doc alone and thanked her for insisting he drive.

Once they piled out of the car, slogging through ankle-deep mud in a cold, pine-scented drizzle pretty much discouraged the gloating. Frozen to the bone, Ben barely managed putting one foot in front of the other. Off to their right, he heard axes on tree trunks. Fearless Chief Macdonald, he took the lead, never so much as raising his voice any of the dozens of times Jason stepped on his heels. Molly trailed Jason, and Doc brought up the rear. Occasionally, he heard muffled voices and the scratching sound of a tree dragged along the path.

Ben's contribution toward scintillating conversation consisted of, "Puddle ahead," and other such witticisms.

Undaunted by the rain, Molly called every few steps, "I'll let you know when I see our tree, Daddy."

The last time she offered this hope, intending to hurry up her selection, Ben turned his head to speak to her, but kept walking backward, watching Doc, luminous, eyeing him.

"Judas Priest!" He leaped a foot off the ground and swiped at the mutant, low-hanging branch that dumped at least a gallon of cold rainwater down his neck.

An invisible flock of birds twittered. Doc hooted. Ditto, Molly. Double ditto, Jason. Triple ditto, the pooch.

Miraculously, Ben didn't land on his ass. Doc giggled, then taunted, "Bet you can't do that again."

Of course Molly and Jason screamed, "Do it again!"

The pup sniffed the ground as Ben clawed his soggy shirt away from his body and wrung it out.

"A gentler woman," he said, "more inclined to bolstering a man's ego, doesn't goad his child into fits of giggles at his misfortunes."

A titter reduced the likelihood of an apology from Doc. Ben shuddered melodramatically when Molly imitated the *tee-hee*. Jason said, "What did you say, Mr. Macdonald?"

"I said, you should take the lead." Molly frowned. "Along with Molly," Ben added hastily.

Doc covered her laugh with a phony cough. Teeth clacking, Ben said, "Such conduct discourages men from protecting their womenfolk."

"S-s-sorry." Doc pounded her chest. "I expected the Marlboro Man to be more at home in the woods. Did you hit your lip? You okay?"

"Just ducky." Christ, he hated the cold.

The dog jumped on Ben's leg. Another snicker. Ben pushed the damned mutt away. Thank God, they hadn't attracted a crowd.

Stamping did not start the flow of blood to his feet. Next to him, Doc fanned her face and unbuttoned two buttons on her slicker. Feeling his toes tingle, Ben said, "Molly and Jason, you lead. We'll follow. Stay on the path."

He waited till they skipped out of earshot. "Dammit," he whispered to Doc. "It's not natural for a woman to perspire in this kind of weather."

"Eat your heart out." She bit down on her thumb, waited a heartbeat, then said, "That extra layer of fat's why we *womenfolk* have the babies."

"You know I was kidding, right?"

"You mean that crack about bolstering the man's—"

"Hey, it wasn't a crack. It was supposed to be funny."

"Would you like my sweatshirt?" As she opened the remaining buttons on her slicker, she held his gaze.

Fearing a brain spasm, he swallowed his pride. "You sure?"

"I love the rain." She spread her arms wide. "Let more than three drops fall, and I run around naked in my backyard."

He felt his eyeballs pop. She arched a brow.

Rain dripped off his brows into his eyes. He cleared his throat twice before croaking, "I'd pay to see that."

"Down, Rover." She handed him her slicker, holding it out tentlike by its sleeves. "I know it's pretty desolate, but there's a chance kids are out here looking for Christmas trees."

An image of her peeling down to bare skin exploded in his head. He mumbled, "It's not the kids that worry me. It's their dads. One of them might see you and chop his foot off."

"The parking lot was almost empty, but I'll stay alert."

"And I'll stay vigilant." He stretched the coat out at arm's length, craned his neck the other way, and focused on Molly and Jason. Hunkered down, they examined something on the path. A bug? Whatever, their intensity saved Ben from peeking over the top of the slicker—even when Doc made the same sound he always made when his head caught in the neck opening.

"Guess what?" he asked brightly, then rushed on before she replied. "We have something in common after all."

Her mumbled reply sounded like, "Such as?"

So he said, "Big heads."

"Thank you for pointing that out, you silver-tongued devil."

He laughed, feeling good, proud and witty. "Need help?"

"You up to explaining that kind of help to Molly?"

"Explain what?" Mr. Innocent, he didn't risk slapping his hand over his heart and exposing a half-naked woman. "Molly's more interested in pine cones than in us."

"I hope you're ready." Risa glanced back at him, her thick braid dotted with diamonds of rain.

"Absolutely." Was her double entendre deliberate?

"I believe coat sleeves traditionally go over the wearer's arms," Risa prompted.

Mouth agape, Mr. Ready stared at the flash of ivory shoulders. "Out of practice," he mumbled, afraid his fantasy of unhooking her bra would get away from him. The waist of her jeans bulged with the dry sweatshirt. Despite the cold, suddenly, he was hard.

"We're in an awkward position." She shoved her arms through the coat sleeves while Ben grit his teeth and managed not to drop her coat in the mud. Closing the buttons quickly, she faced him. "Your turn," she said. "Take your clothes off."

Not easily discombobulated, he said, "Huh?"

She patted her bulging waist. "You're not putting a dry shirt on top of your wet one, are you?"

On the cusp of hypothermia, he didn't blush. He shucked off his coat and handed it to her. "No peeking."

"Hurry, then. I can only fight the Macdonald charisma for so long."

"Not to worry." He tugged his soggy shirt off, struggling into the dry one and his coat in record time. He blew on his hands. "I purposely keep the charisma voltage on low in this kind of weather."

"What a prince."

Grinning, he shrugged. "Can't have women swooning under the Christmas trees, wreaking havoc."

"Wreaking havoc. I bet that's a sight to see."

"Awesome. A force of nature. Like you."

Exhaustion, according to medical school wisdom, dampened the human sex drive. Still hot and edgy, Risa had her doubts. After helping fell two giant firs, then dragging them half a continent back to civilization, she waited impatiently next to Molly inside the cashier's shack. Ben, wet to the bone, had trudged through the rain back to the car. A tired Jason and the bedraggled puppy rounded out the male trio.

The shack felt like a hothouse to Risa. Too bad she'd given Ben the shirt off her back. Now, packed in with three other women and their six offspring, she opted for keeping her slicker on. Holy Hannah, doomed to roast.

"Is that Daddy?" For the tenth time Molly pressed her nose against the rain-streaked window and asked this same question.

Risa wanted to scream. Where was the man?

The anxiety in Molly's heart-shaped face stopped Risa. She said gently, "No, but we can call him. See where he is."

"What if he doesn't answer?"

"I'm sure he'll answer."

At a loss for deeper inspiration, Risa unhooked her cell phone from her waistband, but Molly shook her head. "He might think I have a tummyache."

Despite the perfect segue to suggesting a new doctor, Risa felt sadness seep into her heart. Or maybe it was sweat sliding down her sides. Fanning the dead air, she said, "If he asks about your tummy, you can say you're fine but hot."

"I'll tell him you're hot," Molly said, and Risa felt her cheeks sting.

"What makes you think I'm hot?"

"Your face is all shiny and wet."

"I think that's rain." Risa fished a tissue out of her pocket and blotted her forehead.

"Uh-uh." Molly shook her head. She jutted her chin up at Risa. "I 'member how Mommy looked when she was hot."

Tears glittered in her dark eyes. Guilt engulfed Risa. She went down to Molly's eye level and encircled the tiny waist.

Never lie to a child.

Use extreme caution questioning her judgment and more caution undermining her memories.

With tears running down her cheeks, Molly stuck a thumb in her mouth. Risa's chest tightened. "You're right," she said. "I am hot. I'm sorry I said there was rain on my face."

Molly removed her thumb. "Did you lie, La Ti Da?"

Tempted to lie again by denying her original lie, Risa tasted something bitter flood the back of her throat. "I thought it might make you sad if you talked about your mommy."

"Nooo." Molly refused clean tissues. "I like talking about her. 'Cuz sometimes I don't 'member her face."

Earth to Ben. Adrenaline shot through Risa. "You've got lots of pictures of Mommy, don't you?"

"Uh-huh. But I like the pictures here better." Molly touched her heart, and a montage of snapshots at her own fifth birthday party exploded in Risa's mind. Her father singing. Giving piggyback rides. Throwing his voice. It was the last of her birthday parties he ever attended.

Risa made a leap of logic. "You mean like the pictures of you and Mommy singing?"

"Uh-huh. I sitted next to her. At the piano. I can play 'Twinkle, Twinkle Little Star.' "

"Will you play it for Charlie, Tom, and Harry someday?"

"Yes." Molly swiped the clean tissue over her cheeks. "Can we all go swimming someday? My mommy swimmed like a fish."

Her pride broke Risa's heart. "Do you swim, too?"

"I swim like a fish, too. Mommy teached me."

"Your mommy sounds like a wonderful mommy." The lust building inside Risa all day vaporized, and she decided she'd rather go to her grave celibate than disillusion Molly with Ben.

"My mommy was the wonderfullest mommy." How would Molly handle learning Ben was unfaithful to *the wonderfullest mommy?*

No reason she'd ever find out.

Mom and Kelsy and I found out.

But Amy's dead. Where's the infidelity?

Gazing into Molly's clear eyes, Risa took a deep breath, feeling her heart catch. "What else do you remember besides swimming and singing at the piano?"

"Oh, we singed everywhere. In the pool. In the bathtub. Two songs before bed."

"I sure hope Charlie, Tom, and Harry go to bed at the same time or I'm going to be singing all night."

Snuggled in close, Molly giggled. Another prompt for more memories, and she ran down a list that dazed Risa. Outings to the park. Ballet lessons. Baking cookies.

"We made lots 'n lots 'n lots of Christmas cookies," Molly announced. "Could we bake cookies tonight at your house?"

"Oh, honey, it's late." No use reneging so soon on her new resolve to avoid Ben like the plague. "We have school and work in the morning. I think we'll be too tired tonight. . . ."

"What about tomorrow night?"

Tears clogged Risa's throat. After a breath, she said, "I remember my mommy and I always baked cookies in the afternoon. Close your eyes. Is it day or night in your kitchen?"

"Day." Molly breathed. "Lots of sunshine. All 'round Mommy. Her apron has Rudolph on it."

Feeling like a traitor, Risa pulled Molly closer. "Me 'n Daddy have Rudolph aprons, too."

Too weak to resist pumping a child, Risa said, "Did Daddy bake cookies with you and your mommy?"

"Uh-huh."

Risa maintained a smidgeon of integrity by biting her tongue so she couldn't ask for details.

"Ummmm, the kitchen smells so good." Molly smacked her lips. "I love cookies and milk."

Taking note that Molly used *smells* instead of *smelled*, Risa didn't have the heart to correct the mistake. She said, "I bet Santa loves coming to your house."

Molly opened her eyes and looked beyond Risa, who guessed she imagined Santa eating cookies. Lost in the fantasy herself, Risa ignored the prickle on her neck.

"What's wrong, Daddy?"

Breathing hard, Risa whipped around. Ben towered over her. She swung the frog pendant back and forth on its chain. "How'd that sweatshirt do keeping you dry?"

Wet and shivering, Ben Macdonald buckled Molly into her car seat next to Jason. Praise Jupiter, their heads drooped, their eyelids fluttered. Otherwise, Risa was certain they'd be scared witless. Ben looked more like the Grinch who stole Christmas than he did the Spirit of Christmas. Whether he'd overheard bits and pieces or the entire conversation between her and Molly, he was not a happy camper.

He slid behind the wheel. A shower of raindrops flew

off his slicker into Risa's face. She gasped. Stone-faced, making no apology, he shifted into drive.

His iciness didn't surprise her. In fact, it was par for the course when it came to Molly talking about Amy. But if he thought his little temper tantrum intimidated Risa, she'd show him the error of his ways. She turned to the backseat, saying, "Let's sing a couple of verses of—"

"Silence," Ben interjected.

"Sour grapes," Risa muttered, mutinous since the kids were already snoring softly.

"Mind your own beeswax." He swiped at the windshield.

Taken aback by his vehemence, she inhaled sharply, ready to give him as good as he gave. "I don't believe I'm familiar with that line."

Without taking his eyes off the wet road, Ben waved an invisible baton. "First verse goes, 'Don't distract the driver by defending yourself.' "

Risa snorted. "I bet that's popular."

"Not as popular as the second verse. It begins, 'Sit there, and shut up.' " He combed his fingers through his hair, spraying water drops her way for the second time.

Blood pounded in her head, but she gritted her teeth and refused to take the bait. Instead, she yawned, stretched, laid back, and pretended a meditative state that bordered on catatonic. Not too difficult to attain since the *whap whap* of the wipers induced a near coma. She stole a couple of glances at him out of the corner of her eye, but finally, she felt calm.

Praise Jupiter, she'd outfoxed her hormones the night before. Sending him off on a goose chase for groceries before dawn had been a stroke of genius. Otherwise, she'd be eating her heart out right now.

Ahead of them, taillights glowed through the rain like the eyes of wild animals. Barely turning her head, Risa slitted her gaze at him. His lip, swollen and discolored, must have hurt like hell. In fact, he looked like hell. Positively haggard.

Afraid she felt the first inkling of empathy, Risa stared out the window at blackness. She massaged her temples. *Oookay, driving tonight had to bring back the accident.* But did those memories account for why he'd about ground his teeth down to dust? Or was he mad as hell because he didn't want Risa or anyone talking to Molly about Amy? Lost for an answer, Risa ignored the beep of a cell phone. Ben growled, "It's yours."

In everyday conversation, chatting about the weather, a TV show, the traffic, or a patient, words spewed out of Nurse Em's mouth like water out of a broken water hydrant. Tonight, the words gushed out like water from a broken dam. *Where was Risa? Was her cell phone on the fritz? The answering service had tried her, then called Em. Was Risa alone? Some bad news . . .*

Disbelief paralyzed Risa's mind, but not her vocal cords.

"What's wrong?" Ben checked the rearview mirror.

She didn't answer, couldn't because the roof of her mouth was so dry her tongue was useless. She listened till Em filled in the details, then said, "Hold on." In a surprisingly level voice, she asked Ben, "How long to Saratoga?"

"In this weather?" He paused, and she could see he was taking her question seriously, unwilling to toss out an answer off the top of his head.

Part of her wanted to scream at him, but the steady rhythm of Em's breath calmed her nerves.

"Thirty minutes, best-case scenario."

Numb with misery, Risa couldn't bring herself to repeat the estimate to Em. "Realistically"—he turned the wipers on high—"more like forty-five minutes."

Her mind shifted into overdrive, ignoring Ben's question about why the hell she needed a taxi and figuring how far it was to the San Jose airport from Saratoga while Em used another line to call a taxi. On hold, Risa pretended she was still listening. Right at that moment, her mind couldn't manage details for Ben.

Their tailgater flashed his headlights, eliciting from Ben a string of pithy Anglo-Saxon cusswords. Maybe, Risa marveled, cussing helped him hold their speed steady at 20 miles per hour.

Em came back on the line. The taxi would park across from the Plumed Horse. "He swears," Em said, "he'll wait all night."

"How long before he gets there?" Risa glanced at the speedometer. "We probably won't make it in forty-five minutes."

"Not if you want to get there alive," Ben snapped.

"He'll call me," Em said. "I'll call you once he does, give you his exact location, your flight number again . . ."

Em, ever the optimist, offered several words of hope, then hung up. Risa held the phone under her chin, swallowed tears, then said, "I'm cutting to the chase. No discussion, just the bottom line."

Ridiculously, she thought about freshman English and mixed metaphors. Whatever a metaphor was. Were dangling participles her next worry?

Get a grip. She pushed her thumb against her teeth. "Let me try that again."

He glanced her way. "What's the emergency?"

"In Nashville. Traci's in labor."

Intent on finding a dress to wear in Risa's closet after the best sex she'd ever had, Kelsy almost missed the phone. Wrapped in a bath towel, her hair loose, she answered. Somehow, she held onto her emotions and made herself listen to Risa, blinking back tears and replying like a robot. "Don't worry about the dog. I'm staying here, remember?"

"Yes. I mean, no. I forgot. But what if you and Sam patch things—"

"We won't," Kelsy said, not even surprised at her certainty.

"You might. After you tell Jay—"

Mention of Jason felt like a stick in Kelsy's eye. She said softly, "La Ti Da. Sam and I are history." Thank God she knew *exactly* how she felt about Sam. "The bastard could crawl on his belly from here to New York and back—which he won't—and I wouldn't go back to him."

Silence, then Risa said, "You'll tell Sam why I can't—"

"Just tell me what else I can do for you." Kelsy shook her head. "Don't say nothing, please?"

"I can't think of anything—"

"Call me from the taxi? We can talk right up till you get on the plane and take off. Right now, talk to Ben."

"I can't," Risa said tersely.

"Why not for God's sake?"

"It's raining. Hard."

Cold all over, Kelsy cocked her head. "It's not raining here." If it weren't dark and totally ridiculous, she'd say the sun was shining. Because, thanks to Finn, that's how she felt. Ben should take lessons.

Kelsy said, "Felton's the wettest place in the Bay area. Don't panic and think your plane won't leave on time."

"Em says a winter storm's headed our way. It's pouring in San Jose."

"Is that why you're taking a taxi to the airport instead of letting Ben take you?" *A little rain wouldn't stop Finn.*

"Yes."

"Because? There's a *because* you're not telling me, because this doesn't make sense. . . . Dropping you off in the middle of a rainstorm in the dark . . ."

"It's my call."

"But you could have an acci—" Dimly, a light went on

in Kelsy's head. "You're thinking about Amy and New Year's Eve."

"Yes." Shivering, Kelsy wanted to shake Risa. "Did you ask him to take you?"

"No."

"Are you insane?" Kelsy yelped.

"Em's beeping me. Keep your fingers crossed."

Mind racing, Kelsy tugged on a pair of Risa's pajamas and a baggy sweatshirt, then flipped on the Weather Channel. The smell of pizza drifted into the bedroom. With the forecast droning behind her, Kelsy raced into the hall.

"Honey?" Finn called, drowning out the TV. "I'm home."

She stared down at him, jolted by the sparkly halo framing his wet hair. With a huge grin, he flipped raindrops into the air. "Guess what?" he teased. "It's rain—"

Kelsy burst into tears.

CHAPTER 16

"Wait till I open the umbrella." Ben tapped the brakes so that the bastard tailgating them wouldn't rear-end them twenty feet from the taxi.

"There's no need. It's too windy. Besides—"

"Besides, nothing, dammit! Give it up." His heart beat high in his chest as he made the right turn off the slick pavement. The tailgater hydroplaned by them in a spray of water. Ben snapped at Risa, "I'm in no mood for crap."

"Shhh, you'll wake the kids."

"Good. Then they can hear us argue, and Molly can have a stomachache and—"

"And I suppose that would be my fault?"

"Shhh, you'll wake the kids." He pulled up next to the taxi and jerked the keys out of the ignition. "Don't move till I open your door."

They glared at each other for about a decade, then she finally nodded. *Once. Like a damned princess.* His chest tightened, but he knew she'd never sit still for him to say what needed saying. He cracked his door and slipped through it.

Rain, cold as sleet, slammed Ben in the face, tempering his resentment and knocking the breath out of him. Shock brought absolute clarity.

Amy had always intuitively known his feelings.

Foul.

A second blast of rain cooled his fried logic circuits. How should Doc know talking to Molly about Amy back in the tree shack had blown his short fuse? How should she know, jerk that he was, how he felt about anything for that matter?

"You're right about the umbrella," he shouted over the wind, then remembered the sleeping kids and shut his door carefully.

Christ, it was colder than Montana.

The taxi driver, a turbaned Sikh, smarter than Ben, rolled down his window a hair. Teeth chattering, Ben waved him away, then pulled Doc out of the front seat into the raincoat tent he'd made on the fly. God, he'd give anything if he could make her laugh. Instantly, his humor impairment deteriorated further. He shoved her head down, hoping to deflect a drop or two of rain. His attempt was hopeless, not to mention stupid. In their lurching two-step toward the taxi, she said something he missed, but he thought it sounded like, "Hey, great job of drowning me."

From inside the taxi, the driver pushed open the passenger's door behind his seat before Ben was ready, and he whacked it with his hip. The door swung shut. Damn, Ben ground his teeth. Couldn't he get any cooperation here? Too cold to feel pain, he realized Doc had her head buried in his armpit. Water sluiced off his slicker, down her head, then past her collar and down her neck like Niagara Falls. Any wonder she'd accused him of drowning her?

"God, I'm sorry." Disgusted, he lowered his arms.

She shook herself like a dog, stopped, and damned if she didn't smile. "Good. Now I don't feel so bad about saddling you with Jason and leaving the tree at my house and—"

"Shhh. I'll take care of everything." He buried his face in her soaking hair, then moved his mouth down to hers. His lip instantly protested, but he didn't give a damn. He kissed her, tasted rain, then felt the full sting of killer bees as she returned his kiss, wrapping her arms around him, trembling—but not from cold, he was certain.

"This isn't exactly the way I imagined our third kiss," he said, his voice husky.

"You imagined our third kiss?" Grazing his bottom lip with her fingertip, squinting against the rain, she pulled his mouth closer to hers. "When?"

"Long before you did."

"What makes you think I ever imagined kissing you?"

"Duuuh?" He kissed her again, longer this time, amazed at how right it felt. God, it had been so long. He'd wasted so much of his time with her. Regretfully, he pulled back. "Go."

Pressing her lips together, she nodded. "Traci has great doctors. It'll be okay."

"That's my line." He mentally kicked himself again for not figuring out what to say on the trip down the mountain. Since he couldn't improve on her own words, he repeated them. *Please let her know he meant them.*

"Thank you," she said.

"When you get back, I'll tell you my third-kiss fantasy and you can tell me yours." He couldn't let go of her.

"Deal."

Her smile blinded him. He opened the taxi door. Quickly, she ducked her head and slid inside. Ben slammed her door, then hurried to the other side of the taxi and tapped on the driver's window. He leaned into the warm cab. "Drive this woman as if she were your own mother." Then, in case this was too oblique or in case the driver didn't give a damn about his mother,

Ben added, "Take *no* chances. She's a very important person. If you have *any* problem, call me at this number." He shoved a business card and two hundred-dollar bills at the driver, hoping the man understood Ben would find a way to make his life miserable if Doc didn't arrive safely.

Eighty-three minutes later, both kids woke up a mile from Doc's house. Fully alert after their power nap, they shot a dozen questions at Ben before he reached the cul-de-sac. Where was La Ti Da? How did Ben know she was at the airport? When did her plane leave? What was wrong with Charlie, Tom, and Harry? How was La Ti Da?

During a three-second lull, Ben crossed his fingers and posed a question. "Sweetheart, how would you feel about spending the night at La Ti Da's with Jason while I go to the airport?"

"Yay, yay," Jason screeched.

For once, Molly didn't go bonkers. She said, "Why, Daddy?"

Crossed fingers work every time.

"Because," he picked his words carefully. "La Ti Da's at the airport alone. She's worried about Charlie, Tom, and Harry."

"Is she scared?" Molly asked.

"Yes, sweetheart. I think she is scared."

"I think you should go, Mr. Macdonald."

"Thank you, Jason. Molly?" Ben felt his heart thud. What was Molly's hesitation? She had the softest heart. . . .

"Can I go, too?" she asked.

"I'm going if you go," Jason said.

"Maybe your mommy won't let you go."

"She'll let me." Jason raised his voice over the slap of the wipers.

"Can I go, Daddy?"

"Can I go, too, Mr. Macdonald? My mommy will say yes."

Exactly what Ben was afraid would happen. Without Jason around, Finn and Kelsy could . . . Hit in the gut by jealousy, Ben clamped down on his mind. Finishing the thought bordered on masochistic. He took a deep breath, but his heart kept up its frantic jitterbug. *Do not scare Molly.* He slowed for the turn into the cul-de-sac and knew what he had to do, but it took three deep breaths before he found his voice.

"You can't go, Molly," he said, "because there are too many people driving tonight who scare me."

"Why do they scare you, Daddy?"

"They don't scare me, Mr. Macdonald."

"They should, Jason. Because those drivers scare *me* a lot." Ben choked the steering wheel.

"But *whyyyy*?" Jason demanded.

"First, it's raining." Ben felt his heart speed up, but he kept talking—more to himself than to Jason. "It's raining real hard. So hard—what can you see through the rain?"

"La Ti Da's house," Molly said. "But it's hard."

"I can see some things," Jason said. "I can see trees 'n streetlights 'n rain. Lots of rain."

Patience. "But when I'm driving, Jason, I have to see everything."

"Everything?"

"That's a lot," Molly said.

"It is a lot." Ben checked his rearview mirror and willed Jason to shut up. "I'm afraid someone who doesn't see *everything* might hit our car . . . and hurt you." *Or worse.* He gripped the steering wheel, swallowed the sawdust in his throat, and said carefully, "Remember, someone hit our car and hurt Mommy?"

"You better stay home with me, Molly," Jason said solemnly.

The logic of the situation didn't elude Molly. She said, "But what if a driver hits our car and hurts you, Daddy?"

"That could happen." Tempted to bullshit his own daughter, Ben pulled into Doc's driveway, flipped on the dome light, and realized it was absolutely okay that Molly came first.

Doc wouldn't have it any other way.

An invisible boulder rolled off his back. He said, "If you're scared a car might hurt me, or if you're going to have a tummyache after I go to the airport, I'll stay at home."

"What about La Ti Da?" Jason asked. "She's already scared."

"We'll talk to her on the phone, cheer her up." Ben unbuckled his seat belt, then faced Molly. "Want to talk first?"

"That's not fair," Jason yelled. "I want to talk first."

"Hold on," Ben said, pissed he'd even brought up the subject. "We can work this out."

"Let's draw numbers from a hat," Molly said.

"No! That's not fair." Jason rolled from side to side in his car seat.

Molly said, "Daddy can ask La Ti Da who she wants—"

"No, I want Mommy to ask her."

"OH-kay, Jason," Molly sighed, a sentiment Ben shared till he saw the tears on Jason's cheeks.

At some level, this kid knows his world's about to spin off its axis.

"Okay," Ben said. "Sounds like a plan. Your mommy can ask La Ti Da." And he'd talk to Molly, explain about the divorce and trust her big heart was big enough one more time.

The front door opened. Light—golden, warm, and welcoming—flooded the step. The pooch barked, pranced to the edge, sniffed a puddle, turned, and scampered back inside. *Smart doggie.*

Finn and Kelsy, definitely underdressed for the storm, joined hands and raced for the car, squealing like kids.

Eyes narrowed, Ben gripped the steering wheel. The dome light threw a greenish cast on his fingernails, staining his fingers and hands the color of old limes. And if someone cut him open at that exact moment, they'd find his pounding heart was green, too.

Though neither Kelsy or Finn wore a neon sign, there was no doubt in Ben's mind how much time they'd spent that afternoon walking the dog. In fact, Ben concluded that poor mutt probably never even got a walk to the end of the driveway.

Damn, he thought resentfully, life was not fair.

At the entrance to SJO, impatient drivers hit their horns, and rude ones whipped onto the shoulder and careened around vehicles waiting for the lights to change.

Thank God Molly had, after a bowl of Kelsy's rib-sticking chicken soup, insisted on staying with Jason while Ben trekked off to the airport.

As Ben waited in the stalled short-term parking line at the airport garage, he felt silly. Like a teenage boy about to leave an anonymous note in the locker of the girl he secretly loved. But since he now passed as an adult, he should call Doc. Tell her where he was. Prove to her that modern woman though she might be, she wasn't too independent to need him.

She'd think he'd lost his mind, and he wasn't sure she wasn't right about that.

He dialed her cell phone number. Busy. Saying good night to Molly and Jason, he hoped.

Kelsy had promised she'd put them to bed by eight o'clock. With Finn at work, Ben hoped she'd keep her promise. She'd told him he was insane if he didn't go to the airport. "Trust me, Risa's just waiting for a sign. We women love signs."

Personally, Ben didn't believe in signs. If he did, he'd have stopped roaming the aisles for a parking space and gone home within twenty minutes of entering the garage. Christ, there were just too damned many cars and not enough spaces for them to park in.

On the way to the top floor, he reached for the phone, dialed, and waited on hold for five minutes. The automated airline information system informed him dispassionately that all flights were delayed out of San Jose due to adverse weather conditions.

"Would flights be delayed due to *good* weather conditions?" He hung up and dialed the airport directly.

"Surprise, surprise," he said, wondering why he felt a spurt of anger when the busy signal came on almost instantly. Dammit, he still had no damned idea how long Doc's flight had been delayed.

Cussing, he spied the last empty space in the whole damned garage. The driver of a Bronco roaring in from the opposite direction saw it at about the same time. The other guy was, technically, closer to the space. *Tough.*

His years as a cattle wrangler paid off for Ben. Teeth gritted, he pealed out like a madman, whipped in front of the other vehicle, and laid claim to *his* parking spot.

The Bronco squealed to a stop.

What if a driver hits our car and hurts you, Daddy?

Face livid, the driver jumped out. Square and solid, he was built like an Angus bull. The gold ring in his nose reinforced the image. Ben felt his stomach flip-flop. Legs wobbling, he opened his door and blurted, "Jesus, that was about the most dumb-assed thing I've done in a long while."

"You mean you've done something even dumber?" drawled the driver, maybe ten years younger and sixty, seventy pounds heavier. "What the hell was it?"

Heart still thudding, nerves shot, Ben grinned, mentally apologizing to Molly. He brought his palms up. "I

let the woman I love come to the airport without saying
good-bye to her."

"Had a fight, huh?" The guy rolled his feral green
eyes.

"Not a fight, a misunderstanding. My fault. I was
deeply stupid, but I bet you can't begin to believe that,
huh?"

The guy snickered. "Sure can't. Just like I can't believe I'm letting you leave without kicking your ass. But
what the hell. It is Christmas. Go find your lady."

Without thinking, Ben held his hand out, winced as
he heard a few knuckles crack, but took the abuse anyway. The guy said, "A word of advice. Get your head
outta your ass before you regret it."

Four hours after Risa's arrival at the airport, the pre-
boarding announcement almost drowned out the beep
of Risa's cell phone. Her heart lurched. *Please don't let
anything be wrong.* She smacked the phone to her ear. At
first, she didn't recognize Ben's voice, then she squeaked,
"Praise Jupiter."

"You always cry when you're happy?"

She sniffled. "I was afraid you were Traci's doc—"

"Christ! Risa, I'm sorry. I wanted to surprise you—
not scare you to death."

"It's okay. Honestly." Her knees had stopped quaking, but they still felt like water. She sagged against the
nearest chair. "Where are you? At home?"

"Nope. I'm zooming up the escalator."

"The escalator?" she repeated stupidly.

"Did you think I'd let you leave without saying good-
bye?"

In a word, yes. "Where are Jason and Molly?"

"Still at your house. Where are you?"

"Gate 36. At the end of the terminal," she said, suddenly feeling edgy and ungracious. He deserved a medal,

but no matter how much she daydreamed, he wasn't a part of her life. "They've already called First Class."

"I'm next in line at Security."

"Security?"

"Uh-huh. I bought a ticket."

"You did?" She choked her pendant.

"Round trip. It's the only way . . ." His voice faded, then came back strong and clear. "It was the way I could ensure seeing you to say good-bye."

Perspiration ran down her sides, clinging to her raincoat. "You didn't have to do that," she said lamely.

"Does that mean you're glad?"

"I—I—I—"

"I bet a little exercise would clear up that speech problem right away. Why don't you jog back? Meet me halfway?"

Her heart soared. *He bought a ticket?* "Are you getting on the plane?"

"I'd love to, but Molly expects me to take her to school tomorrow."

"That little rascal. I talked to her and Jason not more than five minutes ago. Neither said a word about her spending the night at my house. Neither did Kelsy."

"Where are you?" Ben demanded.

His sudden change of subject raised the hairs at the back of her neck. So he and Kelsy were in cahoots, and he didn't want to admit it.

"You still in this galaxy?" he asked.

"On my way."

Sure she needed her head examined, Risa flashed her boarding pass at the harried-looking ticket agent, then broke through the amoeba of waiting passengers around her. Mumbling "Excuse me," she struggled against the mass of bodies pressing forward.

Finally, she found an opening, ducked around a young couple with a baby, and started running away from the gate. Like her, several people had cell phones pressed against their ears. Unlike her, they moved *toward* the departure gates.

"I see you!" Ben shouted, putting Jason to shame.

"Could you miss me in this damned slicker?" She must look like a yellow blimp. "Praise Jupiter no one realizes I don't have a shirt on underneath."

"I wouldn't say *no one* realizes."

Her heart caught. "Please don't tell me I'm walking around naked as the emperor? That's my worst-case scenario you know," she babbled, ready to tell him about her childhood nightmare.

"Look up," he said.

"What in the world—"

Two white banners dangled over his head as he ran. She squinted. He held the banners out at arm's length, banked like an airplane, and hurtled toward her.

Closer up, she recognized the sleeves on one of her UC-Davis sweatshirts and started laughing.

CHAPTER 17

"Easy now." In the middle of the airport concourse, Ben felt like the village idiot, his heart slamming into his ribcage so hard he could barely breathe. He kept his arms open.

"Don't hurt yourself or my ego," he said, "with your display of wild exuberance."

"Sorry." Doc's hand fluttered over her heart.

A couple of guys toting shoulder bags and laptops elbowed past them, bumped Doc, and never looked back. She literally fell into Ben's arms. His heart stopped, and his lungs wouldn't expand. He wrapped the sweatshirt around her neck and pulled her closer despite their wet slickers. Tendrils of her hair, silky, still damp, tickled his nose. Sure he'd spook her if he moved too fast, he tucked a strand of hair behind her ear, tempted to kiss her. Holding her felt so right, and he wanted the moment to last a lifetime.

"Coming through," a woman warned, dragging a top-heavy bag.

"Thanks for bringing me a shirt." Her voice deepened.

"Am I a romantic devil or what?"

"I'll get back to you." She ducked into the restroom.

Disappointed she preferred getting dressed to kissing him, Ben leaned against the wall and checked the time every couple of heartbeats. By his watch, he waited one minute, fifty-six seconds. But by the thud of his heart, he waited a couple of decades.

Doc emerged patting her hair, the yellow slicker over her arm. "You saved my life."

He expected more by way of appreciation, but she started trotting toward the terminals. "Saunas are cooler than—"

"I think we've about exhausted the coat; okay?"

Mouth primped, she stared at him—then marched onward, head up, chest out, arms pumping. She dodged around the woman with the top-heavy bag, then broke away from Ben.

He lengthened his stride. "Where's the fire?"

"I should get on—in case there's a problem with my seat."

"Take mine." He caught her elbow. "Let's sit for—"

"No time." The woman with the bag bumped Doc behind the knees. She grabbed his arm, missed, and made noises like a small animal separated from its mother.

The next thing Ben knew, Doc collapsed in the nearest chair, and he landed in her lap. He hooted. Stragglers boarding her flight stared at them, then looked away.

"Get off me!" She lunged forward, trying to unseat him.

"Yahoo!" he cried. Her breasts were almost as hard as his erection.

"You are certifiable," she hissed.

"Don't make a scene," he whispered loudly.

"Advice," she panted, "I'll gladly take from a Neanderthal."

Laughing, he stood, pulled her to her feet, then encircled her waist. "If I miss that plane," she said, "I will kill you."

"Hold on." He tapped his temples. "Flashbacks of roping calves—back in my youth."

She gaped, clamped her mouth shut, then shoved him. "You are certifiable."

"Keep the calf off balance, then tie her down," he murmured.

Scarlet-faced, Doc said, "Tying me down could prove a challenge."

"Nope, and keeping you off balance is a cinch." Before she could give him more lip, he tilted her backward.

"Ben!" she screeched.

He figured he only had a minute before security came down on them. He laid the kind of kiss on her Rhett Butler laid on Scarlet O'Hara.

Stunned Doc didn't pound his back, try to break away, or call him names, Ben sneaked a look at her. She went limp as a cat in his arms. Her dead weight definitely shook his confidence, but not his determination.

He blurted, "Will you marry me?"

"I'd rather kiss a frog." Doc whirled away from Ben and trotted toward the Jetway as if chased by the devil.

Seeing red, he caught up with her in a single stride. He didn't touch her, but demanded, "What kind of answer's that?"

She shoved her ticket at the attendant. "Think about it."

Then she was gone. Down the Jetway. Never glanced back. Mad as a bull, he hung around the gate long after the door closed. No way he could drive. Or think. Think about what, for God's sake? Dammit, he didn't want to think. For once in his life, he wanted to do something wild and crazy. He wanted to *feel* wild and crazy.

After a decade of pacing and mumbling, Ben felt his blood pressure drop. Still, the announcement her flight

was deplaning surprised him and sent his pulse racing
again. Ooo-kay. Now they'd get somewhere. He'd las-
soed cows since birth. If he had to hog-tie Dr. La Ti Da
Taylor, he'd get to the bottom of her rejection.

As soon as she saw Ben, she slipped into the slicker
she had slung over one arm. As a rejected suitor, it wasn't
his place, but someone should tell her the damned thing
fit like a tent. It had the sex appeal of a nun's habit. So,
why wear the coat and rob him of the pleasure of leering at her?

Maybe 'cuz she figured out you are leering at her.
Tough.

Her rejection of his proposal still stung. Wounded
pride absolved him of leering. Rejecting a guy's marriage
proposal so callously means you put up with leering was
the way Ben figured it. Doc stomped past him, cell phone
against her ear, and started yakking to Kelsy. A decade
into the conversation, he butted in. Once Kelsy agreed
she'd take Molly to school, he hung up.

Doc glared. He said, "You didn't tell her I proposed
and you turned me down."

"I don't enjoy poking sharp objects in my eyes." Doc
grabbed her phone with a little more force than Ben
thought really necessary. Why so edgy?

"Hey. I'm the one who got rejected. Not to mention
wounded." As he followed her out of the packed waiting area to a drinking fountain, he ran his tongue along
his bottom lip.

"Boo-hoo, boo-hoo." She bent over, her luscious backside hidden by yards of ugly yellow raincoat. She drank.
Way too long for anyone but a camel. When she stopped,
she faced him, her eyes glittery. She patted her mouth.
"I should've said yes just to see you squirm."

"Why the hell would I squirm if you said yes?"

She moved in on him, radiating heat like a blast furnace. "Because the first thing I'd get straight is why you
shut down every time Molly talks about Amy."

Caught completely off guard, he planted his feet on the slick floor. "I don't *shut down*—whatever the hell that psychobabble means."

"You know what—give me a break." She looked him right in the eye. "You heard me and Molly tonight, didn't you?" She didn't wait for his answer. "You wanted to bite my head off. Then Em called, so you gave me a reprieve. If I'd said yes to your heartfelt proposal, you'd have to give me a dozen reprieves before noon every day."

"Then, I guess it's a good thing you said no."

She sighed, and it hurt him to see the light in her eyes go out. He raised his hand to cup her cheek, but she stepped back. "You're screwing up with Molly. I'm not a shrink, but sooner or later, I think she'll shut down, too."

Her words felt like ice cubes dumped down Ben's back. So, he shot back in a voice like breaking icicles. "I thought modern doctors no longer played God."

Her chin came up, shaky but jutted defiantly at him. "I'm pleading for Molly, not—"

"Pleading? Don't kid yourself, Doc. First, you pronounce I neglect my kid—"

"Didn't you admit you work too much?"

His ears rang. "Now, you proclaim I'm screwing Molly up. Excuse me, but neither comes close to pleading."

"Now you're being a jack—" She pressed her lips together and put both hands over them.

Her eyes telegraphed her misery. With a start, he realized she was right. He was a jackass. She was exhausted, worried about her own kids and near the end of her rope with him baiting her at every step of the way. Thank God she'd said no.

Hands up, he conceded. "Okay, I'll give you jackass. And my first jackass mistake was coming here." Since she didn't protest, he went on. "My second was asking you to marry me. Please accept my apologies."

The misery in her eyes didn't evaporate—or even fade, but she dropped her hands to her sides, flexing her fingers, holding his gaze. "I bet you read cereal boxes with more fervor." She shrugged. "I repeat. You're screwing up with Molly."

It was like being hit by lightning twice. But damned if he let her see she'd ripped a hole in his fucking heart. "You know the wonderful thing about experience?" he asked tightly. She hesitated. He said, "It enables us to recognize a mistake when we make it again."

Hope lit her face, but he said, "The mistake I'm going to correct right now is canceling the promise you made me."

She looked blank. His gut burned. Had she intended all along to renege on her promise? He worked his jaw, then said bitterly, "Forget convincing Molly Dr. Karr is her new best friend. I'll do it."

"I don't mind—"

He shook his head. "Not your problem. With everything on your plate, getting Dr. Karr to take us is more than enough. So, after tonight, you don't need to see me or Molly again."

Without missing a beat, she said, "Don't forget Molly expects to visit Charlie, Tom, and Harry."

That almost threw him, but he said, "We'll see."

"Meaning what?" She slapped her hands on her hips.

"Meaning, I'm Molly's father. *I* still decide what's good for her."

"That's interesting . . . since you don't have a clue."

"You trying to pick a fight?" He felt like grabbing her, shaking her, but figured she'd slug him if he touched her. A nerve ticked under his left eye. He reined in his temper. "I don't want to argue."

"No, you want to dictate. Kids respond so well to orders."

"Get back to me on how it goes when you don't give orders to three boys." He pitched his baritone to falsetto.

"Please, Tommy, stay away from matches. Matches can burn us Tommy—"

"You're being ridiculous."

"Ahhh, yes. We jackasses tend to the ridiculous." Stomach churning, he glanced at his watch. Six minutes past midnight, and he felt like a zombie. "On that cheery note, I'll now correct my mistake of dropping by."

"It's a monsoon out there."

He peered at the dark, rain-spattered window. "Monsoons discourage traffic. I should be at your house in time to take Molly for blueberry pancakes. A tradition she dearly loves."

A tradition, he'd remind Molly, started by her mother.

"You're exhausted. As a doctor, I recommend you wait."

He gave her a half smile, showing there were no hard feelings on his part. "Medical recommendation duly noted."

Tension buzzed in the awkward silence between them, but Ben waited, intending to have the last word. Doc played with the top button on her slicker. "Please," she said, "drive carefully."

"Absolutely." He regretted his flippant tone and realized he needed to say his piece, then get out of town. Wanting to get this right, he swallowed twice, then said, "I hope everything goes fine with your sons. I'll cross my fingers you get there in time for their birth. That's one experience I'll never forget."

Doc blinked fast, then extended her hand. "Thank you."

Despite the danger of electrocution, courtesy demanded he shake her hand. Then he beat a hasty retreat before he could make another big mistake.

Emergency cots lined an area near the concourse exit so Ben knew he wasn't the last man on earth. The only time he'd felt this lost and lonely had been the predawn

hours after the accident. Going home to face Molly—
his mind veered away, but his heart dropped. Suddenly
dizzy, he stood still.

After a couple of breaths, his heart started again.
He'd managed after the accident, he'd manage now.
Losing Doc was nothing like losing Amy—for him or
for Molly.

The closer he got to his car, the harder his heart
thumped. Only a bastard would leave Doc alone. She
was wrong about him screwing up with Molly, but what
would she do till six o'clock besides worry? Christ, less
than twenty-four hours ago she'd saved his butt. What if
she hadn't volunteered to take Molly?

Hell, leaving Molly with Doc had saved the whole
damned company. He rubbed the back of his neck.

Dammit, that act of generosity didn't give her the
right to psychoanalyze him. Especially since she was
wrong. He talked plenty with Molly about Amy.

Behind the wheel, he punched on the radio. He
turned the volume up loud enough to rock the pickup's
front end. He found the news. Flooding around the airport in San Jose. Electrical outages up and down the
Peninsula. He felt his guts twist.

"Shit." Molly was probably scared to death.

Rain and wind—a *gully washer* they'd call it in Montana—hit the windshield like a freight train. *Too bad you
don't believe in signs.*

Ben snorted. Kelsy might consider the storm a sign
he should hightail it back to Doc, but the only signs he
believed in were traffic signs, which were now invisible
in the downpour. Hunched over the steering wheel, he
flipped off the radio and inched along, neck muscles
twanging. The wipers whapped their little hearts out,
but visibility remained zero. How many other idiots besides him on the road?

What if a driver hits our car and hurts you, Daddy?

"No problem, Molly." He checked his rearview mirror. "No one else is on the road except your daddy, the dumb-ass jackass."

A bus stop—the only place he could pull over—loomed ahead. Tiredly, he dialed Risa's number.

"My favorite cop again?" Kelsy answered in a sexy, teasing tone.

Surprised by an undeniable stab of jealousy, Ben cut to the chase. "How's Molly?"

"Sound asleep. I just checked."

Ben sighed. Thank God. "She doesn't like storms."

"She's fine," Kelsy said. "Where are you?"

"Trying to figure out where I can rent an ark."

"Risa said a taxi with oars would satisfy her."

"That's hypothetical, right?" Wind rocked the car. "I mean, she's not going over to the hotel, is she? Oars—"

"No, no. She's coming home."

Kelsy spoke to him as if he weren't too bright. Which was okay because he yelped like someone not too bright. "What?"

"Traci's on her way home, too. False labor . . ."

CHAPTER 18

He proposed. During the taxi ride from hell, through flooded chuck holes, in blinding rain, cell phone dead, Risa repeated the litany so she wouldn't scream or throw up.

Something deep inside her said the proposal didn't matter, since Ben never mentioned Charlie, Tom, and Harry. Something deeper disagreed. Ben Macdonald wasn't short on brains. He knew she came with baggage. Triplets. Bound to be a handful. Unlike Molly.

Water gushed down her driveway. No problem. She jumped out at the curb and tore across her lawn, as if chased by the devil, toward the wedge of light on her front step. What was being soaked compared to being alive and safe? Her heart missed a beat. As long as Ben was alive and safe.

"Where—where is he?" She stamped her feet, spraying Kelsy, who jumped back.

"Hey! You're worse than the dog."

"Kelsy." A scream built in Risa's chest.

"Near Moffett and 101." Kelsy's eyes looked full of stars. "Finn to the rescue."

"To the rescue?" Risa squeaked. "Is Ben—"

"He's fine." Kelsy pointed at Risa's slicker, then offered a scroungy, purple chenille robe. "Sorry, I scared you. I just meant Finn gave him an alternate route. He should be here before you finish a hot shower."

"No shower." Risa pulled on the robe, tottered to the family room sofa and collapsed. The undecorated Christmas tree stood in the corner like an unwanted guest.

"But—"

"No shower." Even on the cusp of exhaustion, Risa knew she and Ben had to clear the air. Five, ten minutes of sleep, she'd work out a plan. One where she didn't back down on Molly.

"Okay, forget the shower." Kelsy patted her shoulder.

"No shower." He proposed, for crying out loud. Her heart pumped. He'd never let it go. He'd demand a reason.

"Good idea on the shower," Kelsy conceded. "You're shaking so hard you'd probably fall and crack your head open."

"Gee, thanks." Yawning, Risa stared into the ashes, felt her eyelids droop, then snap open when Kelsy added, "Bobbye Anne called. Traci's embarrassed, but fine. She'll call you later. At the office."

After that, Risa's pulse slowed enough that her mind drifted. Kelsy faded in and out of focus. Her words ran together. Eyes closed, Risa sensed her leaving and surrendered to sleep.

The snick of a door jerked her upright, dry-mouthed and disoriented by light from the small table lamp. The light exploded, plunging her into the dream of Ben and her in bed. Scrubbing her eyes, she swallowed then swung her feet onto the floor. "Ben?"

Hair stuck to his skull, he peered around the corner. His eyes were dull, his skin stretched tight across his cheeks. The lines in his face appeared etched. "Sorry," he whispered.

"I was awake." In disbelief, she felt her breasts harden.

Supported by the door, he shook his head. "Leaving you. I—I screwed—" He straightened like a drunk trying to get his bearings, and Risa stiffened. Holy Harriet, she wanted to go to him, hold him, let him off the hook. *What about Molly?*

"You need sleep." She needed a new brain. At least get up, think on her feet. She stood. Major mistake. The room spun.

"Uh-uh." He worked his mouth. " 'Pologize first."

"No." No way she was ready yet to apologize for the icy tone she'd used with him. In his near comatose condition, he'd never hear her concern for Molly. Hand extended, she said, "Sleep first."

He met her halfway, grabbed her hand, and held it lightly. Bones melted. "No stairs," he said clearly.

"No stairs." Weak-kneed, she led him back to the sofa. "Take the couch." *Take me.*

The thought came out of nowhere. Disgusted, Risa smothered it and guided him to the sofa where he fell down and dragged her on top of him. Before she could wiggle out from under him, he clamped his arms around her.

Certain, at first, he was faking sleep, she lay still, her heart pounding hard enough to rupture a vein in his chest. Faking or not, he looked like hell. She touched the gray-flecked stubble on his chin with the tip of her nail. He grunted and turned his head but didn't open his eyes.

Who said men were the hornier sex?

The fragrance of rose-scented pine and the click of toenails woke Risa at 6:32 A.M. Dressed in tattooed jeans and a cashmere turtleneck, Kelsy tiptoed into the family room with the dog. Fighting her robe, up past her waist, Risa moaned, then elbowed Ben, whose arms were wrapped around her like an octopus.

"They're awake?" Risa tried to raise her head.

"You'd better believe it." Kelsy peeked over the back of the sofa. "Is Ben dead?"

"Would I know?" Risa pinched his cheek. Nothing. Imagining Molly and Jason finding them on the couch like lovers, she touched his bottom lip.

"Jesus!" His eyes popped open.

"La Ti Da!"

Risa lurched to her feet. She caught both kids in a bear hug, then released Molly, who ran straight into Ben's open arms. The dog, like a wind-up toy, jumped on and off the sofa. Kelsy allowed ten minutes of questions about Charlie, Tom, and Harry, then hustled the kids and their canine sidekick upstairs.

The promise of breakfast at McDonald's set off more screams, barks, and shrieks. The enthusiasm hammered a nerve behind Risa's left eye. Ben stared into space like a mental patient off his meds. For a second, Risa felt the way she did when she was about to give a four-year-old a shot that hurt like hell. Her breath caught. Had she lost her mind? She should read him the riot act about Molly. Instead, she wanted him to lie down and rest.

Talk about insane. With the kids and Kelsy leaving any minute—Risa squeezed her eyes shut. Images of her and Ben in bed with Fergie rolled over each other, flooding her mind.

Get him out of here, she thought, choking her pendant. The sooner, the better. "Would you take the dog out again, please?"

"Sure." He frowned as if he didn't remember her dog from the one next door. "How long?"

"As long as you want," she said too sharply, then added, "I'm going to b—nap for a couple of hours."

Holy Henrietta, she let go of her pendant. She'd almost said *bed*. Visions of tangled covers flashed. She shivered and looked away from Ben. "Naps—naps really keep me going," she babbled. "That's how I got through med school. Naps. Every day. I highly recommend naps. Very therapeutic."

He waited till she finally ran down. "Can you at least wait till I get back? We need to talk."

The thunder of footsteps on the stairs saved her. Dizzy from holding her breath, she jogged into the hall. Five minutes of kisses, hugs, and howls did zilch for her jangled nerves. Worse, Kelsy went stupid on her, grinning as if she knew about the dream.

At the door into the garage, Kelsy asked, "Any word from Maryann?"

Ben got the same dumbfounded look on his face he'd had when Risa mentioned the dog. She snapped her fingers. He flinched. "No message."

"What do you mean, no message?" Risa demanded, hands on her hips. "How can she still be stranded in Tahoe?"

Her canine whined and lay down, nose on his paws.

"What can I say? I've got a big meeting—" Ben threw Risa some kind of unreadable look, then laughed.

Kelsy rolled her eyes. Tempted to touch his forehead, Risa stared at him. Was he delirious, running a fever?

"What's the joke?" Kelsy demanded.

"Private." His wink seared Risa like a laser.

Face on fire, she gaped. He wiggled his eyebrows. Piece by piece, she felt her robe and underwear fall off. A wail from Jason interrupted Kelsy, who offered, "It's fine if Molly comes back here after school."

Stepping over the dog, Ben followed Kelsy into the garage, thanking her repeatedly, and strapped Molly into her car seat. He gave Jason a high five, then waved till the garage door came down. Trapped in the kitchen, suddenly conscious of the purple robe padding her hips, Risa fumbled the leash on the dog and tossed the lead to Ben.

"Poor guy can't wait." Her heart filled her throat. She called over her shoulder, "Close the bed when you—"

"Oh-oh," Ben said. "Now you're toying with me."

* * *

Nose to the ground, the mutt snuffled soggy leaves and storm debris in the driveway, apparently oblivious to the drizzle or Doc's impatience. Big blunder—teasing her about her slip of the tongue, Ben realized and shivered. He'd offered to fix a pot of coffee. After a dozen excuses, she shooed him and Fido into the cold, insisting she'd change, then join them.

Just in case she forgot, he kept Fido on a short leash till she came outside, commented on the drizzle and broken branches, then kept her distance as they side stepped puddles. Ben released more lead. The mutt immediately trotted into mud and muck.

"You're pretty good with dogs." Doc yawned.

Oh, goody, Ben thought. *Let's discuss Fido.* The openings he'd rehearsed evaporated. He said, "I'm better with my hands."

He laughed, she didn't. The fist in his stomach clenched. Not a good start.

"Sorry," he said and meant it because he didn't often use the word and he needed the practice. "Last night—"

"Let's not go there, okay?" Dressed in sweats, she dragged out the damned frog pendant and ran it around the gold chain two, three times till he felt dizzy.

The dog sniffed the fire hydrant. Ben focused on her fingers. She stopped with the pendant.

"If you'd kissed me at the airport instead of kissing me off after I proposed," he said, "I might've morphed into a prince. Instead, I followed my frog script."

"Life is a timing problem." She pursed her lips.

An invitation? Ben's ears rang. He leaned toward her. At the same time, the pooch lunged at a bedraggled squirrel. A little fancy footwork kept Ben on balance. Doc danced ahead of him on the edge of the sidewalk.

"Life is a timing problem," he repeated without pointing out he hadn't fallen down once in the past twenty hours. "Since I don't see you hearing me out tonight—with Jason upset, the tree to trim, the pooch to walk . . ."

Hoping she'd jump in soon, he let his argument hang for a heartbeat. She swiped mist off her chin, then lifted it at him. "Yesterday was a long day—even before the airport. If they'd handed out prizes for maturity?" She stopped walking and faced him. "I meant what I said about Molly, but I shouldn't have gone for your jugular."

"My jugular? And here I thought it was my balls."

"Believe me, you'll know it the day I go for your—"

"Gotcha." He clicked his tongue against his teeth.

"You—you—you—are a—" The dog whipped in front of her, wrapping the leash around her ankles. She tottered.

Ben caught her, inhaled her scent of roses and untangled the leash without letting her go. "Frog?" he suggested.

God, holding her felt so good—even with the damned frog pendant jabbing a hole in his chest.

"Bingo." Her mouth twitched.

Tempted to go with the lightness flooding him, he said, "Being a frog's my only excuse for leaving you at the airport."

"Apology accepted. Worthy of a prince." She smiled, and the lightness spread to his fingertips.

She picked up the leash he dropped, whistled for the dog, then said, "Gotta get crackin' or I won't be ready for Kelsy and Jason. Not to mention Sam." She rolled her eyes. "What time's your big meeting—what was that all about, you laughing about your *big* meeting?"

Ben shook his head. "Another time." She opened her mouth, but he talked over her. "I canceled my *big* meeting. Seems there's this technology—conference calls. Works for me."

"Congratulations." They turned around at the end of the cul-de-sac with the dog in the lead. *"Big* change from Saturday."

"Uh-huh. My CTO may need a pacemaker. I explained we frogs have reps for single-digit IQs, sour tempers, and diminished listening skills."

Doc broke up laughing. They reined in the dog till she recovered. A driver backed out of a driveway, window open, stared at them as if they were insane, then drove on. Inside, Ben gloated. He said, "My CTO suggested I say zip during the conference call and think about staying home for a day or two."

Doc hiccuped. "Seriously?"

"Seriously. The appointment with Nora Karr's at eleven, so going to the city never made sense—except to a workaholic."

"Molly will be ecstatic."

Warmth spread through him as he agreed, pretended interest in the dog for a decade, and kept shifting his gaze to Doc. Each time she caught him, he hemmed and hawed, his chest so tight he couldn't catch his breath. Finally tired of acting like an idiot, he blurted, "Amy's accident? My fault."

Locking eyes with him, Doc let out the dog leash to its full extension. "That's not the way I heard it."

His tongue felt like a knife against the roof of his mouth. "Because no one but me knows she suggested a different—shorter—route home."

Tail wagging, the puppy stopped. He sniffed at something invisible to Ben. "Did you argue about that?" Doc asked softly.

"No." Ben shook his head but didn't feel the movement. "It was our first night out in—in a month. I was enjoying being with her. I wanted more time alone with her. Being a frog, I got ticked, took the long way and . . ."

"It's the *ticked* part that keeps you awake at night, isn't it?" Without missing a beat, Doc answered her own question. *"You* didn't run that red light."

"So everyone's told me, but no one knows I was ticked."

"Being ticked." She snapped her fingers. "Perfect reason to beat yourself up and be miserable the rest of your life."

"Thanks, I needed that." He layered each word with sarcasm.

"You prefer platitudes?" Her eyes blazed.

"Hell no." Why the hell had he thought she'd understand?

"I can't wave a magic wand and absolve you. Get over it."

"I don't expect magic!" he yelled. The dog growled.

She bent down and patted her mutt. "Shhhh." Eyes soft, she studied Ben. "The way I see it? Molly comes before guilt."

His heart thumped. Furious he'd spilled his guts, he snapped, "Thanks for listening."

Her four-legged prince barked. Ben felt like barking back. He said, "For the record, I don't plan on telling Molly about—about the alternate route."

"Makes sense." Doc tossed him the leash, then tucked her arm back through his. Trying not to sound like a wuss, he said, "I do plan on talking to her a lot more about Amy."

"Sounds like a plan." Doc dazzled him with a smile.

He accepted her touch and smile as signs she believed him. Which was almost as good as feeling understood. He'd had enough baring his soul for one day. His stomach clenched. What if she'd had more than enough?

He swallowed, then said, "You still okay with me and Molly at your tree-trimming party tonight?"

"Sure." Her laser smile dazzled him. "Molly's gotta see my frog angel."

"Frog angel?" He wiggled his brows and felt his neck muscles relax. He forced his voice into a casual tone, a plan already forming, his mind racing. "Still taking that nap?"

Her left eye ticked. "Maybe five minutes at lunch."

"Want company?"

"In my office?" Fido turned around and looked at her.

"Why not?" Ben replied playing innocent.

"Why not?" The pulse in her temple pounded.

Ben decided to rattle her a little more. Leaning closer, he whispered, "I bet you'll dream about me."

"I sleep like a baby. I never dream."

The lady protests. "You didn't dream about me last night?"

"Absolutely not." She went from a stroll to a trot.

"Honestly?" He lengthened his stride. Out of the corner of his eye, he caught her watching him out of the corner of her eye. "Careful. Santa's makin' a list. . . ."

CHAPTER 19

"Morning, Em." Risa couldn't help it. She practically *sang* her greeting as she floated through the back entrance.

Em arched a brow and grinned. "Ben Macdonald called."

Two hot spots stung Risa's cheeks. Afraid her eagle-eyed nurse would notice her heart thumping, Risa clutched a plastic shopping bag to her chest. "Did he leave a message?"

"Copied it word for word." Em shuffled the pile of papers on her desk, pulled out a sheet, and held it at arm's length. She cleared her throat. "I'm quoting now."

Risa gritted her teeth. For two cents, she'd grab the paper and—

"I hope it makes sense to you." Em adjusted her glasses.

She's enjoying this. The flash of insight came and went. Em rocked back in her chair and shot Risa another grin. Stone-faced, Risa stood taller, hoping to blank out the snapshot of Ben on the sofa with his arms around her.

"Whoops." Em shuffled papers again. "Wrong message."

What if Ben had called to pass on the tree decorating?

Risa didn't think she could stand that. She had to see him. Be near him. She reached for the discarded message, noticed her hand shaking, and casually let it drop back at her side. "Take your time, Em."

"No need for sarcasm. Love should make us better people."

"Love?" Risa lost control of her voice.

"Don't tell me it's lust," Em sorted more papers. "Not with those stars in your eyes."

"It's . . . your . . . last . . . breath . . . if you . . . don't read me . . . that message . . . this instant." Risa leaned over the desk for emphasis, and the plastic handles slipped from her hands.

Em caught the bag. "Stressed as you are, you ought to think about taking your leave of absence early—"

Risa snatched the damned bag. "Santa's making a list."

"Fine. Fine. Here are the exact words." Em paused, then read, " 'Say I'm using Kelsy's oyster stew recipe for supper.' "

Molly took Ben's bait faster than a shark. He repressed everything he'd ever read or heard about parents bribing their kids. He shamelessly proposed a cookie-baking party at La Ti Da's if Molly would see Nora Karr. As soon as Kelsy okayed using Doc's kitchen, Molly couldn't wait to leave so she could get back and start the baking marathon.

Early fifties, prematurely gray, the pediatrician wasn't Doc, but Molly liked her fine after the older woman explained that La Ti Da was a good friend. Reassured Molly's physical showed zilch and that he should expect perfect lab results as well, Ben shook Nora's hand till she begged for mercy. God, life was wonderful.

So wonderful he burned to share it with Doc. But not by phone. This kind of news demanded face-to-face time. Later, after the tree was trimmed, the kids in bed, the pooch asleep, and Kelsy off with Finn. . . . Listening to Molly chatter about the pros and cons of white or pink frosting, Ben mentally wove graphic details into his fantasy.

Jason greeted them at Doc's kitchen door. "We hafta hurry 'cuz Mommy 'n me're taking cookies to La Ti Da's office."

Caught off guard by a flash of tenderness for Jason's innocence, Ben passed off a box of cookie cutters to Jason, then sidetracked Kelsy in the garage. "Sure you don't need a nap?"

She waved her hand dismissively and unloaded more boxes from the trunk. The dog roamed the garage. "Do you think going to Risa's office will turn Jason against cookies for life?"

"No idea." Which was the truth. "They say kids know when something's going on with their parents. Molly sure knows a lot more about Amy's accident than I give her credit for."

Kelsy squeezed his arm. "You and Molly give me hope."

Stunned, Ben stared. Christ, give him another day or two and he'd be ready for soul-sharing on *Oprah* or *Geraldo* or whoever. He bit his tongue. Excitement now deepened his happiness about Molly. Kelsy piled two remaining boxes into his arms, but blocked the door into the kitchen. "Would you mind if I . . . took a walk . . . later?"

"With Finn?" Ben hoped he was right.

Kelsy rubbed her thumb in the middle of her forehead. "Is his name engraved there, or am I just transparent?"

"Both." Ben laughed. Slowly, picking his words, he said, "How will Jason feel if you leave?"

"Nervous. Insecure. He doesn't know why Sam's meeting us," Kelsy stated bleakly. "Mad. That's how I feel."

"I'd guess Jason picks up on your feelings." Ben Macdonald, guardian of secrets, inspiration to Dr. Brothers.

"As crazy as it sounds, with Finn, I'm fine."

"Then, I say go. Jason will benefit from your walk."

"Of course, going to the park, I won't get what I *really* need." She looked directly at Ben. "Why is sex such a hang-up?"

He laughed. "You ask me—a Montana boy?"

"What else is there to do on those cold winter nights? I mean, forget vibrators since—"

Ben whooped. "Watch it. Don't even mention cows or sheep unless you *really* want to insult me."

"Mommy, what's taking so long?" Jason opened the door, and the pup streaked inside. Kelsy stopped laughing long enough to say, "Mr. Macdonald and I were discussing winters in Montana."

Jason said, "Look what Molly found." He held up an apron with a large Rudolph peering into a gingerbread cookie house.

Ben's heart caught, then he grinned at Molly. "Your mommy bought three of these the year after you were born, sweetheart. We always make our Christmas cookies in these aprons, don't we?"

"Always," Molly said. "It's a *treedition*."

"*Treedition?*" Kelsy echoed.

"That's right . . . because we always eat our cookies when we trim the tree." Ben blinked and set his box down. "It's also a *treedition* for you to tie my apron, remember, Molly?"

"Uh-huh."

She took the apron, giving Ben directions he dutifully followed. Bend his knees. Stick his head through the opening. Hold his arms up. Stand still. Molly doubled the ties around his waist and made a loop in front. "How's that, Daddy?"

"That is perfect." He went down on one knee, took her hand and kissed it. "Not too tight, not too loose. Perfect."

"Ooookay." She threw her arms around his neck, bussing his cheek with a loud smack. "What should we bake first?"

The pup, as if understanding the question and having an opinion, jumped, barked, and chased his tail. The kids' attempts at calming the canine had the opposite effect. Over the din, Kelsy yelled, "Why don't I take him for a walk?"

"Great idea," Ben said. "An hour? Maybe wear him out?"

"This was your mommy's favorite cookbook." Ben opened *The Joy of Cooking*. Misty-eyed, he flipped past several pages—glimpses of Christmases past. He stopped on a butter-smudged recipe. "A friend gave this to us when Mommy and I got married."

"Was I there?" Molly leaned into him.

"No, sweetheart. But Mommy and I were beginning to think about you." Ben kissed the top of Molly's dark head.

"This is Mommy's writing." Amy's neat cursive filled the margin. Ben pulled Molly closer. With shaky fingers, he traced the words and felt their message imprint itself on his heart.

"What does it say, Daddy?"

"It says—" Swallowing, Ben had to stop.

"What's wrong, Mr. Macdonald?"

"Nothing's wrong, Jason. I'm thinking about Molly's mommy."

"She's an angel, you know," Molly said sweetly.

"Uh-huh." Jason tugged at Ben's elbow. "What does this say?" He pointed at the familiar handwriting.

" 'Share these Christmas cookies—with those we love.' "

Doc's smiling face danced in front of Ben. "How about," he said to Molly, his voice husky, "if we make a biiig batch of these cookies? Mommy loved them, and I bet La Ti Da will too."

"La Ti Da likes every cookie in the world," Jason announced.

Somewhere between measuring flour and cutting out the dough, Kelsy reappeared. Flushed, blue eyes sparkling, she danced into the kitchen. The pooch collapsed in the middle of the floor. Kelsy hugged Jason. "Let's call him Lucky Prince—LP for short."

Mildly distracted, Molly and Jason threw out pros and cons as they cut out cookies, then placed the stars and reindeer on cookie sheets. A relaxed Kelsy praised the placement, size, and smell of the culinary masterpieces.

Ben almost convinced himself he wasn't envious of the effect Finn obviously exerted on Kelsy, but images of Doc teased him, fanned his envy into pure lust. Judas Priest, he wanted her. His blood boiled from wanting her. How original. What had she done to him? Messed with his head till he couldn't stop thinking about her. If he didn't know better, he'd swear she'd put a spell on him. That thought sent his heart skyrocketing through the roof of his head. *Christ, get a grip.*

High on butter and sugar fumes, he shoved a cookie sheet into the oven. Heat blasted his face. He slammed the door, stood up, and felt his head swim. Out of the corner of his eye he caught the edges of a fuzzy glow behind Molly. He straightened with a jerk. Kelsy, busy offering Jason and Molly decorating tips, didn't look up. Didn't notice the glow. Didn't notice him, the moron. His heart hammered. Little by little, the glow took form.

A form Ben recognized. Amy. Life-size. Life-like.

The hologram shimmered brighter—like a spotlight. Memories flooded back. The three of them. This same time last year. In their own kitchen. Wearing their

Rudolph aprons. Making, then decorating, Christmas cookies. They'd laughed, sung carols, and dropped hints for Santa. Eager to trim the tree, none of them ever imagined a car running a red light.

"Hold your arms up higher, Daddy." Molly, on tiptoe, struggled with his dangling apron strings, retying them and bringing Ben back to the sugar-filled kitchen.

Arms up, he twisted right, in a complete circle.

No hologram.

Undeterred, he twisted left.

Nothing.

A few dust motes floated on an anemic shaft of sunshine above the sink. Could sunshine explain the warmth filling him?

No, not warmth. Heat. Fire. A white-hot radiance, hotter than the sun. *Some memories last forever.*

Memories with a past and a beginning but no end, for example. Memories . . . for example, of the love of a devoted mother and wife for the child and husband she'd left behind.

Sweet Jesus, Amy wouldn't want him miserable. Why would she? She had loved him. That much he knew. And more.

Amy would want Molly to grow up with happy childhood memories, building on them, living life fully with a man and woman who loved each other as much as they loved her.

CHAPTER 20

At 4:50 P.M., Risa gave up. The faster she worked, the behinder she got. She called Ben. "I've rescheduled Kelsy for six."

The exhale of his breath tightened the band around her chest. "I'll explain to Molly why I won't be home."

"At all?"

"I still have hospital rounds." In her private bath, Risa splashed water on her face. "With luck, I'll drag in about nine. Nine-thirty's more realistic."

"What happened to cheering up Jason?"

Ahhh, the ole guilt button. She scrubbed her face dry. "No reason the rest of you can't trim the tree."

"Any reason your partner can't handle your rounds?"

Risa's throat ached. Ben, more than most men, wasn't used to women whose careers derailed important events like trimming a Christmas tree. She said, "Not a reason, maybe, but a catch."

"A catch?"

The fluorescent lights buzzed, jangling her nerves. She said sharply, "My hospital patients are my responsibility."

"I see."

Obviously not, and she didn't have time or energy to spell it out for him. Molly, however, was a different case. "I'd like to explain to Molly."

"She's in the tub. Primping with Fergie. She's worked hard today. She baked cookies for you all after—" He stopped. She heard him take a deep breath. "Oh, hell. You don't need this from me, do you?"

"Not tonight." Risa folded her towel till it was too fat to fold again.

Em tapped on the door. "Tony de Carlo's waiting."

"Coming," Risa raised her voice, but spoke softly into the cell phone. "I have to go. Three weeks ago we nearly lost this little boy. I'll call Molly before I see Jason."

At 6:23, Risa sent Em home. Kelsy and Jason hadn't arrived yet. Sam could wait. She went into the bathroom, turned on the water, turned it off, then dialed Ben's cell and asked for Molly.

In less than a heartbeat, Molly shrieked, "La Ti Da! You should see all the cookies we baked. I made a biiig, humongous, giant Santa Claus."

"So humongous you can't eat him?"

"I can eat him, but I baked him for you, La Ti Da. We used my mommy's favorite recipe."

"Thank you, Molly." The tears in Risa's throat short-circuited further brilliance.

"You're welcome. Daddy says if I take a nap, I can get up when you come home. Fergie's waiting for me."

Say what? Caught off guard by Amy's cookie recipe, Risa realized a few cylinders had misfired. "Where's Fergie now?"

"In your bed. We had a looong bubble bath." Molly giggled. "LP jumped in with us, but Daddy put him in the backyard."

In the backyard? A bath with Fergie? Had the Macdonalds taken up residence along with Kelsy and Jason?

Molly whispered, "I made you a surprise, La Ti Da. Don't let Jason tell, okay?"

"I don't think he will." Heart aching, Risa glanced at her watch. "I'm sorry, honey. I need to go now. See you soon."

"Bye, here's Daddy."

"Think oyster stew," he said. "Time will fly."

At Risa's suggestion, they sat in a circle in her office. A little too chummy for Kelsy, but acceptable with Risa on her right and Jason on her left. Dickhead across from her looked ridiculous sitting on a kid-sized chair. Hands clenched, Kelsy worried she might knock him backward and scratch the bastard's eyes out.

He adjusted his French cuffs with a flourish. Kelsy automatically glanced at his left hand. Surprise, surprise. No wedding band. She tapped her knee with her own ringless finger. Maybe he'd recycle the two-carat marquis she'd thrown at him on Saturday night. Let him give it to his bimbette.

Eyes narrowed, Kelsy watched him examine gold and platinum cuff links she'd never seen. And she sure as hell had never given him that gold rope bracelet. Fingering it, he sat back, smirking. Mr. Relaxed, clone for stuffed frogs everywhere.

He's up to something. She'd been married to the jerk long enough to read his body language.

The way he sat, for example. One hand positioned inches from his crotch, fingers slightly curved. He'd sat that way the first time they met at a Berkeley football victory party after beating Stanford. Sam strutted around at thirty-six like he was still a big sex god on campus. So damned handsome he'd expected every woman to unzip his pants two minutes after he cast his spell.

Only Kelsy had beaten him at his own game. Or so she thought.

Clearing his throat, Sam tapped his gold Rolex. He spoke to Risa. "We should start. I have to go back to work."

Kelsy snorted, watched Jason's face fall, started coughing, then couldn't stop. Risa informed Sam of the pitcher behind him. Mr. Relaxed rolled his eyes, rose, filled a glass with water, and handed it to Jason. "For your mother."

Furious as Kelsy was, she noticed gleefully that Sam stayed behind his chair till she returned the empty glass to Jason. *So, the man I married isn't a complete moron.*

With the jury still out on this point, Kelsy said brightly, "Why don't you begin, Sam?"

"What's wrong, Daddy?"

Nothing castration won't fix. Enjoying her small triumph—taking the offense—Kelsy glanced at Risa, who shook her head. So Kelsy backtracked. Sort of. "Do you have a cramp, Sam?"

"Yes, yes, I do." He massaged the area around his heart.

Have I always known he was such a bad liar?

"Would a cookie make it feel better, Daddy?"

Oh, God. Kelsy tried not to flinch. Sam *never* ate sugar, said it took away his edge, made him dull. Quietly, she said, "Jason made these and baked them himself, Daddy."

Maybe it was the hushed tone she used, or maybe it was guilt, or maybe Sam had suddenly developed a taste for sweets. Whatever. He sat down and broke a cookie in half. "Someday, Jay, you'll have to teach me how to make these."

"Ooo-kay. When?" Jason moved in between his father's legs.

Tears stung Kelsy's eyelids. Magically, Risa passed her a box of tissues. Sam swallowed. For a second, Kelsy almost believed he was uncomfortable. Then, he said, "Well, buddy, I won't be around much for a while."

Smooth, Dickhead.

Jason placed sugar-coated fingers on one sleeve of Sam's Armani suit. "Do you hafta work, Daddy?"

"Yes—" Swallowing his cookie fast, Sam swiped his sleeve.

Heart hammering, Kelsy edged forward, her hands fisted into tight balls. A head shake from Risa froze her midway to standing. Eyeing her, Sam put a hand in the middle of Jason's back. "But I won't be around because I won't be living with you anymore."

"You won't?" The high-pitched question knifed through Kelsy's heart. She dropped back into her chair.

"No," Sam said. "I'll be living in Los Angeles."

"Where's that?" Jason looked over his shoulder at Kelsy, who said, "Not too far from Disneyland."

"We can go there whenever you visit me," Sam said.

"But I want you to live with us." Jason looked back at Kelsy. This time she bit her tongue. She should have spent some of her hour with Finn rehearsing what to say to Jason.

"Don't you want to live with us any more?" Jason gazed up at his father, who—thank God—was sweating bullets. "Why can't we all live in Disneyland? Together?"

"Because—" Sam threw Kelsy a look of desperation. *Huh.* Apparently, he hadn't rehearsed adequately either. "Because," she said, "Daddy and I are getting a divorce."

A finger squeeze from Risa restrained Kelsy's urge to kill Sam. Risa passed him a tissue, then said, "Do you know what divorce means, Jay?"

"Uh-huh." He looked down at his box of cookies. "It means I've been a bad boy, and Daddy doesn't like me anymore."

Breathing hard, Kelsy shot invisible lasers at Sam's balls. Risa gripped her elbow. Quietly, she said, "If Daddy didn't like you—love you—would he be here right now?"

That's your cue, Dickhead.

"But he hasta go to work tonight."

"Not till you understand I'm not mad at you." Sam scooped Jason up onto his lap, stuffing the box of cookies between his chest and Jason's ribs. "I don't have to go anywhere tonight till you understand I love you."

His attempt at pulling Jason closer met with definite resistance. Kelsy wanted to grab Jason and smother him with hugs. Instinct held her back. Perspiration beaded Sam's forehead. He said softly, "You don't like it when Mommy and I argue, do you?"

Duuh. Kelsy bit down on her tongue.

"No." Jason fingered a cookie. "Sometimes you wake me up."

"Yes, we do. Sometimes you can't even go to sleep." Jason nodded. Unnerved by this public display of their dirty laundry, Kelsy glanced at Risa, who mouthed, "I love you."

"Sometimes, when you leave," Jason confided, "I'm scared you won't ever come home."

The last of Sam's cockiness evaporated, and Kelsy felt almost sorry for him. He kissed Jason on the cheek. "I'm sorry you get scared. That's why Mommy and I're getting a divorce."

Liar. Kelsy pressed her lips together. This was hard enough for Jason without introducing Bimbette.

Jason blinked. "I won't be scared any more, I promise."

His promise dropped on Kelsy's heart like an anvil. Maybe there should be a law against parents arguing.

"I think," Sam said slowly, "the next time we argued and I left, you'd feel scared, but you wouldn't tell us. Not telling would scare you even more."

"Can't you and Mommy stop arguing?" Jason shifted his box of cookies. "Molly 'n me argue, but we make up."

Pent-up tears clogged Kelsy's throat. Blindly, she reached for Risa's hand. Eager to sacrifice her pride to save Jason, she said, "You and Molly are so smart."

He bit his lip. "It doesn't feel good when we're mad."

"No, honey, it doesn't." Kelsy held Sam's gaze. She tried not to think of Bimbette. "But Daddy and I don't really know how to make up anymore."

"Can't you try?" Jason looked from Kelsy to Sam.

Kelsy scrubbed her eyes. "Daddy's moving, remember?"

"Won't you be lonely by yourself, Daddy?"

Kelsy heard her jaw crack and watched Sam for signs of heartache. Never missing a beat, the bastard said, "I'll miss you a lot, Tiger. But I have a . . . new friend who'll help."

Ready to tear his lying tongue out, Kelsy stuffed her hands under her hips. Her mouth took over. "She's moving in with you, isn't she, Sam?"

Wrong question. Jason asked anxiously, "When, Daddy?"

"Not till after Christmas, Buddy." *But?* Mad as she was at her stupidity, Kelsy knew there was a *but*. A beat, then Sam said, "But I won't be here for Christmas."

"How will Santa come down our chimney then?" Jason wailed.

"Oh, he knows you're at my house this year." Risa finally interjected, "so next year, he can find Charlie, Tom, and Harry."

Jason frowned. "Are you sure, La Ti Da?"

"She's positive." Risa wiggled her frog pendant, throwing her voice. "She sent Santa a map, and it has your name on it."

Jason slid off his father's lap, approaching Risa in wide-eyed wonder. "Will you teach me how to do that?"

"Absolutely. How about tonight? I'll teach you and Molly while we trim the tree."

He whirled back to Sam, his little face pinched. "Can you help us trim the tree, Daddy?"

Silence, awkward, uncomfortable. Kelsy bit her tongue. Having Sam there meant no Finn, but she'd live with that disappointment. "We won't start till about ten," Kelsy said to Sam, watching the excuses build in his eyes. He avoided her gaze.

"Yeah, me 'n Molly're takin' naps till La Ti Da comes home."

Steeled for Sam's refusal, Kelsy said, "I can get Jason up around nine if you need to get to the city."

"That might work." His relief embarrassed her, but she willed the muscles in her face to relax. "What about Molly?"

Enlightenment exploded. Kelsy felt like doing a jig. *He's afraid to be alone with me.* "I imagine she'll get up, too."

"It's a really big tree, Daddy. Lots taller 'n you. Taller even than Mr. Macdonald."

"Will Mr. Macdonald be there?"

A big grin got away from Kelsy. Poor baby! After her fit less than seventy-two hours ago, Sam was worried she'd go ballistic if there wasn't an adult referee.

There's always Finn. Kelsy felt a glow in her chest. She said, "Risa should be there around ten. We're going to have one heck of a tree-trimming party."

Jason's eyes glazed with fatigue. He snuggled into Risa. Finally, Sam nodded. "Okay, buddy. See you at nine on the dot."

At the stroke of midnight, grinning from ear to ear, Ben craned his neck and took in the symbols of Doc's Christmases past. The lopsided, clunky, clay ornaments, handmade by patients, contrasted sharply with Amy's exquisite pieces still packed in the attic. Damn, he'd better start weaving ornament stories for Molly.

This realization overshadowed the happiness he'd felt all night. Should he talk about Amy to Molly every day? How gauche would he be for asking Doc her opinion? *She does have her own life.*

Another time. He blurted, "Those two . . . decorations on top . . . make me giddy."

"They are giddifying." On the sofa, Doc laughed, and the sound infused Ben with hot hope. "Have you ever, in your wildest dreams, seen two more gorgeous tree toppers?"

"*Gorgeous* isn't the first word that leaps to mind when I behold that frog angel." Nervous he'd swoop down on her like Dracula, Ben backed away from the tree.

"Oh, pish." Slowly, she looked away from the fire and looked at him. "Giddy *and* narrow-minded?"

He backed into the couch. "Call me Mr. Paradox, but I admit the *frog Santa*, on the other hand—"

"Is far too gorgeous to eat." Doc extended an invisible telescope from her right eye. "Great idea you had hanging it on the tree. Molly loved it."

"Thanks for acting surprised when she gave it to you." He had to stop for breath. "I was sure she'd let the cat out of the bag on the phone."

Doc laid her head back and closed her eyes. "Her frog Santa cookie made my day."

Now or never. He pushed against her legs, parking his butt on the edge of the sofa. "Wanna know what made my day?"

She opened her eyes, but didn't give up more space. "Sure."

Afraid he'd sound pathetic, he didn't thank her, but said, "Nora Karr says Molly's fine."

"Oh, Ben." Doc sat up, pulled her knees up to her chest, and leaned across the barrier. "That's wonderful." The dying fire softened her tear-filled eyes. "I'm so glad. I thought you seemed awfully . . . exuberant all evening."

Since she didn't lower her knees and have her way with his bod, he regrouped before stupidity overthrew logic. "I think Molly helped Jason, don't you?"

"Absolutely." Doc hugged her knees. "I'm still not sure how she distracted Kelsy and Sam when they started snarling at each other, but Molly is one awesome kid. Thanks for letting her spend the night. She's exactly what the doctor recommends for Jason right now."

"When do you think she'll understand she can't sleep with every male who needs her?" Ben rolled his eyes.

Doc giggled. "The day you ship her off to the convent."

"Yeah, well, I'm rethinking the convent thing."

"Really?" Firelight danced in her hair. "Why's that?"

"You're why, of course." Ben flexed his fingers.

No thank you for the compliment, but she licked her lips, a sure sign she was nervous. Like someone who'd never seen fire before, she stared into the flames. She spoke as if in a trance.

"Molly was so proud—showing me Amy's recipe, reading her mother's comments." Doc wiggled her fingers, indicating quotation marks around *reading*.

His heart missed a beat, but the bittersweet twinge barely hurt. "I never realized how many memories she has of Amy."

Doc sighed. "My mother had a talent for mining memories of my dad."

No rebuke of Ben, just admiration for her mother.

"Kelsy told me your mother was great—even during your parents' divorce."

"Mom swears taking Kelsy's folks under her wing helped her survive."

Afraid she'd stop talking, Ben kept his mouth shut, and let Risa continue. "My dad was chronically unfaithful, but Mom gives him full credit for teaching me ventriloquism. In fact, she's the one who encouraged me to practice, practice, practice."

"How long since you've seen him?"

"My fifth birthday. His hot-air balloon crashed six months later."

"Christ. Kelsy didn't tell me that."

"I'm surprised. She slept over at my house a lot. She heard all of Mom's wild and zany bedtime stories about him."

"Your mother sounds like quite a woman."

"She's my hero. She helped me understand a former circus clown and hang glider and hot-air balloonist couldn't be faithful when he didn't know how—anymore than he could be a daddy to someone as 'la ti da' as me."

"I'd like to meet her. Is she coming for Christmas?"

An invisible window crashed down between them. Oh-oh. He'd spooked her. Moved too fast. Forgot his Montana horse-breaking roots. Boldly, he asked, "How long is she staying after you bring Charlie, Tom, and Harry home?"

"Why? You think she's a good nanny candidate?"

The coolness in her tone taunted him, tempted him to kiss her till she gave him a break. "How old is she?"

"Excuse me?"

Amused, Ben said, "Could she mellow out my father-in-law?"

"What?" Risa stared at him as if he'd morphed into an elf.

"Or," Ben got right up in her face, "is she like you? Too independent for a man in her life?" She choked the frog pendant. Her breath—uneven, fast, hot on his face—pleased him. "What is your thing with frogs?"

"It's not a . . . thing."

"No?"

"No." The oboe in her voice box throbbed on the single syllable. Ben wound a strand of her hair around his finger. Heat shot up his elbow, then filled his chest. "I'm ready . . ." he drawled, "for that dream about me."

Her eyes widened. "I can't remember—"

"Santa's listening." He leaned into her, enjoying the quiver of her chin. She sputtered. "Kelsy and Finn should be back any min—"

"You think?" He grinned.

"Lucky Prince won't walk much longer." She released the pendant, and he held the scalding body in his palm.

"We'll hear them." He tucked the frog inside her shirt. "Or not."

CHAPTER 21

Beneath the twinkle of Christmas lights, Risa lay on the sofa up against hard, unyielding male flesh. Ben wanted dream details. Details she had no intention divulging. She knew where that would lead. The same place as celebrating Molly's good health.

Dizzy with lust but determined to shut him up, she interwove a mishmash of story lines from every fairy tale she knew into a dream so hopelessly mixed up, she got lost.

Pretending she didn't notice his hips wedged against her pelvis, she concluded, "Didn't I say my dream made no sense?"

"I disagree. I bet the dance scene comes from Saturday night when we danced in your kitchen."

Physically jolted by the memory of their bodies cemented together, Risa lied. "Uh-uh. That came from *Cinderella.*"

He snapped his fingers. "Then you dreamed the future."

Clueless, frowning, she intoned, "No one sees the future."

He touched her cheek. She turned, blinded by his grin.

"You do. You dreamed about the dinner-dance on the seventeenth."

"Bizzzt." She smacked an imaginary buzzer. "News to me." She'd never let herself imagine, dream, or fantasize such an event.

"For someone who can't really remember, you're damned sure."

"It's coming back to me now." She squinted at the fire. "I definitely didn't dream about you and me dancing at a company—"

"Interesting, veddy interesting, fraulein." He stroked an imaginary goatee. "I didn't say zip about a company party."

"This discussion's insane, 'cuz I'm busy that night."

"Doing what?" Ben countered.

"I can't recall . . . but the date sticks out in my mind."

"Because I asked you on Saturday to go with me," he said.

"Why are you lying?" Did he think he could trick her?

"If I didn't ask you, I meant to." He moved closer.

Her breasts screamed. "Sorry, but I can't read minds."

"Really?" He dragged his fingers across the back of her hand and instantly rendered her mindless. Her whole body shuddered. He grinned—the way the serpent must've leered at Eve.

"Forget mind reading," he said. "Take a wild guess what's on my mind."

"Don't think so." She repressed a shiver as his hand slid up her arm, and his thigh pushed against hers. Forget wild guesses. He wanted her.

"Amy," she croaked.

"Nope. You. You're a Puritan."

A quick shrug covered her flinch, and Risa drew a

kernel of comfort from the insult. "Puritans were virtuous folk."

He arched a brow. "Did you say *folk* or—?"

"The world needs more Puritans." Heart pounding, she glared at him. "Puritans stifle temptations of the flesh, forego wild and crazy sex—especially with two four-year-olds asleep in the house and dog walkers about to return any sec—"

"Did you answer my question?"

"Better a Puritan than a stalker," she said virtuously.

"Stalking has its merits." He grinned, his pupils huge.

"Now you're trying to get a rise out of me."

"I thought I was the one we wanted a rise out of."

Flushing, Risa snapped, "Off the sofa. You're crowding me."

"Good. Never leave a Puritan any wiggle room." He pressed his hips into her, and she wanted to smack him, tell him the bantering and touching were wrong, warn him he wouldn't stand a chance remaining faithful to Amy if she ripped his clothes off.

"Let's talk about Amy," he interrupted the litany of virtuous protests flooding Risa's brain. "She wouldn't want me to go to this party alone and be miserable."

"She wouldn't want you to go—" *With someone who wants your body.* Risa clamped her mouth shut. Where was her Inner Puritan?

Ben snapped his fingers under her nose. "I hear the little wheels turning in your head."

"Then listen up." Through sheer determination, she met his gaze, held it, and pretended she'd raised the invisible curtain between them. She pitched her voice low, throaty, sincere. "I'd be miserable. My mind would be on Charlie, Tom, and Harry." *And everyone staring at the whale in black sequins you brought.*

"Yada, yada, yada." He twirled a circle in the air with his index finger. "Bull." He got right in her face, and his warm breath raised the little hairs at the nape of her neck. Her Inner Puritan swooned. "You won't go because you're afraid."

"Afraid?" She struggled to breathe.

"That, unlike Cinderella, you won't escape."

"That's the silliest—" Like in a movie, the fire leaped.

"Truest, most honest—"

"Ridiculous, egotistical—" Her heart thundered.

"Sexiest, scariest, most exciting fantasy you can imagine." His smirk dared her to lie. Which she would have done, but she couldn't catch her breath.

"It's not like we're both virgins." He winked, and she felt like an idiot—dangerous to herself and others. "It's not like we're hurting anyone."

"What about Molly?" Risa ran the words together.

"She adores you. She'd like nothing better than—"

"You staying faithful to her mother. You promised you'd always love Amy." Risa's fingers, toes, and internal organs felt like live electrical wires.

"Loving Amy doesn't have a thing to do with taking you to the party and then having sex with you after—"

Refusing to cry, Risa blinked. "Exactly."

Ben's hands came up like a traffic cop. "Hold on. That didn't come out the way I meant."

"I understand." Risa kicked herself for sounding so small.

"No, you don't. I asked you to marry me—"

"Do not go there. Please." She massaged the spot above her left breast, caught him looking at her, and laid her hand casually on the back of the sofa.

"Fine. But stop trying to wiggle off the hook. I won't take no on going to the dance. After that . . . its your call."

"That's not fair." She ignored her whine. "I don't want the role as your conscience. You promised you'd be faithful to Amy. Why should I have to remind you of that pledge?"

He sat up with a jerk, looking stunned—as if she'd accused him of kicking puppies or pinching babies. His reaction irritated her. She didn't even try to rein in her mouth. "What is it with men and not keeping their pants zipped?"

"Are you including me in that generalization?"

"Truism," she snapped. "Show me a man who believes monogamy is natural."

"It sure felt *natural* to me. What feels weird is whatever's going on with you. Are you confusing me with your ex?"

"Hardly." She sniffed.

"How about Sam?"

"Absolutely not." She rolled her eyes.

"Then that would leave your father."

"My—? I never figured you for an armchair shrink."

"And I never figured you for an armchair shrinkee."

"Armchair shrinkee?" She laughed, but he didn't shut up.

"I'm not your father. I don't fuck and run." Risa winced, but Ben took her hand, laid it over his heart, and looked her straight in the eye. "I will *always* love Amy."

Risa's heart banged against her ribs. Okay, okay. *This* she got. She swallowed, then said brightly, "What's left to say?"

Declare he wanted to raise three sons and a golden retriever mix was a good start. Or, at least say that, in addition to having the hots for her, he liked her a lot, knew the color of her eyes and understood if she went to bed with him once, she'd *never* leave it. Never put her sons first. Never . . .

"Hellooo?" He leaned into her, and she knew if he kissed her, she'd give in, say yes to the dance, have sex with him right here if he wanted, forget Jason and Molly, Kelsy and Finn, and her own Inner Puritan.

"What?"

He ignored her impatience and covered her mouth with his. His tongue was feverish, deliberate. Mindless, she arched under him.

"To set the record straight," he panted between moans, "I didn't take a vow of eternal celibacy."

She sighed. He stopped talking. Finally. Didn't he know the serpent didn't confuse Eve with logic? How could she consider moral dilemmas when her nerve endings approached meltdown? His grunts and other primal cries of pleasure thrilled her far more eloquently than talk, talk, talk. Or think, think, think. Which she gave up when he skimmed the hollow of her throat.

Making a few primal cries herself, she clutched a handful of his hair and pressed her breasts into his chest. His curse filled her with almost as much pleasure as his erection. *He wasn't kidding about celibacy.* He grazed the pulse in her left wrist and sent her heart rate into acute fibrillation.

"One night, that's all," he whispered. "Yes or no?"

A soft woof, followed by shushing, then giggles at the back door came to Risa from another planet. She struggled to sit up.

"Hold on," Ben said. "I'll tell them to come back in five—"

Risa shoved him. "Are you insane? Get up." In a loud, phony voice, she called, "Hey, guys."

Kelsy called, "Here comes your prince, in need of hugs."

Ben yelled, "Let him loose. I'm in a hugging mood."

"Up." Risa squirmed, but Ben didn't budge. "Yes or no?"

"All right, all right. Yes."

The click of toenails on the tile distracted Ben momentarily and bought Risa a deep breath. Her Inner Puritan sniffed, but Risa consoled herself. She wasn't really lying.

It was a woman's prerogative to change her mind.

* * *

Fifteen minutes later, thinking he might learn a thing or two from Fast Finn about sweeping women off their feet and into bed, Ben suggested coffee at his house.

"Let me leave a message for my mother." Finn pulled his cell phone off his belt. "She worries."

Ben's jaw dropped. Shrugging, Finn said, "I can't afford a dog house on my salary. Ma says I do her a favor living with her."

A light drizzle made standing in the driveway more stupid than macho—even for an ex-cowhand from Montana, but apparently not for a hot young cop. Ben remembered nights like this. He and Amy had steamed up the windows in his ancient Chevy pickup. God, that felt like a lifetime ago.

Pulled by the past, he climbed into his pickup. Sooner or later, Maryann would call him. He entered his voice mail password and heard the area code for his only message. His stomach lurched. Despite the roar in his ears, Ben flinched anyway at the guttural bark he knew so well.

A greeting didn't occur to his father-in-law. "You and I need to talk," he stated. "Call me tomorrow at the Fairmont."

"Ho, ho, ho, and a very Merry Christmas to you, my fine sir." Ben jabbed the delete button and stared out the window. No airline, flight number, or time of arrival. Par for the course—or at least the course Quint Ferguson drove with total confidence.

Finn spoke through the cracked window. "Sorry I took so long. Ma wanted details. She can hardly wait to meet Kelsy after all this time. Is everything going my way or what?"

"Let me get this straight." Finn settled back in a comfortable kitchen chair with a third cup of coffee in a room the size of Texas. Ma would kill for the acres of dark green granite counters. "Your father-in-law—a penniless cowhand who married the boss's daughter—hates your guts because you didn't have a penny to your name and married *his* daughter?"

"Bingo." Ben laced his coffee with cream.

Sure there was more to the story, Finn asked, "Did he love his wife?"

"As much as I loved Amy."

"Why didn't he send you to an orphanage after your mother died?" Finn opened the sugar bowl and removed a single cube.

"Carolyn Ferguson had a big heart, but Amy could've had him standing on his head 24/7 if she'd wanted. Luckily, she wanted me at the ranch, too. We were both eight."

Finn exhaled. "I have a hunch that after Dickhead, Kelsy's parents won't think too much of me as a son-in-law."

"What if they get to know you?" Ben stared into his cup.

The cop in Finn wondered what he saw, but he said, "Maybe if I earn Dickhead's big bucks, they'll get to know me."

Ben straightened with a jerk. "I never gave a damn that Quint Ferguson didn't know me or appreciate me. In the end, I got the girl."

Finn gave Ben a high five. "It'll be great if Kelsy's folks don't treat me like something they stepped in, but I'm marrying her no matter what." He slugged back his coffee. "A couple of kids may help."

"Don't count on it." Ben grimaced. "You may get lucky, but my father-in-law still thinks he calls the shots when it comes to Molly. As soon as she mentions Risa—well, let's just say the shit will hit every fan from here to Missoula."

Finn made a leap. "He blames you for killing his daughter."

"Who else?"

"The drunk driver?" Finn forgot his cop voice—neutral, nonjudgmental—and let regret for Ben Macdonald come through. "Of course," he added conversationally, "you've gotta believe that yourself."

"Uh-huh. Sounds vaguely familiar." Ben shrugged and then pinched the bridge of his nose. "Doc's of the opinion I have more important reasons for feeling guilty."

"I'd pay attention if I were you. Frankly, I'm a lot more worried about her blessing." Finn curled his fingers for quotation marks. "Kelsy's folks will come around. Or not."

Guts twisting, Finn added, "This is where you give me a clue what Doctor La Ti Da thinks about me and Kelsy."

Ben's jaw dropped, then he laughed. "What a pair. I bring you home to pump you on romancing women and you come to pump me on impressing a woman immune to your charms."

"Hey, we're guys." Finn shrugged. "Here's my two cents: don't assume you're moving too fast with Doc. There's always another drunk driver and another red light."

"La Ti Daaaa?"

"Gobactabedjay!" Kelsy buried her head under the sheets.

Head aching, Risa rolled over in the other twin bed. "Kel!"

Kelsy buried deeper into her cocoon. Jason wailed louder. Risa inhaled, opened her eyes, read 6:30 A.M. on the clock radio, and moaned a low, piteous moan. Kelsy didn't make a peep.

"Lucky Prince needs to make pee-pee, La Ti Da."

Holy Harriet, she'd forgotten she owned a dog. Her head felt like a bowling ball. Eyes squinted to slits, she zeroed in on the door and shuffled into the hall.

"Lucky Prince is crying," Jason announced in a tone that left no doubt Risa risked her status as Exalted One. "He's just a baby, you know."

"I'm sorry, Jay." Risa didn't know if she was apologizing for her neglect or for the new reality Jason now faced as a child of divorce. Maybe both. Jeopardizing balance, she bent down. "Could I have a hug, please? Then we'll take Lucky Prince out."

A second's hesitation, then Jason threw his arms around her neck. Awed by his forgiveness, Risa whispered, "I'm glad Mommy 'n you're living with me and Lucky Prince for awhile."

"Me, too, but I wish Daddy—" Jason squeezed Risa's neck tighter, and her heart caught. Certain she knew the answer, she asked, "What's your wish, Jay?"

A bark drifted up the stairs. Jason cocked his head, then ran his words together. "I wish Daddy still lived with us."

Resentment at Kelsy flared. Teeth gritted, Risa said nothing. Jason filled the silence. "Since it's Christmas . . . do you think my wish will come true, La Ti Da?"

Not even if I see a camel on the front lawn. Sorrow for her godson tempted Risa to lie. Or at least duck his question by throwing out a few platitudes. She gazed into his hopeful eyes, took a breath, and went with her conscience.

"No, honey. I don't think so." Her conscience gave her an earful. *But you think Ben Macdonald will suddenly decide he wants three more kids and a new wife in his life.*

Swallowing hard, Jason blinked. "I don't think so either." In the next breath, he asked, "Is Los Angeles like Heaven? Molly says no, but I'm scared I'll never see Daddy again."

The quaver in his voice tightened Risa's chest with a mixture of love and sadness and—surprisingly—optimism. Praise Jupiter, he wasn't numb, or pretending his world hadn't been knocked off its axis. On the other hand, he wasn't hysterical.

Cautiously, she said, "I promise Los Angeles isn't Heaven. It's a big city. Remember Mommy said it's near Disneyland. We can go there—"

"Can we come back?"

Puzzled, she said, "Absolutely."

" 'Cuz you can't come back from Heaven, right?"

Her heart stalled, but she recovered, saying, "I think it's more like we wouldn't want to come back from Heaven, but we'd definitely want to come back from Los Angeles."

Downstairs, Lucky Prince howled mournfully. Jason jerked around. The floor tilted, and Risa pitched against his sturdy body. *What'd you expect, mixing lame humor and awful theology?*

Jason wobbled under her weight but kept his footing. He asked, "Why does Daddy want to live in Los Angeles?"

Risa propped her chin in one hand and massaged her burning stomach with the other. *To follow the circus,* Mom had said, omitting references to Daddy's girlfriends.

"His work is there," Risa said. *As if work explains anything.*

Frowning, Jason opened his mouth, but Risa plowed ahead. "Now, you know what I wish?"

After a beat, Jason shook his head. Taking the risk of falling on her butt, she pulled him closer, then whispered directly into his ear. "I wish you could remember the divorce isn't your fault. Daddy and Mommy love you. More than anything, they want you to be happy."

A long, miserable howl widened Jason's eyes. He said accusingly, "Lucky Prince isn't happy."

Instinct told her they'd reached Jason's limit for psychotherapy. Bummed she couldn't grant his wish, she said, "Let's go make him happy then."

With her head coming apart cell by cell, and with Jason the Deafenator screaming at the top of his lungs, Risa almost missed the doorbell—but Molly's shriek alerted her to Ben's arrival.

Face shining, eyes bright, Kelsy stuck her head into the hall. "That's not Finn at the door, is it?"

"No, I believe it's my worst nightmare."

Barefoot, dry-mouthed, tasting of morning breath, Risa padded down the stairs like an old woman. If Ben gave her one bit of trouble when she told him the dance was off, she'd breathe on him. Then he'd beg her to forget about going.

"He can't change my mind," she muttered. Dancing was sex standing up. One short dance in her kitchen, and they'd talked about condoms, for cryin' out loud. No company dance.

She bypassed the coffee pot and slipped outside. Hit in the face by a stiff breeze, she gawked at the chaos on her lawn. Lucky Prince chased Jason across the damp grass. Stumbling over the hem of the Kermit sweatshirt, Molly reeled in hot pursuit. Ben waved in every direction, issuing commands like a demented football coach.

Worried a few neighbors might still be asleep, Risa clapped, then whistled. The screams and barks, encouraged by Ben, went up in volume. Ticked by his slackadaisical attitude, Risa ventured off the deck. Once she was in his line of vision, she waved an imaginary flag. He grinned. "Join the fun."

Did fun include killing him? "I have hospital rounds."

"How about a bowl of my famous oatmeal? Eat and talk."

"It's a twenty-minute drive to the hospital."

He gave Molly a rolling signal. She fell down, rolling past Lucky Prince. "See the energy oatmeal breakfasts give you."

Another time, another place, Risa might've enjoyed his obvious pride. "Rolling on the ground's not on my agenda today."

"Too bad."

He grinned and looked so sexy Risa snapped, "You and I need to talk."

"How about over a cup of coffee? I'll whip some cream—"

"Whip some cream?" Her voice rose. What planet did the man inhabit? "I don't even have time to smell black coffee."

"Starbucks Christmas blend?" He waved at Jason.

"What's wrong with you?" she demanded.

"Not a thing." He beamed at her like Santa on Prozac.

"Wonderful. Then you're in charge of Lucky Prince, right?"

"Your wish is my command." He bowed deeply.

"Look at Daddy," Molly screeched. "He's a prince."

Daddy's nose touched his knees. "Stop that," Risa hissed, her face on fire, her heart fluttering, her brain faltering. "I'll get dressed." *Careful. Don't mention taking a shower.*

"Sounds good." He grinned slyly.

"I'm not taking a shower," she blurted. He raised a brow. Close to choking, she said, "I'll be ready—"

His grin mocked her. Her arms went weak. God, how she'd love to smack that smirk off his face. "I'll be down in five minutes. Our talk won't take long."

Not long enough for discussion. Her decision was final.

"As you wish." He straightened, throwing her a smile that raised the little hairs on her neck.

Molly, her hair almost as wild as Risa's, her face grimy but glowing with health, tugged at Risa's hand. Nervous as she was, Risa hunkered down. Molly planted a wet kiss on her cheek, then asked, "Can I see your ball dress?"

"My—my *ball* dress?" Risa shot a death glare at Ben.

"Uh-huh." Molly nodded. "Can I go with you when you buy your glass slippers?"

"Glass—" Risa felt a deep neuron fire. *He'd told her.*

"What color's your dress?" Molly prodded.

"I don't have one. Or shoes. So I may not—"

"No problem." Ben put his oar in. "Ten days till the

ball. Plenty of time for shopping. Shoes, a dress. The whole enchilada."

"The whole enchilada?" Molly shouted, her face blindingly luminous.

"The whole enchilada?" Ambushed, Risa stiffened and listened for the sound of a trap snapping shut.

"Can I go shopping with you, La Ti Da? Mommy 'n me loved shopping."

Snap.

CHAPTER 22

Silence and two yellow Post-It notes on the door to the garage greeted Risa downstairs thirty minutes later. Furious at Ben, she skimmed Kelsy's neat cursive. *I'll do your make-up for the ball.*

"Ha, ha." Jaw clenched, Risa slid under the wheel and skewered Ben's note to the mirror. So he'd told Kelsy, then cut and run. "By next month," she told her reflection, "since Molly's fine, he'll be working seventy hours a week. I'll be enjoying breakfast in the park with my sons."

Oncoming traffic was endless, so she read Ben's note aloud. "Call me *ASAP.* At home. Very important."

Sunshine flooded through the windshield, and Risa felt her scalp ignite. *Very important?* So important he didn't bother signing his note? What, he figured she'd *know* it was from him? If he'd had something *very important* about Molly on his mind, why all the chitchat about coffee with whipped cream? He thinks I'm an idiot. He wants to discuss—what else?—that stupid dance.

Unless there's a problem with one of Molly's tests. Risa eased onto Cielo Vista Avenue, then pulled to the curb because her hands were so slick on the wheel. Reaching for her cell phone, she stopped. There was nothing wrong with Molly that having Ben around wouldn't fix. He'd acted too dopey for there to be a problem. Plus, Nora had promised to call if the test results were abnormal. *So here we are*, Risa thought, *back at that stupid dance.*

By noon, she'd seen all her morning patients and started on the endless paperwork. Em stopped at the door. "Tuna sandwich. With or without chips?"

The thought of greasy potato chips turned Risa's stomach upside down. Holy Heloise. She crossed her fingers. Maybe I'm coming down with the flu.

"Soup." She ignored Em's frown. "Preferably vegetable, but any kind's fine."

"Trying to take a few pounds off before the seventeenth?"

"Whaaat?" Risa jerked upright like a puppet on a string.

Em shook her hips like a middle-aged hula dancer. "Ben told me about the dance—or *the ball*, as Molly calls it. Says you and she are going shopping—"

Shaken, Risa sputtered. "Shopping isn't in my DNA."

Em patted her short, sleek haircut. "Want the name of my hair stylist? As long as you're buying a new dress—"

"I'm *not* buying a new dress," Risa said through her teeth.

"That's not what Ben says," Em chanted.

"What's he know? How many times have you talked to him?"

"He knows Molly's happier than he's seen her in a year. We've talked six times—make that seven—since you didn't call him back. Which I think is rude."

The rebuke stung. Risa snapped, "I think it's more rude to take personal phone calls when I'm with patients."

"Well, you're not with patients now."

CRACK! The pencil Risa held broke. "Thank you for

that, Sherlock. Can I expect my soup during my life-time?"

"Your wish is my—"

"Shut up." Risa tossed a stuffed frog at Em's back.

"Want his phone number?" Em called. "Or do you know it?"

"I want a little respect."

"That'll keep you warm at night." Em shut the door.

Teeth gritted, Risa picked up the top file and stared at her notes. The more she thought about Ben's arro-gance, the faster her pulse raced. The guy didn't have a clue. Not a clue. She grabbed the phone, dialed his number, but hung up after one ring. No blistering his ears till she had a plan. She'd agreed to go to the dance. Now, she'd changed her mind. Why?

She tapped the desk with her pen. The truth wouldn't work. He'd never buy she was protecting Molly, because she didn't buy that lie herself. He'd say it's just a dance.

No reason needed, she decided, for *why* she'd changed her mind. She punched the intercom. "Em? My soup?"

Silence.

Nurse Em must really be miffed, leaving without a heads-up.

"She'll get over it." Risa picked up a folder.

The phone said, "Call the guy."

Risa clapped her hand over her mouth. Talking to oneself. The second biggest perk of ventriloquism. The first was—

The door to her office flew open and slammed against the wall. A sixty-something, cleanly shaven, flint-eyed, square-shaped man charged into her office to the give-me-no-shit clunk of cowboy boots. He dropped a Styro-foam cup on her desk. "Vegetable soup. Not the meal I'd expect for a hussy."

Flattered, Risa put her hand over her fluttery heart. "Is hussy worse than slut?"

He narrowed his bullet-gray eyes and leaned over

her desk on his knuckles like an alpha baboon she'd once seen in the zoo. "You like Jezebel better?"

"Not particularly." Where was Em?

"Molly seems to think you walk on water, *La Ti Da.*"

"Only on Monday, Wednesdays, and Fridays." Hands shaking, Risa pried the lid off the cup. "Since today's Tuesday, I'm afraid I have to eat. Fainting usually scares my patients."

"You're nothing like my daughter." His flinty eyes blazed.

"I'm sure you're right." Risa took a sip of soup and burned her tongue, but made no sound of distress. Should she call security?

"On second thought," he curled his lip. "If you're crazy about Ben Macdonald, you're exactly like Amy."

Soup slid down the wrong way. Risa coughed.

"What's his appeal? Those big cow eyes?"

Risa blotted her mouth. "I'm a city girl. I've never been closer to a cow than a gallon of whole milk at Safeway."

"So why does Molly think you're the cat's pajamas?"

Cat's pajamas? Where did this guy live? The stuffed frog on her desk spoke, "Molly's taken because I can throw my voice."

"Huh! Pretty piss-poor trick compared to singing like an angel, wouldn't you agree?"

Without thinking, Risa almost nodded. She shrugged instead.

"Molly wants to learn ventriloquism." His contempt dripped on *ventriloquism.* "Apparently, you're teaching her."

"Ventriloquism isn't immoral," Risa countered.

"What if it ruins her voice? It didn't occur to her idiot father she's too young, but aren't you a doctor?"

Locking eyes with Gramps, Risa counted to eleven. She said in her no-nonsense doctor's voice, "I first threw my voice about her age . . . during a pretty traumatic time in my—"

"Not as traumatic as your mother getting killed."

"No." Risa pinched the inside of her elbow. She'd never admit how much it hurt knowing Daddy was alive but never called or saw her in the six months before he was killed.

"He killed her, you know." Risa shook her head, and her uninvited visitor's eyes lit up. "Didn't tell you that, did he, my son-in-law, the bastard?"

"As a matter of fact, he did." The roof of her mouth hurt when she spoke, but damned if she'd give Gramps any satisfaction. "I told him to get over it. For Molly's sake, you should, too."

"I will—when Molly's living with me."

Risa's heart clutched. "Is that what Amy would want?"

"She sure as hell wouldn't want Molly calling you 'Mommy.' "

"You sure as hel—heck don't have to worry about that, Gramps."

"Risa?" Em's voice came through the private back door. "The front door's locked. I can't get in."

"Hold on." Risa pushed her chair away from the desk. Gramps leaped in front of the door.

Risa stood. What was he going to do? Slug her?

"You *are* a big lady." He raked her from the waist up. "Nothing—"

"Yes, yes. Nothing like Amy. I know. And you're nothing like Molly. Which makes it easy to call security—"

"Risa? Are you on the phone?" Em jiggled the door handle.

"She's busy," Gramps barked, never taking his eyes off Risa. "You weren't expecting me, were you?"

"Hard to expect someone you thought lives in Montana."

"I told Lover Boy this mornin' I was comin' to see you. I figured he'd warn you. Camp out here. Be ready to protect you."

Lights flashed, bells clanged. Seven phone calls in four hours were now explained. "I believe Ben knows I can protect myself."

"Humph. A women's libber. I shoulda guessed."

"Don't worry, I don't break old men's balls—unless they stand between me and letting my nurse into the office."

Palms up, he said, "You *are* going to that dance, right?"

"In a word, no." Risa's throat closed. She willed her voice not to crack. "Doesn't that just make your day?"

Shaking his head, he said, "In a word, no."

"What?" Risa cocked her head at Gramps.

"You heard me." He sighed, worked his mouth, finally said, "I told you. Molly thinks you walk on water. She's so excited about this damned dance—the *ball,* she keeps saying—" He scrubbed his face. "She's had a bad year. The idiot works—"

"How'd you handle your wife's death? Did you work more or less?" *Why are you defending Ben?*

"Amy wasn't three years old," he thundered.

"Risa?" Em's voice went up. "I'm going for security."

"It's okay, Em. I'm fine."

Quietly, Risa said to Gramps, "How old was she?"

At first she thought he wouldn't answer. Mouth tight, he barely moved his lips. "Eleven," he muttered. *He'd make a great ventriloquist.*

"That's probably an adult in Montana, right?"

He straightened with a jerk, and Risa said immediately, "Sorry. That was below the belt."

His shrug seemed automatic, devoid of anger. "I'm surprised the idiot didn't tell you this. He was pretty fond of my wife."

"He said she had a big heart and Amy was her daughter."

"Yes, and he was an ungrateful little bastard—his no-good father's son. After Carolyn died, he turned Amy against me. *My* daughter poured her heart out to him. Said he'd lost two mothers and understood her grief better than I ever would."

A wave of pity for the old man washed through Risa. She heard his jaw crack. As if reading her thoughts of touching him, he took a step backward. "I'd've kicked his ass off the ranch, but Caro felt sorry for him. Left instructions in her will. He could work and live on the place as long as he wanted."

Inside Risa's head, curiosity warred with Ben's right to privacy. Gramps had no such conflict. He grimaced. "My biggest mistake was sending Amy to boarding school. She wrote him every day, called him every other day, and spent every waking minute of every vacation day—and night—with him. She became convinced they were star-crossed lovers."

Dry-mouthed, Risa finally swallowed the lump in her throat. "He still loves her, you know."

"Then why the hell's he sniffing around you?" The raw pain in his tone checked the fury flashing through Risa.

The truth hurt, but the old cowboy wouldn't learn the answer from her. She said, "What a way with words, Gramps. I assume you've made your final point?"

"Never assume," he countered. "Assuming makes an ass of—"

"Okay, okay. What's your next insult—your *last* insult?"

His mouth twisted. "What is it with Ben Macdonald and women? My wife, my daughter? Molly, you? I know damned well his sex appeal didn't hook Carolyn—or Molly."

Amy and I, on other hand . . .

Quickly, Risa said, "It's pretty obvious life has kicked him in the teeth a few times." How had she known that in the Starbucks parking lot before they spoke a word to each other? "Maybe it's because he doesn't whine or complain," she hurried to add.

"Yeah. Caro said the same thing. I'll grant he worked hard. Never asked for favors. But"—he waved his hand as if batting a fly—"none of that matters. What matters is that Molly loves him. She says you make him laugh—" He took a deep breath. "She says you make him laugh the way 'Mommy did.' "

Air whooshed out of Risa's gaping mouth. She snapped it shut. Eyes stinging, she thought of Molly laughing with Lucky Prince, with Jason, with Risa at Fergie's throaty voice. Images of Ben laughing blurred together.

"All the women in your family got that big-hearted gene," she said at last.

"Risa? Why's it so quiet in there?"

"Holy Hannah. I forgot Em." Risa pushed past Gramps.

Red-faced, Em huffed in and zeroed in on Gramps. "You called from the lobby and said the elevator wasn't working—"

"I lied." Gramps took advantage of Em catching her breath. "I took a chance you'd leave and wouldn't lock your door."

"Well," Em fumed, "that is sneaky." She stared at Risa and demanded, "Why haven't you thrown this old coot out?"

Good question. "He's Ben's father-in-law."

Em sniffed. "You made Molly cry after she said she wanted to stay here for Christmas."

"Jesus Christ!" Gramps bellowed. "Another member of the Ben Macdonald Fan Club."

"You'd just love to know why, wouldn't you?" Em shot back.

At which point, Risa stepped in. "I heard the front door."

"Really?" Em tossed her head. Risa felt her cheeks grow warm. "The Old Coot here locked it, but I can take a hint."

No diva of stage or screen had ever made a grander exit. Risa managed to wait till Em closed her door be-

fore laughing. Gramps growled, "I suppose she's a libber, too."

"Whatever she is, is not why you came here, right?"
Risa slugged back the cup of cold soup. "Frankly, I'm
confused to the point of being mystified *why* you came."

"If you'd stop distracting me—"

Risa opened her mouth in protest, but realized she'd
get more satisfaction from banging her head on the
desk and shut up.

Gramps proceeded. "I came here to ask you—beg
you—convince you—to go to that damned dance. Not
only did Molly get her mother's big heart, she got
Amy's romantic streak as well."

"Meaning?" Still confused, Risa lifted her brows.

"Meaning, if you don't go, it will break Molly's heart."

A little melodramatic, but the hard glint in his gun-
metal eyes sent a shiver down Risa's back. Eyeball to
eyeball with him, she didn't blink. *Damned if she'd let him
intimidate her.*

"Have you ever heard of give and take?" She cocked
a brow.

"Bull—" The curl of his lip offended Risa more than
the unsaid cuss word.

"Your point being?" he growled.

"My point being, I'll consider going to the dance—
so as not to break Molly's heart—if you'll consider ne-
gotiating."

They regarded each other, neither blinking. "So
what're you waiting for—Christmas?"

"Your attention," Risa shot back. "Here's the deal . . ."

CHAPTER 23

Halfway through the lunchtime strategy meeting Ben's secretary slipped into the conference room, made eye contact, passed like a shadow behind the speaker, and palmed him a message.

Dr. Taylor available for CB before 1 P.M. Time stamped 12:50 P.M.

His heart kicked up. Eight minutes. Plenty of time. He didn't spare a thought for the presenter. Ignoring the curious stares, Ben pushed his chair back. Heart pounding, he jogged into his office across the hall.

"Your father-in-law left ten minutes ago," Em told him right away. "What a piece of work."

"What'd he want?" Palms sweaty, Ben glanced at his watch. Answers eluded him because Em asked. "You ask me? Risa said call you, so . . . I've never seen her so cranky."

"My esteemed father-in-law brings out the worst in us."

"I feel like a bad wind blew through here," Em groused.

Then, having drop-kicked Ben's hopes into the gutter, she transferred his call. Time dragged out. Ben's anxiety spiked. 12:55. *Thank you, Quint.* Too antsy to sit,

Ben stayed on his feet, punched the speaker on, then opened the top drawer.

A silver-framed picture of Amy and Molly lay faceup. His chest tightened. Behind closed doors after the accident, he'd removed everything from the drawer. Hands shaking, he'd laid the picture inside. Then, he opened his door and got down to work. An open-door CEO, he couldn't risk people coming in, seeing the picture on his desk, and expressing their condolences.

Not if he intended to use work as his therapy.

The speaker crackled. Doc said clearly, "I gather the Oracle of Pediatrics has spoken."

"True, but I'm still not *enlightened.*"

"Maybe I can shed more light at dinner. Can you and Molly join us tonight—if I persuade Kelsy to cook?"

"Volunteer me to help." He tried to sound casual. "Kelsy and I have to talk. I left Molly with her earlier today."

"Still no word from Maryann?"

"No, I may rent a dogsled and go up there if it keeps snowing." Her chuckle swelled his ego, but he checked the impulse to show off for her. Better not push his luck. He said, "I hope you don't mind about Molly."

"Hey, Lucky Prince and Jason need lots of attention right now. They're fortunate Molly wants to hang out with them. Big-hearted females are always in demand."

You would know. "For the record, do you think I'm taking advantage of Kelsy's big heart? She's watching Molly four days a week. Till Maryann emerges from hibernation. I'll take care of Molly and Jason on Wednesdays. You see a problem with that?"

"Do I think you're exploiting Kelsy?" Doc laughed. "Exploiting Kelsy's like catching lightning in a jar. I think she gets the better deal. I assume Finn's day off is Wednesdays."

"Bingo."

"Good thing he's young." She laughed again.

Ben laughed too, but his heart wasn't in it. He glanced at the picture and couldn't believe how much he wanted Doc's approval. Quint, on the other hand . . . Fury squeezed Ben's gut. That old man had ignored Molly's clean bill of health and actually demanded she go to Montana till Maryann returned.

Teeth clenched, Ben said, "My father-in-law doesn't like the arrangement."

"Did he offer to stay here and take care of Molly?"

"Jesus, don't even think that. I'd rather let Molly play in traffic first." Was she going to tell him what Quint wanted?

"What if he stayed but Kelsy was chief pooh-bah?"

"You're kidding, right?" Ben heard his jaw crack.

"No."

"First, there is no chief pooh-bah but Quint Ferguson. He's a legend in his own mind. Second, Jason would drive him nuts. Third, he hates dogs. Fourth—"

"Think about it," she said. "You never know."

Risa eased the Volvo into the garage, cut the engine, and watched the white limo park behind her in the driveway. The driver dimmed the headlights a second before the kitchen door flew open. Jason and Molly descended like miniature barbarians accompanied by their faithful barking canine. They screamed her name and tugged at her, talking over each other. Lucky Prince jumped, landed a lick on her chin, then jumped higher. *Home, sweet home.* Sparing a thought about sanity, Risa checked behind her.

"Who's that?" Jason pointed at the limo.

"A surprise for Molly. Why don't you go with her?" Risa gave the kids a little push, but held onto the pup.

Molly threw her a look. The stone frog at the corner of the house said, "Go on, Molly."

"It's okay." Jason took her hand, and they got almost

to the front fender before Quint Ferguson stepped out of the limo.

Now for the fun. Stomach fluttering, Risa entered the kitchen. "Guess who's coming to dinner?" she called.

By the time Ben finished his first glass of French champagne—a gift from Quint Ferguson—he relaxed enough that Risa stopped worrying about calling 9-1-1. He and Kelsy had outdone Martha Stewart in the food department. Miniature pizzas for the kids. Bite-sized quiches, crab toast, and tiny Vietnamese imperial rolls complemented the champagne. Quint looked mildly stunned listening to Molly describe how she'd made the frog Santa tree-topper. "I used Mommy's favoritest cookie recipe, Grampa."

The tension level between the two men immediately spiked, and Risa immediately took responsibility for the conversation. It went downhill fast. Sure that her brain required protein for sustained talk, she gave Kelsy the dinner signal.

At the kitchen table, Quint and Ben stared at each other like lions over fresh kill, snarling and snapping in a quiet way that frayed Risa's taut nerves. Molly apparently picked up on their machismo. She climbed up on Ben's lap and fed him a forkful of steamed carrots. "Did you have a rough day, Daddy?"

Risa heard Quint Ferguson's jaw crack, but after Molly climbed into his lap with a long story about her and Jason and Lucky Prince, he toned down his snarling and snapping.

Surprisingly, Jason won the older man over by peppering him with dozens of questions about life on a Montana ranch. Confessing he'd like to ride a horse, Jason said, "Maybe I'll come visit you someday—after I visit my daddy in Los Angeles."

Oxygen at the table evaporated. Kelsy looked as if the flaky chicken Wellington was stuck midway down her throat. Brow knit, Quint shot Risa a glance. *What now?*

Stymied herself, Risa shrugged. Glaring at her, Gramps spoke to Jason. "Should I expect you anytime soon?"

What Risa fully expected was tears. Jason looked miserable. Molly whispered, "You can tell Grampa."

Jason laid his fork down. "Maybe. My daddy doesn't live with me anymore. He's moving to Los Angeles. Him 'n Mommy're getting a divorce."

Kelsy definitely choked. Without batting an eyelash, Quint said, "Boy, that sucks, doesn't it?"

The other adults, Risa included, made noises like fish gasping for air.

Jason, breathing fine, nodded. "Makes me mad, too."

"I bet." Quint pointed his fork at Jason. "You're mad 'cuz you don't have any say about the divorce and you can't keep your dad from going away, right?"

"Right." Jason nodded. "How did you know that?"

Risa crossed her fingers. Don't let Quint waffle now.

After a glance at Ben, the old man gave Jason his attention. "I felt real mad when my daughter—Molly's mommy—died. I felt mad 'cuz I wouldn't see her again. Mostly, I felt mad 'cuz there wasn't anything I could do to stop the—the car that hit her."

"And you were sad, too, Grampa."

"Yes, I was, honey."

Ben's eyes widened, and Risa felt herself go tense when he opened his mouth. Would he challenge his father-in-law, discount his grief? He said, "Ever feel like crying and screaming at the same time, Jason? That's how I still feel sometimes."

Holy Hannah, there he goes hiding his feelings again.

"When I feel that way, Molly 'n me talk or we play."

Jason, a hero for Charlie, Tom, and Harry? Risa gave Kelsy a quick circle with finger and thumb.

"I like playing with her and Lucky Prince best," Jason said.

As if on cue, a bark from the laundry room gave them all a laugh—including Quint. He volunteered to go to the backyard with the kids and LP till dessert time. Kelsy, who'd said almost nothing, knocked over a full water glass, then looked ready to cry. Risa excused the mistress of the kitchen from KP, hoping Ben took the hint. Maybe go outside. Bond with his father-in-law. *Riiight.*

Kelsy raced upstairs. Ben leaned against a wall. Arms across his chest, he drawled, "Personally, I like melodrama at the dinner table. It feels so much like movies on TV."

Hands shaking, Risa concentrated on scraping plates. "I know the way to hell is paved with good intentions, but does it help if I swear I thought my intentions were good?" *Please help me keep my hands off his body.*

"Maybe." Ben didn't move, but she felt as if he stood only a breath away. There had to be a reason she couldn't breathe. He said, "I suppose I can give you the benefit of the doubt."

"Good, because I swear—" A plate slipped through her fingers. She caught it at the last second and set it on top of the others. No bending over the dishwasher or the blood would rush to her head and she'd pass out.

"While you're swearing," he said, "why not swear you're going to the company dance with me?"

"I swear." She held up a soapy hand. Warm water slithered down her arm. Ben pushed away from the wall, and her arms felt useless. "Your father-in-law made me see the light."

Wrapping her arm in a dish towel, Ben held it there while her pulse did the cha-cha. "So you invited ole Quint home to dinner as a . . . reward?"

"I thought if he saw Molly with you . . ." She tried to turn back to the sink, but Ben patted the towel, holding onto her elbow. "Also," she babbled, "I needed a reminder."

"A reminder for?"

"For why you and I have to give up all ideas of sex."

His fingers tightened on her elbow. "Your logic eludes me."

The sound of voices outside startled her. She jumped away from him, bumping into the dishwasher.

"We're not doing anything wrong, Doc."

"That's not true." *And he knows it.* Jason screeched. Risa ducked around Ben. "You and Quint Ferguson have to make peace."

"Hey, was I rude? Did I put him down?"

Breathing more deeply, Risa waved his defensiveness aside. "You have to do better, for Molly's sake."

The dish towel landed on the counter. "I'm not eatin' dirt."

"That's not what I meant." She softened her tone. "He still has doubts about how you're caring for Molly."

"That's his problem." Ben stared past her, out the window.

"He can make it your problem." Risa picked up the damp dish towel and flicked it against the counter. Ben jumped. She said, "He let his hair down with Jason tonight. In my office, he let me know how far he'd go for Molly."

"I told you. He's a control freak. He—"

Risa snapped the dish towel again. "*He* convinced me to go to the dance with you."

"How?" Ben shook his head. "Did he hire a PI and dig up dirt? What'd he say?"

"That's between me and him."

Ben frowned his dissatisfaction. Risa elaborated. "If he hired a PI, he kept that to himself. But till he showed up, I had every intention of backing out of the dance."

"There's a news flash." Ben raked a hand through his hair.

"Here's another one. The dance is on, sex is off."

"Really." He grabbed the towel. Risa didn't even try to hold onto it. "Paranoia aside," she said, "don't be surprised if Quint does hire a PI."

"That man needs to get a life." Ben held the towel by two corners and slowly spun the fabric round and round.

Tense from watching him, Risa said quietly, "If you and I sleep together, it'll be that much harder for you and him to bury the hatchet and that much easier to hire a PI."

"Tell me again, why do I want to bury the hatchet?"

Without thinking, she pulled the towel away from him and tossed it on the table. Quietly, she said, "For Molly's sake."

CHAPTER 24

"This one!" Molly's face lit up like a neon sign.

The jeweler adjusted the black velvet pillow. "It's one of a kind, Mr. Ferguson."

"I'll bet it is." Quint handed over his platinum card.

"La Ti Da will love it, Grampa." Molly kissed him.

The frog pin was the ugliest thing Quint had ever seen. Pavé diamonds on the belly, real emerald eyes, sixth-century Chinese enamel, and an optional antique gold chain that didn't justify the astronomical price tag or Molly's infatuation.

Quint sighed. Obviously, she'd inherited her father's lack of good taste. Not to mention fiscal moxie. Her twelve-dollar piggy bank contribution didn't cover a tenth of the sales tax.

Molly declined the free gift wrapping.

Snowed in for a week, dependable, responsible Mary-ann had lost her mind and decided that being a ski instructor at Squaw Valley offered more adventure than being Molly's nanny.

Kelsy dropped this bomb on Risa, adding, "Molly's

good for Jason. Having her's fine till Ben makes different arrangements."

So, every time Risa came home, there he was. In her kitchen. Staying for dinner at Kelsy's invitation. Setting the table. Entertaining the kids or returning from a walk with Lucky Prince. His lemon-scented aftershave greeted her in every room but her bedroom. Praise Jupiter, they were never alone. She felt ready to jump out of her skin. Constantly hot and nervous, wired so tight, she flinched at the slightest noise and felt like screaming. Even after he went home. No wonder people turned to drugs or alcohol. Anything that blunted the electrical force sizzling inside her.

Against her better judgment, Risa made an appointment with a Vietnamese dressmaker who, Kelsy swore, sewed with fairy dust. "Let's make it a girls' day out," Kelsy proposed.

Molly assumed she was included and offered dress design advice fit for Barbie. Asked his plans, Ben suggested a romp in the park with Jason, who asked, "Can Finn come, too?"

Ben's immediate acquiescence set Risa's nerves twanging like dueling banjos. *What was he up to?* Kelsy simply beamed, irking Risa more. *He didn't find a cure for cancer.* Casually, Ben said, "After playing so hard, we guys won't be up to cooking."

"Nope." Jason puffed his chest, and Kelsy laughed. Risa suspected collusion.

Ben caught her staring and grinned wolfishly. "Since we'll all be tired Saturday, how about going for pizza? My treat."

Both kids went nuts. Kelsy kicked Risa under the table, but Molly said something that distracted Ben and gave Risa an excuse for saying nothing.

Later, as Molly hugged Risa good night, she whispered in her stage voice, "I'm going to dream about your ball gown tonight."

Mischief twinkled in Ben's eyes. In an aside to Jason, he said, "What're you going to dream about, Jason? Glass slippers?"

"Pizza!" Jason yelled.

Molly giggled. The adults laughed. Kelsy kissed the top of his head, then purred, "What about you, Ben?"

He locked eyes with Risa. Desire, the last thing she wanted to feel, flashed through her, white-hot and heart-stopping. He waited a beat. The fever inside Risa spread. "Oh," he said, "the dress for sure."

Molly sighed. He asked, "What about you, Doc?"

Weak-kneed, she said defiantly, "Frogs."

"Neither rain, nor sleet, nor dark of night . . ." Risa groused Saturday morning on her third time around the block of Kim Nguyen's tiny shop. "So she sews with fairy dust, I'm not walking a mile in this monsoon for a dress fitting."

"Can't weasel out now." Kelsy swiped at the windshield.

"You have to have a new ball gown, La Ti Da." Molly sounded so stricken, Risa felt her frustration ebb away.

"Honey, I have a perfectly good, black dress—"

"But it's not a *ball gown*," Molly insisted.

"Mrs. Nguyen's expecting you," Kelsy chimed in.

"Always my conscience," Risa mumbled, then outlined dropping her in front and returning when she finished. This plan meant no standing half naked in front of anyone but Mrs. Nguyen.

"Can I go with you, La Ti Da?"

"No, honey." Risa tried to sound regretful. "Kelsy needs your help finding a parking place."

"I hate the rain." Molly stuck her bottom lip out.

Surprised she'd missed how much Molly wanted a part in creating *the ball gown*, Risa said, "I promise I'll choose purple, okay? I'll even bring you a scrap of fabric. You don't like it, we'll go back and choose something else. Fair?"

Another trip around the block, and Molly finally agreed. Risa could tell her heart wasn't in it and fell back on reporting Traci's condition and throwing her voice. By the time Kelsy stopped the car, Molly was almost laughing.

As Risa unhooked her seatbelt, Kelsy patted her on the shoulder. "Imagine the fun with triplets on a rainy day."

The bird-tiny, ebony-haired dressmaker made Risa feel huge. *She's like Amy.* Despite her size and somewhat broken English, Mrs. Nguyen quickly cast a spell over Risa. A dress for a princess, she promised.

First, Risa must choose the right underthings. Caught off guard, she followed the petite woman to a softly lit alcove where she opened an antique, satin-lined trunk. Gold and diamond rings flashed as she pulled out half a dozen sample trays. A kaleidoscope of handmade bras, slips, panties, and garter belts lay artfully draped across the trays.

Heart thumping, Risa shook her head. Absolutely not. Wearing such delicate, frilly, barely-there lingerie required courage. "I'm too big," she insisted.

With irrefutable logic, Mrs. Nguyen countered, "Special dress need special underthings." She proceeded to show Risa how off-the-shelf underwear bunched in all the wrong places. "Will rob dress of magic," she stated flatly.

After that, surrender was inevitable. And so exciting. Feeling totally wanton and risqué, Risa chose a pair of silk and lace panties smaller than a man's handkerchief. The wispy, see-through bra was so decadent her daring must offend Mrs. Nguyen.

Beaming, the older woman showed off the garter belts. Risa gasped. Holy Hannah, any one of these could drive a man insane. But Ben would have no sanity worries.

Risa intended to keep *the ball gown* on from the minute she left her house till she returned—long before midnight.

On the other hand, she wasn't about to embarrass herself with ugly panty lines.

Truthfully, she could no more resist the creations by Mrs. Nguyen than pyromaniacs could resist matches. Mesmerized, Risa touched and fingered one garter belt after the other. She'd never owned one, of course. Never thought she would own one. Didn't they date from medieval days—when men locked their women in similar iron contraptions to ensure their faithfulness?

"Buy two," Mrs. Nguyen advised. "Husbands crazy for them."

"Oh, but I'm not—" Blushing, Risa said, "I'll remember that. Right now, I'll take this one, please."

Her selection, an exquisite, beribboned and sequined scrap of transparent black fabric, was softer than anything Risa had ever touched.

"Everyting ready when you pick up dress." To Risa's regret, Mrs. Nguyen replaced the garter belt and closed the trunk.

For some reason—possibly from already making a fool of herself by buying the sexy underwear—Risa felt almost no embarrassment standing bare-assed in front of Mrs. Nguyen. It's not high school gym class, she reminded herself. No other girls in the communal showers nudging each other, staring, whispering.

Arms at her sides, Risa looked into space and the past. Dolly Parton aside, 38D boobs were not a blessing to a fifteen-year-old gawky girl who never had a good hair day from first grade on. *Carrie's clone.*

Mrs. Nguyen pinned and tucked the silk pattern she made in real time, measuring Risa from every angle. Risa stood as still as a statue, unable to shake off the shower scene from the Stephen King horror classic. *What's the difference between Carrie and Cinderella?*

Cindie didn't get her period before the ball.

Carrie didn't have a fairy godmother.

Cindie was a good girl; Carrie was a very, very bad girl.

A burst of lightning—almost a phenomenon in Silicon Valley—cracked. Risa jerked. A pin pricked skin. Cindie/ Carrie vanished. Risa reassured the older woman that she was fine and had, in fact, barely felt the pin. "Not with my hips."

"Better than bones," Mrs. Nguyen said firmly. "Many girls want only to be skinny, skinny."

With definite thoughts about skinny, she bent Risa's ear and removed the silk pattern. She drew her finger-tips across Risa's collarbones. "Very beautiful. Very nice decolletage."

Very sure way to cause a heart attack. The full-length mirror revealed Risa was red as a brick. Stammering thank you, she snapped on her old cotton bra. Mrs. Nguyen asked. "Ugly, very ugly. Ask Santa for new lingerie."

"Great idea." Certain she couldn't resist another sales pitch, Risa dressed hurriedly.

Ten minutes later, a gust of rain slapped her in the face. Drenched, fighting the umbrella, she jerked the passenger door open. A memory unrolled in her head. Ben shivering as he opened the airport taxi door. In her panic, she'd felt like a princess. Holy Hannah, the weather must have him out of his mind about Molly.

Teeth chattering, Risa fell into the front seat and fought off her slicker. Kelsy and Molly made sympathetic noises. Risa rubbed her arms and then stretched her hands toward the heater.

Another image exploded. Ben at the airport. Racing toward her. The sleeves of her dry sweatshirt flapping over his head.

Kelsy eased away from the curb. "Ben called. Three times."

Showing up at the airport went definitely above and

beyond, Risa thought. She snapped at Kelsy, "It is rain-ing."

"Really?" Kelsy said tightly. "Call and tell him that."

"Why don't you call, Molly?" Risa dialed. Then, chicken that she was, she handed over the phone. She ended up reassuring Ben in clipped syllables that they were all fine, then hung up.

"Is your dress purple, La Ti Da?"

"Yes." Mrs. Nguyen had nodded repeatedly. Yes, yes.

"Can I see the scrap?" Molly asked.

Risa turned. "Mrs. Nguyen has to buy the fabric, honey."

"Cinderella's fairy godmother waved her magic wand!"

Faced with debunking a beloved fairy tale *and* shattering a child's innocence, Risa said, "I think Mrs. Nguyen left her magic wand in Vietnam."

"How can she make your ball gown then?" Molly wailed.

"Biiig mistake." Kelsy flipped the wipers on high.

"This is a private conversation." Risa discarded the idea of banging her head against the dashboard. Bright as a ray of sunshine, she said, "Mrs. Nguyen uses a magic needle."

"A magic needle?" Molly all but spit each word at Risa.

"I've never heard a story about a magic needle."

A laugh got away from Kelsy, but she escaped murder by being the driver. "Well," Risa began slowly, "Want to hear one?"

"Yes, I do." Molly crossed her arms over her chest.

From word one, the story didn't grab her. "The Frog Prince" and "Cinderella" were her literary references, so she kept trying to make a connection between Risa's loosey-goosey story and the timeless elegance of the classic fairy tales. A Carriesque heroine and unprincely hero didn't help, but Risa plugged away—weaving substance from nothing. Molly hated it.

Next, she declined a ventriloquism lesson. Repeated coaxing brought repeated rebuffs. Kelly hummed as Molly posed several questions about the magic needle story, but accepted no answers. Sighing, Risa tried to recapture the delirium she'd felt when Mrs. Nguyen complimented her *very nice decolletage.*

Kelsy pulled into the garage, glanced back at Molly, then patted Risa's hand. "Didn't your mother tell you there'd be days like this?"

"You mean days when it rains on the just and the unjust?"

"La Ti Da." Molly's plaintive cry cut their repartee short.

Professional instinct vaporized guilt and flippancy. Risa turned around. "What's wrong, honey?"

"My . . . tummy . . . hurts."

CHAPTER 25

On Sunday, Ben lied through his teeth that he could take care of Molly and insisted Doc go to the office, but he hoped she'd stay home right up till Kelsy said leave. During stints of mopping Molly's face, he frequently flipped into fantasy. Doc, resplendent in Florence Nightingale white, kissing him passionately while Molly slept. Doc did stop by the guest room at eleven that night, when he reported, "No throwing up for the last half hour."

In his role as nurse, Ben regretfully refrained from slamming Doc up against the nearest wall and kissing her till she dragged him into her bedroom and had her way with him.

On Monday morning, Molly padded into the kitchen with the news that Jason's mommy didn't feel so good. Under the circumstances, Ben called his office, canceled another merger meeting, and took Jake's ear-blistering wrath without a word. Gritted teeth and pride kept him from calling Doc. She did not need more problems. By the time she arrived home at 7:30 that night, Ben was at the end of his rope. The kids hung from the rafters.

Lucky Prince bounded through the house like a dog on speed, and Kelsy moaned from her bed.

"Why in the world didn't you tell me about Kelsy?" Doc turned on the patio lights, put the mutt in the back-yard, then marched Molly and Jason up the stairs to the bathroom.

"The wheels didn't start coming off till about three." Ben caught his breath at the landing. God, he sounded whiny. And he was beat. "I thought I had everything under control."

"But I talked to you at four." Water whooshed into the tub.

Feeling stupid, Ben couldn't admit he'd hoped she'd read his mind and come home—even though home must feel like the zoo. Her request for clean pajamas brought him up short. *Nothing to do but face the music.*

The scent of steamed roses filled his nose. Shirt sleeves rolled up, tendrils of hair framing her face and neck, Doc was bent over the tub. Her jacket lay on a lit-tle padded chair under the vanity. The taut fabric of her slacks molded the firm, luscious roundness of her hips. Ben's pulse immediately kicked up. He sagged against the door.

"Daddy, Daddy. Smell me." Molly held up a soapy hand.

"Where's my washcloth?" Jason lifted Fergie overhead, dripping water on Molly. She squealed. Doc handed Jason a washcloth, rescued Fargo, and sniffed Molly's hand.

Hell, she's probably solving higher math problems in her head as I watch. "Confession time," he said.

"Sounds ominous," Fergie piped up.

"I didn't get around to laundry."

"Oh-oh." Doc threw him a grin. "Better expect the Laundry Police later tonight."

The kids howled. Truly puzzled, Ben said, "I don't know how the time got away from me."

"Time management with kids is an oxymoron." Doc

tossed him a towel. "I'll find something, then check on Kelsy." A water spot over her right breast resembling Iowa had stained her cream-colored silk blouse.

Face burning, Ben fumbled a towel in front of his bulging zipper. "Hop out, Molly."

Some time later, he sort of heard Doc come into the family room, but he was so damned beat he couldn't raise his head from the couch. She said, "I see the sleep fairy's dusted everyone."

"I'm not sleeping," he groused and tried to swing his feet onto the floor, but they ignored his brain's command. "Kitchen's a . . . mess."

"Shh." Her fingers on his forehead felt so cool he couldn't remember what he wanted to tell her. "You don't feel hot."

He knew he was burning up with a fever, but she was the doctor so he didn't contradict her.

On his dinner break at 9:15, Finn called Kelsy and got the skinny from Risa. Within seconds, he asked, "Okay, so how can I get your life back to normal?"

Tempted to laugh, Risa sighed. "Find me a fairy godmother who'll help Ben with the kids and hold Kelsy's head. I could cancel my appointments tomorrow, but—"

"What if I ask Ma to help out?"

"Knowing Kelsy, she'll want your mother to think you couldn't have found anyone better."

"Ma loves nothing better than taking care of people. What if this becomes a good time for her and Kelsy to bond?"

"Kelsy won't be an easy patient."

"Ma loves a challenge."

Yawning and scrubbing her eyes, Risa opened the door the next morning at 7:25. Like fairies, Finn's mother and sister bustled in, took charge, and shooed Risa off to work.

At 10:00 Traci called the office while Risa was touching base with Ben. He'd just gotten up. Sounding rested, he said, "Take her call. The kids and I are fine. Kelsy's sick as a dog."

These words rang in Risa's ears as she reconnected to Traci. "I'm sick of being fat as a cow," Traci complained.

"This is the hardest part," Risa soothed, one eye on the clock. She had four patients waiting. "What's Dr. Wallace say?"

"That for someone big as a barn, I'm doing fine. Normal heartbeats for Charlie and Tom. Harry's is a little fast, but she thinks there's no problem."

Aware her own heart sped up, Risa jotted herself a note. *Call Traci's OB/GYN.* The flashing light signaled she'd left Ben on hold. Frazzled, she scheduled a call-back with Traci that afternoon, then picked up the line with Ben. He whispered, "Sorry I was such a blob last night, but watch out tonight."

The intimate overtones burned her neck. Holy Harriet, where were the Ladies Bishop? Em stuck her head through the door. Massaging her temples, Risa said goodbye.

Gifts from her patients for Charlie, Tom, and Harry picked up her spirits, and she soothed herself that Harry's accelerated heartbeat meant nothing.

The last patient departed with a big hug a little past noon. Head aching, Risa staggered to her office and collapsed. Praise Jupiter, Em had ordered in soup and a sandwich. Mrs. Nguyen called as Risa was sniffing the soup. The ball gown would be finished on Wednesday. Deep down, Risa doubted she'd need the dress. In her medical opinion, Ben was a flu patient waiting for his knockout blow.

Of course a smart woman would come home sick on Friday. Stunned at first by her own deceit, Risa let the thought play out. Two sick kids, her hectic schedule, Ben's exhaustion, and now Kelsy's bout with the flu had certainly doused his fire.

That stupid dance would undoubtedly rekindle the ashes and create unnecessary complications. If, however, she came down with the flu, would Ben risk exposing Molly to the virus again? A couple of deep breaths stopped the flutters in Risa's stomach. If the Macdonalds left, she'd never know if Ben remained faithful to Amy. But, then, so what?

Fidelity was *her* hang-up. Fidelity and accepting that Ben didn't want to take on three more kids.

"Understand from Molly the flu's hit you folks pretty hard down there, Dr. Taylor." Quint Ferguson stared at the snow outside his study and felt its coldness creep into his heart. "Molly says she's feeling fine now but wants to stay at your house since Jason's mommy's sick."

Filled with decisiveness, he didn't give Dr. Taylor time to reply. He said, "Molly's a little nervous the flu bug might bite you or her daddy on Saturday."

"I can't speak for Ben, but the only bug biting me is you."

Ignoring her testiness, he said, "I think I reassured her."

"Not even the Czar of the Universe should make promises he can't keep."

"Of course not. You don't ever want to tell a child such a thing absolutely won't happen."

"Wow! Czar of the Universe *and* Mr. Sensitive."

"No need for sarcasm," he said mildly. Again, he didn't leave time for her response, but he made his point. "I'm sure you agree Molly's had more than her share of disappointment for a while."

He let that hang. She finally said, "You know how I feel."

"That admiration is mutual. If Molly doesn't give you the little gift she bought you for *the ball,* I swear I think her heart will break."

"I believe I got that phrase the first time you hit me between the eyes with it. But let me reassure you, Your Sensitiveness. Even if I'm throwing up my socks on Saturday, I plan to go to that damned ball."

Saturday, 4:45 P.M. Ninety minutes to countdown, Risa sat with a towel around her shoulders in front of the bathroom mirror, eyes squinched shut, terror strangling her, and surrendered to Kelsy's brush, comb, and make-up wizardry.

Downstairs LP howled softly. No walk tonight.

Repeated blasts of hair spray coated her lungs and vaporized her neural efficiency. Oh, God. What if, despite Kelsy's best efforts, she looked pathetic? What if she embarrassed Ben?

Breathe. Breathe. Breathe.

"TA-daaa!" After a decade, Kelsy flicked the towel off.

"You can open your eyes now." Molly's warm hand felt soft as a butterfly on Risa's elbow.

Do not panic. A montage of fright shots fast-forwarded on her mental VCR. "Do I have to wear a paper bag over my head?"

"See for yourself." Kelsy pinched her upper arm.

"You look beautiful, La Ti Da."

Behind closed eyelids, hope fluttered even as Risa silently cursed Kelsy. "Thank you, Molly."

No matter what her hair looked like, she still had *the* dress. It would transform Cinderella's ugly stepsisters into sirens. Even with a paper bag over her head, Risa knew she wouldn't embarrass Ben in *the* dress.

"Stop stalling." Kelsy poked her in the ribs.

Slowly, heart thumping, stomach tight, Risa inhaled.

First, she squinted through her left eye, then her right, then opened both wide. She blinked. Her jaw dropped.

"Seeing is believing," Kelsy announced.

"You look like Cinderella," Molly said shyly.

"Holy—" Air whooshed out of Risa's lungs.

She couldn't take her eyes off the beautiful creature staring back at her. She recognized those eyes. Hers. Bigger, deeper. Framed by shades of mauve and purple eyeshadow. With tons of black mascara, they absolutely glowed. So did her cheeks. And her hair—

"Your hair's beautiful," Molly said.

"Thank you." Risa leaned closer to the mirror and fell head over heels in love with Kelsy's creation.

Kelsy cupped the mass of curls at the nape of Risa's neck. "Do you like these, Molly?" She turned Risa's head like a puppet and fingered a sparkling pin.

"Are they diamonds?" Molly breathed.

" 'Fraid not." Kelsy chuckled. "Earth to Risa. Hellooo?"

Turning her head from side to side, Risa ignored Kelsy's teasing. She was too busy admiring the intricate hairstyle anchored to the stranger's head by several sparkling pins. For the first time she could ever remember, her hair did look beautiful. Hesitantly, she touched a curl dangling above her right eyebrow. "Will it stay up all night?"

"Come rain, hail, sleet, or a tsunami." Kelsy pushed Risa's fingers away and adjusted the curl. "This do's gonna stay put."

A flicker of doubt broke through the happiness rushing into Risa's veins. "You know my hair has a mind of its own."

"Pshaw." Kelsy waved her forefinger like a magic wand over Risa's head. "I'm thinking of patenting my secret potion."

"Secret potion?" Molly's eyes widened.

"A sixteenth of a teaspoon of cement—"

"Cement?" Risa yelped.

"What's cement?" Molly asked.

"Just kidding, just kidding." Kelsy picked up a short silver can and passed it to Risa. "I used this stuff when I was a TV reporter. It kept my hair in place for hours."

"But you have good hair." Panic gnawed at Risa's stomach. "My hair's impossible."

"Daddy likes your regular hair," Molly said.

The can in Risa's hand suddenly weighed more than a ton of cement. The list of ingredients did the cha-cha in front of her eyes. Too giddy to read, she laughed weakly. "He does?"

"Uh-huh. He told me so," Molly whispered.

Where? When? Why?

Each question sent Risa's heart pounding harder. Behind Molly, Kelsy shot both fists to the ceiling but didn't make a sound. Just as she hadn't made a sound when Sam called an hour earlier. Without consulting Kelsy first, he invited Jason for a burger and a visit with his new half brother. Put in the unenviable situation of being the bitch, Kelsy agreed, then threw herself into transforming her fury into an amazing hairstyle.

With that mission accomplished, anything might set Kel off. Risking potential lung damage from the hair spray, Risa breathed in, catching her best friend's eye. *Don't disappoint Molly.*

Kelsy tossed her head. Risa's heart beat double time. "You do guarantee I won't end up bald tonight, right?"

"Bald is *not* how I expect you to end up tonight."

"Me either." Molly shook her head.

Face on fire, Risa set the hair spray down hard. "We all agree. In the morning, my hair will look just like it does now."

Wagging a finger, Kelsy smirked. "We'll see."

The urge to strangle her took hold, but Risa clenched her teeth. "Will *someone* take my dress out of the bag?"

Kelsy hustled Molly into the bedroom. Alone, Risa

growled, "Watch out Ben Macdonald. Here I come. Ready or not."

At 5:45, Ben cruised past Doc's house for the third time. The limo driver probably felt like they were on a merry-go-round. At three hundred bucks an hour, the driver probably didn't give a damn if they circled the house all night.

Pulse racing, Ben glanced at his watch. Fifteen more minutes, then he could ring the doorbell. At 6:00. On the dot. He mopped his brow, switched on the A/C and exhaled. Forty degrees outside, and he felt like an Eskimo in the Sahara at high noon.

Remind Risa to wear a coat.

Not that he intended to run the air conditioning once she got in the car.

By then, he intended to stop sweating. Because if sweat kept pouring off him, he'd have to pop into the nearest mall and buy new handkerchiefs. He had time. Between 6:00 and 6:15 he'd said. Arriving exactly at 6:00 didn't give Doc extra primping time.

Maybe she didn't need primping time. Maybe she'd decide at the last minute she had better things to do. His heart missed a beat. Maybe an emergency came up. *Stop being a moron.*

He ordered the driver to slow to a crawl. "Go ahead and park," Ben instructed, "but not under the street-light or in front of her house . . . yet."

God, what psycho invented *dating*?

His wallet stuck to his sweaty fingers. He plied them off, wiping them on his handkerchief and feeling like a Montana kid in his boxers. He laid the wallet on the console.

Put it back.

Hypnotized, he stared at it. He didn't have to open

it. He knew its contents by heart. Driver's license.
Emergency auto service card. Four corporate platinum
cards. Two photos of Molly. The studio shot of her and
Amy. Five hundred-dollar bills.

His heart clutched. Glad for the tinted window sepa-
rating him from the driver, he sat there in the near-dark
for several heartbeats. Christ, he didn't know whether
to laugh or cry. Dressing, he'd convinced himself he
was doing the right thing.

Dammit, he and Doc were adults. No more cat and
mouse.

Drenched with sweat, he raised the A/C control. His
hand froze in midair. Not because of the arctic squall
blasting him between the eyes, but because his wallet
was glowing in the dark.

"It's magic!" Molly stroked the deep purple gown
glowing on Risa's bed. "You'll look like a princess."

"Very La Ti Da." Kelsy slipped the dress off the
hanger.

To keep from floating across the room, Risa hugged
her waist. "You mean that old rag?"

"Rag?" Molly and Kelsy squeaked in unison.

"Okay. I exaggerate." Risa fingered the hem and let
her mental VCR freeze Ben's face when he saw her.

If Kelsy followed instructions, she'd have a photo of
his eyes wide with surprise, and a grin of lust leering at
her. She'd secretly treasure that picture in the years to
come, showing it to her sons when they were old enough.
Old enough to want a woman with every fiber of their
being—the way she wanted Ben tonight.

"I swear," Kelsy whispered, "fairies sew for Mrs.
Nguyen."

In her heart, Risa knew Ben loved Amy for more
than her looks alone. He'd even convinced Risa that appearance and size were her hang-up. In her head she

agreed, but she still longed for Amy's classic elegance. Not to mention her petite body. Trembling, she smothered her fears and misgivings. This was it. The night she'd waited for her entire life. The night she'd never forget.

Exhilarated by the loud hum in her body, she surrendered to her addictive fantasy. One night. One night only. That was all she wanted. All she needed for a lifetime of wonderful memories. Memories that would benefit her sons. Her feet lifted off the carpet. She and her body floated free as bubbles across the room. Molly and Kelsy waited with the patience of nuns.

It was time. Put on *the* dress. Let the good times begin. She fumbled at the knotted belt on her robe.

"Let me." Molly deftly untied the belt.

The robe pooled around Risa's ankles. Molly's mouth dropped. The soft, silky sexiness of the slip and lacy lingerie teased Risa's bare skin. Kelsy whistled. Pushing her lips out in a pout, Risa raised her arms overhead. *Move over, Madonna.*

Kelsy slid the dress over Risa's head, zipped it, then stood back. Molly gasped. Risa smiled at herself in the mirror.

Nothing could ruin tonight. Nothing.

"Are you wired, La Ti Da?"

Stunned by her decolletage, Risa felt dizzy. She mumbled, "I sure am, honey." Holy Heloise, she might as well have a neon sign around her neck.

"I know a good lawyer." Kelsy grinned. "In case you forgot to buy a license to wear that in public."

Wide-eyed, Molly said, "You're gonna knock Daddy's socks off."

CHAPTER 26

The doorbell chimed at 6:02.

"Daddeeee," Molly shrieked.

"AKA Prince Charming?" Kelsy murmured. "Want me to go down? Did he bring the glass slipper? Aren't you wearing the diamond earrings I lent you?"

"Shut up, yes, shut up, yes." Risa jogged to her closet, her pulse racing like a woman in labor.

"Ten minutes, Kel." She handed a shoe box to Molly, then dragged a silver evening bag off the top shelf.

Once she was sure Kelsy had started down the stairs, Risa asked Molly to take her new silver sandals out of the box. "And I'll go get Kelsy's earrings."

Holy Harriet. Why tell the truth when lying was so easy? Aerobic, too, raising her heart rate to its max. Feeling like a drama queen, Risa clutched the evening bag against her right breast. Halfway to the dressing room, she switched the purse to her left breast. Both breasts were so taut they hurt. But not for long. Not if things went the way she planned.

Anticipation zinged through her, curling her toes. She closed her eyes and hugged her waist. Her pulse dropped to the level of downhill skiers. She opened her eyes. Her reflection startled her. Holy Hannah, so much *very beautiful decolletage.*

Red-faced, she tugged at her bodice. Kelsy was right. She could do serious jail time for appearing in public half naked. Preening, she turned for a view of her back. "Holy—"

There was no back to *the* dress. At least from what Risa could see, only one tiny silver button stood between her and the skimpy bra Mrs. Nguyen had designed.

Weak-kneed, Risa collapsed on the bench in front of the mirrors. Satin seams strained where her waist curved inward. She exhaled. Slowly. Evenly. "How're you doing, Molly?"

"Your shoes are on the bed, but where does the box go?"

"Put it in my closet, will you, honey?"

Amazing, Risa marvelled. She could talk. *Open the middle drawer. Don't look at yourself. Don't panic.*

Not being the dummy everyone thought she was, she knew once Charlie, Tom, and Harry arrived, time, energy, and desire for sex would evaporate.

Till then, she was a red-blooded woman. She'd done everything but bludgeon the insane attraction between her and Ben. Surely she'd earned a few points for refusing his proposals. Excitement burned her throat like hot coals. Ethics she'd worry about later—during her lifetime of celibacy.

The heat spread, bursting into a full flame between her legs. Enjoying every minute of her delirium, she pushed aside a layer of tissues in the drawer. Lightheaded with relief, she sighed, remembered *the* dress, and swallowed noisily.

Footsteps sent her heart swinging from rib to rib. Molly stood in the door. "Should I bring your shoes, La Ti Da?"

"No, honey." Risa snatched three gold and green metallic packages out of the drawer, stuffed them in her bag, and felt the corners of her mouth twitch with satisfaction. "I'm ready."

One look at Risa and Ben was hard.

Her mouth moved, his did not. But his feet carried him across the threshold, into the entry. He doubted hell was any hotter. Christ, if he had the brains God gave a goose, he'd stay outside. Given some time—a decade at least—the cool night air would probably shrink his hard-on. Lightheaded as he felt, it was more likely it was his little gray cells shrinking to zip.

"Isn't La Ti Da bu-TEE-ful, Daddy?

"Bu-TEE-ful." Thank God, his tux pants—unlike jeans or everyday work slacks—bagged in strategic places.

God, he couldn't take his eyes off Doc. Her rose fragrance assaulted his brain. On the sidelines, Molly and Kelsy nudged each other. They were too close or he'd make his move right there. On the stairs. *Like Rhett Butler with Scarlet.*

As it was, he had to pull his eyes back into their sockets, suck his tongue back into his mouth, and shift his brain into think mode. Which meant talking.

The think-on-your-feet button in his brain had jammed. Noises from his throat sounded a lot like grunts. The more he tried to form words, the louder he grunted. A big part of the problem, he realized, despite the fog clouding his brain, was his damn wallet. He didn't dare talk. If he opened his mouth, he'd start gibbering about his wallet. How it glowed in the dark. How he should've left it in the limo. How it felt like a slab of molten steel inside his tux.

A snapshot exploded in his head. Five red metallic packages. Nestled between his five hundred-dollar bills.

Condoms. Protection. Quicksand if he didn't watch his step.

Nervous as he was about the condoms, his bigger worry became holding Doc's coat without touching her.

God save him, he wanted to caress her shoulders, kiss the hollow in her throat, drop lower . . .

"Daddy." Molly tugged at his coattail.

He tore his eyes off Doc's cleavage. "Yes, sweetheart?" Molly started, and Ben felt his heart lurch. *Way to go, Butthead.* Demented with lust, he'd forgotten everything but his desire. He dropped to one knee and opened his arms, but Molly hung back. "I'm sorry, baby."

"You're higher than a kite, aren't you, Daddy?"

Impossible not to return her shy grin. Molly could teach him a thing or two about forgiveness. He said, "Sweetheart, I'm floatin'." Out of the corner of his eye, he watched Kelsy open the closet door and felt panic spike.

"Okay, but can you stop floating for a minute?" Molly looked over her shoulder, then cupped his ear. "I have a present for La Ti Da."

With the blinding light in Molly's eyes, what, when, where faded to the back burner of his mind. Ben hugged her and whispered, "I think now's a good time."

She broke away, pulled a box from her pocket, and held it out to Doc. "Grampa gave me some money 'cuz I didn't have enough in my piggy bank."

"Oh, my gosh, Molly." The slit up the front of Doc's body-hugging skirt didn't give her much wiggle room, so Ben forgot his fury at Quint, extended his elbow, and led her to the stairs. Seated on the third step from the bottom, she threw her arms around Molly. "Did you make this bu-TEE-ful paper?"

Molly nodded. "I drawed the frogs and painted them."

Pulling Molly closer, Doc said, "You are amazing."

Dry-mouthed, Ben stared at the paper. Amazing wasn't the first word that hit him. Resourceful for a four-year-old, sneaky enough for a fourteen-year-old. Damn Quint, what other kind of secrets would Molly be able to hide in ten years?

"Recognize the box?" Kelsy said in his ear. "A very la ti da Union Square jeweler."

Thank you, Quint.

Doc rubbed the midnight blue velvet box against her cheek. "Sooo soft, Molly."

Fire flamed between Ben's legs. He gritted his teeth. Dammit, his daughter was a foot away from him. Doc held the box against Molly's cheek. "Velvet," she cooed.

When Doc opened the box, she gasped.

"Do you like it?" Molly asked, her face pinched, anxious.

"Like it?" Doc turned it so Kelsy and Ben could admire the contents. "I love it."

Ben didn't. He hated the damn thing. Over his unspoken objections, Kelsy and Molly slipped it off the chain and pinned it—where else?—smack between Doc's round and luscious breasts. Was it his imagination, or did the frog look like Quint? Or maybe it symbolized the lust in Ben's heart. Whatever. Its sneer mocked him.

Doc was the belle of the ball.

And Ben enjoyed every minute of her glory. Well, almost every minute. He didn't appreciate Jake or the other young turks cutting in during each dance. Seeing them lay their hands on her bare back and whirl her around the floor almost undid him. His wallet burned a hole in his pocket.

At nine o'clock he reclaimed Doc and signaled the band to take an early break. Showtime. He seated her at their table, stepped up to the microphone in a blaze of lights, and gave his welcome. As it came time to announce the merger, he wasn't ready for the lump in his throat. God, he'd spent so many hours building Kindersoft. How could he just walk away? *Because you can't run it without neglecting Molly.* Sure Doc had spoken, he glanced at his table. Where the hell was she?

* * *

Out in the hall, Risa listened to Traci's OB/GYN. "Five centimeters. Better hop the first plane, Mom."

Risa spared a heartbeat to enjoy the excitement. "Hope I make it in time."

"Traci made the call. Low back pain, five centimeters, and she keeps asking between hard contractions, 'Could this be false labor?' "

After they stopped chuckling, Risa thought, Adios condoms.

The bittersweet fantasy flared, then faded, displaced by the obstetrician's contagious excitement. "My first triplets."

"Mine, too." They giggled, women first, doctors second.

A burst of applause from the banquet interrupted the call to Em. Ah, well, Risa silently admitted. She'd never *believed* she and Ben would end up in bed.

Half listening to Em, Risa fingered the enameled frog and made her way back to Ben in a state of high agitation. The band hadn't returned. Talking, laughing revelers clumped together—a human wall between Risa and her table. No sign of Ben. Anxiety honed a thin, sharp edge on her euphoria. Worst-case scenario, call him from the taxi. In her head, Kelsy chanted, *You gotta leave with him that brung you.*

Her chest tightened with regret. In a perfect world, she'd have had her one night of lovemaking with Ben, but unlike Cinderella, she wasn't going home to the mice and a dirty hearth. She found a dark corner and called him. He answered on the first ring. "You missed my news." He sounded testy.

"Sorry. I got some news myself." She told him— never giving his news a second thought—and it was like Clark Kent stepping into a telephone booth. Ben immediately changed his tune and his tone.

"No taxi. Think limo. I'm on my way to the coat check. Give me an hour, and I'll wrangle a corporate jet."

"Thanks." She repressed the flutter in her stomach. "Em's working on something—even though I'm already flyin' high."

The limo driver waited in the no parking zone with the door open. Breathing hard, Risa slid across the back seat, sank into a leather cloud, and sighed. Ben settled in next to her, and they floated away from the curb faster than Cinderella's coach.

Determined not to check the time every fifteen seconds, she placed her hand over her watch. Ben squeezed her fingers.

"The limo doesn't turn back to a pumpkin till midnight straight up."

"Yes, but can we levitate over the traffic?" Pulse racing, Risa ducked her head and checked the oncoming headlights.

He pulled her backward, and she felt dizzy from the sudden movement and the traffic whizzing past. "Relax," he said. "Let me work on your neck muscles."

He worked her coat down past her seatbelt. She went tense down to her toes. Holy Hilda, she was almost naked. Her neck was way too close to her boobs.

"Is this you being relaxed?" The dim interior lights bathed his face with softness.

"Stop!" Dry-mouthed, disbelieving, she pushed him away, pulled her arms out of her coat sleeves, and probed between her hard breasts.

"Is it your heart?" Ben cocked a brow.

Teeth clenched, Risa looked down at her *very beautiful decolletage.* "I—I can't find Molly's pin."

The limo braked for a car that zoomed in front of them, then swerved onto the exit for 101. Gravity slammed him against her. His hand flew out, resting on the spot where she'd worn the pin. At that moment, she forgot how heartbroken Molly would feel. She knew only how heartbroken she'd feel if he removed his hand.

His hand stayed put. His eyes were all pupils in the dim light. "Sure you didn't put it in your purse?"

"I know I didn't," she said weakly.

"Humor me." He pointed to her silver bag.

Desire, unexpected, unwanted, wiped out memory, turned her mindless. Could he feel her heart thudding? All fingers, Risa wrenched open the fragile clasp. The meager contents spilled out onto the leather seat. Keys clinked on her laminated hospital ID card. She scooped them up. *Holy—*

Frozen, she watched a slender glass cylinder of rose cologne roll over the lip of the seat in slo mo, onto the carpeted floor. Despite his seatbelt, Ben lunged for lipstick and breath mints. Hyperventilating, Risa snatched at the twinkle of green and gold.

"See? Didn't I tell you?" His hand shot out, clipping one of the packets she desperately crammed into her purse.

Naturally, he picked up the packet. Pretty sure he couldn't see her blushing, she went for flippant. "Think a shrink would say I really wanted this to happen?"

"Did you?" He stared at the condom in his palm.

Face on fire, she swallowed, then grabbed the packet, dropped it in her purse, and rebuckled her seatbelt. "Me?" She slapped her hand over her heart, hoping to bring her pulse back into the stratosphere. "A born-again virgin?"

He grinned. "Why'd a born-again virgin bring condoms?"

"I—I was pretty sure we'd both drink a lot—"

"And you think I'm the kind of guy who takes advan—"

"No." She shook her head, but her brain didn't shift into think mode. "I—I thought, I mean, I put them in my purse *before* Molly gave me the pin." *Now, isn't everything crystal clear?*

"Let me see if we're on the same wavelength here." He pressed his fingers against both of his temples. "You were afraid you'd get drunk, make a pass at me, and need *protection.*"

His voice lingered over *protection* in a long, mocking drawl. Risa ground her teeth. "Not drunk. Uninhibited. Yes, I figured you'd make a pass at me. So don't say *protection* as if I'm one neuron short of a synapse and—"

"I meant it as a pun. A *romantic* pun." He grinned, flustering her more. She babbled, "Well, I am a doctor. STDs and unwanted pregnancies aren't stats, they're—"

"About as romantic as you can get without getting clinical."

Stung, Risa tossed her head. "You know what? I'm hours away from becoming a mother—at which time, I then become celibate as a nun. So, listen up. I brought the damned condoms because I wanted one wild night of mind-numbing passion before I stop thinking—once and for all—about sex in my life." She paused for breath and enjoyed his slack-jawed shock. "I ignored my conscience, talked myself into believing a one-night fling didn't make me pond scum or you unfaithful. I figured wine would drown out whatever qualms still nagged me. Then, Molly gave me that damned pin, and I knew my game of self-delusion was up."

Dizzy from her verbal rant, Risa lifted her chin, realizing too late her boobs were popping out of her bodice.

Ben glanced down at the spectacle. Risa grabbed a handful of her coat, and he jerked his gaze upward. Looking a little dazed, he nodded. "Okay," he said, the single word husky.

"Good." Risa rolled her eyes up at the moon roof. Praise Jupiter. *He understands.* More disappointed than she wanted to admit, she stared at the stars. *Or, if he doesn't, he's not going to argue.* She glanced at him, then shifted focus to her hands clasped in her lap and tried to think about Molly's pin. Thinking about Charlie, Tom, and Harry would come later on the plane. Ben sat unmoving, still as a stone. Risa felt sick.

Another heartbeat, and the silence became awkward, uncomfortable, and too loud. Because if Risa could hear the silence over the drums baaa-booming in her chest, it was definitely too loud.

"People don't die of embarrassment," he whispered.

"Easy for you—"

"Uh-huh. I speak from long experience." He looked out the window, then looked at her. "Around our twenty-fifth anniversary, I'll tell you a few of my more embarrassing moments."

"Our twenty-fifth—"

"We'll forget my two or three stupidities with you."

"Two or three?" Tears clogged her throat, limiting her speech.

"I'm hoping you lost count after I offered you money."

Blinded by the glare of cars and buses merging into the lane to the airport, she blinked. "Did you say *twenty-fifth anniversary?*"

"I believe I did." He pulled her close, tucked her head into his shoulder, and trailed his fingers downward. "Now can you relax?"

"Are you insane?"

"About you, yes." He nibbled her ear, his hot breath scalding her ear. "My timing sucks, but will you marry me?"

"Hold that thought." Delirious, she pulled her cell phone out of her coat pocket. "The beep's my phone—not my pacemaker."

It wasn't a total surprise that the Nashville area code glowed on the screen, but Risa's delirium evaporated. Medical judgment kicked in. It was too soon for a call unless there was a problem. *Don't look for trouble.*

"Who is it?" Ben peered over her shoulder.

"Traci's doctor." Irritated by his sudden clinginess, she jumped away from him. He moved in closer, bumped her arm. The phone slipped through her icy fingers.

"Damn it, Ben! Can't you stop pawing me for ten seconds?"

The phone rang again. His shock and hurt faded from her radar screen. She hunched her shoulders, protecting the phone, and punched TALK.

"We're in trouble," Sarah Wallace said.

CHAPTER 27

Reverting to med-school days, Risa coped by compartmentalizing. Call Kelsy. Arrive at SFO. Say good-bye to Ben. Fly to Nashville. Enter Traci's room. Four minutes before they took her into delivery. Someday, like a survivor of a train wreck or cancer, she might unlock the compartments for details, examine her emotions at each stage, and remember. Till then, she was doing fine, thank you very much.

Right up until she saw Traci's heart rate. Then, she felt her own heart drop like an anvil.

For the first time in memory, she wished she weren't a doctor. Young, healthy women could suffer major problems any time their pulse shot past 200. Traci's registered at 210 as Risa jogged through the door. Sarah Wallace met her, let her catch her breath, then whispered, "A *short* pep talk from you might help."

Sparing a thought for Sarah's sanity, Risa clamped down on a wave of panic. *Wrong time for melodrama.* "Okay."

Sweaty, eyes glazed, clutching coach Bobbye Anne's hand, Traci lay in bed, her knees up. The whir and buzz of modern technology constantly recorded her skyrocketing pulse.

Traci whispered, "Sorry I messed up your big eve—"

"Oh, daahling." Risa sashayed into the room, dropped her coat, and cocked a hip on the bed. Head back, she struck a pose. "Think of the stories I'll tell Charlie, Tom, and Harry."

Traci grimaced, then said, "Your dress is majorly gorgeous."

A contraction left her gasping. Her pulse spiked to 220. Weak-kneed, Risa whispered, "This old rag?"

Like Kelsy, a lifetime ago, Traci and Bobbye Anne also laughed. A forty-point drop in heart rate and two thumbs up from Sarah Wallace proved antibiotics and laughter was the best medicine.

Wait, Risa ESPd the obstetrician. Throwing pride to the wind, she went for another laugh—and maybe another drop in Traci's pulse. She began, "Wearing *the rag,* I knew Ben didn't stand a chance."

Heat stung her face. Unbidden and unwelcome, the replay of them dancing froze in her mind. She blinked. The scene faded. "Being a doctor, I took along . . . condoms."

"You didn't!" Traci hooted. Risa tugged at her bodice and slapped her hand over her heart. "Three. Extra silky. Green—"

Bobbye Anne snickered. Between howls, Traci said, "I—I bet you don't tell that to Charlie, Tom, and Harry for a long time."

With Traci's pulse holding steady at 180, Sarah Wallace made her move. "Showtime." She mumbled to Risa, "Good show, m'dear."

Heart pounding, Risa followed the gurney and a giggly Traci into the corridor. The delivery room doors loomed. Bobbye Anne waved her out of the way. Before retreating to waiting room hell, Risa said to Traci, "When you get your figure back, we'll alter *the rag* for your first tour with Bobbye Anne, okay?"

"Ooookay!" Traci sighed. Her pulse read 142.

Risa waited outside the delivery room for five minutes, but the automatic doors stayed shut. Breathing hard, she tottered to the waiting room. Two guys about her age—fathers-to-be, she assumed—openly gawked as she entered.

Duuuh.

She'd left her coat in Traci's room. Too bad. Her feet hurt too much to go back. She fell in the nearest chair, groaned silently, and wiggled her tomato-red toenails, painted with such care by Molly. This must be how the stepsisters felt after trying to jam their feet into that damned glass slipper.

She bent over to unstrap the instruments of torture, and her spine prickled. She raised her head. Two pairs of male eyeballs had about popped out of their sockets. And no wonder. Mrs. Nguyen's push-up bra was pushing up way too much eye candy.

Heat rushed up Risa's bare chest and shoulders to her face. Eyes straight ahead, she sat up slowly and pretended interest in a distant wall. The men shifted their gaze, too. As they searched for the source of her fascination, she pressed her fingers over her jittery heart. Pacing back and forth in front of them would be like throwing raw meat just beyond the reach of chained dogs. If they were women instead, she'd join them. Talk about babies and crack jokes about the demise of the human race eons ago if men got pregnant. Absent females, she stayed put.

For the first time since med school, the familiar hospital smells of alcohol and disinfectants turned her stomach. Plus, the chair was too soft, the lights too low. Compartmentalizing wasn't working so well now. Not with two horny men so close.

Out of the corner of her eye, she caught Curly drooling and recoiled. She glared at the idiot. No wonder his wife nixed him in delivery. Newborns had no defenses against such stupidity.

Brought up short by her sour opinion, Risa recognized her favorite tactic: avoidance. Focus on anyone, anything but Harry. Because what if Harry . . . She clasped her hands in her lap. Do *not* go there. A nurse stopped at the threshold. Risa's heart leaped. Curly rose. "A girl," the nurse said.

Chest out, Curly approached Risa with a cigar. At a loss where to put it, she stuck it behind her left ear, waiting for Mo to step forward on some lame pretext. In which case . . . Her nose quivered. The scent of lemons and limes mellowed the stink of tobacco. Heart fluttering, she whipped around. "Ben!"

"I found Molly's pin." He waved it, then surveyed the cigar and her bare feet. "I forgot an ashtray and the glass slippers."

Doc flew into Ben's arms and laid a full-mouth kiss on him. More gratifying, her breasts pressed into his chest. Her body heat, plus the pungent scent of tobacco, sharpened his gratitude for being there. He wanted her more than ever. But first, he'd show her she wasn't in this alone.

Her hug turned so fierce, it bordered on clinging. Having her all over him exceeded his wildest expectations. He felt drunk with wanting her, but steamy desire could wait. She stopped kissing him a nanosecond too soon, but he stayed cool.

The one sour note was the short, pasty-skinned, rabbity-looking guy across the room. Ben didn't care for the way he rolled a cigar back and forth between his fingers. Also, his eyes flashed a glittery, feral red every time Ben trailed his fingers down Doc's bare back. Reluctant to let her go, he suggested she change into the jeans and T-shirt Kelsy had sent.

"The restroom's in the next county." She pushed away. A memory exploded. Ben understood. After the accident, he'd refused to leave the hospital, arguing with doctors and nurses. He'd felt pissed and trapped and scared and disbelieving all at once as guilt chewed him up. "Just a suggestion," he said reasonably. "I understand."

"Really?" She shied further away from him.

Worried one of the icicles in her voice would break and stab him through the brain, Ben regrouped. "I meant I understand why you don't want to leave the waiting room."

Her raised eyebrows said he was an idiot. Mind whirling, he said, "When Molly was born, I stayed with Amy every minute."

"Lucky you." He heard her bitterness and mentally kicked himself. Ooo-kay. One more shot. "I remember— I—after Amy . . . died, I hated people who compared their experiences to mine." On the off chance he'd actually seen Doc nod, he plunged on. "No one understood. Whatever anyone said, I shot it down."

That got him another death glare. Determination took root. "After the accident, I felt helpless. That pissed me off. I was a CEO. I took charge, made things happen."

"It's different with Harry." Her gaze flitted across his face, resting somewhere behind him.

"Yes, but—" Ben caught himself and shut up. Out of the corner of his eye, he saw Mr. Rabbity stretch his legs and smirk.

Sniffs trouble in paradise, Ben thought.

Trouble easily bypassed if he backed off, gave Miz Independence space. He considered the easy way, then decided, *hell no.* No matter what Doc said, he understood the wall she'd thrown up. He'd been there, done that. "Excuse the cliché," he said, but you sound a little . . . tense. Ready to argue over—"

"Harry isn't going to die!" Her voice broke.

"Christ, Doc—Risa!" His heart ached for her. "I never meant Harry might . . . not make it."

Scrubbing her eyes, Risa stood up straighter. Ben

took her hand, folded her fingers over his, and kissed them one by one. She didn't exactly flinch, but she sure didn't swoon either.

"The obstetrician said Harry should be fine." Every word said and unsaid felt like a land mine, but holding her hand against his cheek gave him confidence.

Risa said fiercely, "I'll take care of him no matter what."

Ben wrapped his coat around her. She twisted away. "I should be in there. In there, I can do *something*. Out here I—"

"C'mon." He led her to a sofa. "It's been a long day."

The cliché fell out of his mouth automatically, but she shook her head. "Sitting's easier said than done in this dress. I'm giving the damn thing to Traci."

Before Ben admitted his disappointment, he asked, "Why?"

"Can you see me in it at the playground? Or at the office?"

"Got it." The pulse in her throat quickened, and he caught Mr. Rabbity suddenly take great interest in the upside-down magazine he held.

Bells clanged, but the wheels in Ben's head fell off. He sprinted across the waiting room. Mr. Rabbity lurched to his feet and gurgled, "Just going for a cup of . . ."

Ben looked at him. Without finishing his sentence, the jerk trotted out the door. Ben sauntered back to Risa. "Amazing how fast guys cut through BS."

Doc had no time for Ben. Not with the endless pow-wows about Harry. The bleeding around his heart required immediate surgery. Risky, almost experimental. Ben understood being shut out. Because if he didn't, he'd have left hours ago for the airport. Instead, he rocked Tom and Charlie in the neonatal nursery and tried to stifle the panic coiled in his gut.

Jesus, he could kill Kelsy. Ordering him to commandeer a company jet so she and the kids could fly to Nashville. Thank God, Molly was fine. He'd talked with her for the third time less than five minutes ago. According to Kelsy, the taxi was two miles from the hospital. Surely, Molly would arrive . . .

In his arms, Tom squirmed. At four pounds and four pounds three ounces, these guys were tiny. Helpless. Defenseless. Duh. Ben wasn't about to admit he felt protective, but for now he could look out for them.

He pulled Tom's blanket back and checked the nasty bruise he'd found earlier. A bump during birth, the nurses guessed. Knowing how he'd feel if Molly had such a bruise, Ben alerted Doc on her first stop in the nursery. To his amazed disappointment, she spent two seconds examining the injury, then never said boo to him or a nurse. *She's the doctor.*

Kelsy made a production of their arrival. Once Ben convinced himself Molly was fine, he blasted Kelsy. "This is no place for kids."

Kelsy rolled her eyes at him. "Hotel reservations?"

Ben bristled. "I'm not your damned secretary." Used to a secretary, he hadn't given a thought to such logistics.

Molly sneaked her hand into Ben's. "Are you and Kelsy having a fight, Daddy?"

"Sort've, sweetheart." Ben thought his head would explode.

"Can you stop?" Jason asked, his eyes big.

Kelsy arched one brow, then said, "Right now."

Despite the fire in his guts, Ben held his tongue. Kelsy stayed in the waiting room with the kids while he checked in with the nurse. Harry's doctor had left the floor. Dr. Taylor should be out shortly. Patient confidentiality prevented the nurse from divulging more details. Her refusal to meet his gaze told Ben more than words could.

Dry-mouthed, he retreated to a spot near the swinging door. If he was smart, he'd get Kelsy. She'd know what to say to Doc. He was clueless.

"What's your blood type?" Risa ripped off her surgical mask. "Harry needs a transfusion before surgery."

As a doctor, she knew the odds. Knowledge tasted like bad coffee in the back of her throat. Ben's B+ didn't fit Harry's type A.

He took a step toward her, but she crossed her arms over her chest. She related the facts without sighing or crying or screaming. The hospital had used their last pint of A+ with Traci. The nearest hospital could spare only one pint. The cardiac surgeon refused to operate without three pints of whole blood. Regular donors hadn't responded to the hospital's emergency call.

"A plus?" Ben broke in. "That's the rarest . . ."

He must've seen her agitation at the reminder. Praise Jupiter, he shut up instead of offering several out-of-the-box ideas that CEOs supposedly spout by the dozens.

"Nobody on the staff has the right type?"

"One doctor," Risa snapped. *He's trying to help.* She swallowed. "She scheduled vacation, but there's a chance—"

"Where's she live?" Ben demanded.

His tone frayed a nerve. Jaw clenched, Risa said, "Halfway to Memphis."

"I'll go pick her up," Ben said quietly. "Montanans would consider this—"

Angry, Risa shook her head. "Word problem du jour. How many miles per hour must a doctor drive before the hole in Harry's heart—" Her throat filled. She blinked rapidly. "If she left home this second, she'd never make it here in time."

"Oh . . . shit!" Ben raked a hand through his hair. "What about another hospital?"

"Someone's checking." This time his obvious question didn't bother Risa, but his nearness threatened to undo her. She stepped backward. "I—I want to check on Tom and Charlie. Could you call Kelsy? Give her an update?"

Groaning, Ben grabbed Risa's hand. "She's here. She—"

"Whaat?" Risa ignored the shush of the neonatal nurse. "Where?"

"In the waiting—"

"Get her!" Risa shoved him, having no time for his wounded look. "Page Dr. Bartholomew," she spit the order at the nurse.

Kelsy rolled up her sleeve before Risa finished explaining. Seven minutes later, on her back in a green-curtained cubicle in ER, she cracked one joke after another. The tightness clogging Risa's throat didn't disappear, but she could breathe.

From time to time, Ben shot her a look, but the adrenaline pumping through her veins was for coping—not for eye sex. When Jason wanted reassurances about the needle, Kelsy insisted it didn't hurt. "We'll go for ice cream when I'm finished."

The kids squealed. Ben shot Risa a look. *Did he remember their trip to Baskin-Robbins? The high-voltage sparks they'd thrown off? Kelsy's matchmaking?* The nurse bustled in. Disgusted she'd let her mind veer away from Harry, Risa focused on removing the needle from Kelsy's vein. The heat of those moments in Baskin-Robbins belonged to another lifetime.

"Aren't you coming, too, La Ti Da?" Jason clung to Kelsy.

Unraveling with impatience, Risa made a noise. Eyes wide, Jason took a step backward. Instantly ashamed for scaring him, she held her arms out. He shook his head and turned his face into Kelsy's thigh. Ben, forgotten, said quietly, "Hey, Jason. Let's give La Ti Da time to visit Tom and Charlie. You and Molly and I'll eat. We'll bring ice cream back for everybody."

The suggestion fell on deaf ears. Jason jutted his chin, bringing back for Risa an image of him in her office listening while Sam and Kelsy turned his world upside down. Now, he must feel Risa had abandoned him, too.

"I'm sorry, Jason." She held her palms up. "I forgot being a mommy doesn't mean the rest of my life stops."

Looking from Jason to Risa, Molly asked, "Are you *real* worried about Harry?"

Without giving herself time to sidestep the question, eyes stinging, Risa said, "Yes, and I'm real scared . . ."

"Why didn't you tell us?" Jason demanded, rattling Risa. God, she'd sound like a fool saying Harry was her concern and hers alone.

"What can we do to help right now?" Ben's dark eyes invited her into his soul.

Her throat felt too tight to speak. Molly slipped her warm hand into Risa's icy one, and words came. First, Traci didn't know yet about Harry. Second, Risa wanted some time with Tom and Charlie. Third, she'd feel better if Kelsy stayed with her. She concluded, "In about an hour, I'd love a small dish of strawberry ice cream."

"You've got it." Ben looked at the kids for confirmation.

Both nodded. Risa said to them, "I'd love a kiss now."

Molly went first, her eyes huge with unshed tears.

Jason went second, squeezing Risa's neck fiercely.

Ben went third, his lips melting away her fears.

CHAPTER 28

So tired she felt cross-eyed, Risa led the way to NIC. At the door, Kelsy hesitated. "Did I screw up big time bringing Molly and Jay?"

"No. They remind me how resilient kids are."

"Four years from now, you'll bring Charlie, Tom, and Harry to the hospital to meet Sofia."

"Sofia being?" An invisible vise squeezed Risa's heart.

"My first daughter." Kelsy glowed.

Momentarily blinded by envy, furious they'd changed the subject from Harry to Kelsy, Risa swallowed. "Whose father would be Finn Bishop, you lucky fool?"

Radiant, Kelsy nodded. "He loves Jason, too."

"Tell her you love her—that you'll take on Charlie, Tom—"

"Thank you, Dear Abby." Ben cut Kelsy off as he balanced dirty ice cream cups.

"The sooner the better." Kelsy got right in his face. "She's never been more vulnerable."

"What every frog prince looks for—a vulnerable babe."

Mad as hell, Ben steadied his tower of cups. "What kind of jerk do you think I am?"

Kelsy jostled his arm. Sticky strawberry milk slopped onto his wrist. Eyes narrowed, she demanded, "Were you born dense?"

"Probably." He wiped his wrist. "Were you born nosy?"

Despite his scorn, Ben listened. Kelsy talked with her hands on her hips. "Risa finally gets everyone's concern about raising triplets alone. She said skiing uphill would be easier."

"Good analogy." Ben stepped around Kelsy.

"Here's the point. She thinks you only want sex. Or, if you want more, being daddy to three boys isn't part of the more."

Ben flushed. "That's a leap."

"Maybe. But I'd bet you don't realize how confused Risa is about fidelity."

He slammed the lid on the trash can. "You're either faithful or you're not. What's to understand?"

"Helllooo." Kelsy sighed. "Her dad? Tim? Sam, too. She believes there's not a man alive who can keep his pants zipped."

"Sure you're not injecting your own bias into what she said?" The ice cream in Ben's stomach tasted sour.

"My bias is that Finn will always be faithful."

Amazed by Kelsy's certainty, Ben swallowed a snort. "Do I get any credit for being faithful to Amy since I was six?"

"A lot of credit in Risa's eyes. I'd say she finds fidelity your best quality. But"—Kelsy paused—"if you and she have hot, torrid sex, that means you're unfaithful."

Ben exhaled. "Is it because I'm from Mars that I'm lost?"

Kelsy ignored him and went on. "But forego hot, torrid sex, and she thinks it's because she's fat and repulsive."

Something popped inside Ben's head. "Give me a break."

"Exactly what I'm trying to do." Kelsy came closer. "I'll take the kids to the hotel. You stay here. Let Risa know your intentions . . . which I assume include Charlie, Tom, and Harry."

Ben's third try in two minutes to get her to leave the nursery annoyed rather than charmed Risa.

"The sofas are pretty comfortable. Maybe you can sleep—"

"No!" Her brain had entered some fuzzy zone where she disputed every word he said.

Tom stirred. She lowered her voice, "If Dr. Bartholomew can stay awake in OR, I can stay awake in here for two more hours."

Ben exhaled through his teeth. "Then, let me hold one—"

"I'm fine. Thank you," she added resentfully. Being civil strained her reserve of energy.

Leaning forward in his rocker, Ben rested his elbows on his knees and propped his cheek on one hand. He looked tired, uncertain, and . . . surprisingly sexy. Without warning, an unwanted jolt of desire uncurled inside Risa.

Caught off guard by a rush of emotions—denial, disgust, delight—she held Tom and Charlie to her chest. The tingle between her legs came from sitting too long, she reasoned. With three infants dependent on her, desire was a weakness. She planted her feet on the floor and rocked harder.

Ben sighed. "There goes the cape."

"Did you say . . . cape?" Overheated from her marathon rocking, Risa slowed.

"Sure did." He grinned, inviting escape for a minute.

Except escape was fantasy. She snapped, "My brain's fried."

His mouth twitched. "I'm a caped crusader-in-training."

Risa snorted. Ben's eyebrows shot up along with three fingers. "Sworn to uphold truth, rock babies, and help their mom. If I succeed in all areas, I get my blue cape."

She laughed outright, and the muscles in her neck relaxed. "Do you already have the tights?"

"Yep. The red boots, the body suit, the Batmobile—"

"The Batmobile? Aren't you somewhat confused?"

"I thought we'd established that. I'm also crazy in—"

In her arms, Tom mewed. Risa held her breath. A warning look shut Ben up. Charlie didn't move. She breathed. Ben opened his mouth. Tom let out a glass-shattering scream. Sound asleep, Charlie jerked fully awake, using his lungs to their max.

Within seconds, everything Risa knew about babies evaporated from her mind. Ben held his hands out, but she shook her head. Feeling clumsy, incompetent, and unfit for motherhood, she suggested tensely that she needed a cup of coffee. "Fresh. Nothing out of the machine."

By the time Ben returned from his wild goose chase half an hour later, he still needed earplugs, and Risa still needed help, which she still refused. "Toss the damned coffee," she barked.

Frustrated, Ben capitulated. Not a good time to declare he loved her. Not when she wouldn't even let him hold her kids. A life together, he realized, looked likely only if Dr. Bartholomew worked a miracle.

Ben's stomach churned. No doubt Risa could deal with repeated surgeries, experimental treatments, or whatever was required for Harry or either of his brothers. What Ben doubted was his own capacity for such love. Sure, he'd do anything, go anywhere for Molly. But could he honestly say he'd do the same for Charlie, Tom, and Harry?

Guilt snapped at his heels, but he left. Outside the nursery looking in, he exhaled. Risa had reached the end of her rope. How much longer could she pace in that claustrophobic cubicle before she collapsed? Memories of taking charge like a CEO came back. Surgical mask in place, shoulders back, arms open, he stepped back inside. "Give them to me."

Her jaw cracked, but she settled the squirmy bodies into his arms. As if afraid he'd pinch them, she watched him like a hawk. Ten minutes later, despite his brother's howls, Tom fell asleep.

Ego boosted, Ben laid the baby in his crib. "Dumb luck."

Red-faced, Charlie alternated between shrieks and wails. Out of the corner of his mouth, Ben said, "The nurse swears their coffee's better than the cafeteria swill."

At the door, Risa hesitated and peered back, her eyes bright with unshed tears. Although tempted to lay the screaming baby in the crib and go hold her, Ben waved her into the hall. After some skilled rocking, the shrieks changed to whimpers, then silence.

On his way out of the nursery, Ben remembered not to tiptoe. Theoretically, babies adjusted best when adults maintained their normal, everyday behavior. Fingers crossed, he peered through the glass. Charlie and Tom lay serenely asleep.

A young nurse wearing a red, fur-lined hat said, "Bet you didn't know watched babies never sleep."

He laughed. "Tell that to their mother."

Out of the corner of his eye, Ben saw Doc. Her hair reminded him of a nest of snakes. The bags under her eyes resembled prunes. Shoulders slumped, she shuffled. The nurse said, "Adopting triplets makes her pretty special in my book."

"Mine too." Ben turned to intercept Doc.

She immediately apologized for her absence, adding, "I suppose Charlie went to sleep as soon as I left."

"Not quite." No use making her feel bad. She swayed, and he took her elbow. "The nurses will get us if there's a problem." She looked over her shoulder. He said, "I'm prepared to arm wrestle you if it comes to that."

"Is arm wrestling legal for a caped crusader-in-training?"

"Yep. Till I get my blue cape, I've got lots of leeway."

"No arm wrestling necessary tonight." She yawned.

Pulling her close, he went with temptation. He pressed his lips against hers, ridiculously happy when she opened her mouth to him. Her arms tightened around his neck. His erection apparently woke her up. She moaned. He whispered in her ear. "We're in this together, Doc."

"You must really want that cape." She laughed, not quite with the gusto he admired so much, but with enough spunk he didn't take offense.

She inhaled between her teeth. "Don't let me fall asleep, okay? I want to be alert when Dr. Bartholomew comes out."

"Okay." Ben caressed her hair and wished he could let her sleep. God, she must be beat. "I'll regale you with stories about your sons that will keep you awake for decades."

"So regale me." Her voice shook.

He tightened his arm around her. "Once upon a time, there lived a red-haired baby doctor. . . ."

"Textbook-perfect," Dr. Jose Barthlomew announced after five hours in the OR.

Hearing the news, Doc hugged Ben tighter than bark on a tree, her face buried in his shoulder, her heart hammering against his chest. No tears, but a series of sighs, followed by murmurs and bursts of laughter. Her hold on his neck tightened with each sound she uttered.

Ben just held her, grateful she allowed him to share her luminous joy. Bartholomew waited several heartbeats before dropping his bomb.

"The next couple of hours are the worst part, but in three, four weeks, Harry should be ready to go home."

"Three or four weeks?" Doc raised her head, her eyes filled with stars. "Holy Hannah."

Three or four weeks? Ben stood there frozen.

He felt the floor shift. Sweet Jesus, would Kelsy, crazy in love with Finn, stay in Nashville for three or four weeks? What if she didn't? Or couldn't? How would Doc manage? Sooner or later, she had to sleep. *Not unless someone's at the hospital.* What about Jason? How could Doc and Kelsy schedule round-the-clock hospital vigils with Jason here?

Feeling like Grinch, Ben didn't have the heart to ask his logical questions. Not with Doc over the moon. It was as if Harry's convalescence presented zero problems for her. She flashed her laser smile as if she owned the whole damn world. Her excitement was so brilliant, the lights dimmed. Determined to focus on Bartholomew's optimism, Ben couldn't avoid one question. It banged in his head like a drum: was he going to desert Doc to hammer out the merger?

Day and night faded into a fog for Risa. At eight o'clock each morning, Bobbye Anne picked up Molly and Jason. Molly had absolutely refused to go home with Ben. With the four-year-olds taken care of, Kelsy went to the hospital for the day shift. One ear always open for a call from the hospital, Risa sank like a rock into bed at the hotel. Nine hours later, Bobbye Anne brought the kids back.

They and Kelsy joined Risa for supper in the noisy, crowded cafeteria. Next, they all visited the nursery where Harry now occupied a crib between his brothers.

If the triplets didn't raise the roof, Risa slipped out and spent a few more minutes with Molly and Jason—so wonderfully loving and optimistic, she couldn't get enough of hugging and kissing them before they went off with Kelsy to bed at the hotel.

The nurses insisted that Risa leave the nursery for at least ten minutes every hour. She generally used the nine o'clock break for visits with Traci, who stayed in her room. Not because she was having second thoughts about the adoption, but because she felt rotten two days after the delivery.

On other breaks, Risa chatted with Ben. Worried about Harry's persistent temp, caused by a post-op infection, she mustered no interest in the Silicon Valley downturn. More often than not, he launched into memories of Molly. Her birth and stay at St. Claire's. Her first day home. The first time she slept through the night.

Hooked on the memories Ben spun out, Risa created images of the Macdonalds akin to the Sunday school pictures she carried in her head of Jesus, Joseph, and Mary. A part of her knew she romanticized the early days of Molly's life. But since her fantasies hurt no one, she treasured them for her own children.

On the third evening, Kelsy, rather than the alarm, woke Risa. Bobbye Anne had brought the kids home early. Jason had a stuffy nose and a temp. The promise of pizza didn't raise his spirits, so Kelsy feared trouble.

"I bet you have a virus." Risa listened to his chest rasp.

"We already had a virus," Molly countered.

Eyes glazed, shivering atop the covers, Jason groaned. Molly asked, "Are we gonna throw up again?"

"Why do you say *we*, Molly?" Kelsy threw Risa a look. "You don't feel sick, do you?"

"Uh-uh, but I wish my daddy was here 'cuz my tummy hurts."

Sharing Molly's wish, Risa said, "Your daddy's coming back soon, you—"

"Careful." Kelsy dropped the second shoe.

After an all-nighter the night before, Ben had run into a major glitch. Kelsy had assured him he should stay in Silicon Valley for as long as necessary.

At the end of this account, Molly said, "I bet he'd come if I asked him to."

Doc's call came at the worst time for Ben.

The legal beagles, HR specialists, and CPAs stared at him like a rabbit among hyenas when he answered his cell in the conference room. His XYZ counterpart groaned.

Tough. Let them figure out what he meant about having family responsibilities. They either closed the deal today, or he was out of there.

Without apology, he stepped into an adjoining office. "What's wrong? Is Harry okay?" He flipped on a lamp, cracked the mini-blinds on the outside wall, and blinked like a bat.

Doc assured him right away that Molly's tummyache was probably nerves. She liked Bobbye Anne but didn't want to leave Jason at the hotel when he was sick.

Update delivered, Doc called Molly to the phone. Before he lost his courage, Ben said, "I have a question for you, first."

He spoke so fast, his words ran together, but he didn't slow down. "Do you miss me, too?"

He heard a soft intake of air, then, "Here's Molly."

Not in the least surprised, Ben laughed. "And here I come," he said. "Ready or not."

Here I come. Ready or not. Risa hurried to the hospital. Despite the chill, Ben's teasing good-bye had her blood boiling. In the lobby, she shook her head several times. She was being silly. His business was in crisis. *He's on his way here.*

Molly needs him. True, but he'd done more for Charlie, Tom, and Harry than Risa had ever imagined in her wildest fantasy.

In the nursery, a twenty-something couple greeted her with radiant smiles. Their twin girls were going home. Hugging and talking over each other, they asked about Charlie, Tom, and Harry. Another perfect family, Risa thought before sanity returned and she gave two thumbs up.

All right, she thought once they left, so she was a single mom. Deal with it. She had so much for which to be grateful. Such as Harry's temp. Down to 100. Pulse steady. Weight up three ounces. Life was beautiful.

Almost perfect, if she didn't make too much of Tom's screams. She picked up her biggest and firstborn son, normally the easiest going of the triplets. He shrieked, drowning out her words of comfort.

Dry diaper. Forehead a little warm. Just in case, she took his temp. Not fun. He kicked and flailed with the strength of a little stallion. The thermometer read normal.

Harry and Charlie lay in their cribs, wide awake, mesmerized by reindeer mobiles. They waved, kicked, and cooed. Risa threw them each a kiss. Mystified, she checked Tom's chart.

An hour early for scheduled feedings. Still, he was growing so fast, maybe he was hungry. One problem. Feed him now, then feed Charlie and Harry on schedule, she'd then have two feedings instead of one. This could cause a big impact on future feedings.

As if he understood her vacillation, Tom raged. Patting a spot in the middle of his back, Risa put him over her shoulder and whispered his name repeatedly. With shaky hands, she tested a drop of milk, then grazed his cheek with the nipple. Face scarlet, he whipped his head from side to side. Gallons of tears dripped into his ears. Not a drop of milk went down his throat.

Her stomach clenched. What if he had colic? Or, what if her excitement at seeing Ben had upset him because her heart rate banged against her chest?

Crooning to her inconsolable son, Risa understood—for the first time, at the most basic level—the fear and anxiety of the mothers who'd come to see her because their child wouldn't eat, wouldn't sleep, wouldn't stop crying. Those mothers had described pain sharp as broken glass in their heads from lack of sleep. Now, Risa got it. Because that's exactly how she felt physically. Emotionally, she felt lonelier than she could ever remember.

At seven o'clock, Traci showed up for her first visit. Right away, she asked what was wrong with Tom. Irked by the question with no answer, Risa snapped, "How do I know?"

Graciously, Traci accepted an instant apology. Wisely, she escaped. Left with Tom, whimpering now instead of bawling, Risa took a deep breath. She was fine, Tom was fine, the whole damned world was fine. The more she lied to herself, the more he cried.

At nine o'clock, the lights in the main nursery dimmed. Risa sank into the rocker, cuddling Tom. *Do not panic.* She kicked off her shoes, closed her eyes, and let her brain slip backward. Ben pacing with Tom. Mouthing soft gibberish. Soothing her son.

Unreasonably, jealousy flared. Ben should have no influence over *her* child. Her throat ached. She felt like crying. Tom beat her to the punch. He hiccuped, then sighed a long sob, then another. His scream raised the hairs on the back of Risa's clammy neck. She knew she'd crashed and burned. How had she ever been so arrogant? What did a single pediatrician know about being the mother of triplets?

Half an hour into her self-flagellation, Harry woke up screaming. He was soaked. Like brother Tom. What's more, Harry wanted food, demanded it, and made his point by bawling louder than Big Bro. Risa made the mistake of checking on Charlie.

Leaning over his crib, she startled him in that zone between sleep and waking. His eyes widened, his body stiffened, and his mouth became a gaping black hole. Charlie was so obviously terrified that Risa forgot the bottles and picked him up. The delay did not sit well with her other two sons. They screamed so loud Risa thought she'd dropped straight into hell.

Into bedlam, Ben came with arms open wide. He took Charlie, kissed her, and said, "Looks like you could use a hand—or two."

On the off chance the triplets were sensitive to roses, Risa stopped wearing her signature cologne, switched shampoos, and used an unscented body lotion, all with disappointing results. Day or night, the babies did not stop crying till she left. No one could offer a theory, plausible or implausible, why each of them cooed like angels around Kelsy and Ben—especially around Ben.

To Risa's chagrin, he and Kelsy took twelve-hour shifts at the hospital. Their glowing reports felt like ice picks in Risa's heart. Like a sulky child, she brushed aside their attempts at soothing her wounded ego. She refused all physical contact with either of them. She rarely threw her voice or played with Molly and Jason, but they dispensed hugs and kisses anyway. Maybe, she reasoned, she wasn't Mommy Dearest after all.

Two days before Christmas, Ben took her aside and promised a surprise if she and the kids stayed out of the hotel until five o'clock.

Being up close and personal with him, she forgot she was the mother of triplets. Lack of sleep, she rationalized, explained her desire to fall on Ben's neck and never let go. When had she started thinking she couldn't live if Ben resumed his own life? Holy Hedda, she didn't even know the outcome of his merger.

Guilt threatened to ruin the spectacle of Rudolph chasing Santa in Peabody Park. But Molly and Jason, along with every kid in the audience, howled, and Risa soon caught the Christmas bug. By the end of the show, fat snowflakes dropped from the sky. Risa stuck her tongue out. Scarlet-cheeked, Molly and Jason imitated her. Passersby smiled. Strangers wished them Merry Christmas as they wandered through the slush, past tinsel and bee lights and greenery decorating most store windows.

Realizing that Molly and Jason had missed much of the best part of Christmas, Risa proposed shopping. They worried about money, and she patted her purse. Whatever their shopping spree cost, it could never equal what she owed them and their parents.

Three hundred bucks later, arms aching, Risa staggered off the hotel elevator at 5:15. Mercifully, she'd called Ben from the lobby. He met them with hugs for Molly, high fives for Jason, and a peck on the cheek for Risa. "Have you been a good girl?"

Desire raced through her. Mercifully, he didn't attempt small talk. When he took the handles of her shopping bag, bones melted in her useless hand. Holy Hannah, the Christmas spirit.

CHAPTER 29

"Santa brought it," Ben said, once the kids stopped screaming.

It was a two-foot Christmas tree, scragglier than Charlie Brown's. Both kids loved the lights and icicles and didn't mind the lack of colored balls or ornaments. Open-mouthed, they marveled at Santa's ability to get from the park to the hotel so fast.

"Are you *sure* you're not one of Santa's little helpers?" Risa moved closer to Ben. Laughter and noise faded.

"FYI, pizza should arrive momentarily."

"Why don't you stay?" Eyes huge, she moistened her lips.

It was as if they were alone, and she'd invited him to an intimate dinner. With asparagus-oyster appetizers, followed by grapes with whipped cream.

Sanity tapped his shoulder. "In five, ten minutes, Tom expects me to rock him."

She hugged her waist. "How will I manage at home?"

Ben went still. "Glad to teach you all my tricks."

The pizza arrived before he could expand on the brilliance of this notion. Molly and Jason screamed as if they'd never seen pizza. Their delight took the edge off

Ben's disappointment at leaving. With one foot in the hall, he suggested casually, "Come over after you eat for a preview of my best tricks."

Kelsy, overhearing, eyed Ben, pushed them out the door, and threw their coats into the hall. As they raced for the elevator, he laced fingers with Risa. "We'll make it up to her."

"We?" Risa's heart dropped faster than the elevator. The door opened. Maneuvering through the crowd allowed no time to think.

In the lobby background, strings and piano accompanied Nat King Cole crooning Christmas carols. Risa's mind floated up near the twinkling thirty-foot tree. Outside, snowflakes drifted downward, turning the street into a Hollywood scene. Being so close to Ben raised her blood past boiling.

Holy Hannah, she'd missed his teasing. And his laugh. She loved his laugh. Her feet felt as if she'd stepped in cement. What was wrong with her? She'd barely seen him for days, and now here she was. Ready to jump his bones simply because he'd said *we'll make it up to her.*

"Over here." He pulled her away from the revolving door, under an overhang protected from snow and wind.

Wherever he wants to go, she thought dreamily. Driving a dogsled across the Yukon presented no problems at that moment.

"You look a little . . . stunned," he said, raising his eyebrows.

"Aren't you cold?" she asked. Snow danced like bees around his head.

"Are you kidding? I feel like my hair's on fire." He cupped her chin, peering into her soul. "Shouldn't you take my temp—or something?"

Her heart stopped. No mind required to read the message in his eyes. Boldly, she said, "You said *we.* In the elevator."

"You noticed."

She wanted to kiss the huge grin off his face. "I notice a lot."

"Such as?"

Shivering from his scalding fingertip on her bottom lip, she said, "I notice you're here instead of in California."

"Took a leave of absence." He wiped snow from her eyes.

Ears ringing, she mumbled, "You—you did?"

He lifted a shoulder. "Negotiations never progressed."

Her heart fluttered. "Sounds like you and me.

"I hope you understand I intend to change that."

She hated feeling so hopeful, so helpless. "*We* implies, could imply—"

"No." He shook his head. "*We* definitely means I love you."

Her heart started swinging from rib to rib.

"Even with all you've had on your mind, I assumed—"

He lifted a shoulder again, leaving her weak-kneed. "Forget assumptions. For the record, I love Charlie, Tom, and Harry, too." He looked like a kid with snow dusting his hair.

"What about Lucky Prince?"

His mouth dropped, then he laughed. Did he know what he'd bitten off? She still wasn't sure he wanted her as much as she wanted him. "You do know the only reason I've lost weight is because—"

He threw his hands up. "Thanks for reminding me *why* I love you. You've lost—what? Three pounds? Or is it thirty-three?" He grabbed her shoulders and gave her a little shake. "Do you have me confused with a snake? Or your ex? Since when does a savvy, funny, beautiful woman get hung up on weight?"

His questions snapped, crackled, and popped, each faster than the previous. Her tongue stuck to the roof of her mouth. He rushed on. "Personally, I wish you'd never lost a pound. I like your curves. I've always liked your curves. This may shock you, but the first thing I noticed about you in that line at Starbucks wasn't your big emerald eyes."

Tempted to wrangle more specifics, Risa savored the compliment in silence for a second, then said, "I know moaning about being a *big* woman is politically incorrect."

Since Ben didn't contradict this statement, she spoke quickly, hoping he hadn't heard her voice quaver. "If I had any sense, I'd swear I'm not really as shallow as a saucer."

His laugh surprised her. Lord, he'd seen right through her and figured out she'd love a few more years of compliments. "What's so funny?"

"You, of course."

Okay, better funny than vulnerable. She threw him a death glare, but he laughed again. "Doc, you don't have a shallow thought in that gorgeous red head. If anything, you think too much. I can see the wheels turning right now."

"I'm not transparent." She looked down her nose at him.

He chucked her under the chin like she was a pouty child. "If I'm wrong, I'll eat dirt, okay?"

"Okay." It wasn't okay, but any other answer and she'd sound like a spoiled brat. "Just remember, you're not the only one who doesn't like armchair analysis," she added.

"I swear," he held up his right hand, "you can tell me to shut up at anytime."

"Uh-huh." Maybe she'd kill him instead.

"First point." He held up one finger. "You think that sooner or later, I'll end up comparing you and Amy."

Shut up! Heat scalded her cheeks.

Apparently, he didn't notice sweat drip into her eyes, because he didn't miss a beat. Just went on making his case. "Point two. You think Amy, of course, will outshine you. Because men always prefer svelte, petite females to *big* women."

Shut up! The bottom fell out of Risa's stomach.

He wrapped his arms around her waist. She held her breath and looked into far space. "Svelte and petite, you are not."

Shut up, please, shut up!

"And never will be, I hope." He kissed the tears leaking out of her eyes, then asked, "Do you compare apples and oranges?"

A head shake didn't satisfy him. "How about night with day?"

His tone was light, but she knew he expected a response, so she shook her head, amazed by the risk he took of making himself vulnerable to rejection.

"I won't ask then why *I'd* compare you with Amy." He held her gaze. "You'll never know I don't . . . unless you marry me."

Married, would he be more supportive? More selfless? More sexy? Seeing his jaw tighten, she said lightly, "Points taken. My answer's yes, on one condition. No, make that two."

"Make that zero," he said. "Life's too short. What're we waiting for? I love you, and I'm pretty sure you—"

"You know I love you. I have since we danced in the kitchen." Paralyzed by her hangups about infidelity and body image, she'd taken so much for granted. "But I can't toss Kelsy—"

"She and Jason are family. They can live with us." He kissed her ear, whispering, "I'm tired of being a frog."

"You're not!" Tears blurred her vision, but her heart saw with perfect clarity. He'd never demanded she acknowledge he was always there for her, her sons, Molly—and even Jason and Kelsy.

"You're sure you want to marry an idiot?" she whispered.

"As long as the idiot is you. Now, let me show you why I can't wait."

His kiss was enough, but the heat deep inside her erased all doubt. "Is Christmas too soon?"